"I absolut... ...bout the Hex books. They a... ...oblem is I race through each one of them b... ...wait to see how they end."
—Fresh Fiction

"Outrageously funny and imaginative ... Vicki Lewis Thompson is a creatively gifted author who can make the reader believe even the impossible as she brings the story alive on the printed page.... Brimming with wit, creative characters, a delightful plot, and plenty of imagination, this story is a delight."
—Romance Junkies

Wild & Hexy

"Each book that Vicki Lewis Thompson pens is an experience that will have you laughing from the start ... simply delightful. *Wild & Hexy* is a zany adventure in romance and magic. Readers won't be able to resist another visit with the inhabitants of Big Knob."
—Darque Reviews

"An excellent addition that makes me eager for more! ... You never really know what might happen in the small town of Big Knob, but you won't want to miss a thing. A must read!"
—Fallen Angel Reviews

"There was so much going on in this book that I really didn't want it to end ... wonderfully fun ... a keeper for sure!"
—Fresh Fiction

"If you thought *Over Hexed* was phenomenal, wait until you read *Wild & Hexy*! ... A rip-roaring good time."
—Romance Junkies

"Get ready for a truly *Wild & Hexy* ride ... brewing with lots of magical fun, mishaps, and most important of all—romance! ... Vicki Lewis Thompson has penned a fun paranormal tale."
—Romance Reader at Heart

"Pure FUN from first page to last!"
—The Romance Readers Connection

"Sassy, fun, and magical, *Wild & Hexy* is pure delight from the first page.... This novel is one you'll want to read in one sitting, and then you'll want to read it again."
—Romance Reviews Today

continued ...

"A fun book to read from start to finish."

—Once Upon a Romance Reviews

Over Hexed

"A snappy, funny, romantic novel."

—*New York Times* bestselling author Carly Phillips

"Filled with laughs, this is a charmer of a book."

—The Eternal Night

"The same trademark blend of comedy and heart that won Thompson's Nerd series a loyal following."

—*Publishers Weekly*

"Thompson mixes magic, small-town quirkiness, and passionate sex for a winsome effect." —*Booklist*

"A warm and funny novel, you find yourself cheering. I would definitely recommend it." —The Road to Romance

"This novel was brilliant. I laughed until I cried, and it was a very fast read for me. This genre is the beginning of a new series for Thompson, and if this novel is any indication of the following books, then Thompson has hit the jackpot."

—Romance Reader at Heart

"Vicki Lewis Thompson has a true flair for humor. Pick up *Over Hexed* and be prepared to be amused, delighted, and satisfied as Vicki Lewis Thompson takes you on an unforgettable ride." —Single Titles

"Vicki Lewis Thompson sure delivers with *Over Hexed* . . . a lighthearted tale that won't soon be forgotten."

—Fallen Angel Reviews

"With her wonderful talent of lighthearted humor, Vicki Lewis Thompson pens an enchanting tale for her amorous characters, steeping it in magic and enough passion to scorch the pages."

—Darque Reviews

"Vicki Lewis Thompson has created another romance blended with humor to make you beg for more."

—Once Upon a Romance Reviews

Blonde with a Wand

A Babes on Brooms Novel

Vicki Lewis Thompson

A SIGNET ECLIPSE BOOK

SIGNET ECLIPSE
Published by New American Library, a division of
Penguin Group (USA) Inc., 375 Hudson Street,
New York, New York 10014, USA
Penguin Group (Canada), 90 Eglinton Avenue East, Suite 700, Toronto,
Ontario M4P 2Y3, Canada (a division of Pearson Penguin Canada Inc.)
Penguin Books Ltd., 80 Strand, London WC2R 0RL, England
Penguin Ireland, 25 St. Stephen's Green, Dublin 2,
Ireland (a division of Penguin Books Ltd.)
Penguin Group (Australia), 250 Camberwell Road, Camberwell, Victoria 3124,
Australia (a division of Pearson Australia Group Pty. Ltd.)
Penguin Books India Pvt. Ltd., 11 Community Centre, Panchsheel Park,
New Delhi - 110 017, India
Penguin Group (NZ), 67 Apollo Drive, Rosedale, North Shore 0632,
New Zealand (a division of Pearson New Zealand Ltd.)
Penguin Books (South Africa) (Pty.) Ltd., 24 Sturdee Avenue,
Rosebank, Johannesburg 2196, South Africa

Penguin Books Ltd. , Registered Offices:
80 Strand, London WC2R 0RL, England

First published by Signet Eclipse, an imprint of New American Library,
a division of Penguin Group (USA) Inc.

First Printing, February 2010
10 9 8 7 6 5 4 3 2 1

To all the compassionate souls who spend their precious time and resources to save homeless pets, with special gratitude for the largest no-kill facility in the world, Best Friends Animal Society, where I spent a fulfilling week one memorable July.

Acknowledgments

As always, I'm deeply indebted to the wonderful folks at Penguin for championing my cause, especially my editor, Claire Zion. I'm grateful for the support of my agent, Robert Gottlieb, at Trident Media, and for the constant encouragement from my assistant/daughter, Audrey Sharpe and my brainstorming partners, Jennifer LaBrecque and Rhonda Nelson. I'm also filled with wonder at the twists of fate that brought me in contact with Romance Writers of America and its founder, Rita Clay Estrada. Rita's vision transformed the romance landscape, and without RWA many of us, including me, might never have published a book. Thank you, Rita.

Chapter 1

The night Anica Revere turned Jasper Danes into a cat started out innocently enough.

They'd dated for nearly three weeks, and tonight lust ping-ponged across the restaurant table. Anica had anticipated this moment since she first glimpsed this dark-haired Adonis with golden eyes. Although Monday wasn't a common date night, Jasper's favorite restaurant was open and he hadn't wanted to wait for the weekend to see her again. All the signs pointed to finally Doing It.

He studied Anica as if he wanted to lick her all over, which sounded great to her, except ... she still hadn't mentioned a significant detail, one that could be a real buzz kill. She hadn't told him she was a witch.

With chemistry this strong she was so tempted not to tell him, but one mistake with a nonmagical man was enough. The image of Edward racing out of her bedroom a year ago still pained her.

He hadn't even bothered to grab his clothes. Sad to say, a Chicago police squad car had been cruising by the apartment building and poor Edward had been arrested using a *Keep Lake Michigan Clean* leaflet as a fig leaf substitute.

She'd heard all about it from her neighbor Julie, who

kept a video camera running from her third-story window in hopes that she'd get something worth airing on her brother's independent cable show, *Not So Shy Chi-Town*. That clip made it on the show, no problem. To avoid legal repercussions, Edward's features had been scrambled so no one except Julie and Anica knew who it was.

"You're frowning," Jasper said. "Anything wrong?"

Good thing he wasn't a mind reader. "No, no. Sorry." She smiled to prove that everything was hunky-dory.

He reached for her hand. "What do you say we get out of here?"

Whoops. She wasn't quite ready to be alone with him. Better to reveal her witch status in a public place, where she could resist the urge to prove that she had special powers.

That had been her biggest mistake with Edward. He hadn't believed her, and she'd worked one teensy spell to convince him and had been inspired by what was at hand, so to speak. He'd left before she could explain that his penis would return to its normal color in a few hours.

"I'm fine with leaving," she said. "But there's chocolate mousse on the dessert menu. Let's get some to go. Mousse could be . . . a lot of fun."

"Mm." His gaze grew hot. "I like the way you think."

As he signaled their waitress, Anica searched for the least-threatening way to explain her unique gifts. After her experience with Edward, she dreaded broaching the witch situation. Maybe she should retreat to a quiet place for a few minutes and ask for guidance.

She pushed back her chair and picked up her purse. "I need to make a trip to the ladies' room."

He stood, a perfect gentleman. "Hurry back."

"You bet." All the way to the rear of the restaurant, she thought about how gorgeous he was and how much she wanted him. She imagined how his eyes would darken during sex. So far his lips had only touched her mouth and neck, but she could mentally translate that delicious sensation to full-body kisses. She longed to feel his dark chest hair tickling her breasts as he hovered over her, poised for that first thrust.

Despite her parents urging her to find a nice wizard boy, she'd always been attracted to nonmagical guys. Because they couldn't wave a wand or brew a potion to create what they wanted, they had to make it through life on sheer grit and determination. She admired that.

She'd noticed Jasper the minute he'd stepped into her downtown coffee shop. What woman wouldn't notice six feet of gorgeous male with a physique that did great things for his Brooks Brothers suit? She'd become his friend once she'd learned he was suffering from a broken heart. Sure, he probably had the ability to recover on his own, but she wanted to help.

They'd progressed from conversations at Wicked Brew to a lunch date. That had been followed by two dinner dates, and after the last one he'd kissed her until she'd nearly caved and invited him upstairs, rule or no rule.

He had a right to know the truth before the kissing started again, though, and most likely he wouldn't believe her. If he didn't she had to let him go. No clever little tricks to convince the guy this time. But letting him go would be very difficult.

The bathroom was empty, which pleased her. She'd been hoping for time alone to prepare. Jasper was special and she didn't want to muck this up if she could possibly help it.

Closing her eyes, she took a calming breath and murmured softly, "Great Mother and Great Father, guide me in my relationship with this man. Help me find the best way to tell him of my special powers. May we find a kinship that transcends our differences. With harm to none, so mote it be."

The bathroom door squeaked open. Anica quickly opened her eyes, turned toward the mirror and unzipped her purse as a tall brunette walked in. Moving aside the eight-inch rowan wood traveling wand she carried for emergencies, Anica pulled out her lipstick and began applying another coat of Retro Red.

She expected the woman to head for a stall or take the sink adjoining Anica's to repair her makeup. Instead the woman clutched her purse and watched Anica. Weird. Maybe this chick needed privacy, too.

Anica capped her lipstick, dropped it in her purse, and closed the zipper. Turning, she smiled at the woman, who didn't smile back. Instead her classic features creased in a frown. Troubles, apparently. She looked to be in her late twenties, about Anica's age.

"It's all yours." Anica started toward the door.

"Damn, I can't decide what to do."

Oh, Hades. Anica tended to invite confidences and she was usually willing to listen and offer whatever help she could. But now wasn't a good time. "I'm sorry. I have to get back to my date."

"Jasper Danes."

Anica blinked. "You know him?"

"Yes." The woman sighed. "I stopped by here for a drink, hoping to run into him, because he comes to this restaurant all the time. I should have realized by now he'd be involved with someone else."

Anticipation drained out of Anica so quickly she felt dizzy. She looked into the woman's soft brown eyes. "You're Sheila."

The woman nodded.

In the spot where hope had bubbled only moments ago, disappointment invaded like sludge. If Sheila was having second thoughts about breaking up with Jasper, then Anica should step aside. What Anica shared with him was mere lust, which might disappear once he found out she was a witch.

She made herself do the noble thing. "We're not really involved." *Yet.*

"I was afraid to ask if it was serious between you two, because it looked as if—"

"We were heading in that direction, but when I first met him he was devastated over your breakup. If you regret leaving him, then maybe there's still a chance to start over." Anica wanted to cry. Jasper was the first man she'd had any real interest in since Edward and she was giving him back to his ex. Nobility sucked.

"Excuse me, but did you say *I* left *him*?"

"Yes. He said that he begged you to reconsider, but you—"

"Oh, my God." Sheila gazed at the ceiling. "It's déjà vu." She closed her eyes and let her head drop. "I thought I was smarter than that. Guess not."

"I don't understand."

When Sheila opened her eyes to look at Anica, her gaze had hardened. "I didn't understand, either, until now. Tell me, did he say that I broke his heart?"

"Sort of. You know how guys are."

"Apparently I don't know enough about how guys are, but I'll learn. Let me guess what he said." Sheila deepened her voice in a pretty good imitation of Jasper. "*I thought we had something special. I was all set to take her home to meet my folks in Wisconsin when she lowered the boom. Maybe I should have seen it coming. Maybe I dropped the ball somehow, didn't live up to her expectations. I tried to get her to reconsider, but she was finished with me.*"

Uneasiness settled in Anica's stomach. Sheila had quoted Jasper almost word for word. What if this woman was a nutcase who'd been lurking in the coffee shop behind a newspaper while Jasper spilled his guts? "That's . . . approximately what he said."

"I'll bet a million dollars that's *exactly* what he said. Because that's the speech he gave me about Kate, his previous girlfriend. It touched my heartstrings, which appear to be directly connected to my libido. A few dates, and we were in bed, where I could mend his broken heart." She blew out a breath. "I didn't leave Jasper. He dumped me three weeks ago."

Three weeks ago Jasper had walked into Wicked Brew for the first time and she'd elbowed her employee Sally out of the way so that she could personally serve him a latte. Jasper had shown up the next morning, and the next, and on the third morning he'd announced that his girlfriend had left him.

But Sheila couldn't be telling the truth about that breakup. Anica prided herself on her ability to read people, and Jasper had been one forlorn guy three weeks ago. If he'd made up that story—no, she couldn't believe that he'd do such a thing.

"I want to hear Jasper's side," she said. "I don't see any reason why he'd—"

"Don't you? He's figured out that women are suckers for a sob story. He hangs with a woman until he finds somebody he likes better. Then he dumps the current girlfriend and works the heartbreak-kid angle with the new one. I fell for it. And the worst part is, if I could have him back, I'd take him, even knowing what I know."

Anica shook her head, still unwilling to accept what Sheila was saying. "I'm sure there's an explanation. Maybe you two misunderstood each other." That still left Anica out in the cold if Sheila and Jasper reunited, but she'd rather see that happen than discover Jasper was a louse.

"It's hard to misunderstand when someone says, '*It's been lots of fun and you're amazing, but it's time to move on.*' That's pretty damned clear, don't you think?"

"Did you two fight about something?"

"No. All was peaches and cream. I'm guessing he met you and decided to trade up."

Had Jasper lied to her? Anica couldn't believe it, but there was only one way to find out. "I'll talk to him."

"You do that, and if you decide you don't want him after you find out the truth, let me know." Sheila thrust a business card in Anica's hand. "He might bounce back my way."

Anica stared at her in disbelief. "You'd still want him, even if he lied to you?"

" 'Fraid so. I shouldn't, but . . . he's just that good."

Jasper tried not to be worried. He'd noticed Sheila sitting at the bar when he'd first walked in with Anica. He didn't know if Sheila had spotted him or not, but he'd asked for a table quite a distance from the bar, just in case. She'd seemed to take the breakup reasonably well, but there was no point in flaunting his new girlfriend.

Sheila was alone, but he told himself that she was probably meeting some guy here. A woman who looked like Sheila wouldn't have any trouble finding dates. She deserved to hook up with someone who appreciated her more than he had.

For a while he'd tried to tell himself Sheila was everything he needed in a woman, but then he'd looked into Anica's startling blue eyes and experienced a zing of excitement he hadn't felt in years. Immediately he'd made a clean break with Sheila. It was the only fair thing to do, and he prided himself on never cheating on a lover.

Sheila had seemed fine with parting ways—no tears, no drunk dialing, no trumped-up visits to the brokerage house where he worked. He hadn't run into her again until now. He was relieved that she'd remained at the bar and hadn't wandered over during the meal, which might have been awkward.

Anica's suggestion about the chocolate mousse in a to-go box had fired his imagination, and he could hardly wait for her to get back from the bathroom. Her apartment was within walking distance, a happy coincidence that meant they could have a romantic stroll to build the anticipation.

Weather conditions weren't ideal for a stroll—icy March winds still blew down Chicago's streets—but the breezes were subtly different these days, a shade warmer than they had been even a week ago. Spring was hovering, ready to swoop in and transform the city. Jasper planned on having sex with Anica tonight, but he'd thought way beyond that.

Spring was a perfect time to start a relationship, with buds opening, sap rising . . . yeah, the sap was rising in him, all right. This time, though, sexual attraction wasn't the only emotion driving him. He admired her body, but he also admired her intelligence and business savvy.

She'd opened a downtown coffee shop in an area Starbucks hadn't mined because there was nothing to draw a nighttime crowd. Anica kept Wicked Brew open weekdays only from seven to four and made a killing from the office workers who didn't have time to walk several blocks to Starbucks.

Admittedly, though, he hadn't been thinking much about her business smarts tonight. Tonight he wanted to peel the clothes from her luscious, long-limbed body. He wanted to take the pins out of her blond hair.

The image of undressing her made his cock hard. Because he'd have to wait a while before doing anything about that, he distracted himself by concentrating on the bill. As always, he gave a generous tip in honor of the nights during his college career when he'd held down this kind of job. God, had it really been ten years ago?

As he signed his name to the credit card slip, he glanced up to check Sheila's seat at the bar. She wasn't there. So maybe she'd left.

Or not. A woman was heading into the restroom. The light was dim back there, but he had a bad feeling that woman going into the door marked with a stylized *W* could be Sheila.

That might not matter, though. Anica was due back any second, and besides, she'd never met Sheila. The woman in the bathroom probably wasn't Sheila, anyway. He was getting paranoid.

He knew why, too. Anica had given him a whole new lease on life, both sexually and mentally. He'd even imagined sharing an apartment, which was major because he'd never spent more than a long weekend with a woman. As serious as he'd thought he'd been about Sheila, he'd never created a mental picture of what their combined lives would look like, which should have told him they weren't right for each other.

Here he was already thinking about living with Anica, and they hadn't even had sex. He pictured eating microwave popcorn and watching old episodes of *South Park* on Friday nights, flying kites over Lake Michigan on Saturday afternoons, battling for sections of the *Trib* on Sunday mornings. The scenes rolled in his head like a chick flick accompanied by a perky sound track.

Of course it was only their fourth date. They had plenty to learn about each other and he wasn't making any stupid predictions at this stage of the game. But he had a special feeling about this particular woman. He wouldn't be surprised if ... but that was jumping the gun. He'd let things unfold as they were supposed to.

He sure wished she'd get back from the bathroom, though. Women did all sorts of mysterious things when they disappeared in there. One of them involved girl talk.

That was the part bothering him at the moment. Having an ex-girlfriend talking to a current girlfriend was never a good idea. He prayed that wasn't going on.

At last Anica came out and started toward him. He stood, smiling, and picked up the take-out carton of chocolate mousse. When she didn't return his smile, his anxiety level shot up about a thousand percent.

"We need to talk."

He groaned. When a woman said that to a man disaster was in the air. Now he was virtually positive Sheila had followed Anica into that bathroom. "Would you rather sit down and eat dessert here after all?"

"No, let's leave." She headed toward the restaurant's foyer.

Jasper had no choice but to follow, but suddenly he craved the protection of other diners. He didn't think Anica was the type to make a scene in a nice restaurant. Then again, he wouldn't swear to it. He didn't know her that well.

When Anica reached the front door, she paused to take her black wool coat from where it hung on a garment rack. Jasper helped her on with it. He'd admired this coat the first time she'd worn it because it was so unusual; more a cape than a coat, with a generous hood. Contrasted with Anica's blond hair, the black coat and hood made quite a statement.

Once she'd settled her hood over her golden hair and was ready to step outside, he handed her the mousse so he could put on his tweed topcoat. Then he took the mousse back before walking with her into the chilly night.

The night was balmy, though, compared with Anica's tone as she faced him on the sidewalk. "Your ex-girlfriend came into the bathroom while I was in there."

"Sheila?" He'd hoped to sound vaguely interested, but the word came out as a croak of alarm.

Anica clutched her hood when the wind threatened to blow it off. "She made some pretty harsh claims, and I need to know if anything she said is true."

"Okay." Jasper turned up his collar as he tried to imagine what complaints Sheila might have had about him. He'd thought that he'd pleased her in bed, but maybe she'd been faking those orgasms. That wasn't really his fault, although maybe he should have—

"Sheila says that you dumped her."

"That's not true." He'd never dumped a woman in his life. Sure, he'd broken up with them, but he'd done it in the kindest way he knew how.

Anica let out a breath. "Thank goodness. I knew she had to be lying. She must be trying to salve her conscience by claiming that you're the one who broke up with her. I apologize for doubting you."

He should let it go at that. It was a harmless thing, this habit he had of using a broken heart as an entrée with a new woman. He should just agree with Anica that Sheila was lying and they could move on to the most excellent conclusion of their evening.

Admitting he had been the one to leave was only going to cause problems. The main thing was that he and Sheila were finished. Yep, that was all that mattered.

"Jasper?" She peered up at him. "Shall we go? It's pretty cold out here."

"Yeah, let's go." He took her hand as they faced into the wind and started toward her apartment building. Maybe Anica wouldn't even care if she knew the truth, and at least that would clear the air between them. Nah, that was stupid. Why buy trouble?

"Does Sheila's behavior bother you?"

"No. Why?"

"You're being very quiet. Listen, if seeing her again has stirred up old feelings, then maybe—"

"It's not that." The wind blew harder, enough to make his eyes water. "You know, it's not that important who does the leaving, is it? I mean, when a relationship is over, it's over. Somebody has to make the move, but what difference does it make who walks out the door?"

"It seemed to make a big difference to you three weeks ago."

"Oh, well . . ." He managed to dredge up a chuckle. "You know how it is. When you first meet somebody, it's like a game. Every guy has some little strategy for breaking the ice. No harm, no foul, right?" He glanced at her to see if she was going along with this line of reasoning, but her hood kept him from judging her expression.

Her voice gave him no clues, either. "What sort of strategy do you have, Jasper?"

"Oh, you know." He gave her hand a squeeze. "Maybe pretending to be a little more broken up over my previous relationship than I actually was. You can't blame a guy for—"

She pulled her hand away and turned to face him, her blue eyes colder than Lake Michigan. "Yes, I can, Jasper. You broke up with her, didn't you?"

"You mean technically?"

"Yes. Let's get extremely technical."

"I guess I'm the one who actually ended it, but it was the decent thing to do, after all. I'd met you, and I thought you were amazing."

She stared at him, her face growing tighter by the second. "So you really like me, huh?"

"Yes." He didn't enjoy admitting his feelings under less-than-optimum circumstances, but maybe if she knew how he felt she'd get over being angry. "I think about you when I'm not with you, and when we're together, time races by. It's only been about three weeks, but you're already a big part of my life."

She nodded. "Good. Then you won't have to lie to the next girl. Be as broken up about this as you want." Spinning away from him, she hurried down the street toward her apartment.

He stared after her in stunned surprise. "You're leaving? Over a little thing like that?"

Instead of answering, she quickened her pace.

"I can't believe this." Had any woman ever left him? If so, he couldn't remember. And for Anica to leave him, the person he thought might turn out to be a life partner . . . This was just wrong. And by God he would fix it.

He had to run to catch up with her, and he could hear

the mousse slopping around in the take-out container—
the mousse he'd hoped to smear all over her naked body.
"Anica, wait!"

She kept walking.

"Hold up a minute." He grabbed her arm and pulled
her to a halt.

She turned and glared at him. "Let go of me."

He knew if he did, she'd start off again. He gulped in
cold air. "Anica, take it easy. You're overreacting."

"*Overreacting*? You start our relationship with a bald-
faced lie, pretending to be brokenhearted in order to
worm your way into my life, into my *bed*, and you have
the unmitigated gall to say I'm *overreacting?* You're a
real piece of work, Danes!"

"Come on. What I did is a small thing, nothing in
comparison to the good times you're throwing away."

"If I'm throwing them away, it's your fault, buddy. If
you're capable of that kind of calculated manipulation,
how can I trust you to be honest about anything?"

He pulled her closer. "Trust your body, Anica. We
have chemistry. You can't deny it."

Her nostrils flared, and for a moment something
closer to desire than fury burned in her gaze. "I won't
deny it," she said through clenched teeth. "Unlike you,
I tell the truth."

"See? Now let's just—"

"No!" Breathing hard, she lifted her chin in defiance.
"Just because a girl has chemistry with a jerk doesn't
mean she has to act on it!" She wrenched free and
backed away from him.

"Sweetheart, you're cute when—"

"Finish that sentence and I won't be responsible for
my actions." She backed away and held up both hands.
"I warn you. Stay away from me, Jasper. I'm in a really
bad mood right now, and you don't know what you're
dealing with."

He'd never seen her so worked up, and he admired her spirit. Surely he could coax her out of this snit and then he could redirect all that passion into more productive channels. He couldn't accept that he was about to lose her. Not over something so trivial.

He moved toward her again. "Come on, Anica. Be reasonable. Let's talk this out."

"Back off, lover boy!" She pulled something out of her purse.

"Pepper spray? Now you're really being ridiculous." Refusing to believe she'd hit him with the spray, he kept advancing. Anger and lust weren't so far apart on the emotional scale. One kiss and he'd tip the balance in his favor.

She pointed the thing at him. "It's my wand."

He laughed. Now he knew for sure she was kidding around. "Not bad, although isn't that a little small? I pictured them as bigger, but they say size isn't everything."

"Stay away from me."

He wasn't about to. She was way too cute. "Hey, if you want to go all Harry Potter on me and play let's pretend, can we go up to your apartment and do it in comfort?"

"I'm serious, Jasper." She shook the wooden stick. "Don't make me use this!"

He grinned at her and kept coming. "Gonna turn me into a frog? How about I kiss you first? Maybe you'll change your mind."

"Stop!"

Instead of stopping he grabbed her around the waist and pulled her close. "Come here, you."

"I said stop." She shoved him away. Then she muttered something in Latin, and light spurted from the end of the wooden stick. He opened his mouth to remark on the cool special effects, but before he could speak, his body began to shake. He dropped the box of mousse as the tremors increased and his heart raced out of control. Good God, he was having a heart attack!

Anica stared at him in horror.

Do something! He tried to scream for help, but his lips refused to work. Her wide-eyed, terrified gaze was the last thing he saw before he blacked out.

Chapter 2

"Dear Goddess, what have I done?" Cold sweat trickled down Anica's spine as she gazed at the pile of clothes on the sidewalk and the hissing cat trying to work his way out from under them. Any minute the cat would be free, and then what?

She had no time to debate the matter. Stuffing her wand in her purse, she scooped up the clothes and the cat, wrapping the whole bundle inside Jasper's tweed coat.

The cat's response was immediate. He struggled harder, clawing and growling in his attempt to get away.

"Stop it, Jasper! I'm taking you home. I'll find the spell to undo this, I promise." She held tight to the bundle and glanced around to see if she'd been observed, if squad cars were closing in, ready to take her to the slammer. No telling what the sentence was for transforming a commodities broker into a cat.

And that was only the civilian punishment. Far greater sanctions awaited her if the magical world found out what she'd done. Twenty-first-century witches and wizards were forbidden to use their powers to change a being from one form to another. Such things may have happened at times in the old days, but things were different now.

Luck seemed to be on Anica's side tonight. The street was deserted except for a couple passing on the other side. The pair hurried along, not looking in her direction, as if wanting to get out of the cold wind.

She hoped she wasn't close enough to the apartment to be within range of Julie's camera. Julie had been saving up for a zoom lens. Anica prayed she hadn't been able to afford it yet.

Anica had worn her do-me shoes with the stiletto heels on this date and now wished she'd chosen her black boots instead. On these ice picks she had to be careful not to turn an ankle. If she'd been wearing the boots she could have made her escape much faster, and she and Jasper might never have had the confrontation that had gone so wrong.

He continued to squirm inside the bundle of clothes, and she hugged him tighter, determined not to let him escape. He yowled in protest.

"Rescuing a cat, are you?" said a voice behind her.

Anica didn't stop, but she half turned to acknowledge Edna Shoumatoff, the seventy-something woman who lived two doors down on her floor. Edna had never married and had a low opinion of men.

Judging from the small paper sack Edna clutched to her chest, she'd stepped out for a burger and fries and was on her way back to eat it in front of her TV. For winter outings, Edna wore a Russian Cossack hat, a red quilted jacket, and sweats.

"Hi, Miss Shoumatoff. Yeah, I saw this cat wandering around with no collar and decided to keep it from getting run over."

"It doesn't seem to like being captured."

"That's because he doesn't know what's good for him." She wasn't sure whether as a cat Jasper could understand everything she said, but she hoped so. Maybe he'd stop struggling if he realized she was doing the best she could to remedy the situation.

"So it's a male, then?"

"Yes." An arrogant, entitled male who had pushed her into an action she deeply regretted. She would make everything right, but losing her temper like that wasn't her style. She'd been furious with him but also at herself, because even knowing his true nature she'd felt a dangerous tug of sexual excitement when he'd pulled her close.

That's why guilt plagued her. She might have turned him into a cat partly out of fear that she'd fall under his spell again and lose all self-respect. After all, Sheila had been willing to take him back. *He's that good.* Anica shivered.

Maybe Jasper did understand that she was trying to help him regain his human form, because he settled down a little, making him much easier to carry.

"I wouldn't have anything but a female," Edna said. "Males are nasty, and I'm not just talking about cats."

Anica had listened to Edna's anti-male rants many times before. The best response was no response.

"Dollars to doughnuts that cat you found is not fixed."

"Uh, no, I'm sure he's not."

"I hope you're planning to take care of that immediately. I can't abide a male cat that's not fixed."

Jasper suddenly went very still.

"I know what you mean, Miss Shoumatoff," Anica said. "I'll take him in pronto." It was the only reasonable response, after all.

With a screech, the cat turned into a dervish again, fighting harder than ever to get loose.

Edna laughed. "You'd think he understands English."

"I have a feeling he does." That could be both good and bad. She was breaking new ground, and she wasn't sure she wanted Jasper to know all her secrets. The spell was an old one, something she'd read years ago in one of her history of magic books. Of course there would be a counterspell. Of course. She ignored the uneasy fluttering of her stomach.

"Your other cat's a male, too, isn't it?" Edna said.

Orion. Anica had forgotten her obstinate, pudgy tabby cat. She'd adopted him thinking he had a touch of magic in him, but Orion had turned out to be an ordinary cat. She loved him to pieces, anyway, and he would *hate* having another cat invade his territory. "Yes, he's a male. I may have to keep them separated temporarily." *Until I get the spell reversed.*

"An orange tabby, if I remember right. You got him fixed, I hope."

"Of course."

"What color's this stray?"

Anica had no idea. Once the spell had taken effect, Jasper had quickly disappeared into the mound of clothing and had been hidden the entire time, so he could be any shade, any breed.

She'd better improvise for Edna's sake. "It was too dark to see very well. He was ... sleeping under this mound of clothes."

"I thought you said he was wandering around?"

"He was ... earlier. I noticed him earlier, before I went to dinner. Then I heard him yowling under this bundle of discarded clothes and decided to take action." For a person dedicated to truth-telling she was cooking up a pretty good lie. The irony wasn't lost on her.

Edna glanced at the bundle in Anica's arms before she started up the cement steps leading to their apartment building's front door. "Pricey coat to be somebody's discard."

"It's amazing what you can find at Goodwill these days." Anica had been wishing Edna hadn't happened along, but now she was grateful for her neighbor's presence. "I'm glad you're here to get the front door. I'm afraid to let go until I'm inside my apartment." With all this talk of neutering, she couldn't afford to loosen her grip on the cat. She'd done this deed, and she had the responsibility for setting it right.

"All right." Edna opened the main door. "I can help you into your apartment, too, if you want."

"That would be great." Anica and Edna climbed the stairs to the second floor. "My keys are in my purse." Moments later, as Edna took her purse from her arm and started fishing around, Anica wondered if that had been such a bright plan.

"This is a strange-looking thing." Edna held up Anica's wand. "Is it a pen? I don't see any point."

Anica laughed. "Oh, *that.* Just a piece of driftwood I picked up and polished because I thought it was pretty. Then I saw something on TV about using a sturdy pointed object for self-defense, so I decided to carry it." The more she had to lie, the less comfy she felt.

"We wouldn't need to defend ourselves if men were all neutered," Edna said darkly. Eventually she located Anica's keys and opened the door to her apartment. Orion was at the door, paws prancing in delight. Then he sniffed the air and backed up, growling. Obviously he'd smelled Jasper.

"Don't forget. First thing, get him fixed," Edna said.

"To be sure. Thanks for the help, Miss Shoumatoff." Anica stepped into her apartment and shoved the door closed with her hip. Orion was gone, probably hiding in the cupboard underneath the kitchen sink.

As she began to lower her bundle to the floor, Jasper gave a mighty heave and broke free, wiggling out of his confinement. Dropping globs of chocolate mousse on her beige carpet, he streaked toward the nearest open door, which happened to be her bedroom.

She ran after him. "No! Don't go under the . . ." A smear of chocolate mousse on her white Belgian lace bed skirt marked Jasper's passage. She dropped to her knees beside the bed. She thought he might be black, although the mousse all over his coat made it hard to tell.

She'd forgotten all about the mousse, but the take-out carton must have been under the pile of clothes. She'd scooped up cat and mousse together. Someday she might have the distance from this horrible experience to laugh about that. But this wasn't that day.

Lifting the bed skirt, she peered under the bed. "Jasper, please come out."

Jasper was nothing more than a dark shadow hunkered under the exact middle of the double bed.

"We have to clean that mousse off."

He didn't move.

"I can't work a spell to change you back to a man unless you come out."

No response.

"Look, I can see why you wouldn't trust me. You may not believe this, but I've never turned a person into an animal in my entire career as a witch. I'm not proud of losing my temper like that, but what's done is done. Now I have to fix you."

Jasper growled.

"Sorry, bad word choice. I have to *transform* you. I won't let anyone near you with a scalpel, I promise. Now, come on out, like a—" She stopped herself before she called him a good kitty. Jasper was not a cat, no matter how much he might look like one at the moment.

Or act like one. That maneuver of running under the bed was very catlike. While she was mostly horrified at what she'd done to another human being, she couldn't help being curious about how this transformation had affected Jasper.

Would he still think like a man or would he think like a cat? Would he develop a taste for cat food or would he crave a human diet? Would he hate the idea of a bath and prefer to lick the mousse off himself?

Yikes. Chocolate was fine for people but potentially bad for cats. "Listen, Jasper, if you feel the urge to lick that mousse, don't. Some cats have a severe reaction to chocolate. It makes them very sick."

She believed he understood human speech, so she decided to add a clincher to the warning. "If you ingest the chocolate, you could end up at the vet, and I'm sure my vet would insist on vaccinating and neutering you."

Jasper hissed his disapproval but didn't change positions.

She was getting nowhere. Maybe she should go to her living room bookshelves and find the musty old book where she'd first read this transformation charm. She could research the counterspell while sitting here minding the cat.

"I'm leaving to get the book I need to help you, Jasper." She stood and took off her coat. "I'll only be gone a minute, and I'll close the bedroom door so Orion can't get in." Laying her coat on the bed, she walked toward the door. "And remember, *don't lick.*"

Lick himself? Eeeuuuwww! Jasper was convinced he was in the middle of a sickeningly real nightmare and he'd wake up any minute safely lying in his king-sized bed in his condo, with his clock radio playing his favorite rock station. But even though none of this nonsense was actually taking place, he wouldn't lick the mousse coating his fur. Gross.

He liked the idea that he had claws, though. He wouldn't mind using them to scratch the hell out of the woman who had put him in this condition.

But he was dreaming. Of course he was. His dash under the bed had been pure self-preservation, and now that he was under here, he wasn't coming out until he woke up.

The whole date with Anica must have been part of this crummy bad dream. He could hardly wait to wake up so he could laugh about it. The part about Sheila being at the restaurant—he could figure that out. Apparently he had a secret fear that she'd arrive unannounced and mess up his deal with Anica.

As for Anica being a witch, maybe it was the black coat that looked like a cape. Or maybe it was that chance remark his buddy Fred had made the other day at work that Anica seemed to have cast a spell over him. The brain was amazing. Somehow it had put the cape and Fred's remark together and come up with witchcraft.

The cat transformation wasn't so tough to decipher, either, now that he thought about it. He'd always considered himself something of a tomcat, a man about town. All that talk about neutering was pretty scary, though. A shrink would probably have a field day with that part.

The door opened and closed. His hearing had improved considerably in this dream, and his sense of smell was outstanding. He knew Anica was in the room even before she spoke.

Her spicy perfume had seemed faint in real life. The scent was so much stronger now. Other smells assaulted him, as well, but two caught his attention. One he identified as belonging to another cat, the one he'd sensed when he'd first arrived in the apartment, and the second distinctive aroma was Anica's. It came across as strongly as if he'd had his nose buried between her breasts.

"Still under there, Jasper?" She was in her nylons, so she must have taken off the sexy black heels.

Kneeling down, she lifted the lace bed skirt and peeked under the bed. "I brought the book." She laid something as big as an unabridged dictionary on the carpet. "I should be able to find the counterspell, no problem."

Now that his panic had eased, Jasper felt like making some sort of response. What came out was a very ordinary meow. It didn't sound particularly manly, either, so he tried again, determined to make the sound deeper. Still too high-pitched for his taste.

"So you're talking! Does that mean you're ready to come out?"

No way, José.

"When I start to do the spell, I'm sure you'll want to be somewhere other than under my bed. I don't think you'll fit once you're human again. Plus you'll be—uh—naked. You might want to be somewhere you could grab a towel, like in the bathroom."

Maybe this nightmare could turn into a good dream, after all. If his cat self transformed into his naked man self, and Anica was still part of the equation, they could have dream sex. Sure, she'd turned him into a cat, but it was all a dream, so he could forgive her.

"Jasper? Come on. Don't be stubborn."

On the other hand, this spot under the bed had served him well so far. Tucking his paws under his body, he prepared to wait her out.

Cats were good at waiting, he discovered. The space under this double bed was very small. He smelled old wood and lemon oil. It was probably an antique. This dream was the most detailed one he'd ever had.

"I really can't leave you under there. I'm going to levitate the bed."

Holy crap! Could she do that? She was a witch in this dream, so anything was possible. Jasper tensed, his tail twitching, as he wondered if his hiding place would rise up to the ceiling. He'd run again if it did. There had to be other hidey-holes in this apartment, and he'd find them. A cat, he was discovering, could fit in very small spaces.

Anica murmured something in Latin, but the bed didn't move. "Huh. That always worked when I needed to vacuum up the dust bunnies." She chanted again. Still the bed remained on the carpeted floor.

She sighed. "All right. For some reason that spell has a glitch in it. I might as well quit fooling around and do this the normal way. Be right back."

Jasper didn't know what the normal way entailed, but

when Anica returned, he found out. She shoved a broom under the bed.

He freaked. Rationally, he shouldn't freak. It was a broom, for chrissakes. As a man, he didn't have a single negative reaction to a broom. As a cat, he *hated* brooms. He hated this one in particular, which had a thick, round handle with carvings on it. Without knowing for sure, he decided it was a witch's broom.

"I need you to get out of there," Anica said. "Come on. Go." She moved the broom back and forth under the bed.

Jasper tried to hold his ground, but in the end he bolted. He ran for the bedroom door, but that was shut tight. He tried to squeeze under her dresser, but no dice. The sliding mirrored closet doors were closed, too. The only escape was through the bathroom door, and that was a dead end.

He knew that but he had no choice. Racing through the door, he leaped into the tub and hid behind the shower curtain, which was, he belatedly noticed, decorated with glittery stars. The bathroom door closed and he was trapped.

Her voice took on a crooning, seductive quality. "Poor Jasper. You were a louse about Sheila, but no guy deserves this." She peeked around the edge of the shower curtain.

He cowered in the corner, hating that he cowered, but he couldn't seem to help it.

"Looks like you're an all-black kitty, with the most beautiful golden eyes. That makes sense, I suppose, with your natural coloring. Well, enough chitchat. Let's see what counterspell I need to invoke."

The sound of Anica flipping through pages of her book was the only noise in the room, except once when the heat switched on. That was the other thing Jasper had noticed when he'd transformed—the bitter cold of a Chicago March night. He'd been covered by a pile of his clothes, but even so, the sidewalk had felt like ice under his paws.

Of course, that hadn't stopped him from struggling to escape when Anica had picked him up to take him home. Better to be freezing and in charge of his life than to be a prisoner sitting in a warm apartment, depending on someone else to provide food and shelter. Jasper hadn't liked that feeling as a kid and he didn't like it now as a cat.

His parents had controlled his every movement until he turned eighteen. He realized now it had been out of concern, but he'd felt smothered and had rented his own apartment the minute he could save enough money. Staying in control was important to him, which made this dream his ultimate nightmare.

"Hm." Anica flipped a few more pages. "Maybe in the index," she murmured to herself.

Jasper didn't like the sound of that. He hadn't heard an *aha* of discovery yet. What if she couldn't find a counterspell?

Then he chastised himself for being a fool caught up in this fantasy. Whether she found a counterspell or not, he would eventually wake up and all this would be forgotten. A nightmare might seem to last forever, but they all had to end sometime. The clock radio would click on at six thirty and he'd hit the snooze button to give himself another five minutes.

Then again, he might not hit the snooze button this time. Not if going back to sleep meant returning to this wacko dream.

"That's weird," Anica said. She sounded puzzled.

Despite knowing that nothing really mattered, Jasper felt his gut tighten. Without him willing it, his tail twitched from side to side. The tail part intrigued him. Swishing his tail was a much better stress buster than drumming on the table with his fingertips.

He became aware of Anica's breathing, which wasn't

as steady as it had been when she'd first settled down to read the book. He would bet a hundred bucks that she wasn't finding what she'd expected to, and she was becoming agitated. When she closed the book with a bang, he knew for sure.

"I'm an accomplished witch." She said it as if trying to convince herself. "I can create my own counterspell. Okay, Jasper. Showtime!"

The curtain swished aside and he stared up at her. She held a pointed wooden stick in one hand. The thing she'd used on him before had been more compact. This one measured at least eighteen inches and was made of some light-colored wood that had been polished until it gleamed.

She raised it like a conductor about to signal the beginning of a symphony. Then she pointed it directly at him and started in with the Latin phrases. They sounded very official, and if anything could do the trick this stream of Latin should. He became mesmerized listening to her.

After about five minutes of constant chanting, she lowered the wand and put both hands on her hips, the wand sticking out to one side. "This is one stubborn spell, Jasper. But I'm going to beat it." Taking a deep breath, she raised the wand again, pointed it at his nose and resumed chanting.

He decided to help. Lifting his head, he began yowling in time to her chanting.

"Great!" She paused for breath. "That's excellent! Keep it up!"

She spoke Latin and he spoke cat for at least another ten minutes, but nothing came of it. He kept expecting his body to stretch and the fur to fall away. He'd already picked out the towel—a light green bath sheet—that he'd use to cover himself once the transformation took place.

Except it never did.

Anica stopped chanting. "Let me test this wand. I'm

not sure it's working." She pointed the wand at the toilet and muttered something. When nothing happened, she jiggled the toilet handle and tried again. No response. "Flush, damn you!" She was clearly getting upset.

Jasper hopped to the edge of the tub and stared at the toilet, willing it to flush.

"It's the wand. I'll try my other one." She stormed out of the bathroom, leaving the door open.

Jasper could have run out, but he didn't see the point. If her other wand worked, then he'd be transformed any minute. There still could be time for some dream sex before the alarm went off, which just might salvage this awful nightmare.

From the door of the bathroom, Anica pointed her short wand at him and chanted with more intensity. After several minutes of chanting with no observable result, she lowered the wand. "I have a bad feeling about this."

She wasn't the only one. He'd been looking forward to dream sex with her.

"Jasper, I'm not sure what's going on here, but my magic seems to be on the fritz."

Bummer.

"I hate, hate, hate doing this, but I have no choice. I have to call my sister, Lily."

Because she said it as if delivering a death sentence, he was immediately afraid of this Lily person. Hopping back into the bathtub, he scrunched down in the corner.

"Oh, Lily's not that bad. It's just that I'm usually the responsible one and she's the screwup. We've had our issues over the years, and although we're not enemies, we're not fast friends, either. Seeing what I've done to myself—and you," she added hastily, "will send her into gloat mode. But she's pretty good at magic, so she might be able to take care of this problem."

Jasper marveled that he'd had dozens of conversations with Anica over the past three weeks and she'd never mentioned a sister. They couldn't be very close.

Then again, this was a dream. The real Anica might not have a sister at all.

She closed him in the bathroom while she went to get her cell phone. He made use of the time to hop up on the counter and look at himself in the mirrored wall above the sink. He'd been wondering what he looked like, and if he was as sleek and elegant as he imagined.

Not so much. The creature staring back at him looked like it'd been put through a food processor. Dull black fur, about a half inch all over, was matted with dried bits of chocolate mousse. He had globs of it clinging to the tufts in his ears. In fact, he was the ugliest cat he'd ever seen. Fuckin' A.

He hated the idea of licking his fur. Hated it. But he hated looking like a Dumpster diver even more. He pawed at the faucet and managed to turn it on. Then he wasn't sure what to do next. Stick his head under it? Climb into the sink?

Just at that moment Anica opened the door with the phone to her ear and spied Jasper. "Wait, Jasper." She picked him up from the counter. "I'll give you a bath instead."

Like hell. He wasn't about to trust her to do that without somehow drowning him. He felt his claws sink into her arm as he launched himself away from her and out the bathroom door. He didn't feel bad about scratching her. She'd brought it on herself.

He scampered through the bedroom and romped down the hall, loving the freedom, ready to do whatever it took to get himself out of this hellacious mess. Then he skidded to a halt.

Blocking his way was the cat he'd sensed earlier when he'd first come into the apartment. He was an orangey color and looked enormous with his back arched and every hair sticking straight out. He was the cat from hell, and if Jasper wanted his freedom, he had to go past him.

Chapter 3

Anica barely heard her sister's promise that she'd be there ASAP. Leaving the phone on the counter she rushed through the bedroom and out into the hall, where Orion and Jasper had found each other and were circling like prizefighters, each trying to out-hiss the other.

"Orion! Jasper! Cut it out!"

Neither cat paid any attention. Ears back, tails swishing, they crouched and circled, ready to rumble. Anica ran back to the bathroom, filled a water glass, and made it back just in time to see Orion and Jasper lunge at each other and go down in a rolling, spitting ball of black and orange fur.

Anica tossed the water on them. With a screech, Jasper abandoned the fight and raced for the living room. Orion followed, and a loud crack signaled that one of them had broken something. Anica arrived to find Jasper on top of the bookshelf. Orion, who couldn't leap that far, waited at the bottom, growling.

Anica's very expensive, impossible-to-replace crystal ball, which she'd put on top of the bookshelf to keep it out of Orion's reach, lay on the floor in two pieces amid smears of chocolate mousse on the carpet. The crystal must have split when it bounced off the marble-topped end table, which now had a large chunk broken off the right front corner.

She didn't know what breaking a crystal ball signified, but it couldn't be a good thing. The carpet could be cleaned, but the green marble-topped table was an antique she'd saved for months to buy.

She glared at Jasper. "Keep this up, fur face, and you'll be eating Cat Chow for the rest of your life."

With a sigh, she went to the kitchen and got a sponge and a bucket of water. She wasn't much good at cleaning because she'd always used magic for that. Sponging up mousse from the carpet sounded disgusting, but for the time being, she had no choice.

She was still on her hands and knees when Lily used her key and came through the door. Anica had given her the key after renting the apartment, probably in some vain hope they'd grow closer. It hadn't happened. Apparently they were too different. Dropping the sponge into the bucket, Anica got up.

Dear Zeus, how she hated to let Lily see her in the middle of such a major screwup. She forced herself to be gracious. "I appreciate you leaving work, Lil."

"Are you kidding? I wouldn't have missed this for the world." She glanced around and quickly took in the disasters. "Whoa! Your boyfriend looks like shit. What's he been rolling in?" Lily took off her backpack and black leather jacket.

"Chocolate mousse from La Bohème."

"Was that before or after the transformation?" She was wearing her bartending outfit—a low-cut black knit shirt and skinny black pants. Her dark hair was piled on top of her head in a loose arrangement. With that hairstyle and platform shoes, she was at least six feet tall. Anica was not petite at five-eight, but Lily was almost five-ten in her bare feet.

"After the transformation."

Lily surveyed the living room. "Uh-oh. Is that what's left of your crystal ball?"

" 'Fraid so. Do you know what happens when you break one?"

"No." Lily crouched and picked up the two pieces. "Do you?"

"Nope."

"I'm thinking Super Glue might not be the answer." She laid the pieces on the carpet again and stood.

"Probably not. I'll research it later. Right now, we have to deal with the cat situation. I'd rather the Wizard Council didn't find out."

"I'll bet." Lily's brown gaze was smug. "Who would believe that my perfect older sister would one day break a *rule*. How does it feel, sis?"

"Not so good, if you must know. Can we get going here? I hope you brought your wand. My two don't seem to be working."

"I always carry one in my backpack." Lily walked over and unzipped a side pocket. "But I have to ask, what sent you over the edge and made you zap this guy—what's his name?"

"Jasper Danes."

Lily pulled out her wand, which was dyed deep purple and covered with glitter. "He can understand everything we say, can't he? I mean, he's a cat on the outside but still a man on the inside, right?"

"I think so." Anica glanced over at Jasper, who stared at her with accusing golden eyes. "It's hard to tell since he can't talk."

"That could be a plus. Want me to try and keep that feature in when I change him back?"

After the lies Jasper had told, Anica was tempted. But it would violate wizard law. "Lily, we can't mess around with people."

"Don't be all sanctimonious with me." Lily pulled a

reference book on spells out of her backpack. "You're the one who turned a man into a pussy."

From his perch on the bookshelf Jasper growled.

Lily glanced up at him and smiled. "Yep, he can understand us, all right. You still haven't told me why you wanded him, sis."

"I'd rather not go into it."

"Was it because you discovered he has a teeny-tiny dick?"

"No, it wasn't!"

Jasper hissed, which made Lily laugh.

Anica scowled at her. "You're enjoying this way too much."

"Yes, indeed I am. For all my twenty-six years, I've been the screwup in the family and you've been the model of perfection. I finally, *finally* have something to hold over your head. Unless you were planning to come clean with Mom and Dad."

Anica thought of their highly respectable parents, who'd taken a year's sabbatical from their teaching positions at the International Magical Academy to research ancient herbal remedies in Peru. "I'd rather not."

"Good choice. My silence can be bought, but it's not cheap."

"Lily! You're dickering over terms while a man's existence hangs in the balance!"

"Who put him in that position, hmm?"

Lily had her there. Oh, how Anica regretted that split second when fury and frustration had wiped out years of discipline. "You're right." The words tasted like vinegar in her mouth.

"Music to my ears, big sis. Music to my ears. Okay, I found something that might work. Stand aside, and let the responsible sister take a shot. Oh, how I love saying that! It's never been true before, but looking at the mangy alley cat perched on your bookshelf, you have to admit it's true now."

Anica closed her eyes and envisioned a lifetime of being blackmailed by her younger sister. "Just do it so we can all go back to our regularly scheduled programs."

"If you insist." Lily sighed. "I would love to stand here and poke fun at you for another hour or so, but—"

"Lily!"

"Okay, okay. I suppose there's some reward in that he'll appear naked. That could be fun. Did you want to get him a towel or something?"

"Yeah, hold on." Anica hurried to the bathroom and pulled a towel off the rack. When she returned, Lily was waving her wand like a symphony conductor, but Jasper was still in cat form. Anica hadn't watched her sister do magic in some time and had no idea how she worked these days. "You didn't start, did you?"

"No. I'm limbering up the wand. I like my men and my wands flexible."

Anica groaned. If she hadn't been desperate for help she wouldn't have called Lily. But she hadn't been able to think of anyone else who could come at a moment's notice and could (she prayed) be trusted, or bribed, not to tell.

Lily cleared her throat. "I've given up on the Latin chants. Too hard to remember. English works fine for me."

"You can chant in Portuguese if it'll break this spell. Go."

"I'm ready." Lily raised her wand. "Mangy tomcat, full of grime, tiny dick your only crime—"

"That wasn't the problem, damn it!"

Lily paused, took a breath and started over. "Mangy tomcat, full of grime, flaccid dick your only crime—"

"It had nothing to do with his dick!"

"I find that so hard to believe. In my world, men either have what it takes or they don't. I can't imagine turning one into a cat unless they come up short, so to speak."

Anica didn't dare look at Jasper crouched on the bookshelf. "I have no idea whether he would come up short or not."

Lily stared at her in disbelief. "No nookie?"

"Not yet."

"What's wrong with you? You've known him for weeks! Okay, I have the chant for this. Don't interrupt this time." She rolled her shoulders and shook out her hands. "I need to concentrate."

"Okay." Beggars couldn't be choosers.

"Mangy tomcat, full of grime, low sex drive his only crime, re-create his form sublime. With harm to none, so mote it be."

Anica doubted that Jasper had a low sex drive, not if Sheila wanted him back on any terms. But Lily was incapable of working a spell without throwing something funky into the mix. Anica had forgotten that until now.

She held her breath and waited for Jasper to appear before them, naked and covered with chocolate mousse. If that happened, it could settle the tiny-dick question once and for all. Anica didn't believe that supposition of Lily's for a minute. Fate wouldn't be so cruel as to make a man as gorgeous as Jasper and give him substandard equipment.

The two women and the orange cat gazed at Jasper, waiting for something to happen. Anica and Lily hoped to see the cat become a man. Orion obviously expected that Fate would deliver this interloper to him once again so he could whip his ass. No cat could stay on a bookshelf forever.

Nothing happened.

Lily examined her wand. "I don't know the problem. It was working before I came over here. I used it to change the TV channel in the bar from ESPN to *American Idol*."

Panic tightened Anica's muscles. "Test it on something else."

"Good idea." Lily pointed her wand toward the kitchen. "I use this one all the time at work. *Tequila smooth and lime so tender, dance a tango in the blender.*"

From the grinding noise that followed, Anica concluded that Lily's wand worked just fine. Her spell must be wrong. "Can you try another spell?" She was almost afraid to ask, for fear the next chant would be even more embarrassing, but they had to keep trying.

"Let me see what I can find." She grabbed the book and flipped through it. "Maybe this one. *Mangy cat so discontent, sorry you are impotent. Change thy form and be a gent.*"

Anica groaned. "Do they all have to insult his sexuality?"

"Actually yes. They recommend getting the transformed being angry, which acts as a kind of catalyst to help reverse the spell. That's assuming the spell is similar to those in this book. It must be not, since we haven't changed a whisker on that cat so far."

"Can I see the book?"

"Be my guest." Lily handed it over.

Anica read quickly and with increasing despair. "These spells are much more elaborate, involving pieces of hair and stuff. I didn't do any of that."

"Where did you get the spell in the first place?"

"Remember that old *History of Magic* text I found in the used bookstore right next to campus?"

"Not particularly. You were the one who went gaga over that musty old thing, not me."

"I'll go get it." Anica walked back to the bathroom and returned with the book, which she opened to the page with the incantation on it. "I memorized this for fun back in my freshman year. I thought it sounded cool. I didn't even know if it would work."

Lily came to read over her shoulder. "Anica, there's no counterspell listed under it."

Worry made Anica impatient. "Don't you think I know that? If there had been one, I'd have used it."

"So why did you use a spell with no counterspell?"

"I forgot it didn't have one! And the spell was a reflex, something I did without thinking it through, a knee-jerk reaction."

"Amazing. That's so unlike you. He must have been a gold-plated asshole to make you lose it like that."

"Well, he was, but that doesn't mean he deserves to be a cat for the rest of his life."

"Or that you should lose your magic for the rest of yours."

"What?" Anica glanced up at her sister.

Lily squeezed her shoulder. "I read it in my spell book just now, but I didn't want to tell you. It said clearly that if a witch or wizard transforms a person into an animal, no matter the reason, they must reverse the spell within ten minutes."

"Ten minutes?"

"That's all the time they have before they lose their magic abilities. And those abilities won't be restored until the person is restored to his or her original form."

Anica slammed the cover on the *History of Magic* and laid it on a chair. "Show me where it says that."

Lily retrieved her spell book and thumbed through until she found the passage. "Here."

Anica's hands trembled as she took the book and read the passage Lily pointed to. Sure enough, that's what it said. "No wonder my wands don't work! My stupid *History of Magic* might have said something about this little side effect!"

"I hate to point this out, but it's a history book, not a spell book. I doubt they expected you to work magic from it."

Anica wailed. "I didn't mean to! It just happened! What are we going to do?"

"What do you mean *we*?"

Anica had no choice but to humble herself. "I can't do it by myself. My magic is gone. I need you to help me figure this out, Lily. Please."

"How sweet it is. But I don't seem to have any immediate answers. Maybe we should call in some experts."

Anica shook her head so hard she felt like she popped a vertebra in her neck. "I have other references we can consult." Returning Lily's book to her, Anica walked over to her bookshelf and pulled out three different volumes. She'd bought them on sale and hadn't used them much, but something was better than nothing.

"I'd feel better if we had an experienced witch or wizard on the premises," Lily said. "Not Mom and Dad, of course. I know you wouldn't want either of them to see this cock-up, but—"

"I don't want *anybody* to see this except you and me." Anica walked over to the sofa and set the books on the coffee table in front of her. If she consulted anyone besides her sister her transgression would be spread all over the wizard world by tomorrow morning. Lily might have the impulse to blab, but Anica had dirt on Lily. Lily could be contained.

"Okay, but this really cool witch and wizard came into the Bubbling Cauldron the other day. He's a little flaky, but she seemed pretty sharp. We talked magic a little, and she knows her stuff. They live in Southern Indiana, and I have their number. They could be here in a few hours."

Anica picked up the first book and turned to the table of contents. "I'd need more information on them than that. For all I know, they'd report me to the Wizard Council the minute they heard what I've done."

"Actually, I think they're on the Wizard Council."

"Lily!" Anica stared at her in horror. "I can't consult somebody on the council! They'd be obligated to turn in a report on me. I'm sure we can fix this ourselves and nobody will be the wiser."

"Whatever you think—you're the one with no magic powers."

Gritting her teeth at the thought of being powerless, Anica turned to the chapter on transformation. Unless she solved this problem, she would have to depend on Lily for any little magic chore she had. And she had a bunch of them.

But that wasn't the most important consideration. She had to solve it because otherwise she had ruined Jasper's life. Why, oh, why had she allowed herself to be carried away on a tide of negative emotion?

She knew better. She'd built up a successful business because she always thought things through, weighed the odds, acted only when she was ready. She wasn't impulsive. Jasper's behavior had caused her to overreact, just as he'd accused her of doing. That wasn't like her at all. He must have gotten under her skin even more than she'd realized.

"Finding anything?" Lily walked over to stand beside the sofa.

"Not yet." She kept searching through the book. "There's information about transforming, but it's all similar to what's in your book. I'm hoping to find a reference to that old spell. I think that's our only chance."

"I think so, too. Maybe—" From inside Lily's backpack, her cell phone played "Born to Be Wild." "Excuse me a minute. That's probably work."

While Lily took her call, Anica picked up the second book, but each reference turned out to have no more information than what they'd already tried.

"Still nothing?" Lily came back over to the sofa.

"Nothing."

"Hey, I have to go back to work. I got Chad to cover for me, but his girlfriend's sick and he has to go take care of her."

"You're leaving?" Anica tried to keep the apprehension out of her voice.

"Yeah, if I want to keep my job. The Bubbling Cauldron is the only wizard-owned bar in town and I prefer working for magical people." She put on her leather jacket and hooked her backpack over one shoulder.

"Surely someone else could tend bar tonight."

"I could already be in trouble for calling Chad. Devon, the owner, doesn't like us to switch places without his okay, but he was unreachable, so I just did it. If I bring in yet another bartender and he finds out, he'll go ape shit. He knows his magic, but he's also a control freak."

"I didn't realize. But if you ever get fed up with him, you know you always have a job with me at Wicked Brew." Anica wasn't sure how that would work, but as a sister she should offer.

"Thanks, but no, thanks. You'd probably make me get up at the crack of dawn."

Anica smiled at that. "Yeah, I would."

"Besides, I have another reason I want to keep this job. There's a really cute guy who's been coming in for drinks. I'd like to see if that can go anywhere."

Anica didn't want Lily to lose her job, either, but she wished her sister had a better reason for wanting to keep it than because she had a crush on one of the customers. That was Lily, though—short-term goals but no long-term plans for the future. Meanwhile Anica had her own business and a healthy IRA. She played ant to Lily's grasshopper.

But her reign of imagined superiority had come to an abrupt end tonight.

Lily paused with her hand on the doorknob. "I can check back when I get off work."

"I'd appreciate it." Anica got up to lock the door after Lily. "I'll call you if I find anything promising in these books. Obviously I won't be able to work the magic myself."

"I'll be happy to come over and handle that chore." Lily winked at her. "Once I do you'll have a naked man in your apartment, which will be my cue to leave. After going through this trauma, you might as well take advantage of the situation."

Anica glanced toward the bookshelf, where Jasper was scrunched up in disapproving silence. "Somehow I don't think he'll be in the mood. I sure wouldn't be after something like this."

"My dearest sister, don't you know about the most important difference between men and women? A woman has to be in the right frame of mind, but a man is *always* in the mood."

Chapter 4

Easy for you to say. Jasper glared at the brunette striding out of Anica's apartment. Clearly no one had ever turned Lily into an animal with fur and a tail. Although he had to admit he was growing somewhat fond of the tail. He liked the way he could flick it around.

In any case, even if Lily managed to transform him back into a man, sex wouldn't be his first thought. He'd be out for revenge.

The longer this business continued, the more he was forced to question his belief that it was all a dream. Yet everything in him resisted the idea that Anica was a witch who had turned him into a cat. Witches were fairy tale beings who didn't exist in real life.

But her bookshelf contained a ton of books on magic. When he'd leaped to the top he'd knocked off a crystal ball. To his immense satisfaction, it had cracked on the way down and taken a chunk off a marble tabletop in the process. He would have been happy to destroy some more stuff, but first he'd have to fight Orion again, and that hadn't been much fun.

That fight was the main thing making a believer out of him. He'd done some damage to Orion but the other cat had managed to scratch him in several places, too.

The wounds didn't feel like imaginary dream scratches. They stung like a sonofabitch.

And he wanted to clean them, but without opposable thumbs that would mean licking, and he so was not going there. It sounded icky and Anica had convinced him licking chocolate would land him on the surgical table of a castration-happy vet. Even in a dream he didn't want to lose his nuts.

But his intense sense of smell also undermined the dream theory. Crouched on the bookshelf with the smooth, lemon-scented wood under his claws, he was on sensory overload. He could smell the chocolate mousse, the dust collected on the books, the lime from the margarita still sitting in the blender. He could smell Orion, and his hackles went up automatically. Underlying it all was the scent of Anica—the soap, the shampoo, the perfume, and a sweet aroma that was all female. Too bad he hated her.

His hearing was just as acute. He picked up Anica's breathing, the flipping of pages, the hum of the heater, water rushing through the pipes in another apartment, the ticking of a quartz clock, even the swish of Orion's tail across the carpet.

Jasper couldn't quite accept that he was making this up in his sleep. He wasn't that good a dreamer. He couldn't quite accept that he was a cat, either, which left him in limbo. He needed to come down on the side of one reality or the other if he wanted to keep from going crazy.

Because this dream, if that's what it was, seemed never-ending, he decided to play it as the cat. He might wake up any minute, or Anica could find a counterspell in one of her reference books. . . . Although it looked as if she wouldn't be able to work the necessary magic. She'd have to rely on Lily.

If he could talk he would ask why they hadn't researched spells on the computer sitting on the delicately carved desk in a corner of the living room. Maybe nothing would be available—it wasn't the kind of thing he'd ever checked out—but everything in the world seemed to be on the Net these days. Then again, maybe her computer didn't work. It did look sort of old.

"Shit!"

Jasper blinked. He'd never heard that word come out of Anica's mouth.

That was only the beginning. With a string of swear words that would do a construction worker proud Anica slammed the cover on the third book, stood and turned in his direction. "I hate to say this, Jasper, but I think we're both fucked."

If he'd still been a guy, he would have laughed. The sight of blond, angelic-looking Anica using the F word was just plain funny. He should be worried about the implications of her statement, but he was getting really tired.

In fact, he could use a nap. Somewhere he'd read that adult cats slept eighteen hours a day. He was probably way overdue for a snooze.

"I'm going to call Lily and tell her we'll tackle this tomorrow, when we're fresh." Anica walked back into the bedroom, probably in search of her phone.

She returned with the phone pressed to her ear as she talked to her sister. "Yes, I'll seriously think about calling the Lowells in Big Knob, but I don't want to rush into anything. Right now let's practice damage control. Promise you won't say anything to anyone." She paused. "Thank you. I really appreciate that."

Jasper could sense the anxiety level in the room lowering. Anica was ready to take a break from the drama and settle in for the evening. His energy level was dropping, too, so he was okay with that program, but he hoped he wouldn't be spending the night on the top of the bookshelf.

"Okay, Lily." Anica shifted her weight as she talked on the phone.

Jasper noticed how her purple silk dress clung to her

hips. He'd planned to take that dress off tonight, but after this episode she could be sexier than Cameron Diaz and he wouldn't give a damn.

"Right," Anica said. "I'll be in touch tomorrow. Yeah, I know. Not until noon. Take care." She closed her phone and looked up at Jasper. "I'm ready to call it a night, but I have to clean you up first. Otherwise you might lick that chocolate mousse while I'm asleep."

He weighed the pros of getting clean with the cons of whatever watery fate she had in mind for him.

"I'll run bathwater for you."

For some reason, the bath concept seemed a little less scary than it had at first.

She gazed up at him. "Jasper, I'm sorry about this. I promise to do the best I can to make everything right again. We'll take care of it tomorrow." With a sigh she turned away and walked into her bedroom.

He could tell she was really sorry. As well she should be. If this was all real, and he was increasingly worried that it was, she'd behaved in a totally irresponsible manner by casting a magic spell she didn't know how to reverse. He had no sympathy for her.

The bath water thundering into the tub sounded like Niagara Falls. He'd had no idea the world could be such a deafening place for a cat. Orion kept his watch at the bottom of the bookshelf.

Jasper didn't relish sleeping with one eye open all night, but he was dependent on Anica to keep Orion from attacking him. It wasn't his fault that he was invading the other cat's territory, but he had to suffer for it all the same. Damn, how he hated this helpless feeling, and it was all Anica's fault.

She came out wearing a white terry robe. Her feet were bare. In spite of his anger, he found himself wondering what she had on underneath the robe.

"All right, Jasper. Come with me." Reaching to the top of the bookshelf, she pulled him down into her arms.

He could have resisted, but he was tired of hugging that narrow plank of wood. Even better, Anica nudged Orion aside. "Not you," she said.

How she managed to get him into the bathroom and close the door on Orion, he wasn't sure. But he'd rather face her than a cat bent on his destruction.

"The water's lukewarm, Jasper," she said. "I'll make this quick, but I have to get that chocolate mousse off of you."

He took a look at the water in the tub as she lowered him toward it. For one panicky moment he pictured drowning in the water, and he struggled. She held him tight in her arms and the terry robe kept his claws from digging into her skin.

Nevertheless he somehow ended up standing in that water while she scrubbed him down with a loofah. His scratches stung and he hated every minute of it, but he understood it had to be done. He searched for a distraction, which he found with very little trouble. As she leaned over to wash him, her terry robe fell open just enough to reveal her cleavage.

Think like a man, Jasper told himself. *Take what bennies you can get and enjoy the view.* He concentrated on the sway of her breasts as she worked him over with the loofah, and for seconds at a time he'd forget that he was a cat getting a bath.

He peered intently at the opening in case he could catch a glimpse of a rosy nipple, but no such luck. Looking up he noticed that her hair was coming out of its arrangement and blond curls clung damply to her cheek. She looked sexy as hell, and he was so engrossed that when the bath was over and she wrapped him in a big towel, he was almost sorry.

"There you go. Such a good kitty." She dried him with the towel while she crooned endearments.

Kitty? He growled at her, damned insulted that she'd called him that. He was a guy, with a manly job navigating the tricky waters of the commodities market. He supported the Bulls and the Bears with season tickets.

What else? He drove a Beemer and played a mean game of pool. He'd been known to smoke the occasional cigar, and he loved a cold glass of beer. He was so loaded with testosterone it wasn't even funny. And yet the more she rubbed him down, the more he had the urge to ... purr.

The sound rumbled up from his chest, surprising the hell out of him. A manly man didn't purr, dammmit! But cats did, and whatever she was doing with that towel was terrific. He couldn't stop the purr from getting louder. It wasn't unlike an erection that wouldn't go away.

"That wasn't so bad, was it, Jasper?" She gave him one last swipe with the towel and set him down on the bathroom floor.

And damned if he wasn't still purring. Apparently it was some sort of cat reflex that he couldn't control. Hanging on to his anger was getting tougher by the minute. If he didn't concentrate he was liable to end up on his back getting a tummy scratch.

No, by God. She was the enemy. Assuming this was real and not a dream, she'd turned him into a cat over some minor infraction. Once he was himself again she'd pay for that. And he would be himself again. No way was he ending up as a cat forever. That was simply unacceptable.

"I'm glad you let me give you a bath," she said in an indulgent tone. "Are you hungry? I have some leftover chicken in the refrigerator. Let me get you some. It's the least I can do."

Spoiling him wouldn't let her off the hook, but he'd take advantage of everything he could while he was in this situation. Besides, he couldn't be expected to eat those dried rabbit droppings that passed for cat food. Surely she'd continue to feed him people food.

She scooped him up in her arms and carried him

out of the bathroom. Being carried meant he wasn't in charge of his movements, which he disliked, but it also meant he wouldn't be attacked by the demon cat who was waiting right outside the bathroom door, ready to pounce. And being cuddled against Anica's breasts wasn't the worst thing in the world, either.

That cursed purr started up again. He sounded too blasted agreeable, and he tried to will the purr gone, but short of hacking up a hair ball, he didn't know how to stop it. Come to think of it, he regretted raising the whole hair ball issue. Other cats might indulge in that disgusting behavior, but he had no intention of doing it.

Orion didn't seem very happy, which made Jasper exceedingly pleased. The orange cat made noises that sounded like a kitty version of swearing as he trotted right along with them toward the kitchen.

From his favored perch in Anica's arms, Jasper gazed down at Orion. *Eat my shorts, fur face.*

Anica set Jasper on the counter. "I'll feed you up here, so Orion can't get to you." Then she crouched down and tried to pay attention to the demon cat, but he wasn't having any of it. He stalked away, out of reach.

"This is only temporary, Orion," Anica said. "You're my main man. Jasper will be gone by tomorrow." Then she muttered something that sounded suspiciously like *I hope*.

While Anica pulled a bowl out of the refrigerator, Jasper took inventory of the kitchen from his position on the beige laminated countertop. His brief time on the floor of this apartment had taught him that he couldn't see shit from ten inches off the ground. No wonder cats sought higher vantage points.

The appliances were standard apartment issue— white and slightly beat up. The cabinets were oak laminate and also a little worn around the edges. Both the kitchen and the living room were on an outside wall facing a neighborhood park, so there was a window over the sink, and Anica had several small pots of stuff growing on the sill.

If he hadn't been factoring in the witch thing, he would have said they were herbs like basil and oregano, but he couldn't imagine she'd take up valuable window-sill placement for something that ordinary. She could be growing something poisonous there. For damn sure he wouldn't chomp on any of them to find out.

She'd added some decorator touches to the kitchen with colorful towels and potholders, plus she had a killer espresso machine sitting on a counter across from him. The blender sat next to the espresso machine. It was filled with a light green mixture—the margarita Lily had created with her wand. Other than the magic margarita, the kitchen was unremarkable-looking.

He wasn't sure what he'd expected—black cauldrons bubbling with evil-smelling potions, maybe. Jars filled with eye of newt or some equally nauseating ingredient. Instead the kitchen looked about the same as those belonging to his previous, nonwitchy girlfriends.

The microwave dinged and she set a warm bowl of cut-up chicken in front of him. "I warmed it up for you," she said. "And here's a bowl of water, too." She put that down beside the chicken.

The food smelled like heaven, which probably explained why Orion was yowling with displeasure as he pranced back and forth in the narrow kitchen.

"I can't give you any," Anica told him. "The vet's orders were very specific. No more table food. Being overweight is bad for your heart."

Jasper tried to enjoy his triumph as he ate the chicken, but Orion sounded pitiful. If the orange cat hadn't tried to rip out his throat, Jasper might even feel sorry for him.

"Hey, Orion, sweetie. Come on over." Anica held out her hand. "Let me give you a cuddle. That's better than food."

Orion must not have thought so, because he danced away from her and kept yowling his complaint about being chickenless. He was making quite the racket.

"Okay, this is not working. You're disturbing the neighbors."

Sure enough, a thumping noise came from above them.

"See?" Anica snatched up a protesting Orion and carried him into the living room.

A door opened and closed, and then there was silence. Jasper couldn't believe she'd just throw her cat out in the hall. He was working very hard not to feel sorry for Orion, but if Anica had given him the boot for a few angry yowls, then Jasper had better mind his manners. He couldn't afford to be tossed out the door. Not if all this was real.

Anica walked back into the kitchen minus her cat.

Jasper stared at her, his heartbeat picking up. He was at her mercy and he didn't really know what she was capable of doing. He prepared to run if necessary, to fight if he had to.

"Don't worry," she said, as if reading his mind. "I put him in the coat closet. He actually loves it in there, and the darkness settles him down."

Some of Jasper's tension drained away. Thinking like a cat, he could imagine how a cozy dark place would appeal. Now that he'd had his chicken and some water, he could go for a cozy dark place, himself.

"Since he's tucked away, feel free to use the litter box if you want."

His brain went on tilt. *Litter box?* Oh, dear God.

Anica continued to explain the setup in a perfectly normal voice, as if she weren't bringing up the most horrific concept he'd yet encountered about this transformation.

She pointed to the end of the kitchen. "The litter box is in there, on the floor of the pantry. I always leave the pantry door open for easy access."

She could have a freakin' red carpet leading through that pantry door. He wasn't going in there. Not now. Not ever. He was a man. He got the indoor plumbing concept.

"I think I might be better off leaving Orion in the coat closet for the night," she said. "He's had a rough time—not that you haven't—but that's his security spot. It'll only be for tonight, anyway."

She paused, her finger tapping her chin. "I'm not sure where you'd rather be for the rest of the night. I don't have an actual kitty bed, because Orion usually sleeps with me." She shrugged. "I'll leave it up to you."

Turning off the kitchen light, she walked into the living room and doused the lights in there, too. When she walked into her bedroom, she left the bedroom door open.

Jasper sat on the counter and contemplated his next move. Where should he spend the night? He could take a chair in the living room, or he could crawl back under her bed. He could also sleep *on* her bed, but that would appear too friendly, as if he actually liked her.

At the moment, though, he had a more pressing problem than where he'd spend the night. He had to pee.

Chapter 5

Anica didn't sleep worth a damn. When she woke up, groggy and disoriented, at five, the misery of the previous night came rushing back.

Having Jasper loose in the house all night had been a bad idea, psychologically speaking. She should have locked him in the bathroom or the kitchen—anywhere so that she'd know where he was.

While half-asleep she could have sworn she'd heard the toilet flush. Then she'd had nightmares that he'd spontaneously changed back into a man, which she supposed could have happened. She'd been so irresponsible to invoke a spell she didn't completely understand.

She'd acted out of arrogance and wounded pride. Because she was so good at her craft and normally had no problem countering the spells she cast, she'd never dreamed she couldn't undo anything she created. How wrong she'd been.

If—no, *when*—Jasper became a man again, he might well be murderous with rage. She couldn't really blame him. Under the same circumstances, she'd be ready to do damage to the person who'd cursed her.

Because she'd never seen Jasper truly furious, she wasn't sure what sort of reaction to expect from him when she and Lily transformed him. She'd take his clothes to the one-hour cleaning service this morning so he'd have something to wear, but that was the least of her worries.

She wasn't afraid that he'd sue her, because no one would believe that he'd been changed into a cat. But he could do something like ruin her business with some well-placed comments to her regular customers, who knew he'd been dating her. He could use the power of the Internet to disparage the quality of the coffee and the food.

She lay in the dark, listening for the sound of Jasper moving around the apartment. To her surprise what she heard was the slow click of computer keys. Her pulse raced and she sat up. Had he regained his human form, and was he already using her computer to find ways to destroy her?

Heart pounding, she listened carefully. Whoever was typing couldn't be Jasper, or at least not Jasper in his normal state. She'd seen him text on his BlackBerry. The guy knew his way around a keyboard. This sounded more like a nontypist, someone laboriously using the hunt-and-peck method.

Her imagination conjured up all sorts of horrible possibilities. Jasper might have turned into something between worlds, half man and half cat, a creature that would make people scream with terror. Or maybe her use of the ancient spell had conjured up some magical monster sent to punish her, and it had begun by typing up a list of her sins to send to everyone in her address book.

How could a magical being get into her apartment, though? She had protective spells cast around every door, window, and vent. Oh, wait. If her magic was gone, then those protective spells would be gone, too. That meant they'd disappeared from her business, too. She hadn't even considered that, hadn't thought to ask Lily to replace those spells for her.

Slowly she drew back the covers and slipped out of bed. Normally she'd grab her wand before going out to face an unknown threat, but obviously her wand wasn't working. She searched the dim interior of her bedroom for a weapon, although mere weapons would be no use against magic.

Still, she couldn't make herself go out there without some sort of defense. Unplugging the hand-painted ceramic lamp sitting on her bedside table, she took off the shade, unscrewed the bulb and wound the cord around the base. Aimed correctly, the lamp could crack a skull— if that skull was human.

As she crept down the dark hallway the sporadic clicking continued. Her chest tightened and she stopped to draw a shaky breath. She needed to calm herself. Whoever was typing must not have her imminent death in mind. Otherwise they would have attacked her in her sleep. *Unless he wants to destroy my reputation before he destroys me.*

Whoever or whatever it was would be facing the screen with its back to the hall. She grasped the lamp by the narrow neck and raised it over her shoulder as she made her way to the end of the hall. Heart pounding, she peered into the living room.

The ghostly light from the monitor revealed Jasper, who was still very much a cat, sitting at her desk. She sagged with relief to discover he wasn't some malformed mix of man and cat, and that no monster had invaded her space.

But her worries weren't over, not by a long shot. The implications of Jasper at the computer were enormous. She understood that and yet she was fascinated by how he'd managed to do it.

His haunches rested on her chair, and he'd braced his left front paw on the desk so he could use his right front paw to press the keys. He studied the keyboard before each tap, the way a touch typist would have to do because they'd long ago forgotten the exact location of each key. He was using Word, which meant he'd successfully navigated the mouse. The scene looked like a video from YouTube that would of course be titled "Cat and Mouse."

Under other circumstances Anica would be laughing her head off as she watched a cat in command of a computer. But this wasn't a trumped-up video, and a cat with the mind of a man—an enraged man at that—was a scary thing.

No telling how long he'd been at this exercise. If he'd managed to use the mouse, then he could have already been surfing the Net. He could have sent a bunch of destructive e-mails while she was asleep.

She'd never imagined he'd turn on the computer, but why not? It was a perfectly logical move given his limited choices. She had to give him points for ingenuity, even if she was worried sick about the consequences to her.

She walked toward him. "Good morning, Jasper. I see you've decided to use the computer."

He turned his head and gazed at her with wary eyes.

In a moment of blinding insight, she realized he was as afraid of her as she was of him. While he was a cat, she had the power of life and death over him. He couldn't know that she wouldn't use that power, although she was seriously thinking she'd restrict his computer access for the time being.

His gaze flicked to her right hand.

She'd been so intent on the computer problem that she'd forgotten that she was carrying her bedside table lamp. He could very well think she meant to brain him with it.

"I couldn't imagine who was out here typing," she said. "I brought this to defend myself." She lifted the lamp slightly. "Lame, I know, but I've never bothered to keep anything around for protection. I always could count on my wand, plus the protective spells I'd placed around the apartment. Now I have nothing but a hand-painted lamp."

Setting it on the floor by the desk, she picked up Jasper and sat at the desk with him in her lap. The message on the screen was obviously to her and amazingly didn't contain any swear words. Considering how he struggled to type, he might not think it was worth it to waste time cussing her out.

Besides, as she'd recently realized, he might be afraid of how she'd react. He needed her in order to revert back, or rather he needed the combination of her and Lily. He couldn't afford to tick her off.

The words were constructed the way she'd expect from someone with only one paw at his disposal. He'd used his texting skills to cut down on the typing, and he'd turned on the capitalization function, so everything appeared in caps.

**CALL WRK NMBR BSNSS CRD IN WALET SAY
IM SCK WAKE LILY UP CHNGE M**

She could guess that had he finished, the last letter would be an E. His demands were reasonable. She couldn't imagine why she'd agreed not to call Lily until noon just because no one ever called Lily before noon. This was an emergency.

"I'll call your work number at nine a.m.," Anica said. "And I'll call Lily this morning, but not right this minute. If I call her at five twenty, even if I get her over here, she'll be of no use to us. An incompetent witch is worse than no witch at all."

Jasper put his left paw on the desk and started poking at keys again. WHT TME

"Eight o'clock. I'll call her at eight."

NO

"Okay, I'll call her at seven thirty."

NOW

Anica sighed. He was right. She'd fire up the espresso machine and pour a couple of cups down her sister. They had to get back to work on this.

"Okay, Jasper. I'll call her."

He repositioned himself in her lap so he could reach the mouse. He dragged the cursor to the bottom of the screen.

"Omigod." She'd been so focused on the message he'd typed in Word that she'd missed the Internet tab sitting at the bottom. He'd been online after all. If he'd been e-mailing ... but no, that would have taken an enormous effort, considering how tough it was for him to type text.

She reached for the mouse and brought up the Internet screen—a Google listing of sites dealing with magic. He hadn't been e-mailing anyone. While she'd been sleeping, he'd been trying to help himself in the only way he could manage. He'd turned on the computer and tried to do research. Ridiculously, her throat tightened.

"I'll definitely check this out," she said. "Thank you. I completely forgot about going on the Internet. Thanks for the reminder." She minimized the screen again. "Is there anything else you wanted to tell me?"

Jasper painstakingly tapped out another message.

LEVE LID UP

*   *   *

Jasper had finally come to the inescapable conclusion that he'd been hexed by a witch's spell, and he wanted it rectified immediately. Working the computer without opposable thumbs hadn't been easy, but at least he'd been *doing* something. Now he was forced to let the witchy sisters take over.

From listening to Anica's side of the conversation when she called her sister, Lily wasn't responding well to the summons. Tough shit.

"She has to take a shower to wake herself up," Anica said as she clicked the cell phone closed. "But she'll be here."

It wouldn't be soon enough for him, but he had limited control in this situation. Very limited control. Then Anica let Orion out, and Jasper's focus shifted from Lily's impending arrival to escaping death. Orion was one scary cat. Plus he hated Jasper's guts, which in all fairness Jasper understood.

To add fuel to the fire, Anica hauled out another chicken breast, cut it up and nuked it for Jasper, while Orion was stuck with something Anica said was low-fat and probably tasted worse than it looked. Once Anica had put food out for both cats, she left to take a shower.

Orion ate the miserable food in his bowl lickety-split, which meant he had plenty of time to pace back and forth in front of the counter and growl at Jasper, who took his time with the chicken. After all, he had nothing else to do until Lily showed up.

He peered down at Orion a few times, and each time Orion hissed and glared his intention to take Jasper apart at the first opportunity. From this vantage point, Jasper could evaluate Orion's bulk. Even when his fur wasn't sticking out, he was big. Fat, actually. He might be lazy by nature, but he probably didn't have much motivation to exercise, either.

Jasper finished his chicken and wondered what else he could do to pass the time. If he stayed here on the counter he'd start thinking about his situation, and that was counterproductive because he couldn't do a damned thing about it without a witch on hand.

He could, however, work off some of his stress and some of Orion's flab at the same time. His leap from the counter landed him right in front of Orion, who hopped backward in shock. Jasper let loose with a taunting hiss. Then he ran like hell.

Because Orion was no match for Jasper's speed and agility, Jasper paced himself so the pudgy cat wouldn't give up. Staying just out of reach, he raced through the apartment. When Orion got a little too close, Jasper launched himself at the first available high place. If a few things scattered, so be it.

Then he was off again, tearing from room to room like a maniac. It was the best he'd felt since Anica zapped him with her wand. An elliptical had nothing on this kind of workout. He'd spent too much time in a gym. Once he got out of this mess, he'd round up some guys and play touch football every weekend.

Anica walked into the living room in her terry robe, a towel wrapped turban-style around her hair. She glanced at the scene of the Great Chase. "Holy shit." She smelled like oranges and flowers, but she sounded like a drill sergeant. "Jasper! Orion! Stop that right *now*!"

Jasper leaped to his favorite spot on top of the bookshelf and studied Anica's thunderous expression. Had he been a man, he could have coaxed her back to the bedroom and made sure she forgot all about the destruction he and Orion had caused.

But he was a cat, not a man, and besides he was furious with her, so he didn't care if she was upset. With a certain degree of satisfaction he surveyed the damage he'd inflicted on her apartment.

Magazines that had been lying on the coffee table were scattered over the floor, and the stack of books she'd been consulting the night before were on the floor, too. Some ivy-looking plant on a wrought-iron stand had been dumped, spilling moist dirt everywhere.

He and Orion must have tracked through the dirt a few times, because black paw prints decorated every piece of upholstered furniture in the living room and most of the carpet. Between the paw prints and the remnants of the dried mousse, the carpet was in sad shape.

Jasper's one attempt to climb the drapes had tempted

Orion to follow, and the weight of both cats had pulled
the rod out of the wall. The rod had dented a lampshade
on the way down, and the drapes, complete with paw
prints, lay in a tangled heap below the window. A couple
of framed photographs had fallen off a side table. The
glass was cracked on one that had landed sunny-side
up.

Jasper smiled, or at least his inner man smiled. Cat
lips didn't work into a smile very well. He hadn't asked
to be here, hadn't asked to be turned into a *cat*, for God's
sake, and he was making the best of a lousy deal. If he
could talk, he would have told Anica the mess was all
Orion's fault.

As a side benefit, some of the belligerence had
drained out of the big orange cat. He flopped down on
the carpet, panting. He might not thank Jasper for the
game of chase, but it had been good for him. He also
might be too worn out to launch into a fight.

Anica stared at the carnage as if she couldn't quite
believe it. From the way she ran the coffee shop, Jasper had assumed she was a tidy person. He'd never noticed trash lying around and coffee spills were wiped up
immediately.

At first Anica wandered around trying to straighten
and pick up, but finally she plopped down on the sofa
and buried her face in her hands. She sounded whipped.
"I'm just not used to trying to clean without magic. I
guess I'll have the same problem at the coffee shop."

That got Jasper's attention. Had she depended on
magic to help her run the coffee shop efficiently? Maybe
Wicked Brew always looked spotless because she'd
waved her wand and made it so. If she was used to solv-
ing her problems with a magic wand she would be very
motivated to return him to normal so she could get her
abilities back.

He had to admit this was justice in its purest form,
and he hoped she'd learned a lesson. He certainly had.

Never assume that your new girlfriend is an ordinary woman. She could be a witch who will turn you into a cat if she gets mad at you. That was his main takeaway from this experience.

A key turned in the front door and Anica got up to greet Lily.

Last night Lily had come striding through the door ready for action. This morning she moved slowly, as if her muscles weren't on board with the concept of being upright. Jasper felt a twinge of remorse and snuffed it out. Lily had the misfortune to be related to Anica, who had created this mess.

He'd never had a sibling, but if he'd been that lucky he would have expected his sister or brother to stand by him in times like these. He was frankly relieved that Lily had shown up. He'd been a little worried she might not.

She didn't look ready to work magic, though. Her dark hair was still damp from the shower and she had a different type of running shoe on each foot. Her red sweat suit had seen better days, and she hadn't bothered with makeup.

She clutched a travel mug as if it contained the elixir of life. She gazed at Anica through heavy-lidded eyes. "The sun's not up."

"I know." Anica hurried into the kitchen. "I'll make espresso."

"Your apartment's completely trashed."

"I know that, too."

Lily wandered over to the computer. "Guess who was on the bus?" she called to Anica.

"Who?" Anica called back.

"Nobody! It's freakin' six a.m., Anica, and I— hello." She stared at the screen. "Uh, who typed this message?"

"Jasper. While I was sleeping."

Lily scanned the words Jasper had painstakingly typed. Then she turned and her gaze met Jasper's. "Well done. I wouldn't have used the litter box, either."

"You see why I had to contact you. He's gone to a lot of work to make sure we get started nice and early." Anica closed a cupboard door and the espresso machine began to rumble and hiss. "He also pulled up a Google site on magic."

Lily inclined her head in Jasper's direction. "I can see we're dealing with a resourceful guy."

"Yep," Anica called from the kitchen.

Lily sat in the desk chair. "I hope you realize that transforming him back could mean a whole lot of trouble for you."

"I'm well aware of that."

"Have you considered *not* changing him back?"

In the silence that followed, Jasper's blood ran cold.

Chapter 6

Because Anica wasn't stupid she realized that Jasper couldn't take his revenge on her if she left the spell in place. She wouldn't get her magic back, but most of the world operated without magic, so she should be able to.

But keeping Jasper in his present state would be immoral and she wouldn't consider it, no matter what consequences she had to suffer. Still, every time she thought about how miserable he could make her life once he'd returned to human form, she shuddered.

Lily was engrossed in whatever she'd found on the Internet when Anica came in with the espresso. A demitasse hadn't seemed adequate to what they were dealing with this morning, so she'd given them each a mug full.

She set one down on the desk next to Lily. "That should set your tonsils to vibrating."

"Thanks. Got any doughnuts?"

"Day old."

"Don't care."

Anica returned to the kitchen and came back with a box she'd brought home from Wicked Brew yesterday. She opened it and put it on the other side of the keyboard. Normally she'd be worried about crumbs in her keyboard, but at this point, needing Lily's help the way she did, she wasn't going to fret about a few crumbs.

She peered over Lily's shoulder. "Anything?"

"This is my favorite site. I should have thought of going to it last night." Lily highlighted a recipe. "Do you have these ingredients?"

"I picked up some mugwort the other day, so yeah, I have everything."

"Think you could get him to drink it?"

"This is a guy who pecked out a message with his paws and went online using the mouse. I think he'd drink ant-eater pee if he thought it would work."

Lily grinned. *"Anteater pee?"*

"Just an illustration. I think he's desperate."

"Notice that it takes at least eight hours to work."

"I did." Anica read through the instructions again. "But I like the way this is presented."

"He should be watched all day."

Anica glanced at her. "If you'd take the first part of this morning . . ."

"I was afraid you'd ask me that."

"Once I get Wicked Brew up and running, I can leave again, but I need to be there first thing. In fact, I should be there in about forty-five minutes."

Lily blew out a breath. "Can you be home by eleven?"

"I should be. It's not like I'll get caught up in traffic or anything. That's why I rented this apartment, so I could walk to work and back."

"Okay, I'll just stay jacked up on espresso until you get home. But leave the shop earlier if you can. I need my beauty sleep before I head off to work at five."

"Deal. Ready to try making the potion?"

"Something's better than nothing." Lily hit the PRINT button and the small unit under the desk started squeaking.

Before Anica realized that Jasper had moved, he was under the desk, trying to grab the paper out of the printer.

"Hey!" Anica picked him up. "We need that."

"So does he." Lily gave the cat a speculative look. "Do you suppose he was trying to get the recipe for himself?"

Anica scratched behind Jasper's ears. "Anything's possible. Orion used to be fascinated by the printer, for different reasons of course, but he's lazier these days."

"Orion's fatter these days. How's the diet working out?"

"I don't think he's lost much. I've tried to get him to exercise, but he's not the type to leap for feathers or chase a jingling ball. He loved chasing Jasper, though."

"So I see from the wreckage he left in his wake."

Anica grimaced. "I hate to ask, but can you clean it up for me?"

"If this potion works, you'll be able to do it yourself."

If the potion worked, the cat in her arms, the one she was so affectionately petting, would soon be a man she used to dream of having sex with. Now she only hoped he wouldn't ruin her life. Feeling less affectionate, she put him down. Orion had climbed on a chair and was sound asleep, so Jasper was safe for now.

"Let's cook us up a recipe." Lily grabbed the printout and stood.

Anica took a deep breath. "Okay."

As they headed for the kitchen, Jasper at their heels, Lily lowered her voice and leaned toward Anica. "Before we do this, make sure changing him back is what you want."

"Of course it is." Shielding her gesture with one hand, she pointed frantically at the cat following them into the kitchen. Jasper's hearing was better than hers.

"Uh, good point." Lily reached for the pocket door and slid it closed in Jasper's face. Then she walked over and turned on the blender, which still held last night's magic margarita.

"This is silly. He'll know we're talking about him."

"But he won't know what we're saying. Anyway, have you thought this through?"

It was a strange comment coming from the woman who hardly ever thought things through, but Anica's world had turned topsy-turvy in the past few hours. "What's to think about? I can't take a life and that's essentially what I'd be doing."

Lily crossed her arms and leaned against the counter. "Noble sentiment, sis. But he's smart and he's pissed. Plus he's capable of shitty behavior. You changed him into a cat for a reason. What was it?"

Anica told her about Sheila.

"So he's a player."

"I guess, although I really thought he cared about me."

Lily rolled her eyes. "Then he's a polished player, which is worse. No telling how many women he's seduced with that technique. I don't blame you for drawing your wand. I would've been tempted, too."

"I didn't draw my wand at first. I wouldn't have done anything to him, except when I tried to end the relationship he followed me and kept insisting that he hadn't done anything wrong, even after I laid out his sins in detail. He still wouldn't take no for an answer, and then he grabbed me and tried to kiss me, even after I told him not to."

Lily threw up her hands. "I would have wanded him just for that alone! And you want to take a chance on jeopardizing your future by turning this guy loose?"

"Yes."

"Look, I admit he's pathetic now, but that's always the way. Some guy finally gets what's coming to him, and then everybody feels sorry for the bastard. I say he'll make a really nice cat, especially after he's neutered."

"Lily!"

She shrugged. "I've had a few men in my life that deserved that fate. Don't blame me for wanting to act out a long-cherished fantasy."

"Jasper is not getting neutered, and no matter what I have to do I'm going to see that he becomes a man again."

"If the issue is losing your magic, then—"

"It's only a secondary consideration."

"We could appeal to the Wizard Council, Anica. There are mitigating circumstances."

"Not really. I lost my temper and invoked a spell I hadn't researched. I don't care what Jasper did; my reaction was irresponsible. I need to set him free again. That may not even be enough to return my magic powers to me, but I have to do it for his sake."

"Oh, Zeus's balls, you're such a Goody Two-shoes! It's nauseating."

Anica gazed at her sister. "Please say you'll help me."

"Yeah, though it pains me, I'll help you. But I want to go on the record as being opposed to this plan."

Jasper crouched by the closed kitchen door, trying to hear what was being said, but the noise of the blender drowned out most of the conversation. What he did hear made him quiver with dread. He'd distinctly heard Lily say *after he's neutered*.

He knew they were deciding his fate in there, and he had no idea how it would go. Sometimes Anica seemed to look kindly on him, but Lily was tougher. If she had enough influence over her sister, his ass could be in a sling.

But wait! The computer was still on. They'd left the magic recipe on the screen, and he could memorize it. How he'd mix the ingredients he didn't know, but if they decided not to brew that potion, he wanted the chance to make it himself.

Trotting back to the desk, he hopped on the chair and

with a whisk of his paw refreshed the screen. Then he looked at the ingredients. Gross. Anteater pee might be easier to swallow than this junk.

Unfortunately it would take about eight hours to work. That was disappointing. Anica had been able to change him in the blink of an eye, so why couldn't he revert back just as fast? Damn magic.

Despite the drawbacks of the recipe, he memorized it, anyway, just in case. Anica was right. He was desperate, ready to do whatever he had to in order to become a man again.

He missed everything about his other life—his condo with its king-sized bed, his walk-in shower, his big-screen TV, his ESPN, his Heineken. Anica didn't seem to own a TV. How could someone live without such an essential piece of equipment?

As he committed the potion ingredients to memory, he smelled something putrid coming from the kitchen. They were brewing a potion, all right, but was it the one to change him back or one to permanently seal his fate as a cat? They'd closed him out of the kitchen, so he hadn't been able to watch them make it.

God, this sucked. And he'd thought his worst nightmare would be a major loss in the commodities market. He looked at the time at the bottom of the computer screen. Still early. Nobody would miss him at the office for at least another two hours.

He should find a way to remind Anica to call in sick for him. If the potion worked, though, he'd only miss one day. By tomorrow at this time he'd be back in his condo, ready to shower and get himself to the office before the market opened.

Needless to say, he wouldn't stop by the Wicked Brew for his usual latte. But to jump on the El and ride it to work would be heaven. He'd never appreciated how great his life was until it had been ripped from him.

When the kitchen door slid open, Jasper leaped from

the desk chair and pretended he'd been lying in the middle of the grungy carpet all along. No use tipping his hand. He'd considered sending out an SOS to one of his buddies, but what the hell would he say? *I've been turned into a tomcat. Come rescue me.*

His friends would laugh and think he'd come up with the most outrageous joke yet. He knew that he had a reputation for being the cool guy who dated the hottest chicks. He was proud of that reputation and didn't want to damage it. Crazy e-mails pleading for help weren't a good idea.

Anica approached him with a bowl. She still wore her terry bathrobe and the turban around her freshly washed hair. Not every woman could carry off that look, but she could, not that he cared. She was no longer a romantic interest. There was a gigantic understatement.

"We have something for you, Jasper," she said. "I can't guarantee that it'll turn you back into your normal self, but the information on the Internet site was promising."

He looked into her eyes and tried to tell if she was lying. He discovered that his cat instincts seemed to detect whether someone was sincerely interested in his welfare or not. Anica gave off sincerity in waves.

The stuff in the bowl smelled like they'd ladled it out of a sewer. Why couldn't a magic potion smell like a bowl of strawberries? You'd think if witches could brew up potions, they could find a way to make them smell good at the same time.

As he was bracing himself for the challenge ahead, someone knocked on the apartment's door. Jasper froze in place. Should he make a break for it if Anica opened the door?

No, that was panic talking. He might have the recipe for the transformation in his head, but he couldn't shop for the ingredients, couldn't use cooking utensils, probably would burn the condo down if he tried to operate the stove.

"I know you're up," called a voice Jasper recognized. "I heard you turn on the blender."

Yikes. It was the woman who'd walked home with Anica while she carried him wrapped in his clothes. It was the woman who had wanted his balls whacked off. He edged toward the bedroom, where he could take refuge under the bed.

Anica scooped him into her arms before he made it to the hall. "It's just Miss Shoumatoff," she said. "Don't be scared."

Scared? Nah, he was *terrified*. Any woman who could speak so casually about turning him into a eunuch was a woman to be avoided at all costs. But Anica held him fast as she walked to the door and unlocked it.

The hateful woman stood in the hallway with a pet carrier in her hand. "I see you still have that stray."

"Yes, I do." Anica scratched gently behind Jasper's ears.

He shouldn't like that, but to his shame he *loved* it. Ears must be an erogenous zone for a cat. His anxiety level decreased the longer Anica kept up the soft caress.

"There's a free spay-neuter clinic today," Shoumatoff said. "So just let me take him and save you the trouble. I'll keep him until you get home later."

Jasper glanced over Anica's shoulder and there was Lily, smirking. Oh yeah, this was hilarious. A real laugh riot. He struggled to get away, but Anica held him tight.

"Thank you, Miss Shoumatoff," she said, "but I plan to take him to my personal vet."

Jasper had to believe that was a lie.

Shoumatoff frowned. "He'll charge a fee, won't he?"

"Yes, but my vet should get to know him if this cat is going to be part of my household."

Surely Anica was making this up as she went along. Jasper prayed that was the case. The thought of becoming part of Anica's household, eating from a dish on the counter every day—he might have to drown himself in the toilet bowl if it came to that.

Then he had another horrible thought. If Anica couldn't change him back, she would feel obliged to keep him, and she really *would* take him to her personal vet. Jasper began to tremble as that potential eventuality played in his mind in excruciating detail.

"It's a ridiculous waste of money," Shoumatoff said. "But if you want to throw your money away, that's up to you."

"I appreciate the thought, Miss Shoumatoff."

Jasper didn't.

"Just trying to help." Shoumatoff stomped back to her apartment.

"Thanks," Anica called after her. She closed and locked the door.

"Bossy bitch, isn't she?" Lily said.

"She's the kind of wild-eyed zealot who gives a good cause a bad name. Now, where were we?"

"I believe we were trying to revert Jasper to his original self before your neighbor has him castrated. That could really ruin a guy's day."

"Right. But she's never getting her hands on you, Jasper."

Jasper certainly hoped not. He shuddered every time he thought about that woman. If he wasn't keen on the potion before, he was all over it now. He'd drink sludge from an oil pan if it would keep him out of Shoumatoff's clutches.

Lily and Anica stood hovering nearby as he crept toward the bowl, his whiskers twitching. The closer he came, the worse it smelled. He'd had a pair of gym shoes years ago that would have qualified for the toxic waste Superfund. Even they hadn't smelled this bad.

Of course, his sense of smell was ten times better than it had been as a guy. Plus if he'd been a guy, he could have held his nose while he drank this swill. As a cat he had no option except to take it like . . . like a cat.

Slowly he lowered his face toward the shallow bowl. He estimated it contained about two ounces of this hideous brew. He couldn't gulp it, either. He had to lap it, one tongue full at a time.

He took a taste and backed away, sputtering. Dear God, that was noxious stuff!

"Remember the goal, Jasper," Anica said softly.

Exactly. The goal of becoming a man again so he could avoid castration and so he could make that witchy blonde pay for what she'd done to him. He forced himself back to the bowl and began lapping. Every time he started to gag, every time he wanted to quit, he pictured Anica homeless and living in a piano box down by the Chicago River.

No court would hear this case but that didn't matter. She might have magic on her side, but he'd have justice on his. With every swallow of this evil-tasting brew he vowed to find a way to bring her down.

Chapter 7

Anica watched in amazement as Jasper powered through the potion. "He drank it all."

"He even licked the bowl," Lily said. "Maybe it tastes better to a cat."

"More likely he's motivated to change after Miss Shoumatoff's visit. You should have felt how he tensed up when she proposed the spay-neuter clinic." She gazed at Jasper.

"He looks like every other cat in the world," Lily said. "No one would ever know."

"I would."

"And you wouldn't be able to live with yourself, would you?"

"Nope."

"He's lucky that you have a conscience as big as the John Hancock building. What if you hadn't snatched him up right away and brought him home? What if you'd let him get away?"

"I don't even want to think about it." With a sigh, Anica turned toward her sister. "Now I guess we wait."

"I wait. You go to work. Get your butt dressed. The sooner you organize the troops at Wicked Brew, the sooner I can go home and hit the hay."

Anica started toward the bedroom and then turned

back to her sister. "You could sleep here while I'm gone. My bed's comfy."

"Thanks, but no, thanks. The recipe said that depending on the potency of the ingredients, it could be longer or shorter than eight hours. I don't relish waking up to find a very enraged, very naked man standing over me. When I meet a naked man, I like him to be smiling."

"All right, then. I'll—" Anica paused again as Jasper bounded over to her, meowing as he ran. "What?"

He charged back to her desk, leaped on the chair, and moved the mouse with his paw. Then he batted at it and his original message from early this morning filled the screen.

"Oh, right. I'm supposed to call his work and say he's sick." She crossed to the bundle of clothes that still lay where she'd tossed them the night before. She needed to gather them up, anyway, so she could take them to the cleaner's on her way to work. His wallet was still in his pants pocket.

She pulled it out. "I should leave this with you. I mean, in case he transforms really fast and needs it."

"I'm hoping that doesn't happen, to be honest." Lily peered over at her sister. "What's in his wallet?"

"I'm not going to snoop through it, Lily. I found his business card and that's all I—"

"You're insufferable." Lily grabbed the wallet away from her.

"Lily. Give it back." She checked out Jasper's reaction, but he seemed intent on typing another message on the screen.

"Come on, don't you have any curiosity?"

"Sure, but I—"

"I doubt he *can* get any madder than he is already." Lily thumbed through the bills. "A hundred and twenty-six bucks."

"You're not thinking of taking it?"

"Of course not. I'm not a thief, just nosy. Aww, look.

Here's a picture of a middle-aged couple. I'll bet they're his parents."

Anica couldn't resist glancing at the wallet-sized studio shot of an attractive, seemingly prosperous but unsmiling couple. He wore glasses and his hair was graying. Her hair was a gorgeous shade of brown that had to be compliments of a good color job.

Lily leaned close to Anica's ear. "They both look like they have a stick up their ass."

Anica choked back a laugh. "Stop it, Lily."

"Well, they do."

"If they could only see him now."

"Dear Zeus, what a thought." Anica hadn't even considered the heartbreak she could cause Jasper's parents. She couldn't look at the picture anymore. "Put it away."

Lily tucked the picture back into the wallet and continued her survey. "American Express credit card, driver's license . . . wow. Is he this cute in person?"

Anica gave the license picture a quick glance. "Cuter."

"Whew. I understand the appeal. Let's check out his stats—weight is one eighty-five; height, six-one; hair, brown; eyes, brown—"

"I would have said his hair is black, not brown, and his eyes aren't brown, either. They're more a golden color."

Lily smirked. "Not that you've been gazing into them or anything."

"I never said I wasn't attracted to him."

"Are you still?"

"Of course not." Anica put plenty of conviction into her denial, but judging by Lily's smile her sister wasn't fooled.

Lily continued to study the license. "He'll be thirty-one on August fourteenth, which makes him a Leo. How appropriate that you turned him into a cat."

Anica felt weird standing here discussing Jasper as if he wasn't in the room. She waved the business card she'd plucked out of the wallet. "I'm calling his work."

"And who are you supposed to be, his girlfriend? Sister? Mother? Cleaning lady? Round-the-clock nurse?"

"I hadn't thought of that."

"You'd better come up with something. You can't make an anonymous phone call announcing that Jasper Danes is sick and won't be coming in today. That's how office rumors start. I mean, how sick would he have to be if he couldn't even call in himself and has some woman do it for him?"

About that time Jasper meowed again while retaining his post at the computer.

"I think he has something to say about it." Anica walked over to the desk.

Jasper had typed EMAL THM. Then he switched screens, where he'd already called up his server and accessed his account.

"He wants me to e-mail and pretend it's him," Anica said.

"Good solution, but I hope he changes back soon, Anica. This is getting creepy. I don't like thinking of domestic pets having human thought processes. It makes me very nervous."

In the midst of composing the e-mail Anica glanced up in alarm. "You'll still stay with him, though, right?"

"I'll stay, and I'll do a little cleanup while I'm at it. If Jasper tries any funny business, he needs to remember I have a working wand, and I know how to use it. Got that, Jasper?"

He got it all right. He'd decided the night before that Anica was the more softhearted sister. If he'd been dating Lily instead, no telling what she'd have done to him with that wand of hers. Being changed into a cat might have been one of the better options.

He was probably as nervous about spending the morning with Lily as she was worried about hanging out with him. Thirty minutes later when Anica left, taking his clothes with her, he turned and stared at Lily.

She'd picked up the two halves of the crystal ball. Retrieving her wand, she murmured something and tapped each half. Whatever she'd done must work like Super Glue, because when she put the halves together, the ball became whole again. Impressive.

Lily replaced the crystal ball in its holder and turned to him. "Don't look at me, pussycat. I may be a witch, but I've never had a thing for cats. I like dogs better, but with my lifestyle dogs aren't a good option, either." She waved a hand at him. "Go take a nap or something. Maybe by the time you wake up, the potion will have worked."

He loved that idea. A snooze might be the perfect way to pass the time. Sitting around waiting for his hair to fall off could send him into loony land. Strolling to the sofa as if it had been his idea, he hopped up on it and found a cushy spot in the corner.

"Before you go to sleep, though," Lily said, "let me impress upon you that I'm an innocent bystander in all this. It's not my fault that you're currently walking on all fours and your whiskers stand out at a right angle to your face, so if I'm the only one here when you transform, don't try to take it out on me."

Jasper wasn't making any promises. Lily hadn't been the one holding the wand in the initial incident, but she'd been the one laughing at the idea of him losing the family jewels. She'd been the one going through his wallet. She wasn't so damned innocent.

Plans for revenge swirled in his head as he closed his eyes and settled down for a nap. He felt as if he'd been asleep for all of two seconds when Lily's "Born to Be Wild" ring tone sounded.

From her side of the conversation, he gathered that she was talking to Anica and all was not well. Jasper opened his eyes to slits so he could stay alert to whatever new disaster was brewing.

"If you say so." Lily didn't sound happy. "We'll be there as soon as we can. Bye." She closed her phone and gazed at Jasper. "We have to go to Wicked Brew."

That was all well and good, but he was a cat. Last he'd heard the health department frowned on animals other than guide dogs in any establishment serving food. How was she planning to take him into a coffee shop?

Lily disappeared inside Anica's bedroom and came back out wheeling a hot pink overnighter. "She told me to put you in her pet carrier and then smuggle you into the back room, but that's a bad idea on several levels. First of all, the health department will shut her down if they get wind of me doing that. Second of all, the pet carrier doesn't have wheels, and I don't want to lug your sorry ass for three blocks."

Jasper wondered why she didn't create some sort of magic spell to handle this. He gazed at her.

"This is spooky. I can almost see you think. I'm not doing this magically because doing magic jacks me up worse than a triple shot of espresso. I'm already a little jazzed from mending Anica's crystal ball, so if I create a magic spell to get us both to the coffee shop, my nap just won't be happening. So you get to roll, buddy."

He didn't want to go to the coffee shop. As Lily advanced on him, he wondered if he could leap off the sofa fast enough to avoid her. But then what? He'd learned that going under the bed didn't work. It was a small apartment. She'd hunt him down eventually.

But he didn't relish being closed inside a hot pink suitcase. One more thing to add to his list of grievances. His day would come, and when it did both these sisters were in deep shit.

"Don't worry." Lily picked him up and carried him to the open suitcase. "I'll leave the zipper open a little bit so you can breathe."

That was big of her. In the meantime he'd be incarcerated in a canvas prison where he couldn't see anything while he was rolled like a load of laundry down a bumpy sidewalk. But she'd let him breathe. Yay. Humans had such a distorted view of what was a bonus for their pets.

"I pray to Hera you don't transform while you're in here," Lily said as she zipped him inside the suitcase. "You wouldn't fit, for one thing."

No duh. She and Anica were taking a huge chance with his potential transformation. Whatever was going on at the Wicked Brew had better be a freakin' emergency to require dragging him down there while the spell was wearing off.

He'd be perfectly happy to stay in the apartment while Lily went, but apparently they were afraid to leave him in case the transformation ... what? Went wrong? He wasn't going to consider that. Lily zipped the suitcase except for a two-inch slit that let in a sliver of light.

"Okay, Jasper. Here we go!"

Oh, joy. She tilted the suitcase so it would roll, which meant he lost his footing. He scrambled to keep upright as they bumped over the doorsill and sailed down the hall.

When they got to the stairs, she bumped him down a couple of steps and then must have taken pity on him, because she picked up the suitcase and carried it the rest of the way.

"I hope you appreciate this, Jasper." She was puffing by the time they reached the street. "And I have to say, you're heavier than you look."

That's because muscle weighs more than fat. Of all the things he missed about being a man, being able to talk back ranked right near the top. Being able to walk along the street instead of being rolled down an uneven sidewalk in a hot pink suitcase was up in the top ten, too. By the time the air coming through the zipper became decidedly warmer and he could smell coffee, he calculated that his eyeballs had been jolted out of their sockets.

He heard Anica's voice laced with frustration, and then a door closed and the suitcase was unzipped. The fluorescent lights temporarily blinded him. He was aware of footsteps walking away, and then a door opened and closed. As his eyes adjusted he found himself alone in a storeroom surrounded by floor-to-ceiling shelves packed with boxes.

Most of the boxes had been slit open and the contents were spilling out onto the floor. It seemed like a strange and wasteful way to handle inventory. When he crawled out of the suitcase to nose around, the spilled sugar made the footing gritty and unpleasant.

Something wasn't right. Walking across the grit to the door leading into the coffee shop, he could hear Anica and Lily on the other side.

Lily sounded worried. "You're sure no money is missing?"

"There was nothing to steal," Anica said. "I'd taken the money out of the cash register when I closed up yesterday afternoon."

"You need to call the police."

"There was no sign of forced entry, Lily."

"Then it could be one of your employees."

"You know what caused it as much as I do. All the evidence you need is spray-painted on the mirror."

Jasper couldn't stand the suspense. By wedging his paw under the door and applying some pressure to the opposite side, he could feel the latch start to give. Good thing he'd worked out at the gym every day. Pulling harder, he tripped the latch. Once the door was cracked he had no trouble pushing his way through it.

Instead of being covered with grit, the floor on the other side was gooey. He picked up his paws in distaste. But he wanted to see the mirror, the one that was fastened to the wall behind the counter. Hoping Anica and

Lily didn't notice him, he crept along the baseboard until he was on the other side of the shop, but he was still too low to get a good look at the mirror. Shortness sucked.

He stopped next to his table, the one he'd staked out when he used to come into Wicked Brew. He'd thought it was such a clever name for a coffee shop when he'd first heard it. Now the name jangled in his brain like a fire alarm.

Jumping up on the table, he got his first good look at the trashed coffee shop. Coffee beans, ground coffee, and chocolate syrup coated the counter and a good part of the floor. Napkins had been shredded and added to the mix, until it looked like someone had intended to tar and feather the place.

He gazed at the message sprayed in whipped cream on the mirror. Whoever had written it had a talent for calligraphy and an ear for rhyme.

SHOP UNGUARDED, HAPPINESS FOUND. WE CAME IN AND MESSED AROUND!

Lily had her back to Jasper as she gazed at the mirror, hands on her hips, legs braced apart. "You think this is the work of teenage fairies, don't you?"

Jasper had a tough time picturing gay teenagers vandalizing a coffee shop.

"I'm sure it is." Anica's posture mirrored Lily's. Looking at their body language no one would doubt they were sisters, despite one being blond and the other brunette. "Those magical kids have too much energy and too much time on their hands. A coffee shop run by a witch who seems to have forgotten to activate her protection spell would have been irresistible to them."

Oh, *that* kind of fairy. Jasper was even more alarmed. Just when he was beginning to adjust to the presence of witches, he was slapped with the knowledge that fairies also were real and capable of wrecking a midtown Chicago coffee shop.

"Messy little buggers," Lily said. "I wish they'd made themselves a few cups of espresso and left. Why did they have to do all this?"

"Because it was fun. I don't think they're malicious, really. They probably assumed I could put it back together in no time."

"This isn't an instant fix, not even using a wand. I think they slit every single box in the storeroom."

Anica nodded. "Pretty much. The thing is, either I close down for the day . . . or longer, considering I'll have to reorder supplies. Or, if you'll—"

"Oh, Anica."

"Okay, never mind."

Lily groaned. "I'll do it, but you know what happens to me after a vigorous magical workout."

"Can't you take a sleeping potion or something?"

"I've tried that and nothing works. I think I'm essentially allergic to wand magic. My system goes on tilt and that's the end of sleep for at least twelve hours."

"Then forget I asked."

"No, no. I can't leave you in this condition." Reaching over her shoulder she pulled her wand out of a pocket in her backpack as if unsheathing a sword. "Since you can't put a protective shield around yourself, you might want to step outside. I'd shield you, but that'll take more time and energy."

Yikes! Don't forget the cat! Jasper let out a plaintive yowl.

Both sisters spun toward him.

"Jasper, you're supposed to be in the storeroom." Anica walked over, her shoes making sucking noises in the glop.

"Just take him outside with you," Lily said. "That way I can handle the storeroom as soon as I'm finished here."

"Thanks, Lil." Anica picked up Jasper, made her way to the front door, and unlocked it. "Oh, and don't forget to fog the windows before you start."

"Don't I always fog the windows?"

"No. There was that time you had the wild party in the department store window, and—"

"Anica."

"What?"

"Let's remember why we're dealing with this, shall we?"

"You're right. Sorry." Anica tucked Jasper inside the folds of her black cape and stepped into the cold morning air.

"I don't know which is worse," she muttered, apparently to Jasper since he was the only one who could hear her. "Being trashed by a roving band of teenage fairies looking for thrills, or being obligated to my sister. Damn it to Hades, why did I have to cast that spell?"

Jasper vowed he was not going to feel sorry for her. He was absolutely not. Never, ever. Except . . . for now.

Chapter 8

Anica deeply appreciated what Lily had done for her. She truly did. But she paid for it by listening to her sister gloat for at least an hour afterward. Lily had to gloat subtly, because Anica had opened the shop on schedule and was busy serving customers, one of whom was her sister, taking full advantage of the free espresso Anica offered.

Caffeine seemed like the last thing Lily needed, but Anica wasn't about to deny her what she asked for, not after walking into her shop and finding it spotless. She'd locked Jasper in the tidy storeroom, making sure the door was truly locked and not just closed. He'd be fine there sleeping in the suitcase until the morning rush was over.

Her employees could handle the business after that, and she wasn't worried about more visits from fairies. Besides cleaning the place from top to bottom and re-placing all the supplies, Lily had restored the protection spells that would keep Wicked Brew safe from both magical and nonmagical break-ins.

Anica realized that her apartment protection spell probably wasn't working, either, but she couldn't bring herself to ask Lily to fix that, too. Lily was already bouncing off the walls in reaction to the magic she'd done so far. Another protection spell would put her on massive overload and increase Anica's debt exponentially. Anica already owed her sister a lot. And Lily reminded her of it every five seconds.

"Hey, sis." Lily motioned her over. "What say you and me do lunch later and maybe go shopping? We haven't shopped together in ages."

Anica recognized the attempt to create more of a bond between them, which she'd welcome under different circumstances. "Nice idea, but I can't."

"Why not? You have good help around here. You can leave the shop for a while."

Until that moment, Anica had forgotten the other side effect of Lily doing major magic. She couldn't hold thoughts in her head for more than ten minutes. Anica lowered her voice. "Jasper, my new cat. Remember?"

"Oh, right, right. Jasper. I forgot about him."

"He drank that special stuff this morning. I don't know how it might affect him."

Lily glanced around at the bustling shop. "Oh yeah!" She looked up at Anica. "I'm getting spacey, huh?"

Anica nodded.

"Oh, well." Lily stood and grabbed her backpack. "Think I'll hit the department stores by myself. I could use some new clothes."

Guaranteed she'd max out her credit card. Anica couldn't stand by and let that happen when it was her fault Lily was in this condition. "Hey, come home with me instead. I'm almost ready to leave."

"What'll we do at your place?"

Anica thought fast. It had to be something active, something Lily loved to do. Anica knew in her heart what it had to be, the area where she'd always been weak and Lily was strong. "I want you to try teaching me to dance . . . again."

"That didn't go very well back in high school. You stomped off in a huff."

"I promise not to stomp off this time, and I'd really like to learn."

Lily got a devilish gleam in her brown eyes. "How about salsa?"

Anica tried not to wince at the image of her attempting salsa. She was so bad at dancing. "Sure, if that's what you want to teach me."

Lily grinned. "It most definitely is. I'm smokin' when it comes to salsa."

"And I'm not."

"I know." Lily looked smug. "This role reversal is working for me, sis. When can we leave?"

"Give me five minutes to make sure Todd and Sally are on top of everything around here. Then I'll go get . . . the suitcase, and we'll leave."

"What suitcase?"

Anica spoke in an undertone. "The one with the cat in it."

"Oh, that's right! I keep forgetting about that."

Anica envied Lily her forgetfulness. Anica was afraid that even after Jasper changed back into a man—and he would, because she was determined to make that happen—this incident would haunt her forever.

Jasper wanted to do nothing but sleep, but that didn't seem to be his destiny. First he was carted back to the apartment in the suitcase, and nobody could sleep through that jolting experience. They made one stop, and from the smell of the place and the rustling of thin plastic, he identified it as the cleaner's. At least he'd have clothes to wear when he transformed.

Back in the apartment with both sisters, he endured a whirlwind of cleaning conducted mostly by Anica. She wouldn't let Lily help by using the wand, which made sense if working magic made Lily hyper. Consequently Anica hauled out the vacuum, which was the signal for Jasper and Orion to dive under the bed, where they had a hiss-off.

Fortunately Orion didn't try to chase Jasper out from under the bed, which seemed like the only spot to hide from the monster vacuum. Jasper tried reasoning with himself that it was only a vacuum cleaner, a tool he'd used himself a million times. But he'd been a lot bigger then. And he hadn't had a tail that could be sucked right into that roaring machine.

He and Orion seemed to bond over their mutual fear of the vacuum cleaner. Jasper was relieved that they'd reached detente. He'd hate to have to fight Orion and avoid the vacuum at the same time. A cat could only handle so much stress, especially when he was desperate for a nap.

As a man, Jasper had never been a napper, and yet that seemed to be all he could think about as a cat. He wanted that cozy corner of the sofa where he'd started his snooze earlier that day, before the whole suitcase trip, fairy vandalism and magical restoration deal had interrupted his shut-eye time.

Finally the vacuum noise stopped, and he ventured out just as a Gloria Estefan tune blasted from Anica's CD player in the living room. Orion stayed under the bed. Maybe the orange tabby didn't care for Gloria, but Jasper had always kind of liked her music.

He crept down the hallway and peered into the living room, where Lily was putting on a salsa demonstration that nearly set fire to the carpet. Jasper recognized the sexiness displayed by Lily during the dance, but he was more interested in Anica, who stood in the kitchen doorway, gazing at her sister with obvious envy.

He hadn't known Anica long enough to find out if she liked to dance. It didn't really matter, because now that she'd hexed him they were so over. He had no reason to be curious about the dancing habits of a woman he had no intention of dating ever again. He should just find a cozy spot somewhere and take that nap he'd been promising himself.

Instead he settled down right where he was and watched to see what would happen next.

"This isn't the best album for dancing," Lily said. "But it'll be okay for starters. Next time I'll bring some of mine."

"I don't think the music matters when you're as uncoordinated as I am," Anica said.

"Of course it does! Everything matters." Lily stopped dancing and glanced down at her sweat suit. "Even the clothes matter. Let's go see what we can find in your closet."

"That's way too much trouble. I don't want to change clothes for this."

"Come on, come on." Lily beckoned to her sister as she started toward the hall. She paused as she spotted Jasper. "Looks like somebody came out from under the bed."

"It's been about five hours since he drank the potion, Lily. Don't you think we should see some sort of change in him by now?"

"I don't know. I'll take a closer look." Lily crouched down next to Jasper and peered at him. "Sorry, sis. He's still very much a cat."

Anica came to stand beside her. "I know, but I wish we'd see *something* that shows he's changing back into a guy."

"Too bad you don't have cable. We could test him by putting him in front of ESPN with a bowl of beer and a package of Cheez-Its."

Jasper hissed his disapproval.

Anica laughed softly. "I don't think he appreciates your stereotyping him like that."

"Oh, bite me, Jasper."

It was a tempting thought.

Lily stood. "Enough of this. Let's raid your closet and find us some hot dancing duds." She continued down the hall.

Jasper glared after her. Lily was so wrong about him. He didn't like Cheez-Its. Onion rings went way better with beer.

He sulked for a while as the women discussed clothes. Lily apparently found something of Anica's she wanted to wear, judging from her exclamations of happiness. Beyond boring. Naptime beckoned, and he was on his way to the sofa to stake out his corner spot when Lily let out a hoot.

"When did you buy *this*? Talk about wicked! I didn't know you had it in you, girl."

"I may not keep it," Anica said.

So much for Jasper's plan to take a nap. He retraced his path to the bedroom.

"Of course you're keeping it," Lily said. "In fact, you're going to wear it right this minute. Take off your pants and sweater while I cut off the tags."

Anica sighed. "All right."

Jasper arrived in the bedroom doorway to find Lily wearing a black dress she must have borrowed from Anica, which made it indecently short. Jasper spared her one glance before all his attention was claimed by Anica taking off the sweater she'd worn to Wicked Brew that morning. She and Lily hadn't noticed him, so he crouched on the carpet and waited for the sweater to come all the way off. He might as well know what he was walking away from when he left this apartment tonight.

Quite a bit, it turned out. Even giving credit to a black underwire bra, Anica was built like a goddess. Knowing he was going to ditch her the minute he was himself again, he probably shouldn't check her out like this. He should go back down the hall and get on with that nap.

Yet he drew comfort from the fact he wasn't sleepy anymore. Maybe the potion was working, because he shouldn't be fixated on Anica while she undressed. But he was mesmerized as she kicked off her shoes, unzipped her slacks and stepped out of them.

"I don't think you're supposed to wear a bra with this." Lily held up a red dress on a padded hanger.

Jasper wasn't much of an expert on dresses, especially when they were still on a hanger, but this one looked promising. The top part was a halter style that tied at the back of the neck, and the skirt sort of floated in the breeze from the heating duct, which meant as it moved it would show off a nice pair of legs.

"You can wear a bra," Anica said, "but it has to be a halter style. I haven't bought one to wear with it yet."

"Then go without."

"Okay."

Jasper held his breath as Anica reached behind her back and unhooked her bra.

Just as the bra came undone, Lily stepped in front of his line of sight. He hadn't meant to growl. It sort of slipped out. Both women turned immediately in his direction.

Anica gasped and held the bra against her breasts. "I didn't realize he was there."

"Me, either," Lily said. "If I didn't know better, I'd say we have a Peeping Tomcat on the premises."

"I'll finish changing in the bathroom." Anica snatched the hanger from Lily and stalked away.

"I don't get it," Lily called after her. "You came really close to sleeping with the guy, so why worry about a little boob show now?"

"Because I never will sleep with him," Anica said from the bathroom. "I don't want some man I never intend to sleep with walking around Chicago with a visual of my bare tits."

"You always were too modest. And speaking of visuals, chances are you'll see *him* naked soon, anyway. You two are going to be on fairly intimate terms with each other, whether you want to be or not."

"I know. I wish there was some way to avoid that, but I can't leave him alone when the change is taking place.

I want to be there in case there's some . . ." She let the sentence dangle there, unfinished.

Some what? Complete the sentence, damn it! Jasper fought down panic. The whole transformation process scared the shit out of him, and she was only making it worse.

Going from man to cat had been like nothing he'd ever experienced, as if he'd driven his Beemer into a wall at eighty miles an hour. There'd been the shock of impact and then a brief period of total blackness before he realized with growing horror that he was suddenly very hairy and quite vertically challenged.

If he'd thought it was real in those first few minutes after the transformation, he might have gone insane on the spot. But he'd convinced himself immediately that he was in some awful nightmare, and that belief had helped get him through the initial hours. Now he was starting to adjust to his new body.

That was a sobering thought. He was getting used to being a cat. That didn't mean he wanted to stay that way. It only meant that he was adaptable.

Yet when he thought of changing back again, a sick feeling formed in the pit of his stomach. Would his skin split like the Incredible Hulk's? Would it be slow and painful, or quick and painful?

Either way he figured it would have to hurt. You couldn't do something that monumental to an organism without causing trauma. It didn't take a medical expert to understand that.

For that reason, he wanted somebody else to be there, so he was grateful that Anica had committed to that plan, even though she didn't want to see him naked. He didn't want her to see him transform, either, but his fear was greater than his ego. He might need help.

"What do you think?" Anica walked out of the bathroom, her feet bare, her blond hair brushing her white shoulders, and the dress doing amazing things for her body.

Jasper swallowed. He'd been sexually attracted to her before, but he'd had no idea she could look this hot. The dress's neckline made the most of her eye-popping cleavage. The multilayered skirt had an uneven hem, and when she moved, the layers parted on one side to reveal a creamy thigh.

Lily clapped wildly. "Bravo! It's the perfect salsa dress. It's as if you'd planned on learning how to dance."

"I only wanted to look as if I could dance." Anica gave her a sheepish glance. "I wanted to fool people into thinking I could step out on the floor any minute, but instead I'd chosen not to."

"Well, that's just silly, to go to all the trouble of dressing the part and then not doing it. I'm going to teach you the moves that will make you worthy of that dress. Got shoes?"

"Oh, sure. I bought those, too." Anica leaned over to rummage in the closet.

Meanwhile Jasper was wishing he could be in the closet, enjoying the view of her leaning over. None of this lusting on his part was good, because he was supposed to hate her. He had a rule—never go to bed with a woman you despise, no matter how hot she is. Naturally he despised Anica for turning him into a cat. Any reasonable person would feel that way.

But how could you despise a woman who was so luscious and so . . . human? Her witchy abilities were intimidating, but not so much now, when she'd lost her magic. He was touched by her worry about her dancing ability, or lack of it. Apparently a witch couldn't fix everything with a magic wand. At the moment, Anica couldn't fix a pot of tea with her magic wand, and Jasper could see how much that bothered her.

He wasn't minimizing the damage to him, not by a long shot. She had plenty to answer for, and he was still a cat, although rediscovering his human libido was encouraging to him. He needed to direct it somewhere else, though, on general principles.

Then Anica brought out the spike-heeled shoes that matched the dress, and proceeded to fasten the ankle straps. God help him, he couldn't look at those shoes without lusting after the perfection of her legs. He didn't want to want her, but he couldn't seem to help it.

"Hooker shoes!" Lily crowed. "Too bad we don't wear the same size shoe, or I'd be stealing those from you when your back is turned. Come on, sis. Let's shake it up!" She shimmied through the bedroom doorway. "I saw you ogling her, pussycat," she said without sparing Jasper a glance. "Don't think I didn't."

Anica walked over and gazed at him for several long moments. He kept eye contact. Staring was what cats did best, he discovered.

"Are you the kind of person Lily thinks you are?" she murmured. "Are you just a tomcat on the prowl?"

"Anica!" Lily cranked up the music. "Get your butt in here!"

With a sigh Anica walked down the hall, her heels sinking into the carpet and the sway of her hips making the hem of the dress dance around her legs.

Jasper watched her go and felt a tug of regret. He wished he could talk so he could convince her that Lily was wrong about him. Sure, he had a line he used on women. Didn't every guy? An innocent line wasn't exactly a criminal act.

Looking back on it, he wished he hadn't done that with Anica, for obvious reasons, but that was water over the dam. Her seductive walk reminded him of what could have been, would have been, if Sheila hadn't picked that night to come to his favorite restaurant. Sometimes life wasn't fair.

He noticed that they'd left the closet door open. He'd be wise to go settle into the closet and seek forgetfulness in a nice long nap. Hanging around Anica was not a productive move on his part. But as he listened to the beat of the music he wanted to go in and see how she was making out with the dance lessons.

The blender whirred again and this time they might plan to drink the margaritas they made. Soon the sisters were laughing, and one of them turned the music up another notch.

Jasper edged down the hall and peered around the corner.

Anica stood with a margarita glass in one hand, and as he watched she drained it. Then she sashayed over to Lily. "Okay, I'm ready."

"Good! Now move your hips like this." Lily undulated like a woman having vertical sex.

"Lily, that's so trashy!"

Lily smiled. "That's the idea. You could do it in bed with a guy, couldn't you?"

Anica blushed. "Yes, but this is—"

"Fun. Try it."

Still blushing, Anica made a halfhearted attempt.

"More." Lily demonstrated again. "Exaggerate."

Anica took a deep breath. "Here goes nothing." She executed the move exactly the way Lily had.

Jasper's eyes narrowed to slits of pleasure as a purr rumbled spontaneously in his chest. She was getting to him. Not good.

He wanted to watch Anica dance all afternoon, but he couldn't seem to shake the desperate need for a nap. That would be the cat influence taking over. With a yawn he trotted back to the bedroom and hopped up on the bed. He fell asleep to the music of Gloria Estefan and Anica's laughter.

He woke up to the scent of warm chicken. A quick check told him that his cat status hadn't changed. It should have by now. A sick feeling of dread curled in his stomach.

Or was that hunger he was feeling? He followed the chicken smell, which took him through the living room and to the doorway of the kitchen. The scent of tequila and lime still hung in the air, but Lily was gone. Anica, wearing a pair of flannel pajamas, stood in the kitchen. Jasper missed the red dress, but he had more urgent concerns than ogling Anica.

Orion wove a figure eight through Anica's ankles. The hiss he sent in Jasper's direction seemed more obligatory than threatening, but Jasper paid little attention. All his focus was on the kitchen clock. Six thirty. More than twelve hours had passed since he'd lapped up that evil brew, and nothing had changed.

Anica turned to him. The look of concern in her blue eyes told him all he needed to know. She was worried.

"I see you're awake," she said. "I fixed you some chicken."

Theoretically, Jasper should be too upset to eat, but that didn't seem to be the case. He was starving. Even so, he didn't want to push his luck with Orion, so he waited until Anica had placed Orion's bowl of food on the floor and the big cat had shoved his face into it. Then Jasper leaped to the counter and began to eat the chicken Anica had warmed for him.

"I don't know what to think, Jasper," Anica said. "We'll see what happens tonight, and if you're the same in the morning, I'll have to swallow my pride and call in that couple, the one on the Wizard Council." She shuddered.

Although he was intent on eating, Jasper listened with one ear. The thought of a governing body called the Wizard Council blew his mind. But if such a thing existed he wanted them in on this. The crisis was at hand.

"In the meantime, I can't do much except wait." Anica kept talking as she started washing the margarita glasses. "Too bad I couldn't ask Lily to renew the protection spell on this apartment, but I didn't dare put her through any more magic spells today. Between repairing my crystal ball and the coffee shop cleanup and protection spell, she was on overload."

Magical people should be able to handle that sort of problem, Jasper thought. Maybe Anica could have cured Lily if she had her own magic working.

"Anyway," Anica continued as if trying to convince herself, "the coffee shop was the interesting place to break in to. They won't be so excited about a boring little apartment."

She dried the glasses and put them in the cupboard. "But speaking of that, I can't even remember if I locked the dead bolt." Putting down the towel, she left the kitchen.

Once she was gone Orion meowed softly. It seemed to be directed at Jasper. He peered over the edge of the counter and sure enough the orange tabby was gazing up at him, a pitiful look on his fuzzy face.

Orion had suffered a lot in the past twenty-four hours, and Jasper thought he needed some sort of reward for that. Anica hadn't offered him one, but she might be too distracted to think of it.

Orion wasn't supposed to have the chicken, but Jasper couldn't stand looking at that sad face. He picked up a bite of meat and dropped it to the floor in front of Orion. Orion scarfed it up at once and licked his chops. Then he glanced up at Jasper in obvious longing.

Jasper dropped the last two pieces of chicken on the floor. He didn't need to worry about food, anyway. If nothing happened tonight, then tomorrow Anica would call in the wizard top brass, which should do the trick.

Once he became a man again he would head for the nearest restaurant and order a steak dinner. Orion would be stuck with those dry little pellets, maybe forever.

"Dead bolt's on," Anica said as she walked back into the kitchen. "Not that a dead bolt will stop fairies, but I doubt they'll bother with this place," she murmured, almost too softly for Jasper to hear.

He hoped she was right about that. He'd seen the kind of destruction a band of teenage fairies could create. He hoped they didn't show up here, especially when he was in this vulnerable cat form.

Anica spent the rest of the evening reading, and Jasper spent it watching her read. Damn boring. He wished she'd try a few of those dance steps instead.

Finally, around ten, she yawned. "Time to go to bed." She gazed at Jasper and Orion. "Can you two guys manage to share my bed without fighting?"

It could have been a line out of a porn movie if the two guys in question hadn't been cats. Jasper wondered if Anica was starting to forget he was a man in a cat suit. He wasn't about to let that happen.

Chapter 9

Anica wasn't sure what woke her, but as she lay in the dark, she heard someone, or something, moving around the apartment. Could be the cats. Rising cautiously on one elbow, she checked in the dim light to see if they were on the bed. Both were gone.

Okay, so it was the cats. At least they weren't fighting, which was a relief. Maybe they were even getting along, becoming friends. Comforted by that thought, she settled back onto her pillow.

She'd barely closed her eyes when the sound of teenage laughter drifted in from the living room. Her eyes snapped open and a chill ran through her. Not cats. *Fairies.*

Throwing back the covers, she jumped out of bed and instinctively reached in her bedside table drawer for her wand. Not until it was in her hand did she remember that it was useless. But the fairies might not know that.

Now that she was fully awake, she noticed a red glow coming from the living room. Where were the cats? Kneeling by the bed, she lifted the skirt and peered underneath. "Orion?" she called softly. "Jasper?"

She couldn't see much at all, but when she groped under the bed as best she could, she didn't come in contact with any furry bodies. They could be anywhere in the apartment. Wand in hand, she crept out of the bedroom. She'd never realized how much she depended on her magic until this moment.

On her way down the hall she told herself that the fairies were only teenagers who had slipped away from their parents and were looking for thrills. They weren't dangerous, only mischievous. If they'd been dangerous, they would have invaded her bedroom.

They'd probably figured out that if she was careless enough to leave her shop unprotected, she might have done the same with her apartment. They might be after her wine and tequila, forbidden to them at their age, and any food she happened to have on hand because, like most teenagers, they were always hungry. They were often destructive, too, but being magical, they considered it only temporary destruction, easily fixed.

Fairies and witches moved in different circles, so a prank played on a witch wasn't as likely to be discovered by fairy parents. As she neared the end of the hall, she caught a glimpse of what was going on in her living room and was not amused. The little snots had decorated it like a sex club.

Nude paintings hung on the walls. Her sofa and chairs were upholstered with images of couples in various sexual poses, and the entire room glowed red. That was bad enough, but many of her magic books had been pulled from the shelf and strewn carelessly around the room. One of her favorites lay open on the coffee table, a page torn.

Three fairies, two boys and a girl, were gathered around her computer ogling an X-rated Web site while they drank tequila shots from three souvenir shot glasses she'd picked up on vacation. They dressed like teenagers everywhere, with the boys in logo T-shirts and baggy pants belted around their hips and the girl in low-riding, skintight jeans and a knit top that hugged her ribcage and stopped short of covering her ruby-enhanced navel.

She looked like a surfer girl with her golden tan and long blond hair. The boys' hair was gelled within an inch of its life and stood up in angry brown spikes. Anica thought the two might be brothers.

Tattoos covered all three, although the kids could make those disappear in an instant if necessary. Likewise their faux piercings. Fairies couldn't tolerate metal, so all the jewels were magically attached and could be removed in no time.

That was one big difference between these three and nonmagical teenagers. If nonmagical teenagers got a tattoo or a nose ring, they were stuck with it. Fairies could choose to add or eliminate body art whenever they wanted.

There was no point in trying to turn on the overhead light. The fairies had surely made the light switch inoperable. Anica tried to catch a glimpse of the cats, and finally found Orion in a far corner, tail twitching, fur sticking out.

He crouched as if awaiting his opportunity to leap on the intruders and scratch their eyes out. His belligerent body posture said quite plainly that he was pissed. His home had been invaded once again and he was plotting his next move.

Anica would rather that he didn't get involved. Ordinarily fairies didn't harm animals, but if these three had consumed enough tequila, all bets were off. Jasper was nowhere around. Maybe he'd freaked at the sight of the fairies and was hiding in a cupboard.

If so she could hardly blame him. The guy hadn't believed in witches until yesterday, and tonight he'd been confronted with hormone-drenched teenage fairies. His sense of reality had been seriously damaged recently.

So she had to put a stop to the fairy mayhem, and she had to accomplish that with a bluff. She wished that she had on the red salsa dress and sexy heels instead of her blue plaid flannel pajamas and bare feet. Too late to do anything about that now.

Raising her wand with as much authority as she could muster, she cleared her throat and waited for them to abandon the computer screen and turn in her direction.

They did that slowly, as if they had no fear. Safety in numbers, maybe, but if she'd had her magic working, their confidence would have been proven foolish. Three wet-behind-the-ears fairies couldn't stand up to a witch in full command of her powers.

Too bad that wasn't her at the moment. She counted on their ignorance of that fact. "You should all be ashamed of yourselves," she said in the sternest voice she could muster. "Put everything back the way you found it, or suffer the consequences."

Both of the boys looked a little worried, but the girl stood and thrust out her tight little boobs. "I'm not afraid of you. We got in here so easy, just like we got in your shop last night. Your magic needs a serious tune-up, witch."

Mouthy kid. Anica longed for the power that she'd had so recently, so she could teach the girl the proper way to speak to someone who had been practicing magic before she was born. She gave the girl her best witch stare. "You might want to reconsider that position."

"Ooooh, I'm so *scared*."

Anica itched to take the girl down, magic or no magic. "Remove your illusions from this apartment and remove them now."

The girl stuck her hands in the back pockets of her jeans and lifted her chin. "What if we don't feel like it?"

The boys must have drawn courage from her defiance, because they both stood and glared at Anica. "Yeah, what if we don't feel like it?"

Anica adopted her most ominous tone. "You will regret it. I promise you, you will regret disobeying me."

"Prove it." The look in the girl's silver eyes said that she'd sensed Anica's lack of magic the way a predator senses the fear of its prey.

Physically Anica was no match for them. The boys were taller than she was, and the odds were three against one, even without figuring in their magical abilities. Their command of magic, immature though it was, made the odds even worse.

She'd failed to intimidate them. Now what? "Your parents would be so disappointed if they could see you now." Even as she said it she knew it was a lame statement. It might have worked for her at that age. It worked for her *now*, in fact. But these three weren't like her, and that was the scary part.

One of the boys, the taller one, stepped forward. "What our parents don't know can't hurt them, can it?"

The girl tossed her golden hair. "And you can't tell them because you don't know who we are."

"I know you're three fairies with no respect for magic," Anica said. "Anyone who can treat magic books that way is—"

"Your books are stupid," the shorter boy said.

"Yeah, totally." His brother picked up the tequila bottle. "Here's what I think of this one." He tilted the bottle slowly, enjoying his power as he prepared to pour tequila on the open pages of her favorite book.

"Put that bottle down, and put it down now!" The male voice rang with authority.

Anica spun around to find the source of that commanding voice and almost dropped her wand. Jasper stood in the kitchen doorway wearing two small towels tied together at each hip to make a kind of loincloth front and back. Other than that, he was magnificently naked.

And no longer a cat—no sir, not even a little bit. Very much a man. A broad-shouldered, narrow-hipped man.

The dark hair sprinkled over his glorious chest was exactly enough. Ditto the hair on his muscled calves.

She gulped. "Jasper, you're—"

"Going to take these three apart, I think." He advanced toward them, his fingers flexing. "I could use magic to do it, of course, but I prefer the satisfaction of ripping their limbs from the sockets with my bare hands."

In a daze of admiration and gratitude, she watched him move. He had a certain catlike grace, but otherwise nothing about him reminded her of Jasper the cat. Everything about him reminded her of why she'd craved him from the moment they'd met.

He'd decided to try his own bluff, obviously, and convince the fairies that he was a wizard. They'd have no reason to think otherwise if he was standing naked in her apartment. Witches traditionally had wizards for lovers. She was the rebel who had bucked the system.

All three teenagers' eyes grew wide as they watched Jasper approach. The tall boy holding the bottle of tequila smacked it down on the coffee table. "Insane wizard approaching! Abort, abort!"

In a flash, all three fairies reverted to their smaller, action-figure size. They sprouted wings and began to glow.

"What the hell?" Jasper stared at the fairies as they flew toward the door.

"They're leaving!" Anica cried. "We can't let them leave until they've changed everything back!"

From a corner of the room an orange streak hurled itself at the last fairy in the flock. With a leap that was astounding considering his bulk, Orion snagged the fluttering creature and landed with it clutched in his paws.

"I'll be damned." Jasper walked over to the cat and crouched down. "Good work, buddy. You got one."

Anica did her best to concentrate on the situation

they were in, which was dicey to say the least. But when Jasper crouched down the kitchen towels shifted tantalizingly. She had to use all her self-control not to try to glimpse what was behind those kitchen towels.

This is not the time, girl. It might never be the time. Even though Jasper had stepped in to save the day, that didn't mean that he was particularly fond of her.

Orion pinned down his trophy with both paws while the fairy protested in a high-pitched voice. Orion glanced over at Anica as if asking permission to eat it.

"You can't munch on the fairy," Anica said. She looked around for the other two, but they were nowhere in sight. They'd probably taken advantage of the distraction when Orion caught their friend and miniaturized themselves to the size of a gnat. Then they could slip out the way they'd come in, through the old-fashioned keyhole in her apartment door.

She gazed at her cat. "Let me amend that, Orion. If the fairy you captured removes the illusion placed on my apartment, he can go free. Otherwise munch away." She guessed that the captured fairy was one of the boys, because the girl was way too savvy to allow herself to be caught.

The remaining fairy continued to squeak, and with some difficulty, Anica made out the words. He begged to be allowed to remove the illusion so he could go home.

"All right." Anica knelt next to Orion. "That's a good kitty. Let me have the fairy."

Orion seemed reluctant to let it go, but eventually Anica held the struggling boy in both hands. "I'm handing you over to the wizard," she said, "and I warn you not to cross him or you'll end up dragon chow for sure."

The fairy squeaked some more as Anica stood and gave him to Jasper. Her breath caught as her hand touched his. He was so damned warm. So deliciously naked.

At this juncture she should have been reminding herself why she'd turned him into a cat in the first place. He'd lied to her. More than that, he hadn't thought doing so was such a bad thing. He'd been unrepentant.

Then she remembered what Sheila had said in the restaurant bathroom. *He's just that good.* She'd always criticized women who had sex with bad boys, men they didn't particularly approve of, just for the promise of sensational orgasms. Criticizing had been easy for Anica because she'd never been tempted by such a man.

But she was sorely tempted now.

It might not matter, though. Chances were he wouldn't want anything to do with her, and that would solve her moral dilemma, now, wouldn't it? Still, she knew that if he'd been willing, she would have abandoned her principles. Quite a comedown for Goody Two-shoes.

Jasper raised the fairy in the air. "Put this room back exactly the way you found it. And make it snappy."

Anica almost giggled. He sounded like a father reprimanding his kid, which was probably the right tone to take with this little delinquent.

With a few high-pitched commands from the tiny fairy, the nude paintings were replaced by the landscapes Anica had chosen for the walls. The upholstery went back to a muted floral pattern, and the red bawdy-house glow changed to normal lamplight.

Orion watched in total fascination. He was especially intrigued when the bottle of Jose Cuervo rose from the coffee table and wobbled through the air on its way back to the kitchen. Like baby ducks, all three shot glasses followed. The computer winked off, and the room was back to normal.

Jasper glanced at Anica. "Should I let him go now?"

"Yes. Thank you."

Jasper opened his hand. The fairy fluttered his wings a moment, as if testing to see if they still worked before he launched himself into the air. In two seconds he was airborne, and then, with a little pop, he disappeared.

Jasper looked startled. "Did he vaporize or something?"

"No. He's right there." Anica pointed to something that looked like a tiny insect heading for the door. "He'll leave the way he came, through the keyhole."

"You might want to stick some gum in that keyhole from now on."

Anica looked at him and smiled. "They'd just find another way. The only thing that works is a magical protection spell. I had one . . . before."

"Before you turned me into a cat."

Her chest tightened as she realized the mood of cooperation had left along with the fairies. They'd faced down a common enemy, and she was grateful for his help. But now he'd leave, and maybe he'd tell her how he planned to pay her back for this, and maybe he'd just let her find out the hard way.

"When did it happen?" she asked. "You changing back, I mean."

"Sometime after those jokers showed up. Orion and I came out to investigate. I was watching them changing everything and I was getting really angry, but then I started feeling weird. Somehow I knew what was about to happen to me, and so I ducked into the kitchen so I wouldn't transform right in the middle of the living room floor."

"Did it . . . hurt?"

"Fortunately no." He flexed his shoulders. "I'm a little sore, but otherwise I seem to be fine."

"I guess that potion took longer than we expected for some reason."

"Right. Thank God it worked eventually."

She gazed at him, unsure what to say. "Does it matter that I'm horribly, terribly sorry for what I did?"

He sighed. "I don't know, Anica. Being sorry doesn't quite cut it when you consider what I've been through."

"I know. I know it doesn't."

"Where are my clothes?"

"Hanging in my closet. I'll get them for you."

"That's okay." He started down the hall. "Give me five minutes and I'll be out of your hair."

She watched him walk away and tried to think of what she could do or say that would make a difference. "Can I make you coffee? Put together a sandwich?"

"No, thanks," he called over his shoulder. "I just want to get home. I want my life back."

That was plain enough. He wouldn't be hanging around for coffee or anything else, for that matter. She couldn't blame him. He'd had a life, and she'd temporarily stolen it.

"I'll phone for a cab." She could at least do that much. She glanced at the clock for the first time and noticed it was a little after midnight.

She put down her wand to dial the phone. Once Jasper was gone, she'd test to see if her wand worked again. She expected that it would, which meant she could re-create the protection spell for her apartment.

She would be happy to have her magic back. She tried to focus on that and forget about the man who was about to exit her life. He wasn't the right guy for her, had never been the right guy. She'd allowed sexual attraction to override her good judgment.

The cab company agreed to have a driver outside her building in twenty minutes. Unless Jasper chose to wait down by the curb, which he certainly might if he was angry enough, twenty minutes was the outer limits of her remaining time with him. She might never see him again in person. If he had anything more to do with her, it might come in the form of revenge, blackmail, or something equally ugly.

His cry of alarm startled her out of her morbid thoughts. She raced down the hall, terrified that something had gone wrong with the transformation after all.

Something had. In a frightening replay of the previous night, Anica first saw a pile of Jasper's clothes on the floor. Then she watched in horror as a black cat crawled out from under the clothes. Jasper was a cat . . . again.

Chapter 10

Fuckin' A! Jasper hissed in fury when Anica burst into the room. If he didn't need her, or rather her witchy sister, he'd give in to the urge to scratch the living daylights out of her. He'd been a man again! Why hadn't it lasted?

"Oh, Jasper." Anica's eyes filled with tears.

As if her tears would do him any good. It gave him little satisfaction to know that she was so upset. Her upset was nothing compared to his upset. He was ready to chew the carpet.

Although the worst part was that he'd found when he was a man, he was still attracted to Anica, even in those dopey flannel pajamas she was wearing. Her blond hair had been mussed and her cheeks pink, giving him a preview of what she might look like after a brisk round of sex. He did *not* want to want her. For one thing, she was a witch, not exactly his dream girl choice. And for another thing, she was a witch who'd turned him into a cat.

What kind of romance would that be? He'd be afraid to cross her for fear she'd zap him with her wand again. Talk about a total imbalance of power. And yet knowing all that, he hadn't been able to stop the flow of sexual chemistry between them.

Looking around for some way to vent the frustra-

..on he felt on more than one level, he spied the delicate posts of her antique bed. *Yes.* Walking over to the nearest one, he stretched his front claws as far as they'd go and began to systematically mark up the wood. Let her try to stop him. Just let her try.

She didn't, and eventually the thrill of ruining a precious piece of furniture faded. He wasn't naturally a destructive person. In fact, he was a little ashamed of himself, even if she did deserve the memento of what she'd done to him.

Tearing up furniture wasn't getting him anywhere, though. He bounded into the living room, hopped up on Anica's desk chair, and turned on the computer. While he waited for the program to boot up, he considered sinking his claws into her desk, as well.

But his heart wasn't in it. If he was ever part of an invading army, he would be lousy at sacking the city. Mindless destruction wasn't his thing, even when he was furious.

Instead of scratching the desktop he leaned over and watched Orion batting a felt mouse around. Maybe Orion was becoming inspired to be more active. That would be a good thing.

Anica had followed Jasper into the living room, as he'd expected she would. She leaned over and helped him with the keyboard so he could bring up Word. She smelled really, really good. He wished she'd scratch him behind the ears. . . .

No! Forget that stuff. He didn't care about ear scratching anymore. He'd had a taste of being a man again, and he would focus all his energy on getting back to that. Once he had a screen to work with, he typed a message to Anica.

CLL LLY.

"You're right." Anica picked up her cell phone out of a holder shaped like a dragon. "I should have thought of that immediately. She'll still be at work."

Jasper was already on to the next thing. MKE POSHN.

"Right, right. Obviously we didn't give you enough." Anica put the cell phone to her ear. "I need to speak to Lily Revere. It's an emergency."

Damn straight it was an emergency. And he was ... getting his ears scratched by Anica while she waited for Lily to come to the phone. He was also purring. Shit. He needed to knock that off, but he couldn't seem to stop the rumbling noise, especially when she scratched her finger along his jawline. Yeah, like that. *Nice.*

How could he react this way when he was so angry with her? Apparently his human mind could be boiling because he was trapped in a cat's body, but his cat body loved being caressed by a woman who knew exactly how to do it.

"Lily, it's me," Anica said. "Jasper changed back for a few minutes. Yeah, I know. It was exciting, except that now he's a cat again, which frustrates both of us."

As she continued to rub behind Jasper's ears, he had to remind himself why it was so bad to be a cat, and specifically Anica's cat. He recalled the thrill of manipulating the commodities market and pulling down a sizable profit. That was increasingly harder to do in this economy, but that only ramped up the challenge.

He loved a challenge. Being a pampered cat living in Anica's apartment was a sick joke compared to the life he'd had before, no matter how good it felt when she smoothed a finger over his nose.

"I need you to come help me mix up the potion," Anica said. She paused to listen. "I suppose I could do the actual mixing before you get here, but I think you need to do that chant thing. Okay, good. See you then."

After tucking the phone back in its dragon holder Anica stroked her thumb along Jasper's jaw, and he arched into her touch. "She'll be here as soon as she gets off work," Anica murmured. "In the meantime I'll mix up the brew and start it simmering. I'll make a lot this time."

He wanted plenty of that brew, no matter how nasty it tasted. But if one bowlful had given him only about ten minutes, he hated to think how many he'd have to drink to get an entire twenty-four hours. And then what? Would he have to keep chugging the stuff to keep from growing hair and claws? Had he turned into some kind of werecat?

Just then he noticed Orion lying on his side next to the sofa, reaching with his paw as far as he could underneath. The poor chump had lost his felt mouse and was too porky to squeeze under there and get it.

Anica walked into the kitchen to collect the ingredients for the potion, and Jasper leaped down from the chair to follow her. Then he glanced over at Orion, who was struggling mightily. Jasper remembered how the orange cat had valiantly attacked the retreating fairy, which had kept Anica from having to live, even temporarily, with nude paintings and X-rated upholstery.

Orion's heart was in the right place. Yeah, maybe he'd tried to kill Jasper initially, but Jasper would have felt the same if his space had been invaded. Walking over to the sofa, Jasper dropped to his stomach and made himself into a very flat cat so he could wriggle under the sofa.

Once there he found the mouse right away. Funny what becoming a cat could do to a guy's perspective. Losing control of his life had made him a lot more sympathetic to the kinds of concessions Orion was forced into every day. If Orion wanted the mouse, Jasper would provide the mouse.

With a swipe of his paw he sent it skittering out from under the sofa. He had a limited view from under there, but he could see Orion pouncing on the felt toy, then rolling over and kicking at it with his back claws. Watching Orion enjoy the mouse gave Jasper a good feeling. Life in general still sucked, but Orion's playfulness had turned out to be a little spot of happiness in the middle of a swamp of despair.

After watching Jasper slurp at least a gallon of the potion she and Lily had concocted, Anica expected him to change back into a man again sometime during the night. Instead she woke at five and found him still very much a cat curled up at the foot of her bed next to Orion. The two cats weren't exactly touching, but they were lying less than two inches apart. The war between them appeared to be over.

But if Jasper was still a cat Anica hesitated to leave the apartment, and yet she needed to go into work for a couple of hours. Probably everything would be fine and the two cats would sleep undisturbed. But if something went wrong, if Jasper had some unanticipated problem, she'd never forgive herself for being unavailable. She'd like to have someone here who could notify her in an emergency, but she couldn't make herself call Lily again.

Her upstairs neighbor Julie, the one who kept her video camera constantly focused on the street, would be awake, though. Julie slept in the middle of the day because she thought the most interesting events on the street happened between dusk and dawn.

Leaving both cats asleep on the bed, Anica padded into her living room and picked up her cell phone. Sure enough, Julie was awake and seemed delighted to be asked to do a neighborly good deed.

Thirty minutes later she was at Anica's door, dressed in her usual Goth black, her hair spiked and her eye makeup heavily applied. Anica hadn't figured out Julie's financial situation, but the girl was about twenty-two, wasn't going to school and didn't seem to have a job other than filming segments of anything interesting that might show up, doctoring them to disguise identities and then airing them on her brother's cable show.

Julie also wrote scripts, which explained the small laptop she had tucked under one arm. To Anica's knowledge none of the scripts had been produced, not even on her brother's show. Anica suspected that Julie and her brother were living on trust funds of some sort, but it wasn't the sort of question a person asked.

"So you have a new cat?" Julie walked in and looked around.

Belatedly Anica remembered she'd never invited Julie into her apartment. They'd only talked when passing each other on the stairs. Anica was usually careful about who she let into her place because they might become curious about the magic books and the crystal ball. Advertising her status as a witch wasn't always a wise move.

"The cat's only temporary." She prayed that was true. "I hope to find him a good home." Like his own, for example. "But he doesn't seem to be feeling all that well, so I've closed him in my bedroom."

"Oh." Julie's gaze traveled eagerly around the living room, pausing to linger on the bookshelf and the crystal ball, which Lily had magically repaired last night. "Okay."

"It's probably better if you don't go in the bedroom, because he won't know you. But I wanted someone to be around in case . . . well, in case he gets upset. Call me if you have any problems." If Jasper transformed, he'd probably put on his clothes and come out of the bedroom, which would startle Julie and bring up all sorts of awkward questions, but at least Anica would be notified of what had happened. She'd deal with the questions if and when necessary.

Julie nodded. "I can do that."

"I've made espresso, and there are some leftover doughnuts from the shop."

"Cool."

"I've left Orion out here and he's a pretty friendly

cat." Anica gestured toward Orion, who was lying in the hall just outside the bedroom door, as if keeping tabs on his new friend. She wondered if maybe now that he'd decided Jasper was okay, he liked having a friend around. Or maybe he was waiting to pounce and renew the hostilities. Better to keep them separated until she knew for sure.

"Orion's a neat name. I've seen him in the window sometimes. What's the other cat look like?"

"All black."

"Like a witch's cat."

Anica couldn't tell if it was a chance remark or whether Julie was fishing for information. "I suppose, if you go with the stereotype."

"I guess it's a cliché." Julie fiddled with one of her skull earrings. "Were you having a party in your house last night? I heard some loud noises."

"Must have been the movie I loaded onto my computer," Anica said. "I probably turned the sound up too loud. Sorry about that."

"I keep forgetting you don't have a TV, just the DVD player on your computer."

"That's it."

"Listen, you know that one DVD I loaned you of my brother's show? I can get you some more if you want. It's free entertainment."

Anica nodded as she edged toward the door. "Sounds great," she said, although she'd rather gnaw off her left arm than sit through another cable show produced by Julie's brother. Her one experience had taught her that Julie's brother was a little short on editing and cinematography skills.

"See you later, then," Julie said. "Oh, I forgot. Have you heard the rumor that someone in this building is a witch?"

Uh-oh. So the eagerness to cat-sit might have been eagerness to take a look inside this apartment. Anica managed to look amused. "Somebody's been reading too much Harry Potter. If anyone around here could cast spells, you'd think they'd update the plumbing."

Julie grinned. "It is obnoxiously old. I keep expecting Moaning Myrtle to come out of the toilet."

"As I said—the Harry Potter books have us all thinking that witches and wizards are real. I'd be amazed if anyone in this building is capable of magic." And that, for today at least, was the truth.

She kept her wand in her purse, in case it was suddenly activated, but she'd begun adjusting to the reality of not having magic at her disposal.

"I'll probably give you a call in an hour or so to check on things," Anica said as she headed for the door. "Thanks again for doing this."

"No problem."

Not for Julie, maybe, but Anica hoped she hadn't just created an even bigger one for herself by letting this girl into her life.

Jasper listened to the conversation taking place outside the bedroom door. So Anica was leaving for the coffee shop. He could be really lucky and transform while she was gone. A man coming out of the bedroom would probably scare the shit out of the girl who was supposed to keep tabs on things, but he'd figure out some story to give her.

Maybe he'd bill himself as the irresponsible brother who liked to sleep in and therefore couldn't be counted on to take care of the new cat. It wasn't much of a story, but he wouldn't worry about what this girl, whose name seemed to be Julie, would think of him. Yes, he'd really like to transform right now.

And he couldn't understand why that wasn't happening. He'd taken in enough of that evil slime to make him sick to his stomach. He thoroughly agreed with Anica's statement that he wasn't feeling that well. The transformation potion was gross. He wouldn't care, though, if it worked.

It had worked before, although not until about eighteen hours later. He'd hoped that lapping up twenty times as much would speed the process. So far, all he had was massive indigestion . . . and nothing to do.

So in the manner of cats everywhere, he slept, until voices outside the door woke him. The hackles on the back of his neck rose. Anica's voice wasn't one of them. The person talking to Julie was that Shoumatoff person who was dead set on relieving him of his precious boys.

Julie's voice got louder, as if she and that horrible woman were coming down the hall. He could also smell tuna, which if he happened to be a real cat would probably smell like ambrosia.

"Miss Shoumatoff," Julie said, "Anica doesn't want anybody bothering her new cat."

"Anica will be grateful to me for taking care of this. I came by to see if she'd done it and renew my offer to handle it for her. Obviously she's too busy, so I'm taking charge."

"Miss Shoumatoff, I don't think Anica's going to be happy if you—"

"Of course she will."

As the voices drew closer to the door, Jasper decided he'd better head for cover. By the time the door opened and Shoumatoff the Castrator came through it, he was under the bed in the very middle. He could see two pairs of boots—one black pair that looked capable of stomping on kitty toes and another that looked as if they'd come from the Salvation Army. He could guess which ones belonged to Shoumatoff.

Orion had arrived, too, and was winding himself around the combat boots and meowing his head off. The smell of tuna was overpowering.

"I'm calling Anica," Julie said. "This is not right."

"Go ahead. I'm sure she'll be thrilled that I'm handling this chore. I'll bet he went under the bed." Shoumatoff's jowly face appeared, framed by the lace bed skirt. She looked like she was wearing an old-fashioned cap, sort of like Whistler's mother.

"I see you under there, you sneaky cat. Come get the tuna. Not you, Orion." She shoved the orange tabby out of the way.

Jasper was outraged that she'd push Orion around like that. Tuna or no tuna this woman was bad news, and by God he was going to do something about it.

She edged the tuna under the bed, keeping hold of the can. Once Jasper thought he had enough of her arm to work with he attacked, sinking his teeth and claws in.

It wasn't the wisest plan. She yelled, but she was more agile than she looked. She reached under the bed with her free hand and grabbed him.

Hissing and spitting, he tried to use his claws on her, but she was bigger and stronger. She manhandled him into a carrier and slammed the door, but as she picked it up and started down the hall, he heard Julie yelling something about Anica's instructions.

"Now, Julie, you know this is for the best."

"Anica said you're not to take him! Give me that!"

Jasper was flung around inside the carrier as the two women wrestled for it.

"Look, you left the front door open!" Shoumatoff said. "What if Orion got out?"

"Oh, my God!" Abruptly Julie let go of the carrier. "Orion, where are you? Stay right there, Miss Shoumatoff. Please don't leave. Orion! I can't lose *both* cats."

Jasper's hope faded. He doubted Orion would leave the apartment, but he knew Julie would feel obligated to track down Anica's main cat, not the temporary stray. While Julie searched for Orion, Shoumatoff headed out of the apartment.

Jasper was so screwed.

Chapter 11

As Anica ran down the sidewalk, her shoulder purse banging against her side, she dodged pedestrians as best she could, but she bumped into several people and almost knocked over an older man. She called an apology over her shoulder and kept going. She was half a block away when a taxi pulled up in front of her building.

Edna Shoumatoff came down the steps with a pet carrier in one hand. Anica was out of breath from running and her attempt to call out was worthless.

If she'd ever needed magic, she needed it now. But there was no magic and Edna was getting into the cab headed for some clinic. Anica didn't even know which one. By the time she tracked Jasper down it might be too late.

She couldn't let that happen. With a burst of speed she reached the taxi and grabbed the door as it was closing. She gripped the carrier handle with both hands and braced her feet against the pavement.

Edna peered out at her. "Anica, what's the problem?"

She could barely speak as she gulped for air. "Don't . . . take . . . him."

"Someone needs to!"

Anica managed to speak without gasping. "You can't

just take someone's cat to be neutered without their permission."

"You got a tomcat in there?" The cabdriver turned toward the backseat. "Poor slob. I don't think you women fully appreciate how that affects a guy."

"He's not a guy," Edna said. "He's a cat."

Technically, he's also a guy. But Anica couldn't very well say that out loud.

"Cats have feelings, too," the cab driver said.

They were gathering a crowd, and Anica was ready for this episode to be over. She reached in and grabbed one end of the pet carrier. "Miss Shoumatoff, I promise you this cat is not an overpopulation problem. Let me have Jasper back."

Edna held on to the carrier with a surprisingly strong grip for a woman her age. "No!"

The cabdriver sighed. "Make up your mind, okay, ladies? I'm not getting any richer sitting here by the curb."

Anica pulled harder. "I've made up my mind."

"So have I!" Edna jerked the carrier from the other direction.

"Oh, thank God you're here!" Julie cried out from behind her. "I'm so sorry, Anica!"

Anica had no breath to waste on Julie. She was in a tug-of-war that had to go her way. She yanked harder and there was a loud crack. The plastic carrier, which wasn't very sturdy to begin with, came apart.

Jasper exploded out of it, scratching anything in his way.

Anica made a grab for him and felt his claws dig into her arm. Then he launched himself from the cab to the sidewalk.

"Stop him, Julie!" Anica cried.

But Julie wasn't quick enough. Jasper darted around her and raced down the sidewalk, with Anica, Julie and Edna in hot pursuit. A block later, they all stopped, panting.

Jasper was nowhere in sight.

Edna leaned over and put her hands on her knees as she tried to catch her breath. "See? See what you've done?"

"What *I've* done?" Anica longed to put her hands around the woman's chubby neck and squeeze. "If you hadn't interfered, Jasper would still be safe in my apartment!"

"It's my fault." Julie looked miserable, even more so because her mascara had smeared, turning her into a frightening sight indeed. "I shouldn't have let Miss Shoumatoff through the door in the first place, but she seemed so sure of what she was doing. She brought the carrier and tuna, and then the door was open and I was afraid Orion got out. But he didn't."

"It's not your fault, Julie, it's all Miss Shoumatoff's doing." Anica glared at the older woman.

Edna was unrepentant. "Since you weren't handling your responsibility, I took on the job."

Anica clenched her jaw. A shouting match in the middle of the street wasn't going to accomplish anything. She shouldn't have left Jasper, or she should have asked Lily for help instead of putting that kind of responsibility on her young neighbor. This was her fault, all of it.

She pulled her cell phone out of her purse and speed-dialed her sister.

Lily took a while to answer, and when she did, she sounded groggy. "What's up?"

"Jasper got away."

Lily gasped and seemed instantly more alert. "What do you mean, *got away*?"

"It's a long story, Lil. But I'd really appreciate it if you'd come over and help me look for him. Come to the front of the apartment and then call me. I'll give you my location at that point. I need to keep looking."

"Sure, I'll help. I'll make up a thermos of coffee and be right there."

"Thanks, Lily." Anica snapped the phone closed. "All right. You two are free to go home."

"I want to help you look for him," Julie said. "I feel partly to blame."

"Julie, you're not. Truly." Anica was the screwup. How she hated to apply that label to herself, but there was no avoiding it.

Julie sidled closer. "Even if I'm not to blame, I want to help. I looked through your bookshelf, and I—"

"All righty, then! You're helping! Thanks!" Anica needed to get Julie off that topic immediately.

"I'll look, too," Edna said.

Anica faced Edna and prayed to Hera that she could control her temper. "I don't want you to. He won't come within a mile of you, anyway."

"That's nonsense. He didn't know where I was taking him."

Anica couldn't tell her that Jasper had understood every word and had been convinced that if Edna won the tug-of-war he'd be robbed of his family jewels in short order. She couldn't blame him for running. "You'd be surprised what animals know," she said.

Jasper hunkered down in an alley next to an old metal trash can and tried to figure out where he was. The alley mostly contained Dumpsters and large plastic garbage bins, the kind a truck could lift with a mechanized arm. But for some reason, this normal-sized trash can was sitting here, too.

He wanted to orient himself before he did anything. The world looked completely different when you viewed it from twelve inches off the ground. He could get a better view from on top of the trash can but then he'd be more visible, and he sensed being visible might not be the best thing for a stray cat.

That's what he was now, a stray, and the thought sobered him quite a bit. He'd run on pure instinct, knowing he had to get away from the woman who planned to de-ball him. Freedom had felt great for about the first five minutes, but now he wasn't sure what ground he'd gained. The potion might still work, but becoming naked in the middle of the city with no ID could be a problem.

That was assuming the potion worked, but what if it didn't or only worked for a little while, like last time? If he separated himself from Anica and her sister, he might end up stuck this way forever. He desperately needed to get back to Anica's apartment, while making sure the Shoumatoff woman wasn't anywhere in the vicinity.

If Anica came looking for him, that would be better than him trying to get back to the apartment. She might, but then again she might figure finding him would be nearly impossible. The city had lots of alleys, lots of places where a cat could hide if it didn't want to be found. She might give up the idea as hopeless. She might be relieved to be rid of him, to be honest.

Briefly he considered trying to make his way to his condo, but then he realized that wouldn't work out very well, either. The condo, by his design, had bucket loads of security, including good locks and a state-of-the-art alarm. He wouldn't be able to go inside.

His best bet was slowly retracing his steps to Anica's apartment and then figuring out the easiest way to get in. Shoumatoff lived right down the hall from Anica. He'd have to be very careful.

"You mangy sonofabitch! Get away from there!"

Jasper looked around to see what mangy sonofabitch the guy was talking about. A brick whizzed by his head and smacked against the wall behind the trash can, and then another one hit the trash can itself with a loud *clang*.

He was the mangy sonofabitch? Shit. There was nothing mangy about him. But he'd better get the hell out of there before he got beaned.

The brick thrower had a mouth on him. Jasper was impressed by the creative string of curses the guy sent his way. He didn't take time to look, but from the sound of boots smacking pavement and the brick that landed inches behind him, Jasper decided that the guy had retrieved his bricks from beside the trash can and was firing them off again.

Scooting around a corner and down another alley, Jasper looked for a place to hide and spotted a partially collapsed cardboard box leaning against the side of a building. He ducked through the opening and heard a cat hiss. He was not alone.

Anica's imagination ran wild as she pictured Jasper flattened by a truck, attacked by stray dogs, trapped at the end of one of the blind alleys that crisscrossed the downtown area. She'd taken one route, while Julie had gone in another direction and Lily in a third. They kept track of each other by cell phone.

Anica called Lily for probably the tenth time since they'd started looking.

"What now?" Lily sounded short-tempered. She probably needed more caffeine.

"Any luck?"

"Anica, I told you last time. I'll call you if I see a black cat, any black cat." A blender whirred in the background.

"You're in Starbucks, aren't you?"

"Yeah, I stopped at Starbucks. You wanna complain about it?"

"No, it's okay, Lily." Having her sister buy an espresso from the competition was the least of her worries right now. "Are you sure there isn't some way you could use magic to find him?"

"Not in broad daylight on a crowded street. I tried chanting a discovery spell on Michigan Avenue and a cop followed me for a block. I didn't dare go down an alley looking for Jasper at that point or the cop might have taken me in for suspicious behavior."

"It's been an hour. I'm scared that something's happened to Jasper."

Lily's tone softened. "I know you are, An. Don't give up. We'll find him. Gotta go. My triple shot is ready."

Anica closed her phone but kept it in her hand instead of tucking it back in her purse. Calling Jasper's name, she continued down yet another alley lined with smelly Dumpsters. She was about to cross the street when her cell phone vibrated. She flipped it open, desperate for a scrap of hope. Julie!

"I found him, but he won't come to me."

Anica's heart hammered. "It's him? You're sure?"

"Pretty sure. He's all black, short hair, yellow eyes. His coat's shiny. He doesn't look like a stray."

"That sounds like Jasper. Now that he's cleaned up, he's a good-looking cat." A flash of Jasper wearing only two kitchen towels flashed through her mind.

"I'll bet it's him. He came close, but he won't let me pick him up. He keeps going back to this cardboard box."

"Give me your location." Anica made note of where Julie was, disconnected and called Lily. "Stop at a deli and get a chicken sandwich."

"You want me to take a lunch break?"

"It's for Jasper, in case we need an incentive. I think Julie's found him." She told Lily where to go as she ran down the street, her black coat flapping in the wind. On her way to meet Julie, she prayed to every Wiccan power she knew that the cat would be Jasper and he'd let her take him back to the apartment.

Julie wouldn't know what to say to him, but Anica had some ideas. Having Jasper escape had brought home the point that she couldn't mess around with this anymore.

Jasper might have lost faith in what she and Lily could do about reversing the spell. He also might have lost faith in her determination to protect him from people like Edna Shoumatoff. That had been a total cock-up, as Lily liked to say.

As Anica approached the alley, she saw Lily hurrying toward her from the other direction. Lily had chosen to dress for the search in hooker boots with three-inch heels, a slinky black jumpsuit and a red leather trench coat. She wore cat's-eye sunglasses decorated with rhinestones.

Sometimes Anica wondered if either she or Lily had been adopted, because they had such totally different styles. But at the moment she was grateful that they were in fact sisters and that Lily was willing to help, even if she grumbled about it. Lily held a paper sack in one hand and a Starbucks cup in the other. When she was within ten feet, Anica smelled the chicken.

"You got it. Great." Anica was winded and her words came out chopped and breathy.

"Of course I got it."

"I'm glad I met you before we go in there. Let me have the sandwich."

Lily handed over the bag. "You're welcome."

"Sorry. Thanks."

"I've never seen you this rattled, not even when you lost the spelling bee in seventh grade."

"Look, assuming the cat Julie found really is Jasper, I've decided what I need to do about him. I want to talk with him privately, so I wonder if you could distract Julie while I do that. I don't want her to hear what I have to say."

Lily's brows arched. "You're going to promise to be his love slave after he transforms? Whoops, you're blushing. Don't tell me that's it."

"No, that's not it." Anica was embarrassed by how positively she reacted to that idea.

"I don't know, An. From the way you described his personality, he might go for that. It would be a whole lot better than having him trash your business reputation. And a whole lot more fun."

Anica looked her sister in the eye. "I'll keep it in mind as an alternative." She wouldn't consider such a manipulation, of course, but pretending she would, even for the shock value, sent lust shooting through her system.

"I don't believe you'd ever do it but I'm impressed that you didn't lecture me for suggesting such a thing." Lily gazed at her with new respect. "This experience is having quite an effect on you. Welcome to the world of fallible beings, big sister. Life's a lot more interesting here."

"I'm not sure *interesting* is the right word. *Terrifying* is more like it. Come on, let's go see if Julie's found our boy." She started down the alley.

"Your boy, Anica," Lily said. "Your boy."

He wasn't her anything, but Anica didn't bother to contradict her sister. During the time that he was a cat Jasper was her responsibility. She'd mucked that up, but no more.

"Julie," she called out. "Where are you?"

Julie came around the corner, her hands shoved in the pockets of the black pea coat Anica had insisted she go back for. She'd been ready to search the city wearing nothing but her skinny black pants and a long-sleeved black T-shirt. Anica was becoming fonder of Julie by the minute.

"He's still here." Julie kept her gaze trained on a point on the far side of the wall, a spot Anica couldn't see. "I've been keeping watch over him, but he won't let me come close enough to grab him." She sniffed. "Is that chicken in the bag?"

"Yep. I asked Lily to pick up a sandwich in case we needed something to tempt him with."

"Smart."

Anica went around the corner to see the box. Her breath caught. There sat Jasper, gazing at her with his golden eyes.

She wondered how others could miss the glow of human intelligence in those eyes. He didn't look like an ordinary cat to her, but then she knew he wasn't one.

He didn't approach her. Instead he sat near the cardboard box Julie had mentioned and watched her. His nose twitched, which probably meant he'd caught the scent of chicken.

"It's him, isn't it?" Julie said.

Anica had forgotten the girl was there. By now Lily had joined them, too. "Yes, it's him, all right. Hello, Jasper."

Jasper didn't even blink.

"He's a very good-looking cat," Julie said. "Pretty sleek for being a stray. Do you think he belongs to someone?"

"No," Anica said. "No, I don't."

"Well, yeah, I suppose him not being neutered is a giveaway. Most owners would have taken care of that by now. He looks like he's at least five or six years old. I love cats. I would have one, but my brother's allergic and he comes over all the time."

There was a spell for that, a combination of hypnosis and magic that cured pet allergies, but Anica would have to let Julie and her brother know she was a witch in order to use it. And she'd have to get her magic back.

"Julie," Lily said, "we haven't met, but I'm Lily, Anica's sister."

"Glad to meet you." Julie seemed a little dazed by Lily.

Anica didn't blame her. Lily often had that effect on people.

Lily lowered her voice as if letting Julie in on a secret. "I think it's best if we move back down the alley and let Anica see what she can do without all of us standing around."

"Oh. Sure, sure." Julie began retreating immediately. "That makes perfect sense."

"Besides, I want to ask you where you got those fabulous skull earrings."

"They belonged to my great-aunt."

Anica decided to think about that fascinating bit of news later. She waited until Lily and Julie were out of sight and their voices had faded. Then she pulled the sandwich out of the bag and took off the paper it was wrapped in.

Jasper didn't move from his spot. It almost seemed as if he was guarding something.

Anica looked at him. "I had Lily buy this sandwich as a gesture of goodwill, but you don't care, do you? The thing is I need to take you back to the apartment."

Jasper stared at her without moving.

"I apologize for not keeping you safe," Anica said. "I needed to go to the shop and I hated to ask Lily to come over again. I thought Julie would work out. I never dreamed Edna was such a nutcase. I'm sorry for the trauma, Jasper."

Still he didn't come to her.

Anica sighed in frustration. "Look, I have something to say, and I don't want Julie to hear it. Could you come a little closer? I won't make a grab for you, I promise. It's just that this is a sensitive topic."

Jasper stood, stretched, and moved another three feet toward her.

He was still out of reach, but if she lunged at him, she might be able to get her arms around him and hold on. She'd promised him she wouldn't, though, so she resisted the temptation.

Keeping her voice low, she laid out her proposition. "I've been selfish to try and solve this on my own. Or just with Lily's help. I wanted to keep it quiet so my parents wouldn't find out, or the rest of the magical world, for that matter."

Cocking his head to one side, Jasper seemed to be listening intently.

"I can't keep making you drink that potion when I don't know if it will ever create a permanent change. I'm shooting in the dark, Jasper, and I've finally admitted that's not good enough." She took a deep breath. "I'm going to call the couple that Lily met, the ones who are on the Wizard Council, and ask them to help me reverse this spell."

Jasper's chest heaved as if he, too, had taken a deep breath.

"Will you come home with me so we can get to work on that?"

Instead of moving forward he looked over his shoulder at the cardboard box.

"Come on, Jasper. Everything will be okay." She really thought he'd come over to her, but instead he turned and walked back to the cardboard box.

She slumped in defeat. She'd promised him that she wouldn't trick him in order to capture him, but maybe she shouldn't have made that promise. "I don't know what to do, Jasper. Tell me what you want me to do."

Sitting down near the opening of the cardboard box, he meowed in a way that was almost a command.

"Do you want me to come over there?"

He meowed again. Then he crawled inside the box.

Curious now, Anica walked over to the cardboard box, got to her knees on the dirty pavement of the alley and peered inside. Jasper sat near the opening, but farther in a pair of cat eyes glowed in the shadows.

The unknown cat hissed a warning. But that wasn't the only noise coming from inside the box. Soft mewling sounds mingled with the warning hiss.

Anica turned to stare at Jasper in wonder. "You brought me over here so I could help them, didn't you?"

Jasper met her gaze and began to purr.

Chapter 12

Transporting the mother cat and her two kittens back to the apartment building was more of a project than Jasper had anticipated. He'd been so tempted to leave them there, go home with Anica and forget the home-less family ever existed. Although he wasn't normally into acts of charity, the sight of that emaciated mother trying to nurse her hungry babies probably would have haunted him forever.

Lily had gone off to buy a carrier, and by the time she returned the mother cat had devoured every bite of the chicken sandwich that had been meant for Jasper. He tried not to mind too much. After all, Anica was about to risk public humiliation in front of her magical com-munity for his sake, so he should be able to sacrifice a little chicken. Besides, Anica would feed him as soon as they got home.

The chicken helped soothe the mother cat's fears, but she still might not have gone in the carrier if it hadn't been for Julie. That girl had a way with cats, it turned out. She talked to the mother in a soft crooning voice as Lily and Anica transferred the first kitten.

There were only two, so it shouldn't have been tough, but the moment the first was in, the mother cat leaped after it and tried to take it back out. Anica managed to get the second kitten in the carrier before that could happen, and the family was confined.

"I'm taking them." Julie picked up the carrier and started out of the alley.

"We can trade off," Lily said. "They'll get heavy."

"I don't mind," Julie said. "But I meant I'm taking them to my apartment. They can stay with me until the kittens are old enough to adopt out. Then I'm keeping the mother. Come to think of it, I might keep both kittens, too."

"What about your allergic brother?" Anica scooped Jasper up in her arms and he offered no objection. He was happy to be going back to a warm apartment where no one would throw bricks at him.

"You know, I just realized that I don't want to go through the rest of my life not having cats because of my brother's allergies. He doesn't have to have animals if they bother him, but that doesn't mean I shouldn't get some."

Jasper thought that was a fine attitude indeed. From his new perspective of having bricks thrown at his head, he could see that pets needed all the friendly humans they could find. He'd never realized how dangerous the world could be for an animal. To think he'd come damn close to losing his boys. Too damn close.

In a restored Victorian house on the edge of the town of Big Knob, Indiana, Dorcas Lowell was trying to get an oil stain out of her husband Ambrose's good designer slacks when the phone rang. She detested laundry and had tried various magic spells to get rid of the stain, but she'd only smeared it. She would have turned the job over to her husband, but he was worse at laundry spells than she was and he'd ruin the slacks for sure.

She wouldn't have to be doing this if he'd give up that ridiculous red scooter he'd insisted on buying a couple of years ago. He thought he looked like a biker dude on that contraption, which was now acting up and throwing out oil on his good slacks.

"Ambrose! Phone!" Working on the stain wasn't the sort of job Dorcas wanted to interrupt for a phone call and return to later. Once she'd launched herself into the task, she wanted it over in three minutes or less, not dragged out by interruptions.

Finally she realized that Ambrose wasn't going to answer and, even more irritating, he'd forgotten to turn on the answering machine. He hadn't mentioned going out, but for all she knew he was riding around town on that blasted scooter, deep in his Hell's Angels fantasy, getting more oil stains on his clothes.

"Zeus's balls." She abandoned her stain duty in the laundry room and walked into the kitchen. She could just let the phone ring, of course, but intuition told her the call was important. The caller was persistent, at any rate. Dorcas had a habit of counting rings, and this was the tenth. The caller still hadn't given up.

Dorcas picked up the cordless from the wall mount beside the kitchen window. "Hello?"

There was a slight hesitation, as if the caller was deciding whether to speak or hang up. "This is Anica Revere," a woman said at last. "My sister, Lily, tends bar at the Bubbling Cauldron on Rush Street in Chicago."

"I remember Lily." Dorcas had been quite taken with the tall brunette. Lily might need to ground herself a little more but she had spunk. Dorcas admired that in a witch.

"She gave me your number. I . . . I have a problem and I need some help."

As Anica told her story, Dorcas gazed out the window toward the lake. The ice was melting, which meant that the two lake monsters, Dee-Dee and her mate, Norton, would soon want to come out of their cave under the water and take moonlit swims with their growing children.

The lake monsters had to be careful that the residents of Big Knob didn't see them, which was becoming more of a challenge now that there was a whole family of them living in the lake. Ambrose had erected a flagpole down by the shore, which he'd billed as a patriotic gesture. In reality it was a signaling device. When the flag was right side up the lake monsters had to stay hidden. When it was upside down they were free to come out.

But as Dorcas concentrated more fully on Anica's problem, she decided the lake monsters would have to wait another week before they began their swimming season. Dorcas and Ambrose were needed in Chicago.

"We'll be there first thing in the morning, Anica," she said. "In the meantime I'll do some research on the spell you cast. Because I don't know what we're dealing with, I think it's better if we meet you at a place where Jasper can't hear what we have to say."

"Then come to Wicked Brew." Anica gave the address. "Can you make it by eleven?"

"I think so." Dorcas winced at how early they'd have to be on the road, but she shouldn't complain. Not so long ago they weren't allowed to leave Big Knob at all. They'd been sent here—banished, in fact—to rehabilitate George, the dragon who had been shirking his job as Guardian of Whispering Forest. The Wizard Council had decreed that they couldn't leave, not even for a vacation, until George had earned his golden scales.

Dorcas and Ambrose had finally helped George accomplish that and now they could travel. They'd bought a Toyota Prius and had made several trips to Chicago for the plays, the food and the nightlife. On their last trip they'd discovered the Bubbling Cauldron, run by wizards and staffed by magical people.

"I'll look for you around eleven, then," Anica said. "Also, I probably don't have the right to ask you, but . . ."

"What is it?"

"I know you're both on the council and I suppose you're required to report everything to them."

Dorcas laughed. "They might like that, but I don't see it as my sacred duty."

"Then would you mind not saying anything about this to anyone except your husband, at least for now?"

"You know an alert came down to the Wizard Council when you lost your magic. Most likely there's already a note in your file."

"But they don't know why I lost my magic unless somebody tells them, right?"

"I'm pretty sure that's how it works." Dorcas was sympathetic to those who screwed up. After all, she'd done it herself. She'd messed up a spell involving the Grand High Wizard's brother-in-law, which is why she and Ambrose had been shipped off to Big Knob, the Wizard Council's version of Siberia.

"I'd appreciate it if you didn't tell anyone, then," Anica said.

"We can be discreet."

A relieved sigh traveled across the miles between them. "Thank you."

"Don't thank me yet. We haven't solved your problem."

"No, but I have faith that you will."

Dorcas wasn't so sure. Transformation spells were tricky, especially the older ones. She didn't want to rub that in, though. Anica Revere sounded as if she might be at the end of her rope and Dorcas knew exactly how that felt.

"See you tomorrow, Anica. Give my best to Lily." She replaced the phone in its cradle. Hera's hemorrhoids. Now she had to finish working on that stain. Maybe she'd have to resort to Spray 'n Wash, but that would be admitting she couldn't do laundry magic. No self-respecting witch would ever admit that.

*   *   *

Once Anica got Jasper back in her apartment, she wasn't willing to leave again until the next morning when she went to meet Dorcas and Ambrose Lowell at Wicked Brew. She'd thought keeping the shop operating smoothly was important to her until she'd almost lost Jasper, but her priorities were clear now. Her employees would have to handle things at the shop, and if they couldn't, well, she'd shut the place down temporarily.

She sent Lily home to sleep and gave Julie enough cat food and litter to get her through a couple of days with her new charges. Fortunately the responsibility of a mother cat and kittens had distracted her new friend from the subject of witchcraft, but Anica knew Julie would ask again. If she'd been given skull earrings by a great-aunt, then she might come by her curiosity naturally. She might have a few magical people lurking in the branches of her own family tree.

After Lily and Julie left, Anica sliced up some chicken for Jasper, who had certainly earned it.

His self-sacrifice surprised her. After the way he'd manipulated her affections Anica had categorized him as a self-serving jerk. A sexy jerk, but a jerk nevertheless. Yet he'd been determined to save this mother cat and kittens before going home with her to fix his own problem.

When she went into her bedroom to change into sweats, she left Jasper scarfing up chicken from the bowl she'd set on the counter, and Orion pacing underneath, meowing his protest.

By the time she came back out, Orion and Jasper were at opposite ends of the sofa, grooming themselves. She sat down next to Orion and leaned over to give him a good scratch. "Poor guy. I know it's tough to be the one with your nose pressed against the candy store window, so to speak. Your life should be back to normal soon. You . . . smell like chicken."

She knew Orion couldn't hop up on the counter, or else he would have done that while she was slicing the chicken. Jasper certainly had. He'd been right by her elbow while she unwrapped the package.

So there was only one way that Orion could have eaten any chicken. Slowly she turned to Jasper, who gazed at her innocently. Now she had to know for sure.

Standing, she walked into the kitchen and crouched down to examine the floor underneath Orion's thoroughly cleaned bowl. Sure enough, there was a damp smear on the linoleum. Jasper had drop shipped chicken to his buddy Orion.

She walked back into the living room. "Jasper, I appreciate your generosity, but Orion's trying to shed some pounds. I realize you won't be here long enough to thoroughly corrupt him, but please don't get him started on any bad habits."

Jasper might not be able to talk, but there was no mistaking the look he was giving her. Quite clearly it said, *Bite me.*

After the morning he'd had, Jasper was exhausted. He slept all afternoon and only woke up when he smelled chicken warming in the microwave. This time when Anica fed him she watched him like a hawk, so he couldn't share any with Orion. To make up for that he played hide-and-seek with Orion for a good half hour afterward.

Orion obviously loved it, creeping around corners and pouncing on Jasper, then trading off and letting Jasper skulk around and leap out at him. There was no animosity between them anymore. The chicken-sharing event had obviously clinched the deal as far as Orion was concerned.

Jasper played with Orion partly for the cat's sake, but mostly as a demonstration for Anica. He hoped she was getting the message that Orion needed a playmate and

Jasper wouldn't be around much longer to serve in that capacity. Instead of putting her cat on a diet she should get him a friend.

Playing was fun but Jasper was still low on sleep. When Anica turned in early, he was more than happy to settle down on the end of the bed along with Orion. He didn't even have the energy to sneak into the bathroom and catch Anica taking off her clothes and putting on her pajamas.

He heard her brushing her teeth, and then she came out in a flannel gown buttoned all the way up to her neck. She'd also braided her blond hair loosely and tied it with a ribbon. The getup seemed designed to discourage a man from thinking about sex.

Jasper wished he could feel discouraged by her efforts to look plain, but instead he noticed how her nipples made two of the flowers on the gown stand out in 3-D. His still-active human male brain took that outfit as a challenge, not a turnoff.

He was still a cat, though, which meant that it didn't matter what his libido wanted at the moment. Would he transform again tonight? He had no way of knowing.

If he'd only get another ten minutes, though, he'd rather it didn't happen at all. Reentry was just too hard on the psyche. When he changed the next time he wanted it to be for good. He'd pinned all his hopes on the witch and wizard from Big Knob. Surely they could pull that off.

He dreamed, as he had ever since his transformation, that he was a man again. His past dreams had involved his condo, the office, and his normal routine. But tonight his dream had to do with sex.

No wonder—he'd gone several weeks without any. Quite naturally the dream centered on a certain blonde, one who owned a sexy red dress and knew how to dance a mean salsa. His erection throbbed as he dreamed that he'd peeled off that dress and lifted her onto a bed that was sort of like his at home except with antique posts like Anica's double bed.

Eagerly he climbed into bed with her and moved between her thighs. When he caressed her he discovered how wet she was, how ready for him. Thrusting deep, he felt the immense satisfaction of that ultimate connection.

They writhed together, hot and slick with sweat, both yearning for a mind-blowing climax. He moaned and called out her name.

"Jasper?"

The dream drifted away and he kept his eyes closed, wanting to sink back into the dream, back into Anica's lush body. If he opened his eyes he would see her bedroom through the eyes of a cat, which meant he could see extremely well, but it also meant he was still a cat. He didn't want to know that right now.

A warm hand touched his shoulder and shook him gently. Anica's voice hummed with excitement. "Jasper, wake up. You transformed again!"

His eyes flew open, and instead of his cat night vision, he saw the room as shadowy and indistinct. Human sight! He also had the granddaddy of all erections going on, a holdover from the dream. Grabbing a corner of the quilt he covered his woody as he gingerly pushed himself to a sitting position.

Then he looked at the clock. Eleven thirty. He was a man again but he didn't know how long that would last. He didn't know how long his erection would last, and that was a more immediate problem.

Waking up in the same bed with the woman he'd been having dream sex with wasn't helping. He could smell her, almost taste her. She'd moved her hand and was no longer touching him, but his skin remembered how warm she'd felt. He wanted her to touch him again. He wanted her touching him all over, but he had a specific spot that really demanded attention.

"Should I turn on the light?"

"Not . . ." Using his voice felt weird. He cleared his throat. "Not yet." He had to think, decide what to do next, but all his blood had drained south.

"I could get your clothes, leave them on the bed and go out into the living room while you get dressed."

"I'm afraid to get dressed. That's when I changed back last night, while I was trying to put on my clothes."

"I doubt it was the clothes that made the difference. I think the potion only worked for a short time."

"You're probably right, but I just—I just don't want to take a chance." Besides, bringing this sexual desire under control was the first order of business. Murmuring together in the dark wasn't helping, either. But if he let her turn on the light, she'd probably guess what his problem was.

"Can I get you anything? Something to eat? Something to drink?"

He thought about it. Not knowing when he might suddenly revert back to his cat status, he was reluctant to make big plans, like heading over to his condo. Going through the change in the backseat of a taxi didn't appeal to him. In fact, going through the change while being anywhere but here was a dicey proposition.

Maybe he should set his sights low. "You got any beer?"

"Um, yes, I think so." She seemed taken aback. "Maybe one or two. I don't even know what brand they are."

"I don't care about the brand. I'd just like to taste some beer. It's either that or have sex." He heard the words come out of his mouth and couldn't believe he'd actually spoken them aloud.

Anica sucked in a breath.

"Whoops." He had the inappropriate urge to laugh, so he coughed instead. "I didn't mean to say that."

The mattress shifted as she slid out of bed. "I'll get the beer."

Chapter 13

Anica's heart thumped crazily as she hurried into the kitchen, Orion close at her heels. Orion always followed her into the kitchen with the optimistic hope she'd feed him something yummy. Instead, she picked him up and carried him back into the living room, where she closed him in the coat closet.

She wasn't sure what had prompted Jasper to say what he did, but she'd been thinking about that very subject from the minute she'd become aware of his transformation. She hadn't expected *him* to be thinking about it, though. Yet the more she considered the matter, the more it made sense that he would.

First of all, he was a man (again!), and weren't they supposed to think about sex every four minutes? Something like that. Second of all, he might be a man now, but after last night's experience he couldn't count on staying that way.

She certainly wouldn't advise him to leave the apartment, at least not until several hours had gone by with no change. Essentially he was trapped here with her while he waited to see what would happen. A man with nothing much to do but wait, when finding himself naked in a woman's bed—well, it just stood to reason what he'd be thinking.

Anica walked back to the kitchen, opened the refrigerator and found two bottles of Sam Adams. She held them to her hot cheeks. Whew. So how about her? Was she seriously considering going back in there specifically to have sex with Jasper?

Yes, she seriously was. After all, he'd woken her up with what was definitely a pre-climax moan and then he'd called her name. She'd bet anything he'd been dreaming about having sex with her, and if he hadn't covered himself with the quilt no doubt the evidence would have been overwhelming.

She longed to be overwhelmed. When it came to Jasper Danes, legendary lover, she might never have this chance again. A good game of mattress bingo would serve many purposes. It would pass the time, get rid of a boatload of frustration—his and hers—and it might soften his heart enough that he wouldn't try to ruin her once he regained his human form permanently.

There was no downside to jumping into bed with Jasper right now. Okay, he might turn into a cat during the event, but there were worse things. Many men turned into pigs in bed, even though they didn't actually grow a snout and tail.

She'd take a cat transformation any day over a couple of other sexual misfits she'd had the bad luck to go to bed with. Better a guy who turned into a cat than one who had a foot fetish or was a premature ejaculator.

She wasn't about to waste precious time drinking beer beforehand, either. Neither of them knew how long before he would change again. She put the bottles back in the refrigerator.

Too bad she'd worn this granny gown, but at least she could unfasten all seven buttons that ended where her cleavage began. She could untie the ribbon holding her braid and fluff her hair, tossing it around to give herself a tousled look. She could dab some vanilla behind her ears and between her breasts.

When she'd done all that, she went through her sexual readiness checklist. Legs shaved—check. Recent shower—check. Condoms in the bedside table drawer ... were there condoms in the bedside table drawer? She hadn't had sex since Edward, and hadn't thought to restock. There had to be at least one left, though, and one might be all they had time for.

Shoot, they might not have time for that if she didn't get on with it. She might even walk back into the bedroom and discover he was a cat again, which would be a bummer. *Spontaneous*—that was the watchword tonight. She was going in.

She noticed that the bedroom light was on when she entered the hall. She decided to start the conversational ball rolling before she walked in there, mostly because she wanted to hear his voice and reassure herself that she wouldn't find a cat in her bed instead of a man.

"Jasper, I've been thinking about what you said a couple of minutes ago."

"It was uncalled for." He came to the door wearing a towel wrapped around his hips. "I ..." His voice trailed off as he stared at her.

"I think it was totally called for. I think it's the best idea I've heard in ages." Dear Zeus, he was gorgeous. He'd transformed back into exactly the man he'd been in the restaurant—except for the being-naked part. He was clean-shaven, with great hair and a terrific body. Add to that the obvious benefit of wearing nothing but a towel and you had the perfect setup for outstanding sex.

Jasper's gaze traveled from her unbound hair to her unbuttoned nightgown. Her nipples peaked under the soft flannel, and she was quite sure he noticed. His nostrils flared and the intensity in his eyes reminded her of the way he'd looked at her across the restaurant table ... was it only two nights ago? It seemed like a lifetime.

He swallowed. "You didn't bring the beer."

"Nope." She advanced, backing him into the room and toward the bed.

His chest rose and fell as his breathing grew more labored. "I don't think you want to do this."

"Oh yes, I do." If he took a moisture meter reading about now, he'd know exactly how much.

"But something could happen right in the middle of—"

"That's why we can't fritter away valuable time drinking beer and debating the issue." She surrendered to basic instincts and hooked a finger inside the knot of his towel.

He looked into her eyes. "I hope you know what you're doing."

"I have a working knowledge of the subject but I'll bet I could take lessons from you." Holding his golden gaze she loosened the knot until the towel fell to the carpet with a naughty whisper.

She wanted to look but she was afraid if she broke eye contact, he might bolt. She recognized performance anxiety and it must be a novelty for him, the man who, as Sheila had said, was *that good*.

In this situation, though, he didn't have total control of his body, and at any time it could betray him. He might be willing to abandon the idea of sex in favor of avoiding potential humiliation. She didn't want to give him that chance.

So instead of feasting her eyes on his endowments, she took matters—and his considerable endowments—into her own hands.

When she touched him, his eyes darkened from gold to mahogany. His penis was thick with desire and his balls tightened as she cupped them in her other hand. Feeling the heft, she shuddered to think that he'd almost lost them to the vet's knife today.

He cradled her face and leaned close to brush his lips over hers. "I guess you're committed to this."

"You betcha."

"It's a really bad idea." His breath caught as she stroked the length of his penis. "But I guess we'll do it, anyway."

"I'm counting on it." She closed her eyes when he leaned down to nuzzle the base of her throat. This was familiar. They'd made out before, and she knew he was good at that.

Then he took the open neck of her gown in both hands. "This is just wrong." In one swift movement, he tore the material right down the middle. He kept ripping until he broke through the hem and had the whole thing apart and every inch of her exposed. "Much better."

That was totally unfamiliar! The thrill of such an unexpected assault left her gasping and even more drenched with need.

His gaze moved hungrily from her aching breasts to the curls between her thighs. "I believe you said we had no time to waste."

She wanted him so much she could barely speak. "We don't."

"Then let's get to it, woman." Turning her so her back was to the bed, he gave her a firm push that left her sprawled across the mattress, breathing fast, her legs open, her body completely available to him.

He followed her down, his mouth first at her breasts, then sliding down her rib cage to lick the indentation of her navel and finally coming to rest at her juicy center, where he lapped at the bounty there with a groan of triumph. Dimly she remembered that she'd meant for this to be a mutual event, not one geared specifically to her pleasure.

Then any thought of a plan, any idea of an agenda was swept away on a tsunami of sensation. With an artistry that left her squirming helplessly against the quilt and bunching the material in her fists, he brought her to the brink and eased her back down, took her up again and let her slide back. The roller coaster careened around one curve only to dive headlong into the next roaring free fall.

She was reduced to incoherent babbling, whimpers, and at last, when he finally took her all the way home, she erupted with wild cries of unrestrained bliss. Only as she lay spent, dragging in each breath as if she'd run a marathon, did she think about the neighbors. And promptly dismissed them again.

Easing himself back up her body, he kissed her, going deep with his tongue, imprinting her with the taste of her own climax. It was the sexiest thing any man had ever done to her. As he plundered her mouth she felt the tightening begin again.

Miraculously, she wanted more of him. He was a fever in her blood and she wouldn't be satisfied until he was buried deep within her, touching the very essence of who she was.

His lips left hers and moved close to her ear. "Condoms," he murmured.

Her brain had officially checked out, and she couldn't remember the names for things. "Table," she muttered, but she couldn't for the life of her think what to call the sliding compartment that held the precious condoms. "Inside table." She sounded like a warrior chief in a bad Western.

He chuckled and briefly left her. She was bereft. She wanted his body covering hers for the rest of recorded time. After what seemed like eons he was back, his warm skin sliding over hers. And then what she'd craved since the day she'd met Jasper Danes finally happened. His cock thrust deep inside her and life was complete.

Or so she thought until he started a seductive rhythm. Okay, so life wasn't totally complete yet. But if he would increase the pace a little, and shift the angle a bit, exactly like *that*, and if he'd lift her legs and tuck her ankles around his neck, and hold her hips so that she could arch against him while he stroked even faster, and faster yet, then maybe, at last, life would be ... oh, dear Zeus .. yes ... yes ... *yes. Complete.*

She erupted in a rainbow of colors that seemed to shower them like confetti. With a low growl he drove home once more and held her tight while his body shuddered and pulsed within her. She offered up a silent prayer of gratitude for a fabulous lovemaking session that no one could take away, no matter what happened later on. She also gave fervent thanks that she'd stopped Edna from taking Jasper to the spay-neuter clinic.

Jasper hoped he hadn't just allowed his pecker to lead him into a ditch. Sex was one thing, but he sure as hell didn't want to get emotionally involved with this witch. So he simply wouldn't do that. He'd practice containment.

Sex without commitment, that's what he'd just had. And he couldn't have ignored the temptation, either. Once she'd walked into the bedroom with her hair down and her nightgown unbuttoned, he was beyond stopping himself, except for the niggling fear that he wouldn't be able to finish what he started. Then she'd taken hold of his penis and he'd decided to risk a potential disaster.

But just because he'd dipped his wick in enemy territory didn't mean anything had changed between them. They had no future, with her being a witch who would eventually get her magical powers back. That would make her capable of all sorts of weirdness, things he didn't even want to know about.

He liked being a commodities broker with a normal American lifestyle. If something about this sexual experience felt all happily-ever-after, then he'd blame the transformation for crossing some wires in his brain. She was just a good lay. That's all she meant to him at this moment and all she'd ever be.

She seemed lost in a daze of satisfaction and he felt

pretty much that way himself, but he was the guy with the condom, so he was assigned the job of getting out of bed and heading for the bathroom. He glanced at the bedside clock as he went by and noticed it was almost twelve thirty.

Maybe he was getting tuned in to this magic stuff, because after he saw the time he had a strong feeling that his interlude as a man was about to end. Sure enough, he'd no sooner disposed of the condom than the dizziness started. He dropped to the floor so he wouldn't fall and crack his head on something when he blacked out. He really, really hated this part.

When he regained consciousness, he was crouched on the floor, back to viewing the world from the feline angle. He was pissed that he'd transformed back, but not quite as pissed as he had been the night before. Great sex could mellow a guy out, even when he faced returning to life as a housecat.

Besides the sex, he had another reason for optimism. He'd extended his time from ten minutes to an hour. He hated to think how much of that glop he'd have to drink in order to get two hours of human time, but at least there was a ray of hope that he wasn't stuck like this forever.

"Jasper? Are you okay?" Anica walked naked into the bathroom, spied him crouched there and began to cry.

He hated that she was crying, even though, looking at it realistically, this was all her fault. Still, she'd been so happy a moment ago, lying there flushed and smiling in the light from the bedside table lamp.

"Jasper, I'm so, so sorry!" She scooped him up, cradling him against her bare breasts as she buried her face in his fur and cried some more.

He was sorry, too, but she was getting him wet. Her breasts were cushy and nice, though. She'd be good to cuddle with after sex, but he hadn't had that chance.

That was also her fault, but he wished she'd stop crying about it.

She sniffed and raised her head to reveal eyes that were red and still leaking. She wasn't a delicate crier. "I'll bet you don't like this emotionalism, do you?"

He gazed up at her and tried to signal in the affirmative by blinking at her.

"I mean, you're the one with the big problem, and I'm the one falling apart over it. You didn't fall apart when you changed back." She gulped. "Instead you made wonderful love to me."

Not love. Sex. He wasn't about to confuse the two, and he didn't want her to, either. They'd had sexual chemistry from the get-go, and even though she'd changed him into a cat he still craved her body, especially when he had a body that matched.

He might always crave her body, but she wasn't destined to be his mate for life, not with that witch thing going on. Their sex tonight had been a good use of time and he was glad they'd done it, but he could easily give her up once he was fully released from this curse she'd put on him.

She carried him back into the bedroom. "At least you changed for an hour this time." She sniffed again. "We're making progress. Maybe you'll change back once more before the night's over."

Nice thought, but he doubted it. Although he'd only changed twice, it had followed a pattern. The first time he'd been allowed five minutes on each side of midnight. Tonight he'd had thirty minutes on each side of midnight. Midnight seemed to be the key.

Still holding him, Anica climbed into bed. He struggled to get away, but didn't use his claws because of her silky bare breasts.

"Humor me, Jasper," she said. "I need someone to hold."

Jasper looked around for Orion. Orion could be the

man for the job. But the orange tabby wasn't in sight. Come to think of it, he hadn't been seen since Anica had left to get the beer.

Then Jasper figured it out. He'd dated a few women with cats, and usually they closed them away if things got hot and heavy. On one memorable occasion, a woman hadn't done that. Jasper had been pumping away when he'd felt an excruciating pain in his balls. Seems the cat had mistaken them for a dangly toy.

Thank God Anica had used good sense and apparently tucked Orion in the closet. An incident like that might have seriously affected the budding friendship Jasper felt for the orange tabby.

Keeping her grip on Jasper, Anica reached up and switched off the bedside lamp. Then she snuggled him close and sighed. "Thank you."

Jasper admitted it wasn't horrible being nestled against Anica's plump breasts. She seemed to need him there. He didn't really care whether she did or not, of course, because he didn't really care about her. Yet it seemed sort of mean to leave her alone when she was so upset.

Slowly she began to scratch behind his ears and under his chin. "I just want to say what I didn't get a chance to before you went into the bathroom. I want you to know, whatever happens, I'll always treasure tonight."

Oh, shit. She *was* mixing up love and sex. He'd do well to remember that next time. If there was a next time. He'd like that, from a sexual satisfaction point of view, but it wasn't like he *needed* to have her again.

Anica kept scratching his chin, and although he didn't want to, because it sent exactly the wrong message, he began to purr.

Chapter 14

Lily arrived at ten thirty the next morning to cat-sit for Jasper while Anica went to meet Dorcas and Ambrose at Wicked Brew. Lily was early. Lily was never early, which told Anica how much her sister was worried about the situation.

The steady rain falling outside had prompted Lily to break out her favorite purple raincoat that reached to midthigh, the exact point where her boots stopped. Underneath she had on a short denim skirt and a tight red sweater.

She shook the rain from her coat onto Anica's carpet, stomped the water from her boots and propped her dripping black umbrella near the door. "You didn't call last night. Does that mean he didn't transform at all?"

Anica glanced over toward the sofa, where Jasper and Orion each occupied an end. Jasper seemed to be sleeping, but she didn't trust him not to be listening with both highly tuned cat ears. "Let me make you some coffee before I go." She walked into the kitchen.

Lily followed her and lowered her voice. "You didn't want him to hear you, right?"

"Right." Anica fired up the electric coffee grinder. "We had sex."

"Sex?" Lily's one-word exclamation would have

carried over the sound of a jet engine, let alone a coffee grinder.

Anica sighed and poured the ground coffee into the basket. "Yes, and now I'm sure he knows we're talking about it."

"Sorry. But we're sisters. He should expect we'd talk about it."

"I guess, but—"

"Come on over here." Lily put an arm around Anica and led her to the far end of the kitchen. She leaned in close, as if they were calling plays for the big game. "How long did he transform for?"

"An hour."

"Wow. So the potion must have done something." Lily glanced over her shoulder toward the living room and then huddled again with Anica. "At what point did he change back? Were you still—"

"No. It was after. He'd gone into the bathroom and then . . ." Anica couldn't revisit that moment without choking up. She'd thought she'd been prepared for it to happen, but after the way he'd touched her, kissed her, made such sweet love to her, the change had hit her hard.

Lily gave her a fierce hug. "Poor An. Sounds rough."

Anica nodded.

"Was it great, though? The sex?"

"Yeah, it was great."

"Well done, sis. Now he might think twice before he goes after revenge."

"That's what I thought before I made the decision to go to bed with him. But now . . . now I think he probably deserves to have whatever revenge he wants. What I did was awful, Lil."

"Hey, let's not forget why you did it, okay? You found out he was a lying scumbag who manipulates women into feeling sorry for him so they'll agree to have sex."

Anica looked her sister in the eye and smiled. "Yeah, but it's damn good sex."

Lily laughed. "Then I'm glad you had some."

"Me, too." Then Anica was laughing with Lily, and it felt good. Not as good as sex with Jasper, but nice.

Lily gave her another hug and released her. "You'd better get going. I don't want you to be late for Dorcas and Ambrose."

"That would be bad after they drove all the way up here. Lily, I didn't even think about this, but should I offer to pay them something?"

"Nah, they'll just ask for your firstborn child."

Anica gasped.

"Not really! Honestly, you're the most gullible person I know. No wonder Jasper could hoodwink you so easily."

"Seriously, should I pay them something? I mean, they're taking their valuable time, and there's gas to consider and meals, too. It's not like any of that's free."

"I think the Wizard Council takes care of their expenses."

The very thought of the Wizard Council made Anica quiver with dread. "That's the point. I've asked Dorcas not to mention this to the council. I think I'd better offer to pay them."

"I'd wait to see what they have to say first."

"Okay." Anica took a deep breath. "There's something else I can't handle by myself, but I hate to ask you."

"Go ahead. I love having you in my debt."

Anica rolled her eyes. "Never mind."

"Oh, come on. What is it?"

"I still don't have a protection spell on the apartment. I don't think those particular fairies will be back, but I'd feel better if—"

"Say no more. I'll handle it this morning."

"Thank you. That relieves my mind." Her sister could be wonderful sometimes.

"By the way, you look terrific today. That blue sweater and skirt complement your orgasmic glow."

And she could also be a pain in the ass. "Stuff a sock in it, Lily." Smirking at her sister, Anica left the kitchen and walked over to the closet to get her hooded black coat.

"Oooh, some spunk!" Lily followed her. "Glad to see it. So, is everything fine here? Did you e-mail Jasper's work again?"

"I do it every morning." Anica buttoned her coat. "He has some work-related things piling up, and I'm wondering if somebody needs to check his condo and collect the mail, but if Dorcas and Ambrose can solve this today, he'll be able to handle it."

"Then again, having it take a little longer wouldn't be so bad, would it?" Lily winked at her.

"No comment. And thanks again for doing the spell." Grabbing her purse, Anica left the apartment. She knew perfectly well that once Jasper was completely cured she'd never see him again.

That might take place today. She hoped it would, even though that meant she'd never have sex with him again. If that consequence made her sad, she'd deal with it. Jasper's return to human form was the only thing she'd allow herself to think about right now.

Jasper watched Anica go out the door. He'd figured out that she was meeting her witch and wizard friends at Wicked Brew because he wasn't supposed to be privy to what they said to each other. That ticked him off. He was the primary one involved, after all.

But once again he wasn't in control of his destiny. All he could do was stay curled up on this sofa and pretend to sleep, when inside he was a seething mass of worry. Another day had gone by, another day when he'd been

AWOL at the office. Pickens, the nerd in the office next to his, had his eye on several of Jasper's clients. If Jasper didn't get back there soon Pickens might start stealing those clients out from under him.

As he lay there picturing that unwelcome scenario, Lily came over carrying a steaming mug of coffee.

She sat down beside him and adjusted her short skirt. "So, fuzz face, you made it with my sister last night, I hear."

Jasper kept his eyes closed, pretending to be asleep. He'd been irritated that Anica had told Lily about last night, even though her comment about how great the sex was had soothed him somewhat. Fortunately Anica hadn't gone all mushy when she'd mentioned the incident. Maybe in the light of day she realized it was just sex and nothing else.

"I'm glad you made her happy for a little while," Lily said. "Because she's headed to Wicked Brew to lay her reputation on the line for you."

Jasper thought that was only fair.

"I'm sure you have a mental list of grievances longer than the line at the DMV, but I wonder if you've considered the advantages of being a cat?"

Oh, sure. He'd especially loved the Shoumatoff incident.

"Some people see their glass as half-empty, and I wonder if that fits you, Jasper. Let me show you that your glass is half full. For example, as Anica's cat you don't have to worry about paying a mortgage or buying groceries. Your food is provided free of charge. You have somewhere to live that's warm in the winter and cool in the summer."

He hoped to God he wouldn't be around to experience seasonal change in this apartment.

"Anica makes sure you have a soft place to sleep and that your food dishes are always clean. And here's a bonus. You have the flexibility to lick your balls. I would think an oversexed guy like you would love that to pieces."

If he could talk he'd let her know that contrary to what she might think, he had no interest in that activity.

"Anyway, my big sis is worried that once you're a man again, you'll seek some kind of revenge against her for all your supposed injuries. I hope that's not your plan."

He hadn't decided yet. If Pickens had stolen some of his clients, then he was going to be pretty damned unhappy about it, and pretty damned unhappy with Anica.

Lily sipped her coffee and leaned back against the sofa. "Just in case that is your plan, I need to let you know something. You go after my sister, and I'll go after you. I'm a witch, too, and I don't have nearly the scruples Anica has. And while you don't know if she'll get her magic back, I still have mine."

How dare she threaten him! Jasper slowly opened his eyes.

Lily smiled. "Got your attention, didn't I? I thought you were playing possum. Anyway, lover boy, you'd better do my sister right, whether we're talking in the bedroom or elsewhere. You made some points yesterday when you led us to that mama cat. Very heroic."

He waited, because she obviously wasn't finished.

"But I'm not convinced that you won't try something underhanded with Anica. I'm watching you." She gave him the two-fingered watching signal.

He was determined not to be intimidated. She'd cleaned up the destruction at Wicked Brew inside of fifteen minutes, which had been impressive. But she hadn't been able to fix him, so he knew her powers were limited. Yeah, no doubt she was bluffing.

"I sense you might not believe me. Let's see if I can change your mind. *Doggie, doggie, bold and bright, give this kitty cat a fright.*" She snapped her fingers.

A giant mixed-breed dog came boiling down the

hallway, headed straight for Jasper. *What the hell?* Jasper leaped up, every hair on his body extended as he scrambled over the back of the sofa and fled for his life.

The dog snapped at his heels and almost had him, but he made it to the top of the bookshelf just in time to avoid certain death. He crouched there, shaking, as the dog stood snarling below. Then Lily snapped her fingers again and the dog disappeared.

Breathing hard, Jasper met her gaze. Maybe she wasn't bluffing, after all.

Soon after Anica stepped out on the sidewalk, the wind picked up and blew the rain sideways into her face. She adjusted her hood. When she'd been blessed with magic she'd never worried about arriving wet and bedraggled. A quick spell and her hair and makeup had been restored to the way they'd looked when she'd left her apartment.

She'd taken those magic powers for granted. Too bad it'd required a major screwup like this for her to realize how cocky she'd been about her well-ordered life. She dreaded seeing the condition of Wicked Brew. Although her employees cleaned reasonably well, she'd used magic every hour or so to make it white-glove spotless. But her spotless place of business, her spotless life, were no more.

When she pushed open the door of Wicked Brew, she saw an ordinary coffee shop with ordinary spills on the tables, ordinary straw wrappers on the floor, ordinary sugar scattered on the counter. The place wasn't dirty or in danger of failing a health inspection. But the magic was gone.

The chaos she'd found after the fairy vandalism had been horrible, but this was almost worse because it hadn't been caused by magic. Instead it had been caused by a lack of magic, and that broke her heart.

She hated for Dorcas and Ambrose to see her shop

in this condition, but then again, they wouldn't know the difference. They'd never seen it the other way.

Several of her regular customers called out to her as she walked in, and she returned their greetings with as much enthusiasm as she could muster. She picked up a couple of straw wrappers from the floor and threw them in the trash. If she'd had time, she would have grabbed a rag to wipe down the tables. Todd and Sally were busy filling orders behind the counter and couldn't do it.

But she wasn't here to tidy up the place. She was here to meet a witch and wizard who had the experience she lacked to fix the mess she'd made of her life. Lily had given her a description of them, so they weren't hard to spot. She saw them over at a corner table, sipping on lattes.

They seemed like the sort of boomer couple who would live in Lakefront Towers and have season tickets to the symphony. Dorcas could be a head buyer for Nordstrom, and he could be the CEO of some innovative ad agency. They dressed in a style that never went out of date—sport jacket and turtleneck for him; cowl-necked sweater for her. He was graying at the temples, while Dorcas's chin-length hair looked as if she'd just spent a few hours with a top Chicago stylist who understood all the secrets of color and cut.

Anica knew about Big Knob, of course. Everyone in the magical world had heard of that peculiar little town filled with people clueless about the town's magical heritage. When Anica and Lily were small, their parents had taken them for a drive down to Big Knob so they could see the streets laid out in the shape of a five-pointed star and the pentagon-shaped gazebo in the middle of a five-sided town "square."

Anica remembered the place as quaint but not the least bit sophisticated. Dorcas and Ambrose didn't look as if they'd fit in with the good folks of Big Knob, but somehow they'd managed to survive down there. Anica was grateful they'd stayed, though, because that placed them close enough to help in her hour of need.

Taking a deep breath, she walked over to the corner table.

Dorcas glanced up and smiled, but there was nothing jolly about her expression. Sympathetic was more like it. "You're Anica."

She tried not to read too much into that smile. "Yes. Thank you for coming."

Ambrose pushed back his chair and stood. "It's our pleasure." He pulled out a chair. "Have a seat. Can I get you some coffee?"

"Uh, no, thanks." She thought it was cute that he was offering her coffee in her own shop. "But is there anything more you'd like? On the house, of course. We have all sorts of pastries in the case." She hoped that was true. She hadn't been around to oversee reorders.

"We'll probably go out for lunch after we talk with you," Dorcas said. "So we're fine."

That reminded Anica of the expenses they were incurring on her behalf. "Listen, I've never asked for this kind of intervention before, and I'm willing to compensate you in whatever way you—"

"Wouldn't hear of it," Ambrose said. "We're always glad for an excuse to get out of town. Big Knob's okay, but after a while a person wants to— Dorcas, that was my foot you just kicked."

"Was it? Pardon me. I just wanted to clarify how much we love our little adopted town of Big Knob."

"Uh, right." Ambrose blinked. "Love the place. Love. It."

Dorcas leaned toward Anica. "I'll admit that we were a little dissatisfied with the move to Big Knob in the beginning, but now we've made so many friends, and I'm godmother to several babies."

"Ah yes." Ambrose rolled his eyes. "The *babies*. When

one of those babies comes to the house, everything has to stop, and I— Ouch, Dorcas! Quit kicking me."

"You know you love those babies, Ambrose. Anyway, I'd hate for the council to hear that we weren't thrilled to be there. They might transfer us."

"But aren't you both *on* the council?"

"We're the most junior members," Dorcas said. "That means we could be outvoted if the rest of the council decides we'd be more useful elsewhere. I don't want them getting the slightest hint that that's a good idea." She glared at Ambrose.

Anica had a disturbing thought. "Is there a chance that you'll get in trouble with the council by helping me and not telling them about it?"

"We're not going to worry about that," Dorcas said quickly. "Now, about your situation, I've—"

"No, wait." Anica had enough guilt already, without adding the Lowells to the list of people she'd wronged. "I asked you to keep it quiet, but never mind about that. I've done some soul searching recently and I've decided that I've been way too concerned about my reputation getting ruined. If the council needs to know about this, please tell them."

Dorcas laid a hand on her arm. "Listen, sweetie, I know how it feels to have the council pass judgment on you, and it's not pleasant. I'd like to save you from that."

"But not at your own expense." She was determined not to cry. "Promise me you won't put yourselves in a bad position because of me. I've created enough havoc already."

"Okay, I promise." Dorcas squeezed her hand. "Besides, I'm afraid there's not much we can do to help you."

Chapter 15

Anica left Wicked Brew in a daze. The rain pelted her and she didn't even bother to put up her hood to protect herself. What a stupid fool she'd been to invoke that ancient curse when she'd known nothing about it. She'd spent her whole life avoiding impulsive behavior, and the one time she'd done something reckless she'd created a tangle that might never be undone.

By the time she walked back into the apartment her hair was soaked and water had dripped inside the collar of her coat. She was shivering with both cold and reaction to the news Dorcas had given her. They'd wanted to take her to lunch, buy her a stiff drink, or at least walk her home, but she'd politely refused. This was her problem, and she'd figure it out . . . somehow.

Lily took one look at her and dragged her back into the bathroom, shutting the door after them. "You look like shit on a stick, girl." She helped Anica off with her coat before grabbing a towel and making Anica sit on the closed toilet lid while Lily dried her hair as if she were four years old.

"Oh, Lil. It's a hundred times worse than we thought."

Lily stopped drying. "Hang on a sec." She went out the door and closed it after her. Within a minute she was back. "Jasper was right outside listening. I put him in the hall and closed the bedroom door, too. But just to be safe, let's turn on the shower and keep our voices down."

Anica nodded, ashamed that Lily had to do all the thinking.

"Now, tell me."

Anica hoped she could without bursting into tears. Clenching her hands in her lap, she gulped back a sob. "The spell was created for rakes and scoundrels back in the 1700s. There is no counterspell, which is why I couldn't find one."

Lily sat down on the edge of the tub, the towel forgotten in her hands as she stared in horror at her sister. "So the spell is *permanent*?"

"No."

Lily's shoulders sagged. "So there is a way to lift it. Whatever it is, we'll do it. We'll dance naked in the moonlight on Michigan Avenue if we have to." She brightened. "Is nakedness involved? Because naked magic is becoming a lost art that should be revived, in my opinion. We could—"

"We don't have to do anything." For once Anica was glad her sister was a fruitcake who loved the idea of dancing naked on Michigan Avenue in the moonlight. Lily was a great distraction.

She was also clearly disappointed her naked magic wouldn't be called for. "What do you mean, we don't have to do anything?"

"Jasper has to do it all."

"Jasper?"

"It makes perfect sense when you know why the spell was created." Anica's love of history kicked in, which also helped calm her down. "In order to revert from being a tomcat, the man has to perform acts of kindness. In that way, he buys back time, which is granted to him in chunks on each side of midnight."

"Okay, so saving the mommy cat gave him an hour last night."

"I think so. I'm not sure what he did to get the first ten minutes the night before, but I'll bet it had something to do with playing with Orion."

Lily tossed the towel on the floor and stood. "So it's tricky, but doable. Let's go tell him." She started for the door.

Anica jumped up and grabbed Lily by the arm. "You can't do that."

"I didn't mean *I* would tell him. I think you should do the honors."

"We can't tell him at all, or the reversal won't happen."

"So how is he supposed to . . ." Her eyes widened. "He has to figure it out for himself."

"Yes."

Lily groaned. "Apollo's ass. That could take freaking forever. What about your magic? Do you get it back in the same increments?"

"Unfortunately, no. My magic won't return to me until the spell lifts completely."

"Bummer." Lily regarded her sister with pity. "Can you, like, give him hints?"

"Nope."

"How about setting up situations where he's likely to do the right thing?"

"Nope. Once he correctly identifies the method by which he can change, we can help him search out good deeds, but not until then."

Lily groaned again. "What a nightmare."

"Dorcas has researched this problem. According to what she's found, if he guesses what's happening and asks me to confirm it, I can do that."

"Whoopee. By the time that happens you'll be climbing the walls in frustration." Lily paused and glanced over at Anica. Slowly she started to grin. "Then again, maybe not."

"Lily, this isn't the time to be thinking of sex."

"Why not? Seems to me he could do many acts of kindness in bed."

Anica blushed. He already had, and she wondered if his gift of oral sex would count toward his minutes, and if it did, what he'd choose to do with all his extra time. . . .

Jasper wasn't sure what he'd been expecting from Anica's trip to see the witch and wizard, but he'd thought something would change around here, preferably him. Maybe he'd hoped she'd bring them back to the apartment for some kind of super session of magic with lightning bolts and stuff. At the very least he'd expected her to come back with a bag of evil-smelling but highly effective potions.

But so far this important face time with the witch and wizard had yielded a big fat goose egg. Anica hadn't looked very happy when she'd come home, and then she and Lily had hidden in the bathroom for a long time. He'd hoped they'd come out with a plan, but if they had one, they weren't telling.

Matter of fact, they both *left*. It was as if they'd given up on the whole program and abandoned him to his fate. At least he'd figured out one small part of the puzzle. So far whatever minutes he had as a man had been equally distributed on either side of midnight. That would likely continue, but unfortunately he couldn't predict how much time that would be.

But worrying about his lousy situation didn't help, so he slept a little. The rain continued to fall, and he spent a fair bit of his day on the windowsill, watching the drops hit and travel uphill. When he had no chance to be productive, he was amazed at the insignificant things that amused him.

Still, he had the urge to do *something* to improve his

situation. Hopping onto the desk chair, he turned on the computer.

E-mail was out of the question. There was too much of it, and he couldn't be his usual glib self one paw at a time. Besides, if he responded to one thing, people would expect him to respond to the rest.

Better to keep to the cover story that he had a flu bug that was hideously debilitating plus contagious, and he didn't want to see or hear from anybody until he was himself again. Ha. If only his friends knew how unlike himself he was at the moment.

He could type a big-ass message to Anica, though. He had plenty to say to *her*, and he didn't have to worry about hitting wrong keys or trying for that breezy tone his friends and work buddies were used to.

Once he'd typed the message, he cruised the Net and ended up going to sites involving animals. Inhabiting a cat's body had made him far more interested in the animal world than he had been before. He discovered a site where clicking a button prompted a pet food company to donate a dollar to animal rescue. Back in his real life, friends were always suggesting he go on some site or other and do something like this.

He'd never taken the time, but today he didn't have much else to do, so he clicked the donation button a few hundred times. Couldn't hurt, and it felt good to do it, sort of like he'd felt when he'd led Anica to the mother cat.

Then he noticed a second button. This was for anyone who felt compelled to donate something themselves, in addition to what the pet food company was giving for the clicks. He thought about that for a while.

If he typed very slowly, he could probably enter his American Express number, which he still remembered. He'd never been much for giving to charity, except now he found himself thinking about the mother cat and her tiny, helpless babies whose eyes hadn't even opened yet.

So he'd give twenty bucks. So what? Making sure he had the right numbers and expiration date filled in took some doing. He had to provide his address, which probably would mean more junk mail, but he was into the process now, so he painstakingly did that, too.

When he had the thing all ready to go, one more screen popped up and invited him to increase his donation and receive a free newsletter and a bumper sticker, neither of which he wanted. His twenty bucks looked a little puny sitting there in the donation space, though. He could certainly afford more.

Very carefully he added another zero, right at the moment he heard Anica's key in the lock. She was home! He could finally get answers to the questions he'd typed. In his eagerness, he turned toward the door and his tail twitched, whacking the keyboard.

The distinctive click of a computer key made him glance back at the screen. What the hell? Had his damned tail accidentally added another zero to his donation? Fuckin' A! He wasn't giving away two grand to these people he'd never met!

Agitated beyond belief, he went back to the keyboard and tried to hit CANCEL, which was a small button. Instead he hit COMPLETE MY ORDER, which was a humongous button. He watched in horrified fascination as all that money disappeared into cyberspace.

Then a message flashed on, complete with a picture of a soulful-looking puppy. The cheerful message thanked him for his generous donation. It reminded him to expect his newsletter and his bumper sticker within the next two weeks.

Two thousand bucks. There went a flat-screen TV. Or a new sound system. Or season tickets for the Cubs. Or a trip to the Bahamas.

"Playing on the computer, I see." Anica walked over to the desk.

Oh yeah, he'd been having big fun. He closed down the Internet connection, not wanting her to see what an idiot he'd been.

She set down a small bag before taking off her wet coat and draping it over the desk chair. Then she crouched down and stroked Orion, who had roused from his nap to come and greet her.

Jasper didn't like Orion getting attention first. From his perch on the desk chair, he reached out a paw and batted at her hair.

"Hey!" She glanced up at him and laughed. "Jealous?" While continuing to pet Orion with her right hand, she scratched behind Jasper's ears with her left.

He was truly embarrassed that he liked that so much, and even more embarrassed when he responded with a loud purr. Had he no pride? Apparently not, because he arched into her caress and purred louder.

"I went to your condo today and picked up your mail," she said. "It's in this bag, and I'll open it for you if you want. I also took the messages off your answering machine and wrote them down."

That was good news and bad news. He was glad she'd brought over his mail and snagged his messages, because even a guy down with the flu would do those things. But it was bad news because she must have abandoned the idea that he'd be able to do those things himself anytime soon.

She stopped petting both cats as she stood. "I also watered your plants." She slipped off her shoes and wiggled her toes in the carpet. "Before I realized they were fake."

Jasper knew he should be thinking about the mail, the messages and the questions he'd typed for her on the computer. Instead he was staring at her toes.

He hadn't noticed before that her toenails were painted red. On their dates she'd always worn boots or closed-toe shoes, so he'd had no reason to notice. And last night he'd been too busy to pay attention to her toes.

But now he realized toes were the sort of thing that he could appreciate as both a cat and a man. If he were truly a cat he'd want to jump down and possibly play with them, especially if she wiggled them again. As a man, he wanted to suck them.

Then Orion suddenly leaped on him, but it was a friendly leap, a *Let's wrestle* sort of leap. Jasper decided to oblige him. It was a satisfying outlet for his excess energy. As Jasper rolled around on the carpet with the orange tabby, he was vaguely aware of Anica humming in the kitchen. He could smell hamburger cooking.

This isn't so bad, living here with Anica and Orion. The second the thought floated through his head he wrenched free of Orion and leaped up to the desk, thoroughly appalled. Good God, was he starting to *like* this situation?

Before Anica had come home he'd had a plan, which was to get her to answer some hard questions. Those questions were sitting there on the computer, but he'd allowed himself to be distracted. He'd made no effort to get her to read them and respond.

That was going to be remedied immediately. He touched a key and brought them up on the screen. Then he began to yowl as loud as he could, which sent Orion scurrying into a far corner of the living room.

Anica came running out of the kitchen. "Jasper! What's wrong? Did Orion do something to you? I thought you were only playing!"

Jasper stopped yowling and put a paw on the computer screen.

"Apparently it's not about Orion." Walking over to the desk, Anica glanced at the screen. "That's it? You wanted me to come and read what you've written?"

Jasper meowed.

"Sheesh. You didn't have to scare me half to death, cat."

Cat. Aiming with his paw, he slapped at the keys.

NT A CAT

"Yes, I know," she said quietly. "Believe me, I know. Let me turn down the heat on the stove," she said. "Then I'll come back and read this."

As if he had a choice. As if he had any power in this situation whatsoever. But he wasn't going to let her forget about reading his questions. If she didn't come back in two minutes ...

But she did. Drying her hands on a towel, she came straight over to the desk and peered at the screen. "Uh-huh."

His heart pounded faster as she hesitated. They weren't hard questions, but she wasn't leaping right out there with answers. He also noticed she was twisting the towel. She was nervous, which made him nervous.

She cleared her throat. "First question, Lily and I aren't making any more of the potion we gave you before because Dorcas and Ambrose have told me it's pointless for you to drink that. It won't do anything."

He'd been afraid of that, had anticipated it, in fact, which was why he'd typed the second question. IF NT POSHN, WHT

Anica sighed. "I can't answer that."

A fountain of swear words erupted in his brain, but he couldn't say them out loud, so he had to be satisfied with growling, which he did. Repeatedly.

"I know, Jasper. It sucks. As for your third question, what caused you to change back the two times you did, Ambrose and Dorcas say it wasn't the potion, but I can't say what it was."

Now he almost wished he hadn't forced her to look at the screen. And he was really afraid of her answer to the last question.

She stared at the question for a long time, so long that he was afraid he knew the answer. Still, he had to hear it from her. Better to know the truth.

At last she met his gaze. "I don't know, Jasper. I honestly don't know. Listen, I have to go get dinner ready." She went back into the kitchen.

He felt sick to his stomach as he gazed at the last question he'd typed.

WLL I EVR B A MAN AGN

Chapter 16

Anica didn't see much of Jasper for the rest of the evening, and she wasn't surprised. In his position, she'd be off somewhere brooding, too. He was stuck in a mess with no clue how to get out. Even the people who were supposed to have a clue weren't helping him.

She thought about opening his mail to see if anything was urgent, but decided she didn't have the right to do that. She'd have to ask him first, and he'd retreated to the depths of her bedroom closet. It didn't take a mind reader to know he didn't want to be disturbed. Even Orion left him alone.

Although she hadn't had much sleep recently and was tired, she wasn't about to go to bed. Now she knew, even if he didn't, that he'd become a man again for at least an hour and maybe for longer. Unless he figured out the reason, though, she couldn't imagine how he'd extend his time. He couldn't accomplish many acts of kindness when most of his existence was spent as a cat cooped up in an apartment.

By ten, nothing had happened. She kept peering into the closet, but Jasper was still huddled way in the back, curled up as if sound asleep. She'd had so much coffee that she was jittery and tense. A hot shower was the answer, but what if he transformed while she was in there?

Not that she was afraid of him, and he'd certainly seen her naked the night before, but she still didn't want him suddenly walking into the bathroom. She decided to go for the shower and lock the door.

Dear Zeus, this was a hellish position to be in for both of them. She wondered if he'd thought about the stress she was under. Probably not, and if he did, he might think she deserved it. Maybe she deserved some of it, but that spell should have come with a warning in twenty-point type.

Once she was under the hot water, she felt marginally better. She had to deal with an unanticipated side effect, though. Because she expected him to transform at any time, and because of what had happened the last time he'd become a man, she was naturally thinking about sex.

She came out of the shower wide awake in more ways than one. Maybe she should have taken a cold shower, but she wasn't that much of a masochist. Besides, she'd been sexually frustrated before in her life. It wasn't the end of the world.

He was probably still in the closet, anyway. By the time he transformed, she'd be over this shower-induced sexual hunger and would be curled up in the living room, drinking herbal tea. She liked that image of her—cool and collected, glancing over with only mild curiosity when he walked down the hall wearing ... whatever he chose to put on. She would—

The doorknob turned slightly, stopping at the lock point. Her pulse rate skyrocketed.

"Anica, open the door."

She clutched the towel against her breasts and gulped for air. *He was right there.*

No time for cool and collected. No time for tea, a good book and a casual response to his sudden appearance.

She glanced at the tiny clock sitting on her bathroom counter. Ten thirty-two. Somehow he'd gained another two hours. And judging from the urgency in his voice, he wanted to spend it exactly the same way she did.

Jasper didn't understand how he could resent Anica so much, be so absolutely furious with her, and crave her body at the same time. He'd come out of his cat form once again with an aching erection and a primitive surge of lust he couldn't remember feeling for other women. He'd always before maintained a certain detachment, but not this time.

Maybe the tomcat psyche carried over somehow when he became a man. Anything was possible. That statement meant more to him now than it ever had before. Literally anything was possible.

He'd headed for the bathroom, knowing that she'd just showered and would be naked in there, knowing what he wanted to do once he found her. But he wasn't totally consumed with his need, because he'd stopped to open the bedside drawer and take out a condom. He'd counted how many were left—three—and run a hand over his jaw. Still no beard stubble. He took note of the time—ten thirty-two.

Why he had another two hours was a mystery, but he wasn't going to question it now. Maybe, after he'd exhausted himself with Anica's body, maybe then he'd think about why he seemed to be adding time.

He waited impatiently for her to unlock the door. If necessary, he'd break it down. Whoa! Had he actually thought that? Had Mr. Cool, the guy who made sure he never invested more than he could afford to lose, contemplated destroying a door to get to the woman he wanted?

Yes.

He would think about that later, too, because the door opened.

Anica had wrapped herself in a thick white towel that covered her from armpit to midthigh, and she'd piled her golden hair on top of her head in an arrangement that was quickly coming loose. Without jewelry or makeup she looked young and vulnerable, but so sexy that he shuddered with eagerness. Her blue eyes were wide with an emotion he couldn't read. Surprise? Anticipation? Fear?

He reached for the towel and yanked it away. It fell unnoticed in a heap on the tiled floor between them. At first all he wanted was to look, to drink her in visually while he was firmly in his own skin and could see her the way a man would see her.

Had he ever really looked at a woman before? Had he appreciated the wonder of her body, or had he been too busy planning his next move? Tonight he had three hours. A sinfully luxurious number of minutes. So he would take his time. And look.

Her skin was pink from the hot water and dewy in spots where she hadn't finished drying off. He watched her nipples go from soft and full to puckered and rigid. Her breasts quivered with her rapid breathing.

She had a tiny, flat mole above her right nipple. In his frenzy to experience her, he hadn't noticed it last night. Soon he would lick and kiss that spot, but first he wanted to make sure he saw her, really *saw* her.

He longed to span her small waist with both hands and lift her to the counter, but he would do that later, too. For now he admired how her hips flared, creating a graceful curve down to her firm thighs. At last he allowed his attention to settle on the blond curls between her thighs, and he almost lost it.

Tiny drops of water left over from her shower trembled there, silently inviting him to the feast he'd enjoyed the night before and wanted to savor again. First he would capture each drop of water on the tip of his tongue, and then he would—

"I want to touch you."

His gaze lifted to discover that she was looking at him with equal intensity. Her eyes were no longer wide and innocent, but heavy-lidded and sultry. He remembered how fantastic her hands had felt on him last night, and instantly his cock jerked and his balls tightened.

She ran her tongue over her lips and her smile was pure seduction. "And this time, Jasper, I plan to taste you, too."

Oh, God. If a man lived who could resist that kind of suggestion, Jasper hadn't met him. But then he had an awful thought, that she was offering oral sex because she felt terrible about the whole cat situation. That would take the zing right out of the experience, if that was her motivation. Well, not *all* the zing. He'd still enjoy it, but not in the same way.

He found himself hesitating. "You don't have to."

"I want to."

"Because of what's happened to me?"

She shook her head, still smiling that temptress smile.

"I don't want a pity blow job."

Her low laughter was the sexiest thing he'd ever heard. "That's not the kind I had in mind."

Moisture pooled in his mouth as he imagined what she *did* have in mind. "I . . . then . . . yes."

Holding his gaze, she knelt on the towel that he'd dropped at her feet. As she wrapped her warm fingers around his penis, he thought he might come on the spot. He clenched his jaw and curled his hands into fists. The condom wrapper crinkled under the pressure, and he tossed it to the counter. Later.

She extended her tongue and licked the drop of moisture from the end of his dick. Then she glanced up at him. "I've heard it's even better if you watch."

His response wasn't even a word, really. It was more of a strangled acknowledgment that somehow she'd read his mind and probed his deepest fantasies. He'd met women who didn't want to do this at all. He'd met women who only wanted to do it in the dark. Some were willing to do it when they could use a dimmer switch to mute the glare, or by candlelight, with soft music playing.

But this woman . . . this woman not only knelt before him under the bright lights of a bathroom, she'd invited him to watch her take his eager cock into her luscious mouth.

Apparently he looked as awestruck as he felt, because she laughed again.

Then she reached over and pushed the bathroom door closed. "That will help."

He couldn't imagine why until he glanced over and discovered a full-length mirror on the back of the door. That's when he almost forgave her for turning him into a cat.

For a porn movie, it would be the perfect camera angle. He could see everything—her lips sliding back and forth over his happy cock, her hands fondling his lucky balls, and her breasts bobbing in time to the whole maneuver. He wasn't going to be able to take more than ten seconds of that combination of visual and physical stimulation without coming.

So he closed his eyes and concentrated on not coming. Even then she was slowly destroying him. She'd suck for a while and then she'd lean back and use some sort of twisting motion with her fingers that had him gasping in delight.

Then she'd lick him as if he was an ice cream cone about to drip all over the sidewalk. Which he was. It was hotter than the Fourth of July in this bathroom.

Ah, but a cool breeze tickled the head of his penis, and he had to look. Sure enough, she had pursed her lips and was blowing on him, which was another kind of crazy-making, climax-building, torturous ecstasy. She began to lick again, and he groaned and closed his eyes again.

"Don't close your eyes," she murmured.

"If I watch I'll come."

Flattening her tongue, she rubbed it back and forth over the underside of his penis before hitting that spot with another burst of cool air. "Why hold back?"

He spoke through clenched teeth. "Because I want to do you."

"You can do me later." This time she ran her tongue up and down the ridge that contained about a billion nerve cells, judging from how he was shaking.

"But I want you on the counter." The selfsame counter he was now hanging on to for dear life so he wouldn't fall on her.

"You can have me on the counter." She paused to lick him thoroughly. "And you can have me on the kitchen table." She took him in, all of him, in one long, slow, slide. She spent the same amount of time on the return trip and finished with a kiss on the very top. "You can also have me on the living room floor." She circled the tip of his penis with her tongue. "Just come now."

He moaned. "I want to wait."

"No, you don't. Open your eyes. Watch me."

Cautiously he opened his eyes.

"That's better. Here we go. Home stretch." When she started sucking this time, she obviously meant business.

What was a guy supposed to do? He came. No more cool dude, either. He was loud. He was quivering. He was . . . her slave.

Jasper had been willing to slump to the bathroom floor and stay there while he recovered, but Anica coaxed him back to the bedroom so he could recover in comfort. She was inordinately proud of herself for that last episode. She wasn't normally a femme fatale, but the drama of this situation with Jasper seemed to be inspiring her to new heights of sexuality.

If her relationship with Jasper had gone the way she'd expected and they'd come back here after dinner the other night, she had a feeling the sex would have been okay, but nothing out of the ordinary. Now her entire life was out of the ordinary, so things occurred to her that never had before.

For example, until tonight she'd only used the full-length mirror on the back of the bathroom door to check her hemline or see if her shoes looked okay with her outfit. Even tonight she hadn't remembered the mirror until she was already on her knees. The person she'd been three days ago would have canceled the idea as too outrageous.

But Anica wasn't that person anymore. One reckless act had launched her into a whole other space. Because she couldn't put the world back the way it was, she was learning to take advantage of whatever opportunities came along, such as giving head in front of a full-length mirror and blowing a guy's mind.

She had done that. Whatever the consequences of her turning Jasper into a cat, he would never forget that experience in the bathroom. She was honest enough to admit that was one of her goals.

But it hadn't been her primary goal. Pleasure had been her primary goal when she'd opened the bathroom door and found him naked and aroused. He might think he'd had the lion's share, but she'd loved every minute of that seduction. She'd felt sexy and powerful, which had mended some of the recent damage to her self-esteem.

Now they lay face-to-face in her bed under the covers, smiling at each other. She'd already closed Orion in the coat closet. No sense taking any chances that Orion would interrupt the scheduled activities.

As she'd picked up her cat, she'd noted that he wasn't getting any lighter, but that could be because Jasper was sharing his meals whenever her back was turned. If there was a chance that might count as an act of kindness, she'd look the other way. More hours with Jasper would be a blessing, especially if they could spend them like this.

Jasper shifted his weight and moved closer to her. Then he brushed his index finger over her lower lip. "That's some talented mouth you have there."

"That's some talented dick you have there."

He gave a snort. "Yeah, well, you wouldn't know that from my contribution so far tonight."

"No, but I have an excellent memory for what your dick can do."

He grinned and tweaked her nose. "You're not the woman I thought you were, Anica."

"Because I'm a witch?"

"Well, that too, I guess." He combed her hair back with his fingers. "But I'm talking about how sassy you've become recently. In the times we dated, I never picked up on you being sassy."

"That's because I wasn't. I let my sister have that playing field."

"And now?"

She shrugged. "If I'd been able to cancel the spell right away without anyone knowing, I probably would have continued to play the good-girl role. But I couldn't cancel it, so why not see what it's like to be a bad girl for a change?"

"I hope you're not going to sell the coffee shop and open a strip joint."

"I said I wanted to be bad, not stupid." She sighed. "Not that I haven't been stupid, as well."

"You got mad. We all do stupid things when we're mad."

She recognized that was a concession on his part. Although he might never admit that he'd driven her to take that action, she wanted to acknowledge any ground gained in that direction. "That's nice of you to say, considering."

"You've put me in a mellow mood."

"You look good in mellow." It was a joke, but she meant it. She liked this relaxed version of Jasper, when he wasn't thinking about the market and how he could score big and retire early.

"Ha, ha."

"Yeah, I know. Lame. I'm just passing time until you perk up."

"See, that's what you get. I warned you not to make me come."

"I could go fetch your mail for you to read."

"No, thanks." He reached for her under the sheet and cupped her breast. "I'd rather fondle you than a pile of junk mail."

"Mm. I'm sure the post office would be devastated to hear that." She arched her back a little and pushed her breast into his hand. "More."

"Hussy."

"Bite me."

"Think I will." Easing back the covers, he scooted down and took her nipple into his mouth.

She arched her back a little more. "Good, very good."

"Um-hm." He became more enthusiastic, rubbing his chin against her breasts.

"I can feel your beard."

He lifted his head and gazed at her. "Does it hurt?"

"No." She rubbed her thumb along his jaw. "I like that tiny bit of scratchiness. It's sexy."

He looked into her eyes. "If I were a cat right now I'd be purring."

"But you're not a cat so it probably doesn't do anything for you at all."

"You'd be surprised." He captured her hand and guided it under the covers.

Her fingers closed around his firm penis. "Nice."

"It will be." He rolled her to her back. "Okay, bad girl. Show me what you got."

"In the missionary position? Are you kidding?"

"Then tell me what you want."

"You, on your back, big boy." Anica could hardly believe the suggestions coming out of her mouth, but she liked them.

He followed orders, rolling them both the other way in a tangle of sheets.

"We need to get rid of this mess." Scrambling to a sitting position astride his thighs, she wrenched the sheets away and tossed them to the end of the bed.

He laughed. "Won't you get cold?"

"Not considering what we're going to be doing." She leaned forward, deliberately dangling her breasts in his face as she opened the bedside table drawer and took out a condom.

"Oh, I like this already." He reached for the treats she so casually offered.

Before he could avail himself of the opportunity, she sat up again, the condom packet in her hand.

"Come back down here," he murmured.

She ripped open the packet. "When I feel like it. First I intend to get you suited up."

His golden eyes burned with eagerness. "I can do that."

"Yes, but I can do it better." Leaning down, she took his penis into her mouth.

"Anica . . ."

After giving him some playful licks and sucks, she released him and sat back on his thighs again. "That was just for starters. See how much easier the condom goes on now?" She rolled it on very, very slowly.

A quick check of his expression told her that her technique was having the desired effect. Soon she'd have him crazed with lust yet again.

"Come here." His voice was husky as he bracketed her hips and attempted to lift her up. "I want to be inside you."

"In due course." She gently removed his hands. "Keep these to yourself until I say so."

He frowned. "How soon will that be?"

"When I'm ready." She cupped her breasts with both hands. "I'll now proceed to get ready."

This was uncharted territory for her, but a bad girl would have this in her repertoire, so she decided to try it. Squeezing her breasts, she pinched her nipples and moaned softly. A quick peek at Jasper encouraged her to go on. He was riveted.

Time for Act Two. Keeping one hand on her breast, she reached between her thighs.

His voice sounded strangled. "You're not really going to . . ."

"Yes." She gazed at him as she massaged her clit. This was more exciting than she would have thought. Before long she was whimpering, moaning and writhing against his thighs.

"That's enough!" His hands seemed made of steel as he grabbed her and lifted her onto his cock.

She should probably scold him for jumping the gun, but she was too busy enjoying the sensation of sliding down onto the most rigid penis in the world. She'd take bets on it.

Her climax had almost arrived even before she took him deep inside her, so she knew it wouldn't be long. Bracing both hands on his chest, she looked into his eyes and rotated her hips. "Time to ride, pardner."

He gazed back at her, his eyes glowing with heat and his fingers pressed firmly against her bottom. "You are such a bad girl."

"Told you. Now giddyup."

"My pleasure."

And with that, the two of them rode off, whooping

and hollering, into the most brilliant, mind-shattering sunset imaginable.

Later, as she lay slumped over him, wishing she didn't have to move, she turned her head just enough so that she could see the clock.

He must have felt her movement and guessed her intent, because he spoke without hesitation "What time is it?"

"Almost midnight."

"The halfway point," he said softly. "Damn."

Chapter 17

Jasper tried really hard to bask in the afterglow of great sex. While he made a trip to the bathroom to get rid of the condom, Anica brought in the two beers they hadn't bothered with the night before, along with cheese and crackers and a bowl of chips.

Ideally they should be able to picnic in bed, then brush the crumbs off the sheets and go another round. Jasper figured he had until one thirty in the morning before he reverted back to cat status. He should milk that remaining time for all it was worth. He should also read his mail, but he'd put that off until the last ten minutes or so.

The thing was, during sex with Anica, he'd forgotten about the time. Now he couldn't seem to think about anything else, and his good mood dribbled away like the sand in an hourglass. This whole deal was so unfair.

Why couldn't he enjoy this time in bed with Anica until morning, then get up, get dressed and go to his office? Why wasn't there a way to lift this blasted curse? As he swigged his beer his mind kept at the topic, worrying it the way Orion toyed with his felt mouse.

He'd seen Disney movies as a kid and watched his share of movies about magic as an adult. For every spell there was always a counterspell. For every poisoned apple there was true love's kiss. For every riddle there was an answer that would free the person trapped in the riddle's spell.

There had to be one in this case, too. He looked at Anica, who was happily munching on chips. She was the magic expert in this room. Besides that, she'd consulted with a witch and wizard who were supposed to be like tribal elders or something.

He couldn't shake the feeling that she was holding out on him. "Anica, I'm going to ask you straight out. Do you know what would lift this cat spell?"

She paused, a chip halfway to her mouth. Her deer-in-the-headlights expression gave her away.

"Shit, Anica!" He slammed his beer bottle onto the end table so hard it probably made a dent in the wood. He didn't care.

Leaping out of bed, he began to pace the floor beside it. "You're a real piece of work, you know that?" He pointed an accusing finger at her. "You're willing to screw my brains out, but you won't give me the most important information of my life. What's wrong with this picture?"

"But I—"

"Is it because you want to keep me tied to you? Are you afraid if I leave, I might come back at you for hexing me in the first place?" The ugly words spilled out and he couldn't stop them. "Or maybe you haven't had a good fuck in a while, and me showing up for a few hours every night is taking the edge off?"

Tears filled her eyes. "Stop. Please, stop."

The tears did it. He never had been able to deal with a woman's tears. He'd have been happier if she'd thrown the bowl of chips at his head, but of course she wouldn't do that. She might be getting more adventurous in bed, but he suspected at heart she was still very much a good girl.

And he'd obviously inflicted pain. He took a deep

breath. "Hey, I'm sorry to make you cry. But, Anica, if you know how to break this curse and you're not telling me, then—"

"I can't tell you!" Her words were edged with anger and frustration equal to his. "If you think for one minute that I enjoy keeping you captive, that all I'm looking for is a love slave, then please never touch me again, because I can't imagine what sort of horrible person you think I am."

He wasn't about to tell her that his hunger for her defied all logic. No matter what he thought about her character or her behavior with the hexing thing, he couldn't seem to stop wanting her. It was life's little joke at the moment.

He wanted to despise her for turning him into a cat, but in the first place, she was a tough person to despise. He liked her. And in the second place, how was he supposed to hold on to his rage when his cock wanted nothing more than to be eternally buried in her sweet pussy?

Instead of landing himself in that briar patch, he circled back to the first thing she'd said. "Why can't you tell me?"

She took a ragged breath and swiped at her eyes. "If I tell you, then the counterspell won't work."

"What kind of crazy deal is that? How am I supposed to know what to do if nobody—" The light dawned. "I have to figure it out for myself?"

"Yes."

"Shitfire." He swiped a hand over his face. "Can you give me a hint?"

She shook her head.

"How about if you write it on a piece of paper, I read it and then we burn it? Nobody will know, right?"

"It doesn't matter if nobody knows. It's the nature of the spell that if you're told how to break it, you never will be able to."

His blood ran cold. What kind of hell would that be? They'd both be doomed. They'd be tied to each other, neither of them able to live a normal life because he'd be a man for only a few hours every night, which would be just long enough to keep her from having a relationship with someone else.

Then another horrific thought came to him. "Suppose you accidentally tell me?"

"I wouldn't do that."

"What do you mean, you wouldn't? Let's say I keep showing up every night and we keep having sex."

"After the way you've spoken to me, that won't be happening again."

Now, there was a sucker punch to the gut. The thought of being denied was pretty much unbearable. "Anica, I lost my temper. I shouldn't have accused you of using me for your own selfish purposes. You're not that kind of person. I know that. I'm sorry."

She didn't respond, just kept gazing at him as if he was something she'd scraped off the bottom of her shoe.

He could barely believe that this was the same woman who had lovingly given him the most spectacular blow job of his life an hour and a half ago. Just thinking about that made his penis stir.

Running his fingers through his hair, he wondered how to regain some of the ground he'd lost. Somehow, even though he was the wronged party, he'd now become the villain of the piece.

To his surprise he didn't like seeing her miserable, either. At one time, very recently, in fact, he'd imagined it would be quite satisfying to see her miserable. He'd pictured finding some way to ruin her business so that she'd lose all the money she'd invested. The punishment had seemed justified, considering what she'd done to him.

Yet now . . . maybe she was as much a victim of the situation as he was. She'd bravely tried to make the best of it by giving him some of the greatest sex of his life.

Then he'd accused her of doing it because she was desperate for a decent lay. Not nice.

He sat down on the bed. "Let's start over."

"Where did you want to start over? At the point where we were having a lovely mutual orgasm, or at the point where you accused me of being a manipulative, scheming, not to mention horny and pathetic bitch?"

He gazed into her eyes. "I was a bastard to say those things to you."

"Yes, you certainly were."

"You've given generously of your body, and I should fall on my knees in gratitude. I should beg you to forgive me for being such an insensitive creep."

The corner of her mouth twitched as if she might be holding back a smile. "That would be entirely appropriate."

He took heart from that little twitch. "So I will." Sliding off the bed, he dropped to his knees beside it and gazed up at her. "Anica, please forgive me for acting like a total idiot. I've loved every millisecond we've had sex, and after what I said to you, I completely understand if you kick me out of your bed. I hope you don't, but you'd be absolutely justified in cutting me off."

"Oh?" Her blue eyes sparkled with mischief. "Do you mean that literally?"

He scrambled to his feet and put both hands over his crotch. "I'm sorry, but not that sorry! Who are you, Lorena Bobbitt?"

Finally her laughter broke through. "All right, you're forgiven."

"Thank God." He climbed back in bed with her, took away the bowl of chips and set it on the table next to his beer.

"I was eating those."

"I know, but I was afraid you'd choke." He eased her back onto the stack of pillows.

"Why would I do that?"

"Because it's really dangerous to eat chips while I'm screwing your brains out."

He did exactly that. Anica didn't have a single brain cell working by the time he finished with her. That explained why she forgot to remind him to get out of bed and go read his mail.

He was the one who remembered it. They lay facing each other again, gazing into each other's eyes. He leaned over and kissed her softly. "You have my permission to open my mail."

"Sheesh, your mail! Let me go get it!"

"There isn't time."

She realized that he could see the clock on the bedside table behind her and she couldn't. If there wasn't time for him to read his mail, then it must be almost one thirty. Her heart squeezed.

"If anything's urgent, like a bill, just get out my credit card and pay it that way."

"All right." She was determined not to fall apart on him. After all, he'd still be here. He'd just be ... a cat. She cupped his face in both hands. "Your beard's growing."

"Yeah. If I keep extending my time, eventually I'll have to shave." A shadow crossed his face. "If I keep extending my time."

"Maybe ..." She stopped herself just before she said *Maybe giving me a wonderful orgasm is an act of kindness.* Hera's hickeys! She'd almost blurted it out in bed, exactly as he'd been afraid she would!

"Maybe what?"

"Nothing."

His eyes narrowed. "You almost said it, didn't you?"

She couldn't lie to him, not after what they'd been through. "Yes, yes I almost did!" She sat up and put her face in her hands. "Dear Zeus, you were right. I was all relaxed and happy and I almost said something, and if I had ..." She pressed the heels of her hands against her eyes to hold back tears of frustration and despair. "We shouldn't have sex anymore. I shouldn't spend *any* time with you at all!"

"I couldn't stand that." He sat up and started rubbing her back. "You're the person who keeps me going."

"I'm the person who put you in this state!"

"Well, there's that." He kept rubbing her back. "Don't blame yourself for almost messing up. The point is you didn't mess up. I have to figure out the secret."

"By yourself."

"Right. But you have a ton of magic books out there in the living room. Assuming I change back tomorrow night, then that's what I should be doing—studying those."

She had to admit it was a good idea, although she knew the answer wouldn't be in there. Still, he might get some ideas that would help him discover what he had to do. "All right. I'll make you coffee and . . . do you like brownies?"

"Love 'em."

"Then I'll bring home fresh brownies from work."

He put his arm around her and nuzzled behind her ear. "Just so you know, brownies and coffee won't even begin to substitute for sex with you. But a guy has to do what a guy has to do."

"I know." She lifted her head and turned to gaze at him. "You're smart. You'll get it."

"I absolutely will get it. If I think I know and I ask you, can you confirm it?"

"Yes."

He let out a breath. "Good. That's good."

"But I don't think we can play twenty questions. You shouldn't ask until you're virtually sure. I don't know how many questions you get."

"Can you find out?"

"I'll find out."

"Okay, then." He glanced over her shoulder. "Stay here. I'm going to go look for something in the kitchen."

She didn't believe that for a minute. He'd seen the time and he didn't want to change in front of her. "It's okay, Jasper," she said softly. "You don't have to leave."

"Yeah, I do." He smiled as he climbed out of bed. "It can't be an appealing sight, and I want you to remember me as I am now. Underneath all this humility I'm kind of vain."

She felt honor-bound to play along with him and keep the mood light. "Humility? You're about as humble as The Donald."

"One of my heroes, except I'm better-looking. Feel free to check out my ass when I leave the room."

She watched him go, but she had trouble seeing his most excellent ass through a blur of tears. They rolled unchecked down her cheeks as she continued to stare at the door into the hallway.

As she waited she tried to comfort herself with alternate scenarios. Maybe it wouldn't happen at one thirty, after all. Maybe the spell didn't work the way they both thought it did, and he'd stay this way until morning. Maybe he'd walk back in the room with a glass of milk, a day-old doughnut from Wicked Brew, and a jaunty smile on his face.

When a sleek back cat appeared in the bedroom doorway, she broke down completely. "Oh, Jasper," she sobbed. "I don't know if I can stand this."

The cat walked quietly over to the bed and leaped up on the mattress. Making his way over to her, he crawled into her lap, put his paws on her shoulders, and began licking the tears away.

Anica was in a terrible mood the next morning, and Jasper hated that. She'd always been such an upbeat person. He especially hated the sad way she looked at him.

So before she left for work he goofed around with Orion for a while, just to see if he could make her laugh.

He'd hide behind the curtains or around a corner or behind the sofa. Then he'd leap out at Orion when he strolled by. Orion's reaction was priceless. He'd squeak and jump straight into the air like a cartoon cat. Either Orion liked being startled or he wasn't very smart, because he fell for the joke every time.

It took about three times before Anica laughed, but she finally did, and Jasper was proud of himself.

"You're crazy, Jasper," she said, and leaned down to scratch behind his ears. "Thanks."

He purred, like he always did, but this time he didn't resent showing that kind of contentment. He had a feeling that when he purred, she liked it, as if she wanted reassurance that he wasn't completely miserable even though he was still a cat.

She went off to work looking a little happier than she had when she'd first gotten out of bed. Now that she was gone, Jasper could concentrate on this spell that he had to figure out all by himself.

He considered pulling the books off the shelf and trying to read those, but he'd have a much easier time of it as a man than as a cat. Cruising the Internet wasn't quite as difficult as reading a heavy book, so he decided to research online.

Besides researching, he planned to spend part of the day thinking about why his time had been extended already. Anica had assured him it wasn't the foul potion he'd had to drink. So if the potion hadn't taken him from ten minutes the first night to an hour the second night and three hours the third night, what had?

He was obviously doing something that caused his time as a man to lengthen. But he had no freaking idea what that something was. What the hell was the X factor here?

Calling up the sites where Anica and Lily had found the god-awful potion he'd forced down, he started reading about magic spells and how they could be reversed. A lot of the reversals involved the phases of the moon. Maybe the moon had something to do with it.

He checked what phase they were in now, which turned out to be a waning moon that was at the one-quarter mark. Nothing about that seemed significant. Anica hadn't put the spell on him during a full moon, so nothing pertaining to full-moon spells applied. Finally he decided that he was headed down a blind alley with moon phases.

Besides, the moon was an external thing he couldn't control. From what Anica had said, the cure would be entirely within his control if he could only pick the right suspect out of the magical lineup. Damn. He hated needle-in-a-haystack situations.

Anica's landline rang in the kitchen. She didn't use that phone much, he'd noticed, preferring her cell phone, which she carried with her. But she had an answering machine hooked up to the landline, and it clicked on.

He listened to her cheery little message and felt sad all over again. That was the woman he'd been attracted to, that optimistic person who'd built a business from scratch and seemed to know what she wanted from life. Until she'd found out about Sheila, she'd wanted him.

She wanted him again, at least in her bed, and he thought she might not be so focused on the Sheila issue anymore. Living with her, being able to see the world through her eyes, he realized she'd been right to hate that about his approach. He'd lied to her to get her interest.

His real shame was that she wasn't the only one. He'd done the same thing . . . a few times. He cringed to think how many.

Anica's caller left a message, and he recognized Ju-

lie's voice on the phone. "Hey, Anica, I didn't want to
bother you at work, but I have to tell you these kittens
are soooo adorable. I know having Jasper get loose was
scary, but if he hadn't done that, I wouldn't have Persephone and her babies!"

From his short association with Julie, Jasper wasn't
surprised that she'd choose a name like that. He vaguely
remembered the name from one of his classes in
school.

"I'm gonna name the kittens, too," Julie continued,
"but I want to let their personalities develop first. Anyway, just wanted you to know this has totally changed
my life for the better!"

Jasper let that joy sink in for a while. Cool. Something
good had come out of this disaster. He thought about the
animal rescue site, the one he'd given so much money to.
He didn't intend to give any more money, but he might
just go over there and click the button a few times so the
pet food company had to give some more.

Once he was there and had cost the pet food company a few hundred bucks, he had the strangest urge.
Giving that money yesterday had been horrifying ... at
first. Now, not so much. He wouldn't get carried away
like last time, but his info was already in the system. He
gave them another two hundred, being careful about the
zeroes. Nice feeling. If he weren't a cat, he'd be smiling
right now.

In an increasingly good mood, he continued with his
research. As he was clicking back to the Google page
listing sites about magic, he noticed a business card lying
on the desk. He thought it might have been there before,
but maybe the name registered this time because he'd
been thinking about Sheila.

The card had her e-mail address on it. He probably
would have remembered it regardless. In fact, he had a
good memory for e-mail addresses. If he concentrated

he could probably come up with an e-mail contact for the women he'd dated—and misled.

Slowly a plan developed, one that had nothing to do with reversing the spell, but everything to do with his peace of mind. Tonight, besides reading Anica's magic books, he'd write some e-mails.

Chapter 18

Lily came by the coffee shop around two, and Anica was thrilled to see her. Nobody besides Lily knew the hell Anica was going through—well, some heaven mixed in with the hell—and she was relieved to talk to someone who would understand.

Lily breezed in wearing her do-me boots, her red trench coat and a slinky black dress under it. She glanced around the coffee shop as she walked over to the counter to get in line. Anica was manning the counter because she'd given her two employees, who happened to be dating each other, a half-hour break. They'd missed getting those breaks during the days she hadn't been spending much time at the shop.

"The place looks a little ragged around the edges," Lily said when her turn came to order.

Anica sighed. "I know. I never realized how much I depended on my powers to keep the place tidy. What can I get for you? The usual?"

"You bet. I love those triple shots and they love me back."

Anica felt energy pouring into her just by being around Lily. Maybe it was because Lily still had her magic, but Anica thought it was mostly because Lily was so full of life. "Want a brownie? It's on the house."

"Sure, but can you come and sit with me? I don't see Frick and Frack around anywhere."

Anica laughed. "They're in the break room." She lowered her voice. "Probably making out. But they're due back on duty in five minutes. Take a seat. I should be freed up soon."

"Good. Interrupt them if you have to. I don't much care about their sex life, but I'm dying to know how yours is coming along."

The customer behind Lily, a middle-aged secretary who arrived every afternoon about this time, widened her eyes.

Anica ducked her head to hide her blush. "Gee, Lily, could you say that a little louder, please?"

"I could, but I'd hate to embarrass you in front of your customers."

Anica looked up and gave her sister a big fake smile. "Sure you would."

"I'll just go sit down right over there." Lily cocked a hip and pointed dramatically to a table by the front window. "And wait breathlessly for a description of your latest orga—"

"Yes, I'll have that triple shot right up for you, Ms. Revere. Thanks for coming in." She turned immediately to the secretary. "Ellen! The usual? Decaf latte with skim?"

Ellen glanced over at Lily sashaying to a table. Then she turned back to Anica, her eyes sparkling behind her cat's-eye glasses. "Actually, I think I'll change my order, shake things up a bit."

"Really? What can I get you?"

"A triple shot. Just like the one you're making for her."

"Absolutely." Anica grabbed the smallest paper coffee cup, which was what Ellen usually ordered.

"The next-biggest size, please."

"You bet." She put down the first cup and picked up the medium.

"No, wait. I'll take the largest one."

"Coming up." Anica wasn't surprised. Lily had this effect on people. She gave off attitude in a way that made others want to imitate her. Anica used to envy that about Lily, until she realized that underneath all that bravado her sister was confused and had no idea what she wanted out of life.

Lily returned to the counter using her runway model walk just as Ellen was paying for her coffee. "Can I have the brownie now?" Lily asked. "I need something to nibble on while I wait."

"Sure. Just let me finish this and I'll get it for you." Anica took Ellen's five-dollar bill and opened the cash register.

"No problemo. I'll wait right here." Lily twirled the end of the red belt hanging from her trench coat.

Ellen took her change from Anica and dropped some coins in the tip jar. Then she leaned forward. "Glad to hear you have a boyfriend, dear. I hope he's a sweetheart, like you."

"He's great," Lily piped up, uninvited. "In fact, he's a real pussycat, isn't he, Anica?"

Anica took a brownie out of the case and congratulated herself on handing it to her sister instead of throwing it at her. "You could say that." As she turned to make the two drinks, she wondered why she'd been so happy to see Lily, who was such a total pain in the ass. How could she make fun of such a serious thing?

But by the time Anica's besotted employees returned and she was free to join Lily, she realized what Lily had been doing when she'd deliberately joked about the situation with Jasper. She was daring Anica to maintain a sense of humor in the face of potential disaster. Anica needed to be reminded of that. A sense of humor would most likely save her sanity.

"Did he change again?" Lily asked the minute Anica sat down.

"Yes. For three hours this time."

"Ooh la la!"

Anica felt herself blush for the second time in ten minutes. How irritating. So what if they'd spent three hours in bed and she started to burn all over again when she thought about what she'd done to awaken her inner bad girl? Lily wouldn't let herself blush over a little thing like that.

"That good, huh?"

"Yeah."

Lily seemed to have forgotten all about her espresso as she leaned forward. "So what else?"

"We had a fight."

"My, you two were busy little bunnies, weren't you? Does he know that breaking the curse is up to him?"

"He does now."

Lily nodded and picked up her espresso. "Given three hours to work with, I would hope you'd get that settled and not spend the whole time boinking. But I'm proud of you for grabbing the opportunity when it was offered, sis." She lifted her cup in a toast.

"Thanks. Oh, and I called Dorcas to check out a technicality. She'd said I could confirm the cure if Jasper guessed it, but I didn't know if he had a limited number of tries."

"I'm thinking yes." Lily took a sip of her coffee.

"Three tries. I already told him we couldn't play twenty questions, but now I can clarify that."

"Dear Zeus, yes. At this point, you don't want something going wrong on a technicality."

"Sure don't." Anica sighed and did a modified neck roll to loosen up the tight muscles of her neck.

"Poor baby." Lily reached over and patted her arm.

"I'm just trying to figure out what the heck he did that took him from one hour to three hours."

"Hm." Lily drank more coffee. "It must have been a big-ass act of kindness to get him that much time. He saved the mother cat and kittens and only got fifty minutes more."

"He's been giving Orion some of his dinner."

"Yeah, that's worth about three minutes each. It has to be something bigger." Lily gazed at her. "Was he doing acts of kindness in bed that first time?"

Anica wasn't sure she could discuss oral sex in the confines of Wicked Brew, with customers and her two employees milling about. "I . . . uh, I'm not really comfortable talking about—"

"I'm just sayin' that if he got another two hours while he was doing you, I'm going to be consumed with jealousy."

Anica shook her head. "He was good, but compared to saving the mother cat and her kittens . . . not another two hours' worth of good."

"I still think I'm jealous, considering that I'm currently alone with only a vibrator to keep me company."

"TMI, Lily."

"Oh, I keep forgetting that you're the prudish sister. Pretend I never mentioned the vibrator. We were discussing Jasper, who obviously is better than any old vibrator. So how does he do it?"

"Lily."

"I mean *acts of kindness,* Anica. How does he do acts of kindness when he's so limited by his circumstances?"

"I don't know."

Lily tapped the side of her cup with a manicured finger. "Let's look at the facts. This is like one of those locked-room mysteries. He was in the apartment all day, by himself except for Orion, correct?"

"Correct. And Orion sleeps all day. I don't see how Jasper could accomplish any acts of kindness for a sleeping cat."

"And no visitors, right?"

"No visitors," Anica said. "Nobody has a key except

you, and thank you, by the way, for putting that protection spell in place yesterday morning. I was so upset when I came home after seeing Dorcas and Ambrose that I didn't notice at first."

"No problem. It was perfect timing. I was in the magic mood after jerking Jasper's chain a little."

"What?"

Lily waved a hand. "No biggie. I just worked a little spell to convince him that if he messed with you, he'd have to deal with me."

"What in the world did you—" Then she stopped herself. "You know what? I don't even want to know. But thank you for sticking up for me." Lily's sisterly concern settled like a warm blanket around Anica's tense shoulders.

"Sure. No problem. But this mystery of Jasper getting extra time somehow is going to drive me crazy if I don't figure it out." Lily stared out the window at people hurrying along the windy sidewalk. "The computer," she said at last, glancing back at Anica. "It's his only way of reaching the outside world. Could he accomplish acts of kindness on the computer?"

"Maybe. It wouldn't be easy, but it's the only thing that makes sense. I just hope he's able to figure out that whatever he did, whether it was on the computer or not, is what he needs to keep doing to gain more time."

"He's a smart man. I'm betting he'll come up with the answer." Lily popped the last of the brownie into her mouth.

"So what's up with you?"

"Nothing compared to your life, sis." Lily rolled her cup between her palms. "There's this guy . . ."

"The customer at the Bubbling Cauldron."

"Yeah. His name's Griffin. Griffin Taylor. He's a divorce lawyer."

"Mm." Anica wasn't going to say it, but she had a

hard time imagining a serious professional guy being interested in Lily. Lily tended to attract the professional gamblers, the musicians, the nightclub owners. People like her, in other words. "So what do you like about this Griffin guy?"

"He's hot."

Anica laughed. "I'm sure. You wouldn't look twice at him otherwise."

"But he's hot in a cool way. Not obvious, you know? Low-key. I like the way he jokes around with the other lawyers who come in for happy hour. He has a nice smile, a great laugh."

Anica could read the signs. Lily was crushing on this divorce lawyer with the great smile. "Have you had any conversations with him?"

Lily gazed into her coffee. "Not so much. I've tried to catch his eye, get him interested, but he just . . . isn't. He's polite and everything, but there's no flirting on his part. Only on mine."

"That must be rough, particularly if you're really attracted to him." Anica was thinking it would be especially rough on Lily, who usually got any guy she went after.

Lily shrugged. "I'll get over it." Then she looked up and gave Anica a high-wattage smile. "When do you want another dance lesson?"

Anica thought of her complicated life. "Well, I'm not sure if I—"

"Yeah, I know. It's a busy time, a strange time. That's okay. Never mind."

Anica picked up on the disappointment Lily quickly tried to hide. For the first time Anica wondered if Lily might need her more than she'd let on. She might be lonely. "The shop's closed on Saturday. How about Saturday afternoon?"

"You're sure?" Lily looked cautiously hopeful.

"Yep, I'm sure."

"This deal with Jasper could bust wide open, and then you might not want to."

"If that happens we'll talk about it," Anica said. "But for now let's plan on Saturday afternoon."

"Cool. I've been practicing some more moves I want to show you. We'll have margaritas again."

"What's a dance lesson without margaritas?"

"Way too boring. Well, sis, I gotta go." Lily stood. "Keep me informed of any developments."

"I will." Anica stood, too. Then Anica did something that she hadn't done in a while. She hugged Lily good-bye.

"Oh, I see we're getting all touchy-feely, now," Lily said. But she hugged Anica back really tight, and when she left, she was smiling.

Jasper could tell Anica was in a better mood when she came home from work. He was in a pretty good mood, too. He was working on a theory about the spell, and if it panned out . . . but he wasn't going to get his hopes up too high.

He'd typed a message to Anica on the computer, so he sat—sort of patiently—on the desk chair while she took off her coat and hung it in the closet. He waited—not quite as patiently—for her to greet Orion. But he refused to be jealous that she'd petted Orion first.

After all, Orion was only a cat. And Orion would be here long after Jasper was gone. She should love him up before she moved on to Jasper.

Yet when she stood next to the desk chair and stroked his head, when she rubbed that spot on his chin that made him feel so great, he purred louder than ever before. He admitted it—he was glad to see her.

She put a paper bag next to the computer. "I see you have another message for me, Jasper." She leaned down and looked at what he'd typed while she continued to rub her finger along his chin.

WELCM HOM. HW MNY GESSES?

She answered without hesitation. "Three. I called Dorcas and that's what she said."

Three sounded about right to him, especially with what he'd been reading about magic on various Internet sites. That meant he needed to test his theory before he used up one guess. He'd spend some time with her magic books, too, and look for corroboration of what he thought might be the key to his escape.

He hadn't found any clues until he'd gone back to old fairy tales about magic. There he'd found a common theme. If someone had been hexed, they could sometimes earn their way out of it by doing good works.

Jasper started putting together his recent activities— coming to Anica's rescue when she'd faced the fairies, saving the mother cat and kittens, accidentally giving away two grand to animal rescue. Those things might have been what had awarded him extra time on the clock.

It was only a theory at this point, though, and he needed to test it through his actions tonight. If he extended his time significantly the following night, he'd ask Anica if he was on the right track.

He'd definitely decided to write e-mails of apology to his exes tonight, although he was still debating exactly what to say. His original intent had been to clear his conscience, but those e-mails might help his cause. Maybe he'd give more money to animal rescue while he was on the computer, too.

Besides those two things his theory had another angle, one that made it his absolutely favorite theory of all. Maybe he'd unknowingly earned minutes giving Anica great orgasms. If he concentrated on her pleasure in bed, that ought to count, right? It certainly would in his world, so he'd go with it. Tonight would be all about good works.

While Anica cooked dinner he paced the apartment,

impatient for the twinges that would signal he was changing. He thought about the animal rescue site. Leaping up on the desk chair, he called it up and gave another five hundred bucks. If he knew for a fact that worked, he'd be willing to empty his bank account.

But he didn't know, so he'd keep it reasonable until he was sure. The clock ticked with maddening slowness.

Chapter 19

For the first time in years, Anica wished she had a television and cable. Once she'd cleaned up the kitchen after dinner she couldn't settle down to anything. Jasper's impending change hovered in the air, keeping her from enjoying the book she'd started a few days ago. Flipping through channels with a remote would have been the perfect distraction.

She tried putting on some calming music, but turned it off almost immediately because the insipid sound made her want to scream. Pulling out her favorite deck of tarot cards, she shuffled them and started to do a reading. Then she realized she didn't want to know what the future held. Too scary.

Jasper's pacing didn't help matters. She knew he was antsy, too, but she wanted him to just *settle* for Hera's sake. She wasn't settling, either, but at least she hadn't started to pace. When she caught herself walking back and forth in the living room, she knew something had to be done.

"I'm going up to see Julie and the kittens," she said, knowing Julie would be there because Julie was always there, and now she'd be even *more* there because she had caretaking duties. "I'll take my cell phone. In case you've forgotten the number, here it is." She wrote it on a slip of paper and put it on the coffee table. "You can use the landline to call me . . . if you . . . well, just call."

Anybody watching her say that to a black cat would think she was insane, but that cat would—she hoped—turn into a man sometime this evening. In the meantime she and the cat were driving each other bonkers, and she was the only one who could leave. She could be projecting, but she swore Jasper looked relieved as she went out the door.

Fleeing the apartment seemed right, but maybe she should have called Julie first. Thanks to the wonders of cell phones and having Julie's number stored, she could. She sat on the stairs and made the call.

"Hi, Anica!" Julie sounded like a whole different person. "Did you get my message?"

"I did, and I was wondering if I could come up and see how Persephone and her babies are doing."

"Absolutely. I'd love to show them off." Julie sounded like the proud mother of a newborn.

Smiling, Anica climbed the stairs to Julie's apartment. She'd been in it only once, and she remembered it being a dark and spooky place with dark paint on the walls and college-kid furniture—a futon that had seen better days, brick-and-board bookshelves, one rickety floor lamp and a scratched metal desk. Julie's computer, flat-screen TV and sound system, though, had been state-of-the-art.

Julie answered her knock immediately, and she was wearing a pair of old plastic-rimmed glasses and no makeup.

"I didn't know you wore glasses," Anica said.

"Mostly I wear contacts, but I just couldn't be bothered with them today. Too busy. Come on in!" She ushered Anica into a room that was much better lit than Anica remembered.

It took her a while to figure out that the living room had been turned into a stage set, with movie lights ringing the perimeter. Julie's video camera, which had always been trained on the street, was now pointed at the center of the room where Persephone and her babies lay like royalty in a nest of pillows covered with a blanket. Persephone's food dishes sat within easy walking distance, and so did her litter box, which looked like it had started life as a turkey roaster.

"I borrowed the lights from my brother, Pete." Julie pointed to a large carpeted scratching post with multiple perches. "He brought this over in his truck, too. It's a present for Persephone and the kittens."

"So he's not upset that you have cats?"

Julie laughed. "He's totally fine with it. He had no idea I didn't have cats because of him. He thought I just didn't want the bother. When he comes over, he'll dose up on some OTC meds and not worry about it."

"Perfect." Anica thought she might be imagining things, but Persephone already looked as if she'd put on weight. Her gray coat looked glossier, and her white paws were no longer covered with dirt.

The two kittens nursed greedily, kneading Persephone's tummy with their tiny paws. One was gray, but with only three white feet instead of four, like Persephone. The other one was a black-and-white tux.

"You can go over and pet her if you want," Julie said. "She won't care. Once she got used to being here, she's been very loving."

"But she doesn't know me." Anica crouched down to cat level as she looked into Persephone's eyes. "Do you, sweetheart?"

Persephone meowed softly.

"I think she recognizes a kindred spirit," Julie said.

Anica stood and moved slowly and carefully until she could kneel next to the bed of pillows. "What a good mommy," she crooned, reaching out to gently rub behind Persephone's ears.

The cat leaned into the caress.

"She belonged to someone," Anica said.

"I think so, too. She's not wild at all. Should I . . . put a notice in the paper or something?"

Anica glanced up and saw the yearning in Julie's expression. She'd only had Persephone and her babies a short time, but she'd already bonded.

"I see no reason to do that," Anica said. "She was so skinny when we found her that she's been on her own a long time. It's a good guess she was abandoned on purpose."

"That's what I think, too." Julie hesitated. "Do you like her name?"

"It's a great name. Persephone's the one who got taken to the underworld by Hades."

"I know. I've studied all that. And I wanted her to have a magical name."

"You did, huh?" Now, there was a brilliant response. "I mean, that's interesting." Even more brilliant.

"Anica, I have something to show you."

Anica wasn't as intuitive as she would have liked, but she had a strong feeling this wouldn't be something she wanted to see. "You know, maybe next time. I should probably be getting back."

"It'll only take a minute." Julie flicked the power switch on her DVD player and the flat-screen TV. Then she pulled a DVD out of a cabinet under the screen and loaded it into the system.

If only this DVD could be another one of Pete's lame cable shows, Anica would be grateful. She didn't think that was it, though.

Julie hit PLAY, and Anica recognized the street in front of their apartment building. Down the street a ways, near the little park, a man and woman faced each other, obviously having an argument. Even before the camera zoomed in on the couple, Anica recognized who it was. She'd known all along, from the moment Julie had suggested showing her something.

Anica watched, holding her breath, as the most fateful moment of her life played out on the screen. The woman pulled a small wand from her purse and pointed at the tall, good-looking man. A moment later, the man pulled the woman into his arms, she shoved him away and the man became a pile of clothes.

Someone whimpered in the room, and then Anica realized it had been her. She covered her mouth and stood as she tried to imagine what she could say to this girl who had captured her worst moment on camera.

"I didn't mean to upset you," Julie said. "I wanted you to know that I know. And I want to help!"

"If only you could." Anica gazed at her.

"I have a great-aunt who is a witch," Julie said. "Once my parents found out, they would never let me visit her. But now that I'm on my own . . . sort of . . . I keep in touch with her by e-mail. She lives in California, and I'm not big on traveling by myself so I haven't gone out there, but I've been studying and . . . I think I . . . that is . . . I might be a witch, too. But I can't let my parents know or they'd stop sending money."

"They support you?"

"Yeah, both me and Pete. It's no big deal. They have a ton of money, and I still don't know what I want to do with my life. Well, I do. I want to practice magic."

"But I doubt you'll be able to support yourself on it."

"I know. I was thinking since you're a witch, too, you could help me figure out what's the best job for people like us."

"Well, I—" Her cell phone kept her from having to come up with a response. "Excuse me a minute." Her heart hammered as she flipped open the phone. "Hello?"

"I'm about to make coffee," Jasper said. "Do you trust me with this machine?"

He could have been her live-in boyfriend calling with a simple comment. Except nothing about Jasper was simple. "No." Her voice wasn't quite steady. "I'll be right there." Flipping the phone closed, she glanced at Julie. "I have to go."

"Were you talking to him?" Eagerness shone in Julie's dark eyes. "Does he change back for a while?"

"I have to go." Anica turned and headed toward the door. But she couldn't leave without offering Julie something. "I'll call you tomorrow," she said. "We'll talk."

"I'm serious. I want to help."

Anica glanced at her. "If you can, I'll let you know." Then she went out the door and hurried down the steps. She glanced at her watch. Nine forty. If Jasper was ready to make coffee, he probably transformed at nine thirty. Through good deeds of some sort he'd gained another two hours.

Jasper was wearing clothes for the first time since Tuesday night. He'd expected to be happy about that return to seminormal living, but instead the clothes felt restrictive. He left them on, though, because he had e-mails to write and donations to make.

First he rummaged through the refrigerator and found the other half of the chicken breast Anica had cooked for his dinner. She'd probably saved the rest for tomorrow, but he gave it to Orion.

"Eat fast, buddy. The diet police will be here any minute." He hadn't really needed to say that. Orion always ate like a teenage boy at an all-you-can-eat buffet.

The key turned in the front door lock. Jasper walked out of the kitchen as Anica came through the door, clutching her cell phone in her hand.

She looked rattled. "You're dressed."

"I thought I could risk it." He wondered if she was disappointed not to find him naked and ready for sex.

He wasn't naked, but the moment she'd come through the door he'd felt a familiar ache in his groin. After all, that was the primary activity they'd engaged in while they'd been together in the apartment. She hadn't been around when he'd transformed this time, and he hadn't immediately started thinking about sex. But he was thinking about it now.

He liked that red sweater and skirt on her. He'd like it a whole lot better off her, though. The sweater buttoned up the front, so that wouldn't be much of a challenge. She'd worn knee-high boots today, so maybe that meant that under her skirt she didn't have on a pair of those god-awful pantyhose that were worse than a chastity belt.

Anica locked the dead bolt and turned back to him. "Julie has a video of me changing you into a cat. I just saw it."

A sense of being personally violated wiped out his fantasies of pulling off Anica's sweater and skirt. He didn't want anybody to see that transformation, ever. "How the hell did that happen?"

"Julie's hobby is pointing a camcorder at the street outside the building and seeing what she gets."

"Isn't that illegal? I'm impressed that she took in the mother cat and kittens, but that doesn't give her the right to invade people's privacy."

"She's a kid, and she thinks it's an art form. She always scrambles the image so nobody can tell who it is before she puts it on her brother's cable show."

"*Cable* show?" Jasper felt steam coming out of his ears. "She has a video of me turning into a cat, and she's planning to broadcast it?"

"No, I'm sure she's not." Anica walked over to her antique desk and tucked her cell phone into the ceramic dragon holder. "She's been waiting for a chance to broach the whole subject of witches. By showing me the video, she eliminated any chance I'd deny I'm a witch."

Jasper found this extremely alarming. "So what now? Blackmail? People coming with burning torches?"

"I doubt it. I think she wants me to be her mentor."

"Good grief." Jasper had enough problems with the idea of witches in the city without imagining the concept spreading.

Anica approached him. "What are you afraid of, Jasper?"

"Oh, I don't know. Dating a witch who turned me into a *cat* shouldn't be a big deal, I suppose. A guy should take that kind of event in stride, shouldn't he?"

"You're talking as if such a thing could happen at any time with no consequences. Have you forgotten that once I did that, which is strictly forbidden under current code, I lost my magic?"

Sometimes he did forget that she'd been penalized for her behavior. He got so caught up in his own frustration that he forgot about hers.

"Witches and wizards are not a danger to society," Anica continued. "All our prayers end with the words *with harm to none*. I broke that vow when I changed you into a cat, so I'm no longer allowed to work magic." Her lower lip trembled. Not much, but enough to hint at tightly contained emotional distress.

He closed the distance between them and took her by the shoulders. "It wasn't all your fault."

"Mostly my fault."

"You held the wand, but I provoked you to use it. Nothing happens in a vacuum." He hadn't been willing to admit that until now, hadn't been willing to take responsibility for his present situation. But he'd arrogantly assumed that she wanted him even though he'd lied to her. Now that he'd lived with her and knew her better, he understood that he'd pushed her into reacting.

She took a shaky breath. "I appreciate your saying that," she said. "It helps."

"Good." He gazed into her blue eyes and then, out of habit, his attention moved down to her plump lips, which looked so kissable right now.

She could use a kiss, and he knew that as surely as

if he'd been reading her mind. But if he started kissing her, he would never accomplish anything he'd promised himself he would do with his time.

He'd tucked a condom in his pocket to replace the one he'd had there Tuesday night. No doubt the cleaners had thrown that one away. Just because he had a condom handy, though, didn't mean he had to use it now.

"I have some work to do on the computer." He massaged her shoulders and watched her eyelids droop. "But you must be tired. You haven't been getting much rest."

Her eyes opened, and her gaze was definitely not sleepy. "Adrenaline's kicked in."

"Oh." It would be so easy to say to hell with his program and take her to bed. But tempting as that was, he had a plan and he would stick with the plan. "Did you mention coffee?"

"I'll make some." She stepped smoothly away from him and walked into the kitchen. "How do you want it?" she called over her shoulder.

"Strong and hot."

"Don't flirt with me, Danes. Not unless you're planning to take your clothes off."

He was glad to hear the sass coming back into her voice. "I'll take my clothes off." He'd turned on the computer the minute he'd transformed, so now he was able to walk over and pull up the animal rescue site. "But not yet. The way I have it figured, we have until two thirty in the morning. We should pace ourselves."

"Speak for yourself, wimp." She bustled around in the kitchen, talking trash as she put the coffee on. "If you have no stamina, just be a man and admit it."

He clicked the donation button and gave the organization another two thousand bucks. If he was right about good deeds being the answer, it was a cheap price.

Then he stood and walked into the kitchen. Plans were made to be broken. "You shouldn't taunt a man who's packing a condom in his pants pocket. Especially when you promise him counter sex and then welsh on the deal."

She gave him a saucy look guaranteed to get her laid. "Don't you have something to do on the computer?"

"I'll get to it." He swept the cat food bowl out of the way and lifted her up on the counter. "I have until two thirty in the morning." He fished the condom out of his pocket and handed it to her. "Open this."

Her breathing quickened. "What happened to pacing ourselves?"

"See how you like this pace." Cupping the back of her head with one hand, he began kissing the daylights out of her while he undid the buttons on her sweater with the other hand.

She kissed him back with a very gratifying moan and then anticipated his next move by unbuckling his belt.

He lifted his mouth a fraction. "Have you had counter sex before?"

"No. You're my first."

"Then you must be a natural at it. Just keep working on that project." He hoped she'd hurry. His cock was not happy trapped inside his pants.

Once he had her red sweater unbuttoned, he was overjoyed to discover her bra had a front clasp, almost as if she'd known he'd undress her tonight. *Good guess*, he thought as he flipped open the catch of the bra. The earlier he started showing up in the evenings, the less likely he'd find her running around in a nightgown or a towel.

This sort of clothing challenge worked for him, though. Thrusting aside her bra, he fondled her breasts and felt his dick jerk in response. She'd managed to unzip his pants but his knit boxers were holding up progress. Ah, but a man appreciated something more if he had to work a little harder to get it, and Jasper appreciated the hell out of massaging her warm skin and gently pinching her nipples until they were rock hard.

Then she coaxed his bad boy out of his briefs, rolled on the condom, and it was showtime. Hiking up her skirt he moved between her thighs, and her booted feet nudged his bare butt. Kinky. The feel of leather against his skin inspired him.

He'd never ripped up a woman's clothing until the night he'd torn her nightgown down the middle, but that had turned out well. Might as well reach up under her skirt and rip the crotch out of her panties.

He happened to be kissing her at the time, and whether on purpose or by accident, when he ripped her panties, she bit him. Breathing hard, he lifted his head and gazed into eyes burning with a blue flame. "Did you mean to do that?" he murmured, tasting a drop of blood on his lower lip.

"Did you mean to rip my panties?"

"Yes."

"Then I meant to bite you." Her voice was low and urgent, rich with barely restrained lust. "Bring it, Danes. Bring it right now."

"Oh yeah." Sliding her to the very edge of the counter, he lifted her hips slightly, found her sweet spot, and drove home. "Happy now?"

"Marginally." Wrapping her legs around his waist, she locked him in tight as she looked into his eyes. "I've missed you."

"Me or this?" Damn, where had that come from? Wasn't he the one who wanted to keep this strictly sexual? "Silly question." He began pumping slowly.

"It is a silly question." Her fingers dug into his shoulders.

He reached between her thighs and pressed his thumb against her clit as he continued to thrust. "Forget I asked."

"You keep that up and I'll forget my own name."

"So we'll go for mindless sex." He felt her clench her muscles. She was close.

"Sure." She began to pant. "Mindless sex it is."

He moved faster, watching her eyes. His vocal cords thickened as his climax neared. "Not enough mindless sex in this world."

"Right." Her breasts quivered with every jolt of his body against hers. "Good. Very . . . oh, please . . . Jasper . . ."

"That's it. Let go." He moved his thumb in a rapid circle, wanting her to come soon, because the longer he looked into her eyes, the more he craved release. With her. With Anica.

"Yes . . . ah . . . *yes!*" The spasms hit and her eyes darkened with pleasure, but she didn't close them, didn't look away.

What a gift, to witness the powerful emotions he stirred in her. In a rare moment of openness, she'd let him see all the way down to her soul. The rush of that was all it took to send him over the edge with a growl of animal satisfaction wrenched from deep in his gut. He didn't look away, either. He wanted her to see the effect this surging, desperately sought climax had on him. He wanted her to see inside his soul, too.

Mindless sex. Yeah, sure. He'd never been so mindful of another human being in his entire life.

Chapter 20

Anica knew what words usually followed the kind of emotion-packed sex they'd just had. She couldn't speak for Jasper, but she wasn't ready to say those words, in spite of how he was looking at her, in spite of how she was no doubt looking at him. Given the intensity of their situation, she didn't believe either of them could trust the urge to pledge undying love.

He needed her in order to survive, which had to be coloring everything he did. She needed him to recover her magic, something that became more urgent every day she was without it. Of course she'd feel she needed him. But once the crisis was over, what would bind them together?

The sex was great, no question. Yet even the sex had to be more intoxicating when they were involved in such high drama. When you knew that your lover would turn into a cat within the next four hours, you tended to make good use of your time. You tended to cherish every moment when he was human and capable of giving and having orgasms.

So she wouldn't say the words that would come so naturally to her now. And she'd fix it so he wasn't likely to blurt them out, either. First step, break eye contact.

She glanced down at the counter supporting her. "That was fun. This counter is sturdier than I thought."

"Um, yeah. Anica, I—"

She forced herself to smile as she deliberately lightened her tone. "Quite a multifunctional thing, this counter. I just hope you don't have flashbacks of this at mealtime."

"Ha. Very funny."

Her heart broke watching his radiant expression fade. But one of them had to watch out that they didn't head into an emotional ditch. This time she'd accepted that assignment. Someday he might look back on this moment and be grateful that she'd broken the mood before either of them said something they'd regret.

He eased away from her with a crooked smile. "That's the thing about cats. We live in the moment."

She gazed at him in shock, her eyes recording a smile that reached in without warning and captured her heart. His soft words finalized the takeover, and she was suddenly, irrevocably, his.

Dear Zeus, I do love him. The knowledge punched her in the chest and she gasped softly. She loved him, and she'd ruined the moment when she could have told him so.

Maybe they wouldn't make it once the problems were solved. So what? They could have shared words of love now, in the moment, and let the future take care of itself, which it always did, anyway.

How ironic that an impulse had landed her in this mess and an impulse might have made it all worthwhile, if only she'd had the courage to go with her first instinct. Now the chance was lost, possibly forever. She suspected that a man like Jasper didn't open up very often, and once discouraged from sharing his tender thoughts, he might never try again.

When he left for the bathroom, she scooted down from the counter, determined not to cry as she fastened her bra and buttoned her sweater. She stepped out of her torn panties and threw them in the trash.

All the while, Jasper's face haunted her. She could see the adoration in his golden eyes, the softness of his expression once his fierce climax had ebbed. He'd been a man in love, a man on the verge of declaring that love.

She, on the other hand, was a total idiot worried about making mistakes. That anal behavior had caused her to make a gigantic mistake, and now she would pay for it.

But she vowed that if she could be lucky enough to have a second chance to tell him how she felt, she'd grab it with both hands.

"Bathroom's free," he called from the living room. "I have some work to do on the computer."

"That's fine." She wondered if they'd be like this for the rest of the time he was in human form tonight— casual friends respecting each other's need for space. It was very catlike behavior on his part to back off and claim his own territory.

As she walked down the hall toward her bedroom, she thought again about what he'd said. *That's the thing about cats. We live in the moment.* He hadn't said *they live in the moment.* He'd said *we.*

It made sense that after a while he'd begin to identify with his cat persona. She found that intriguing, one more thing to add to the list of reasons why she was fascinated with Jasper Danes. Too bad she'd deliberately driven a wedge between them, but she couldn't repair that situation easily, if ever.

She spent way too much time trying to decide what to wear for the rest of the evening. Whatever she put on was either too dowdy or too obviously calculated to turn him on.

In some ways she envied him having only one out-fit. He didn't have to worry about what kind of signals he was sending. He had two settings—dressed and undressed. She had at least twenty possible variations, from Victoria's Secret to L.L. Bean and everything in between.

Finally she chose a purple knit lounge outfit that was soft enough to sleep in. Once that was decided, she had to deal with the underwear issue. To wear or not to wear, that was the question.

She settled on a definite *yes* for panties. If she spent much time walking around the apartment without any on, she'd work herself into a frenzy of lust. A woman couldn't be expected to go without panties when a sexy man was on the premises and not want to jump him. But she could skip the bra, couldn't she?

And yet the top half of her sweat suit was a zip-front jacket. Spending four hours knowing she was one zip away from flashing her tits at him would probably send her into hormonal overdrive in the same way a lack of panties would. She found a white tank top in her drawer and put that on under the jacket. Then she left the jacket unzipped, because after all, she didn't want to seem uptight.

By the time she left her bedroom she was doing a mental eye roll. Life wasn't supposed to be this complicated, and it wouldn't be if she hadn't stopped him from speaking what was in his heart. At this point they could have been relaxed and open with each other. Instead he'd probably stuffed his feelings down as far as they would go.

He sat at the computer with a cup of espresso on his right and the open bag of brownies on his left. Then she remembered what else she'd purchased on the way home and dropped into the brownie bag. The box of condoms rested on top of the terminal.

Now, that was funny. She couldn't help smiling as she watched him typing away with a box of condoms balanced front and center at the top of the screen. The box hadn't been carelessly tossed there. It had been placed there with precision. At least he hadn't given up the idea of having sex with her. That was something.

"I see you found my other contribution," she said.

"Uh-huh." He kept typing. "Didn't want to lose track of them, either."

"I see that."

He clicked the SEND button for his current e-mail, reached for the box and turned toward her. "I appreciate your buying these." His gaze traveled over her outfit. "Nice."

"Thanks." Oh yeah, she was hooked on him. One warm look, one word of praise and she was tingling with pleasure.

"These should probably go in that drawer where you keep them." He tossed her the condom box.

She caught it one-handed. "You don't want to leave them up there as a carrot?"

His golden gaze held hers. "You're the carrot."

"Oh." Heat sizzled in her veins. "Then I'll just go put these where we'll know to find them later."

"Or sooner. I'm about done here."

"Weren't you going to read through some of my magic books?"

He glanced over his shoulder. "I like to read in bed."

"All righty, then." Feeling positively juicy with anticipation, she hurried back to the bedroom, quickly opened the box and dumped the contents loose in the drawer. Might as well make the process simple.

She returned to the living room and walked over to the desk. "Checking on your work e-mails?"

"I probably should." He kept typing. "But I can't get excited about doing that."

"Really?" She didn't want to be nosy and read over his shoulder, so she picked up a brownie and walked back to the sofa. "I thought your job was very important to you." She took a bite of the brownie.

"I thought so, too." He clicked the SEND button again

and pushed back the chair. "All done. Do you need the computer for anything?"

"No. You can turn it off." She was still processing his comments about work. This was a guy who used to come into Wicked Brew charged up about the latest developments in the national and international economy. He'd have the *Wall Street Journal* tucked in his briefcase and check his BlackBerry for breaking market news while he was waiting for his coffee.

Standing, Jasper carried his coffee mug and the bag of brownies over to the coffee table. "I don't mean to be all mysterious about what I was doing on the computer." He set down the bag and mug and gazed at her.

"You don't have to tell me. I respect your right to privacy."

"You're the person I should tell. If it weren't for you, I wouldn't have sent those e-mails."

For one nauseating moment she wondered if he was capable of having sex with her one minute and trashing her business reputation the next. No, she was being paranoid. His feelings had changed and she didn't have to worry about that anymore. She hoped.

"Then maybe you should tell me." The love she felt for him was new and untested, and she didn't completely trust him not to destroy her.

"I e-mailed my last three girlfriends."

She hadn't expected that at all. *Three.* The way he said it made them all sound fairly recent, or at least recent enough that they'd have the same e-mail address. If Anica tried to contact her last three boyfriends, she'd be going back five years. Lily had called it—Jasper was a player.

Feeling a little out of her league, she gazed at him. "Why did you e-mail them?"

"To apologize for being a complete jerk. Just like you, they didn't deserve to be lied to. It was time I told them so. Sheila and I've only been broken up three weeks, but

Kate was a good six months ago, and Deb was—God—almost a year."

So he didn't have a history of long-term relationships. Good to know. But as for this recent move on his part, Anica couldn't help be nervous. "Do you . . . want to go back to any of them?" She held her breath.

"Hell, no! I left each of them because I realized we weren't as good together as I'd thought we'd be."

He might come to feel the same way about her, and she had to accept that. "Did you tell them that in this latest e-mail?"

"Why would I say that? I don't want them to feel bad all over again. This is supposed to be about healing old hurts."

"Or creating new ones." Anica sighed. "You don't want them to get their hopes up, Jasper. Um, did you notice that Sheila gave me her business card?"

"Yep. It was seeing her card that got me thinking about this idea." He sounded very proud of himself.

"Do you have any idea why Sheila gave it to me?"

"Not really." He shrugged. "She's a consultant for a window covering company. I thought maybe she was drumming up business."

Anica didn't like revealing another woman's vulnerabilities, but Jasper needed to understand the impact he'd had on his former girlfriends. "She was trying to drum up you."

"I don't get it."

"She still wants you, Jasper. She told me if I wasn't interested, to let her know so she might be able to catch you on the rebound."

"But I made it clear that I—"

"Doesn't matter." Looking at him standing there, confused, rumpled and so very sexy, she had no trouble imagining that women would forgive him anything if they could have one more round of sex, one more chance to convince him they were the perfect match.

"Sure it does. We said our good-byes and that was that."

"People change their minds all the time. Sheila hopes that you'll change yours, and she'd love to help that process along by coaxing you back to her bed."

Jasper groaned. "Maybe that happens with other guys, but not me. When I leave, I leave for *good*. No do-overs."

"I'll keep that in mind."

He met her gaze. "I haven't left you, Anica."

"No, but it's a good bet that you will once my magic comes back. Admit it, the magic freaks you out."

"It used to." He shoved his hands in the pockets of his slacks as if uncomfortable with the topic but determined to discuss it, anyway. "You said yourself that witches and wizards are pledged to do no harm."

"That's true. We are." If she'd gotten that much across, then she'd done the magical community a favor. Not many nonmagical people accepted that basic premise. They still thought of witches as evil.

"I've seen how that works. You broke the rule and you lost your magic."

"Yes."

"So like you said, I don't have anything to be afraid of from you other than the usual man-woman stuff like rejection, misunderstanding, power struggles, hogging the bathroom mirror, using my razor to shave your legs—stuff like that."

She thought he might be saying that he no longer saw her witch status as a problem. Funny how that was the issue they'd started with on Monday night, and now, apparently, it wasn't an issue anymore. No, they now had other issues.

First there was the obvious physical problem of whether he would ever revert permanently to his human form. A great deal depended on that, and there were no guarantees. Then they had to wonder whether they'd want to spend time with each other if he did regain his status as a man. Finally, there was the biggie, the super-duper issue of all—whether, if after all that transpired, they could trust each other with their hearts.

But they'd wandered off the track and she knew a time bomb could be ticking away inside that computer. "You need to send more e-mails," she said.

"I do?"

"Yes. You must e-mail each of those women and let her know that you have no intention of getting back together. You can wish her well, and apologize again for the initial lie you told to get her in bed, but make sure she understands this isn't an invitation to reunite."

"They won't think that's what it was."

She gazed at him and shook her head. "You may understand more about cats than ever before, but you still have a lot to learn about women."

As if to make that point, a muffled cell-phone tune sounded in the apartment. Anica recognized "Brown-Eyed Girl."

"That's my BlackBerry," he said. "Where is it?"

"I left it in the pocket of your wool coat." She motioned toward the coat closet by the front door. "It's in there."

"Damn."

"Someone you know?"

"Sheila." He made no move toward the coat closet.

"You need to answer it, Jasper. If she's calling you at this hour of the night, immediately after you sent her an e-mail, she's in a world of hurt. She's misinterpreted what you said in the e-mail."

Jasper looked like a man going to an execution as he walked over to the coat closet. But he did it. Opening the door, he reached inside the pocket of his coat, pulled out the BlackBerry and answered it.

"Hi, Sheila," he said. "I . . . uh . . . didn't expect you to call."

Anica thought she should duck out on this conversation. She was halfway to the kitchen to get coffee when

Jasper caught her by the wrist. She turned and looked into his eyes.

"No, Sheila, that's not why I e-mailed you," he said.

Anica didn't have to be a mind reader to interpret his pleading glance. He wanted her to stay for moral support. He might even want her to feed him lines.

He cleared his throat. "No, the e-mail was only meant to let you know that I'm sorry for the way I began it." He winced at something Sheila must have said, looked at Anica and mouthed the word *Help*.

She kept her voice very low. "You deserve to have somebody who appreciates you more than I did."

Jasper said that.

Anica tried to think of what she'd want to hear under these circumstances. "Someone who clicks with you on a deeper level."

Jasper repeated her words.

"Someone who's not such a self-centered jerk."

Jasper lifted his eyebrows and she simply smiled at him.

"Uh, Sheila, you need someone who's not such a self-centered jerk. That's right. Yep. If I were you I'd be mad at me, too." He nodded. "No, I don't think it's a good idea if we meet to talk it out. Seriously, no."

Anica racked her brain for something that would discourage Sheila. "We'll both heal quicker if we stay away from each other," she murmured.

Jasper gave her a thumbs-up. "We'll heal quicker if we stay away from each other." He paused to listen. "No, I really believe that. Absence doesn't make the heart grow fonder. It makes you forget all about the person. Absolutely. And besides . . ." He glanced at Anica.

She was running out of happy talk. She shrugged.

"Besides, Sheila, I, um, I hate to tell you this, but . . . I'm tired of sex."

Anica clapped a hand over her mouth. He would never get away with that whopper.

"I know it's hard to believe, but there you have it. For me it's the same ol', same ol'. You can spice it up with whips and chains, threesomes, foursomes, a whole orgy, and it's still a yawner." Jasper turned away from Anica, probably so he wouldn't crack up in the middle of his heartfelt explanation. "Definitely. You need to find someone who isn't sexually jaded. Uh-huh. Right. Thanks for calling. 'Bye."

"Don't tell me she bought that line of bull?"

He faced her with only a hint of a smile. "Maybe it's not a line of bull."

"Jasper, not an hour ago you were—"

"With you. Yes, I know. That's the only part I didn't mention to Sheila. See, although I haven't tried the whips and chains and group sex—"

"I'm relieved to hear it."

"Nah, that kind of stuff doesn't interest me. I'd rather have one-on-one. But that said, I *had* become sort of bored with sex."

"I see." She folded her arms and waited to see how big a hole he'd dig for himself.

"No, seriously! I was beginning to wonder if something was wrong with me because I wasn't into it anymore. But guys don't like to admit a thing like that. We're supposed to be ready for it all the time."

"Sheila seemed to think you were into it. She couldn't have been more complimentary about your performance."

"That's nice, but you just nailed it. I was putting on a performance."

"You mean after a while, after the thrill wore off." The longer he talked, the heavier her heart grew.

"No, I mean from the beginning. Same with Kate and Deb."

"So once the chase is over, the conquest is made, then—"

"No, that's not it!" He gripped her arms, his gaze intense. "I talked myself into going to bed with all three of those women because they were smart and hot, and I thought eventually I'd get the thrill back. It wasn't about making a conquest; it was about trying to feel a little old-fashioned lust."

"That's crazy."

"I thought I was going crazy. Then I met you and the old feeling was back. Lust was back, baby!"

"But what if it goes away again?"

He pulled her close. "How about this? How about we enjoy it while it's here?"

That's the thing about cats. We live in the moment. He hadn't said the words, but they echoed in her head, anyway.

"You have a couple of e-mails to send first."

"You're right. And now I know what to say."

"Jasper, I wouldn't count on fooling anybody else with that sexually bored routine."

"No, that was lame, but I hadn't thought it through. Now I have." He walked back to the computer and switched it on.

"So what are you planning to say to Kate and Deb?"

He sat down in the desk chair and stared at the screen as the computer booted up. "That I've found someone who makes me feel sexually alive again, and I wish the same for them."

Sexually alive. That certainly described how he made her feel, too, and that was a huge gift. She glanced at the antique clock on the wall. Earlier tonight they'd seemed to have so much time, but it was dwindling fast. If she didn't take his suggestion and live in the moment, she'd be all kinds of a fool.

"When you're finished," she said, "you'll find me in the bedroom."

He typed quickly. "Asleep?"

"No. Naked."

Chapter 21

Jasper typed those e-mails with a hard-on. He typed them as quickly as he could before turning off the computer, choosing a few magic books from Anica's collection and walking down the hall. Orion followed him.

Soft light spilled from the bedroom doorway, but it had a different quality from the kind created by her table lamps. He was curious as to how she'd created that effect.

The air smelled like warm honey. Although his human sense of smell wasn't as acute as when he was a cat, he seemed to have learned to pay more attention to his environment. He stepped through the door and found her surrounded by what seemed like a hundred beeswax candles. Tapers, pillars and votives covered every available surface.

The ivory glow made him catch his breath. She lay in the center of a bed stripped of everything but the bottom sheet and two pillows. She waited, this ivory and golden goddess, for him. *For him.* That crack she'd made in the kitchen reminding him about how soon he'd be eating off the counter where they'd just had sex hadn't really fooled him. She was in as deep as he was.

Orion trotted over and hopped onto the bed, where

he curled up next to Anica. She scratched behind his ears, but her gaze remained on Jasper. Jasper had to admit the orange tabby fit nicely into the scene if somebody had canvas and paints to capture it. But he wasn't an artist. He was a man with an erection that felt bigger than the Hancock building.

Setting the stack of books next to the bed, he reached over and picked up the cat. His fingers grazed her skin and his dick twitched in anticipation.

"You'd better put him in the coat closet."

"I hate sticking him in that tiny space. The hall will work." He set Orion on his feet outside the door and closed it. Then, keeping his attention focused on Anica, he pulled his shirt from his slacks and began unfastening the buttons.

Orion began to meow and scratch at the door.

"Coat closet," Anica said with a smile.

"Right." Jasper opened the door.

Orion shot through it and dashed under the bed.

With a groan, Jasper dropped to his hands and knees and tried to reach the cat, but Orion backed into the exact center of the space.

Laughing, Anica broke her pose and climbed out of bed. "I'll get the broom."

Jasper enjoyed the view as she walked out of the room, but then he peered under the bed and glared at the cat. "If it weren't for you I'd be a happy man right about now. I was trying to do you a favor, you ingrate. I'd hate to be closed in that tiny closet, so I figured you would, too. And this is how you repay me for being a pal."

Orion stared at him, unmoving.

"This should help." Anica arrived with the broom.

Jasper recognized the broom. It was the same one she'd used to chase him out from under the bed that first night. This was no O-Cedar brand of broom, either.

The handle was thick and had a pentagram carved into it near the top. The bristles were gathered in a bundle instead of the flat brooms he was used to using.

Where had he seen a similar kind of broom? Oh yeah. Kate had been a Harry Potter fan. She'd dragged him to the movies. Harry and friends rode on brooms like this, but of course that was all fake.

Anica gave him a puzzled glance. "Is something wrong?"

Hell, he needed to ask these kinds of questions sooner or later, but he was afraid it would ruin the sex. He hated to do that, because every time he looked at her walking around with no clothes on, he wanted to—well, do everything in the book with her. And a few things that might not be in any book.

"Jasper?"

"I . . . um, do you . . . ride that?"

Her brow cleared. "You're freaked out by the broom."

"I wouldn't say that."

"I would. You're staring at it as if it might start moving around the apartment on its own."

"Can it?"

"No," she said gently. "And right now, when I have no magic, it's just an ordinary broom, the kind you can use to get a cat out from under the bed."

He realized he was buying trouble, worrying about things that weren't a factor yet. He was less and less willing to do that, so he decided to drop the subject of the broom as a potential flying machine. "I don't want to use the broom to get Orion out."

"Why not?"

"Because it's no fun being chased out from under the bed with a broom."

"Oh." She seemed to be holding back a smile. "Then what do you suggest?"

"Let me get him something to eat instead."

"You know I'm trying to keep him from—" She interrupted herself and shook her head. "Never mind. Sure. Get him whatever you want except tuna. I really don't want to start with that. Cats can get to the point where they won't eat anything else, which isn't good for them."

"Okay. Be right back." He went into the kitchen with the image of her standing there naked, holding the broom that might or might not be able to fly. He was so effing confused. He wanted her more than he'd ever wanted a woman before, and she'd jump-started his libido, which was huge. But could he deal with flying brooms and magic wands?

He'd said the magic wasn't such a factor now. Maybe he hadn't been honest with himself about that. The idea of Anica flying through the night astride a broom was a little disturbing.

He found some deli meat in the fridge to tempt Orion out from under the bed. As he carried it back to the bedroom, he was met with a sight guaranteed to fry a guy's brain and send all the blood rushing south. Anica was on all fours beside the bed, which was interesting enough.

But her pose was even more erotic than that. With her fanny in the air, she laid her cheek on the carpet so she could see under the bed and call to Orion. Jasper almost came when he saw her positioned like that. Forget the cat. He'd grab a condom and be buried deep before the cat could blink.

She must have heard his footsteps, though, because she pushed herself upright and stood. "I can't get him to budge without the broom, so let's see you try with the food bribe."

He was so aroused he could barely talk. Apparently she had no idea what she'd looked like to someone coming through that door. He doubted he'd ever forget that moment.

Then again maybe she'd known exactly what she was

doing. She glanced up at him and smiled. "I was just thinking, we haven't tried it doggie style."

He gulped. "Uh, no, we haven't."

"Get Orion out from under the bed and maybe we can remedy that omission."

Given that possibility, he was ready to drag Orion out with a grappling hook. No, no, he wasn't. Cats were people, too. Well, some were, him in particular. Some were people wannabes, and that would be Orion's category. He didn't deserve the broom treatment.

Fortunately the deli meat worked like a charm. Once Orion was mostly out, Jasper grabbed him. Orion would still get the meat, of course, unlike the sneaky behavior of that Shoumatoff woman, who had brought tuna without any intention of giving it to him. Jasper knew he'd probably been guilty of similar tactics with pets, but he wouldn't treat an animal with that kind of disrespect ever again.

After closing Orion in the closet with his deli meat, Jasper strode down the hall, shedding clothes along the way. He was shirtless before he made it through the bedroom doorway, and shoeless before he got to the bed.

She was back on the bed again, bathed in flickering candlelight. This time, instead of lying on her back as if ready to receive him between her thighs, she was propped on her side watching him undress.

"I love seeing you naked," she said.

"Same here." Then another thought came to him. As he stripped off the rest of his clothes, he wondered if she danced naked in the moonlight.

What were those groups of witches called? He'd read it on the Internet. Then the word came to him. "Do you belong to a coven?"

"How would you feel about that?"

"I don't know. I picture people dancing naked in a circle out in the woods somewhere."

"I have done that a few times."

He was a little shocked by that and a lot turned on.

"Basically, witches and wizards are nature buffs," she said.

He climbed onto the mattress. "With an emphasis on the *buff* part."

"Yeah." She grinned. "I haven't noticed that you have any problem getting naked."

"No." He caressed the slope of her breast. "But I kind of like my undressing to be confined to groups of two."

"So do I." She leaned closer and pressed her mouth to his neck, where she began trailing kisses from there to his collarbone. "I haven't been naked in a crowd for years. Not my thing. I'm not part of a coven, either. I'm what you call a solitary witch."

Her explanation eased some of his anxiety. Besides, they'd spent more time on the subject than he wanted to give it. He slipped his hand between her thighs and discovered her hidden springs rising to the surface. "You seem pretty happy to be entertaining company tonight."

"Mm." She moaned softly as he probed her dampness with his fingers. "You're reminding me of my hostess duties."

"Is that right?" He hoped she'd remembered her promise.

"Uh-huh." Wiggling closer, she reached around him and opened the bedside table drawer.

He could have her wiggle and reach all day, considering how the movements caused her to rub her breasts against him and open her thighs to give him more access for his fingers.

Apparently she had a purpose other than that, though, because she produced a condom that she held between two fingers right in front of his nose. "You'll need this for the next stage," she murmured, her voice turned husky by his caress.

He loved that he could affect her that way. But he

positively adored the way she rolled to her stomach, even though she dislodged his fingers in the process.

She more than made up for that when she pushed herself to her hands and knees and glanced sideways at him. "Whenever you're ready, Jasper."

If he hadn't fallen in love with her before, her saucy behavior now would have done the trick. He couldn't get that condom on fast enough or find his spot behind her soon enough. Then, sweet heaven, he was living a fantasy.

In the light from a host of flickering candles, he took her in the most basic, primitive fashion. If ever a sexual position was designed to emphasize sex and only sex, this was it. Yet by offering herself to him this way, she'd triggered that emotion he'd nearly revealed earlier tonight.

His need for her was raw and hungry, no doubt about it. But threaded through that urgency was a tenderness that prompted him to lean forward, even in the midst of his rampant lust, and kiss her shoulder.

"Thank you," he whispered against her skin. Then all rational thought evaporated in the surge of sexual excitement as he grasped her hips and pounded into her. The rhythmic slap of his thighs against hers filled the room. The candlelight seemed fitting, as if they were in a cave deep in the earth.

For this moment she was his mate and he was hers. Her back arched as she tensed beneath him. He reveled in the music of her cries as she came, and only then did he allow himself the release he craved. At the moment of orgasm, he knew without a doubt that he loved this woman with a fierceness that shook him to his core.

But he wouldn't tell her. She'd made it clear that she wasn't ready to hear it.

They tumbled to the mattress and lay, panting and covered with sweat. He put his lips close to her ear. "Do you fly on that broom, Anica?"

"Yes," she murmured. "Yes, I do."

"Is it as good as this?"

Her laughter was breathless and filled with the satisfaction of good sex. "Not even close."

He smiled. Maybe the magic wasn't so threatening, after all.

Anica woke with a start. She hadn't meant to fall asleep. She would bet Jasper hadn't meant to, either. He'd planned to go through her magic books in the time he had left and search out more clues for breaking the spell.

But they'd decided to cuddle for a few minutes and she'd nestled into the curve of his body, spoon fashion. She'd been asleep before she took three breaths.

That was irresponsible on her part. She knew better than to fall asleep with candles burning, but all was well. She'd been asleep only an hour, and the candles were in protective holders. She'd lost a precious hour with Jasper, though. He was within five minutes of his changing time.

She started to turn toward him to see if he was awake, but before she could do that, his arm tightened around her and pulled her close.

"I know," he said. "I know."

"Did you sleep, too?"

"No." He nestled his beard-stubbled chin against her shoulder. "I didn't think we should both sleep with all these lit candles."

She was mortified that he'd had to take over the job that should have been hers. "I lit them, so I should have put them out. I can't believe I just fell asleep like that, as if I had no responsibility."

"I'm glad you did. I'm sure you were exhausted. And I covered for you."

"Thank you." She seemed to be depending on other people a lot more recently—first Lily and now Jasper. It was a novel and not altogether comfy feeling to give up that control.

"My pleasure." He gave her a squeeze that was more friendly than sexual, which was wise considering the ticking clock. "I liked lying here with you, watching the candles flicker while you slept. Gave me time to decide something."

Her pulse rate picked up. "Oh?"

"I'm going to take a guess about the spell. I was afraid to waste one of my three in case I'm wrong, but on the other hand, I don't want to waste an entire day, either, in case I'm right."

Her chest tightened with fear and she hoped he couldn't sense it. "You're sure? I thought you wanted to do more research first."

"Don't worry." He laughed. "If I'm not right, I won't make another guess until I've read every damn book on your bookshelf."

She was impressed that he could laugh when the stakes were so high. He had more courage than she'd given him credit for. And they were almost out of time for him to make that guess. "What is it, then?

"That I gain minutes every time I do a good deed."

Relief flooded through her, and she rolled over to pull him into a fierce hug of triumph. "You're *right*." She nearly choked on the words, she was so excited for him. "Oh, Jasper, you guessed it!"

"Thank God!" He hugged her back so tightly that her spine popped. Then he kissed her hard on the mouth before scrambling out of bed. "I have to leave."

"Jasper, it's okay! Please don't feel as if you have to leave when you—" She stopped talking, because he was gone. She could follow him, of course, but he obviously didn't want that.

She lay there staring at the candles. Now he knew. Now they could talk about it. Now she could help him lift the curse. It was wonderful, wasn't it? Why should she be worried?

The answer wasn't pretty. Right now, while he was still partly a cat, he needed her. He stayed in the apartment, stayed with her, because he had to have a safe place to live when he returned to his cat status.

Anica had told both Lily and herself that she hated having his fate in the palm of her hand. She was ashamed to admit that maybe she secretly liked having that much control over him. Once he managed to transform himself back forever he wouldn't need her anymore. Her control would be gone. He might be gone, too.

Chapter 22

Jasper barely made it to the kitchen before the change hit him. He'd learned to go with it instead of resisting, which made the crossover ten times easier. He'd be glad when this didn't happen to him every night, but he wasn't horrified the way he had been the first couple of times he'd changed back into a cat.

And this change was the sweetest of all, because now he knew the secret for lifting the spell. Soon he'd be in charge of his life again. He'd already decided it wouldn't be the same life, though.

Living as a cat, he'd come to appreciate some things he'd never paid much attention to before. He'd been too busy rushing from one thing to the next, going for the big score in the market, making sure he had tickets to opening night of whatever play was hot that season, hurrying to the gym and staying on the phone the entire time he was working out.

He'd never bothered to stop and enjoy whatever was right in front of him because he'd been too busy looking ahead to the next great thing, which was bound to be so much better than what he had going on at the moment. He knew now that nothing could be better than making love to Anica in a room filled with candlelight and then lying quietly, watching over her while she slept.

Staying with her all night would be a bonus, though, and he wanted to get to that point ASAP. When he was fully transformed into a cat, he trotted out to the living room, hopped on the desk chair, and turned on the computer. Typing wouldn't be nearly as smooth as it had been four hours ago, but there were compensations. Cats didn't get carpel tunnel or stiff necks. At least he hoped cats didn't.

Now that he knew he'd be changing back permanently, he could allow himself to appreciate the good things about his feline self. He could leap to heights five or six times taller than he was. Even Michael Jordan hadn't been able to do that.

He was now a champion nap-taker, too, and he had to acknowledge that naps lowered his stress levels. He also had meditation skills to rival the Dalai Lama and the patience of . . . well, of a saint. As a man he used to sit and drum his fingers on the desk while his computer booted up. Now he simply sat and waited.

Would any of his cat skills transfer to his human self? Not the leaping ability, of course, but he had hopes for a calmer approach, a more in-the-moment philosophy once he returned to his other life. He realized with some surprise that there were things he'd miss about being a cat.

Not the lack of opposable thumbs, though. Computers were designed for people and he struggled whenever he had to use this one. Yet he'd learned how, and the computer could be one of his main sources of salvation now. He signed on to the Internet.

As he was calling up the animal rescue site, he heard soft footsteps and knew Anica was up. Her scent drew nearer as she approached the desk, and the rustle of silk told him she'd put on a bathrobe.

He'd learned to depend on his cat senses and had missed them during those times when he'd transformed into a man. Consequently he'd learned to compensate by paying better attention. He'd like to hang on to that tendency, too.

"I heard the computer boot up." She yawned. "I thought I'd come out and see what you're doing."

Jasper opened a Word file so he could type a message to her. He clicked on the lock function and typed in U NED SLP.

She laughed softly. "You know, that last word could be *slap* instead of *sleep*. I might need a slap more than I need sleep, come to think of it."

R U IN2 S & M

He didn't think that at all, but he was feeling good and wanted to tease her a little bit.

"Nope."

GD

"But I have a confession to make, Jasper. A part of me has enjoyed the past few days."

PRT OF ME 2

"That's nice of you to say."

MY DCK

She hooted with laughter, and he was proud of himself for making her lose it. That was another thing he wanted that had largely been missing in his human life. He wanted more play. Naked play with Anica would be even better.

"Okay, Jasper, my hoo-ha has certainly enjoyed the past few days, but I've also discovered that I've enjoyed the control I've had over this situation, which is not good. I'm going to work on that, which would be especially important if I'm about to get my magic back."

YES

She took a deep breath. "Yes. Sex with you is a good practice ground for giving up control."

NCE

"It is nice. Very nice." She paused. "Jasper, I . . ."

He waited, wondering if she would choose this moment to reveal the depth of her feelings. Now wouldn't be the best timing in the world, when all he could do was type his response. But he'd take the words whenever he could get them.

Telling him how she felt about him would be the ultimate loss of control, though. She might not be there yet. He'd just been mentally bragging on his increased patience, so this would give him a chance to test it.

"I should let Orion out of the closet," she said at last.

With a little sigh, Jasper minimized his Word file and went back to the animal rescue site. If only he knew the amount to give that would do the trick. He didn't seem to be getting hours in proportion to what he was giving.

Other factors must be at work, and he was still holding out hope that each orgasm he gave Anica counted. That would be sweet. His e-mails to Sheila, Kate and Deb might do something for him. At least he hoped they were in the good-deed category. He'd meant for them to be.

Still, the animal rescue site offered the most clear-cut opportunity for good works. His American Express was a no-limit card, so theoretically he could put anything he wanted to on there. He'd have to pay it next month, though, and he'd rather not empty his IRA and savings to do that. The condo didn't have much equity yet.

He might strike gold at work, but the market was like a temperamental lover. Whenever he tried too hard to woo her she turned into a bitch. So no guarantees from that corner.

He was talking about his freedom, though. He had five hours, and he needed nineteen more to make a whole day. Logic said to charge whatever amount he thought might buy him nineteen hours and worry about how to pay for it later.

Yeah, but what would that amount be? He didn't want to overshoot it by thousands. He'd never know whether he did or not, which would be frustrating in itself.

Anica's footfalls were almost noiseless on the carpet,

but Jasper could smell that combination of sugar and spice coming closer. The scent of male cat came with her this time, which meant Orion was out of the closet.

"What has you so mesmerized, Jasper?" She paused to glance at the screen. "Aha! You're going to make a donation. Smart."

Jasper didn't feel all that smart. He'd love to talk to that witch and wizard and find out if they could be more specific about how this worked. If he knew for a fact that nineteen grand would buy him nineteen hours, he'd probably just do it. But he didn't know that, and he would have a hell of a time paying that money back.

"I would help you navigate the computer." Anica crouched down next to the desk so she could stroke Orion. "But I'm afraid if I did the typing for you that might counteract the value of your good deed."

He sure didn't want that happening, especially because he was toying with the idea of giving ten grand. Even if it didn't take him all the way, he should get a huge chunk of time for that. If he transformed early enough in the day, he might be able to use those extra hours to do more good deeds.

Still, ten grand was a lot of money. He could probably get an equity loan for that amount, but that would add significantly to his debt load. Of course, if he didn't transform back into a man soon, he could kiss his job goodbye and then he'd be in real financial trouble.

And if the worst happened and he never completely made the transition, he would have far bigger problems than being in debt. He typed in the numbers before he lost his nerve.

Behind him, Anica gasped. "Jasper! That's a small fortune! It's a good cause, but I'm sure you don't need to give them that much." She reached around him and tried to grab the mouse.

He batted it away, something he was especially good at.

"Jasper, behave. I'm sure that lifting the spell doesn't require that you spend ten thousand dollars." She reached for the mouse again.

But he had cat reflexes. Leaping to the desk, he threw himself on top of the mouse. Growling, he gathered it underneath his body.

"Don't be crazy." Anica began pulling on the cord connecting the mouse to the computer. "Let me have the mouse before you do something really dumb."

He stared at her while gripping the mouse with the claws of his back feet. Too bad he couldn't talk. He'd tell her that she hadn't quite given up that habit of hers, the one where she wanted to control things. He was a grown man—well, at least for a few hours every evening—and he had the right to donate whatever money he chose to whatever cause he chose.

She pulled harder on the cord, and he growled a warning. He didn't want to scratch her, but she was messing in his business.

"You're being incredibly stubborn. Tomorrow night we can brainstorm ways you can earn minutes. Now that you know how the spell can be reversed, I'm free to help you strategize. I'm sure we can come up with things that don't require some massive infusion of money."

Little did she know. He'd already given $4,700, and his five hours of being a man wasn't all due to that donation, either. He didn't think $10k would even be enough, but it was the amount he could give away without hyperventilating.

It might at least buy him enough human time to work on less expensive goodwill projects. True, he wouldn't get daylight hours to work with until he earned the first twelve, but good deeds were possible at night. He could figure that one out.

Anica tried to stare him down, but as he'd discovered, he was an expert at staring contests. The whole time he looked at her he tried to send a message from his mind to hers. If mental telepathy worked it should work from a cat to a witch. Of course, she wasn't technically a witch without her magic.

Even so, something must have penetrated her brain, because she sighed and backed away. "I suppose it's your decision, isn't it?"

No shit, Sherlock.

She threw both hands up. "All right. I tried to talk some sense into you, but I can see you're determined to do it your way."

Maybe not being able to talk had saved them both. He could easily imagine the brouhaha if he'd been able to get in his licks. Instead, silent resistance had worked. He'd have to remember that technique for later, because he had a feeling this wouldn't be the only time they had this kind of argument. Anica wouldn't give up being bossy overnight, and maybe not ever.

He was fascinated to discover he didn't care. If he was very lucky, he'd get to ride herd on her bossiness for the rest of their lives. Now, there was a concept.

"I want to meet him." Lily sat across from Anica at Wicked Brew, her face alight with excitement. "This is sounding like a serious relationship, and I want to check him out, see if he's good enough for you."

"But you have work, and I have no idea when he'll change." Anica had called Lily midmorning to catch her up on Jasper's progress and to report the large cash donation. Lily had rushed down to the coffee shop to discuss it in person.

"If he threw down ten thousand smackeroos, he could be sitting in your apartment, sipping coffee right this minute. For that matter, he could walk through the door of the shop!"

Anica shook her head. "Before I left, I made sure he had my cell number and asked him to call if something happens, like he did last night. I don't need to have him walk in here and scare the living daylights out of me."

Lily munched on a chocolate cake doughnut, her idea of breakfast. "For that kind of money, I'm surprised he didn't immediately zap back to naked manhood." She dampened her finger and speared some crumbs.

"He might have wished that would happen, but obviously it didn't. I hope he got some extra hours, though. It would suck if for some reason that donation didn't count toward anything."

Lily licked her finger. "Why not call Dorcas and ask her? For all you know there's some chart that tells how many points various good deeds are worth."

Anica doubted it, but calling Dorcas was a good idea. "Thanks. I'll do that right now."

Lily seemed pleased that Anica took her suggestion. "I'll get Sally to give us each a refill." She picked up both cups and carried them back to the counter.

As Anica made the call to Dorcas, she tried not to notice the way the shop looked. The windows needed cleaning and dust had collected in the corners. She should stay late tonight and work on the place, except that she didn't want to spend any more time here than absolutely necessary. Lily was right—Jasper could transform at any minute, and she wanted to be available to help him with his good-deed list. Then she smiled. Maybe helping her clean the shop would count.

Dorcas answered on the third ring. "Hi, Anica. I was wondering if I'd hear from you."

"I'll bet you used magic to find out it was me calling."

"I used to use magic. Now I use caller ID. Far more reliable. How's Jasper doing?"

Anica filled her in on the latest developments.

"Wow. That's a lot of money."

"I tried to talk him out of it, but he was determined." Anica could still see that gleam in Jasper's golden eyes as he'd defied her. "Will it give him more time?"

"It should. I'd be surprised if it didn't. Now that Jasper knows what he's supposed to do, let me ask Ambrose to research the acts-of-kindness angle again. Maybe we can find out more detail."

"Lily thought there might be a chart of good deeds and their respective point value." She halfway expected Dorcas to laugh at that.

"For all I know, there is. That spell is so old that it's tough finding related research materials. But Ambrose will love digging around the magical archives online. He's such a nerd at heart."

"That would be great." Anica thought again of all the time they were putting in. "Will you send me a bill for that?"

"Of course not. But I might send you some cards for our matchmaking service, Hot Prospects. We'd be willing to travel up there if anybody in the Chicago area wanted to hire us."

Anica lowered her voice. "My sister needs your services, but I doubt she thinks so."

"Troubles?"

"Just a guy she's stuck on who isn't interested."

"We could do a scrying, see if he's the one for her. We have a sale going on right now, buy one scrying session, get one for free."

"Then I'll buy two, one for me and Jasper, and I'll save the other one for a while. Maybe she'll give up on this guy, so I don't want to waste a session. How do I pay you?"

"We take all major credit cards."

That struck Anica as funny, but she managed to keep from laughing. "I'll call you back with the numbers. Thanks, Dorcas. Bye."

"What numbers?" Lily sat down and slid Anica's latte over to her.

"Credit card numbers. I bought a scrying session to see what comes up about me and Jasper."

"Huh. Could be interesting. What did she say about the good-deed criteria?"

"She'll have Ambrose research it and get back to me. I guess info on this spell is tough to come by."

"I tell you, sis, when you screw up, you do it royally."

Anica would have loved to argue with Lily about that, but she didn't have a leg to stand on. She *had* screwed up royally. But she wasn't furious with herself anymore. If she hadn't put the spell on Jasper, they both would have stayed exactly as they were. Instead they were growing and changing. She could feel it. She wasn't sure if they'd grow apart or together, but at least they were growing.

"So, can I meet Jasper when he changes this time?"

Anica could tell Lily wasn't about to let this go. "What about work?"

"Let me worry about that. Just promise me that when he changes, which surely has to be before nine thirty this time, you'll call me."

Anica resisted the idea. "He could be in a bad mood, especially if he doesn't get as much time as he'd hoped for that big donation."

"I don't care. Come on, sis, you can't keep him to yourself forever."

No, but she wanted to.

"Anica, you don't think I'll try to steal him, do you?"

"Uh, no. Of course not." Anica took a big swig of her coffee and scalded her tongue. "Ouch. Hot, hot." She waved her hand in front of her mouth.

"You do! You think I'm going to try and steal him! That's so unfair. When have I ever stolen one of your boyfriends?"

"Back in eleventh grade."

"Yeah, okay. Guilty as charged. I was a kid and full of myself."

Anica smiled. Lily wasn't a kid anymore, but she could still be full of herself when it came to men.

"The point is, I haven't stolen a boyfriend from you since then."

"Because you didn't want any of them."

"No." She looked offended. "Because I realized that was a disloyal and mean thing to do."

"And you didn't want any of them."

"That's not the issue. Anyway, I'm not coming over to steal your precious Jasper. I just think somebody from the family should get a look at him, and the 'rents are out of the country."

Anica regarded her sister with amusement. "Gonna bring your shotgun?"

Lily grinned. "I dunno. Should I?"

Maybe. Anica would love to have a way to guarantee that Jasper would stick around once he was free to go. But that was yet another thing over which she had no control.

Chapter 23

By the time Anica came home at four thirty, Jasper was pissed. Ten thousand big ones, plus those e-mails to his exes, plus being nice to Orion, plus giving Anica some really outstanding orgasms—and the most he could possibly get out of it, even if he changed immediately, was ten additional hours. When he did not change immediately, he cut his estimation to eight hours. Not a very good return for his outlay.

Anica gave him a sympathetic glance as she took off her coat and hung it up. "I'm sorry, Jasper," she said as she walked over to where he was curled up in a corner of the sofa, hating life. "I'm sure you're disappointed."

Disappointed? DISAPPOINTED??? Try effing furious. He was ready to chew a bag of nails and spit bullets. All that happy horseshit he'd been thinking yesterday about how evolved he was, how patient, how good at meditating, was out the window, baby. This was war.

"I called Dorcas today. She's the witch who came up with her husband to consult with me about the spell."

Jasper gave her a baleful glance. *Tell somebody who gives a damn.* That witch had been no help whatsoever. What good was being magic if you couldn't fix anything with it?

"She's convinced you'll get some return for your donation. She's just not sure how much. I sure wish you hadn't—" Anica stopped, pressed her lips together, and looked away.

Lucky for her she hadn't just delivered the equivalent of *I told you so*. He was ready and able to shred her lovely flowered upholstery. She must be feeling righteous about now, because she'd warned him not to risk ten grand on this deal. But it should have worked! Why the hell hadn't it?

"I need to mention something else."

He waited for her to announce that Shoumatoff was about to show up and cart him off to the spay-neuter clinic. That was the way his day had gone so far, so he wouldn't be surprised if Shoumatoff had gotten up a petition signed by all the apartment residents protesting his continued possession of balls.

"I promised Lily that when you changed form tonight, I'd call her and let her come over. I, um, told her about the donation, and she's convinced you'll change any minute."

That made one of them. He was quickly giving up hope.

"She wants to meet you. When you're a man, I mean. Obviously the two of you have met as woman and cat."

They had, and as he recalled Lily had threatened him if he didn't do right by Anica. She'd probably be happy to come over and gloat because his ten grand had earned him ten minutes.

"So that's it. Are you hungry?"

He wasn't, but Orion perked up at the other end of the sofa. Orion could always eat.

"Guess I'll start thawing the meat in the microwave." Anica stood and headed for the kitchen.

Jasper settled down and tried to nap. He'd been good at that yesterday, before he'd sunk himself into debt for a transformation that showed no sign of happening. Today the urge to snooze wasn't the same. Today he was picturing the lien on his condo and his clients leaving in droves because he never seemed to make it into the office anymore.

Oh yeah. This sucked.

In spite of that he must have needed to cop a few Zs, because the next thing he knew, good smells drifted from the kitchen, and the clock in the living room pointed to five fifty-five. So he'd missed the five thirty changeover, too. Ducky.

Now the best he could hope for was six thirty, which meant only an additional six hours added to . . . hello. He had that pre-change feeling again. He'd been so used to the half-hour change that he'd assumed it would be then. Maybe now he was on an hour schedule, because he could definitely feel the stirrings that preceded his transformation.

Six in the evening to six in the morning. He could live with that. Twelve hours of human shape. Yeah, he'd been a little grouchy because it hadn't happened sooner, but twelve hours was halfway there. That was significant.

Hopping down from the sofa, he made his way to the bedroom. Anica didn't seem to notice, but Orion caught sight of him and followed him down the hall. Orion trotted faster, as if he wanted to play chase.

Jasper turned and hissed at the orange tabby, but Orion kept coming. He'd found a play buddy and he wasn't discouraged by a little hiss. Putting on speed, he tried to catch up with Jasper.

This was not working. Jasper wanted privacy for what was about to happen to him. To say he was self-conscious about this process would be a gross understatement. But how could he get rid of Orion?

If he went in the closet, he'd change in there, which would send clothes tumbling off the hangers and generally leave chaos behind. He could get away from Orion by leaping to the dresser, but once he changed, he might crack the top of that antique with his weight, not to mention scattering the family pictures Anica had carefully placed there. She hadn't moved her array of candles, either. He'd break something for sure if he went up there.

The dresser was out, then. Ducking under the bed wasn't a solution, either. He'd end up wedged there like a rubber doorstop. Maybe he could wear Orion out by leaping around on the bed, and then when he ducked into the bathroom, Orion would be too tired to follow.

Gathering his haunches beneath him, he launched himself up on Anica's bed. He loved jumping like that, as if he had springs for legs. He waited until Orion made it up, and then he jumped down and ran around the room.

Once Orion landed on the floor with a loud *thump*, Jasper hurled himself back on the bed. He waited a beat for Orion to catch up before hopping down again. Over and over he repeated the pattern, and Orion started to pant. Good.

"What are you two cats up to in here?" Anica appeared in the doorway as Jasper hit the floor for the umpteenth time.

Shit. He hadn't counted on that and the change was almost here. Feeling dizzy and disoriented, he dashed into the bathroom.

"Jasper?"

Getting behind the door, he managed to swing it shut. Then he lay against it, panting as much as Orion, but more from stress than exertion. Okay . . . let go . . . let it happen . . . The temporary loss of consciousness was the worst part. Anica wasn't the only person who liked to maintain control. But at least this time, he'd have twelve hours. Twelve blessed hours . . .

When he came to, he was sprawled naked on the cold bathroom tile, the weight of his body keeping the door closed. Maybe it was the mirror on the back of the door reminding him of the best oral sex of his life. Maybe it was the testosterone that had flowed through his system prior to the change, because he'd been so damned angry about the money. Maybe it was Anica's soft voice calling to him as she tapped gently on the door.

Whatever the reason, he was aroused.

"Jasper, are you okay? Can I do anything?"

He almost laughed. Yeah, she could do something. The way he felt, it would only take about three minutes of her time. Or he could suggest that she strip off her clothes and put Orion in the coat closet. Then they could do something together.

But once they were in bed he wouldn't want to leave. Despite having twelve hours to work with, he realized how quickly that time could disappear if he allowed himself to take Anica to bed now. His first priority had to be finding ways to earn the other twelve hours.

He was making progress, but he wasn't there yet. He also owed a bunch of money and he'd have to make plans to cover that expense. Besides, Anica had promised Lily she could come over. They should get that obligation out of the way. Sex would have to wait.

"I've, uh, changed again," he said.

She gasped softly. Then there was silence. "That's good, isn't it?" she said at last. "You should have twelve hours this time. Are you encouraged? I think you should be encouraged."

Mostly I'm horny. "Sure, I'm encouraged. Listen, why don't you call your sister? I'm going to take a shower." A very cold shower.

"Okay. She probably won't stay long. She'll be taking off work to come over here. Oh, I just thought of something."

"What's that?"

"You haven't been out of this apartment in days, except for that one time when Edna tried to . . . well, anyway. Would you like to go see Lily instead of having her come here? Would you like to go out?"

Jasper's first reaction was eagerness. His second was

fear. Could he trust this change to hold? Because he wasn't willing to admit that fear to Anica, he put more heartiness into his answer than he felt. "You bet! That would be great."

"Good. I'll call Lily and tell her to expect us. We'll just take the bus down to the Bubbling Cauldron."

"Call a taxi." If he changed form in a taxi, he and Anica could do damage control. On a city bus, no way. He'd be an urban legend before tomorrow morning.

"All right. A taxi it is, then." Her footsteps moved away from the bathroom door.

She probably knew he was scared once he'd asked for a taxi. Oh, well. She'd sense it sooner or later. He understood how a newly hatched chick might feel leaving the protection of its shell. But he had to do this sometime. It would be good for him to get out. Rejuvenating.

The discussion about leaving the apartment had eliminated the need for a cold shower, so he took a hot one instead. He would have thought he'd really need a shower after all this time, but no, he was actually clean. He didn't need a shave, either. Apparently when he changed back into a man he regained the body he'd had at that particular hour on Monday.

At six p.m. on Monday he'd been leaving his condo to meet Anica at the restaurant. He'd showered and shaved after work because he'd hoped they'd end the night in her apartment and in her bed. He didn't feel at all like the same man who had walked into that restaurant.

Yet his body was exactly the same as it had been then. His fingernails and toenails hadn't grown and he still had the little nick on his chin where he'd slipped with the razor. On the outside he hadn't changed at all. No one looking at him would be able to tell that he viewed the world completely differently from the way he had on Monday.

Turning off the shower, he reached for one of the towels hanging from a hook on the wall. The towel smelled like Anica, so he took a second to bury his face in it. He wanted to spend the rest of his life with her, and yet he wondered if he was being honest with himself by thinking he could handle the concept of her magical abilities.

He had no way of judging, because she wasn't using magic now. When she'd regained her power he might be forgiven for getting nervous every time she picked up a wand. That wand, once it was operational again, would be a potent symbol of what he'd been through.

He finished drying himself and wrapped the towel around his hips before walking out into the bedroom. He hoped Anica wouldn't be there. She was too much of a temptation. Now that they'd decided to leave the apartment, he didn't want to be sidetracked. Time to face the challenge of stepping out into the world for the first time since his transformation.

She wasn't in the bedroom. She might have figured that if she happened to be there when he walked naked out of the bathroom, they'd never make it to the Bubbling Cauldron. He dressed quickly, borrowed a brush he found on her dresser to tame his hair, and walked out into the living room.

Anica was in the kitchen putting away the food she'd been cooking. Her face was flushed as she bustled around filling containers and shoving them into the refrigerator.

"You were in the middle of making dinner. I didn't think of that."

She glanced up and smiled. "No problem. I finished making it, so I can heat it up later."

"Or wait until tomorrow night. I could take you out to dinner."

She paused to gaze at him. "That's a nice offer, but the truth is, I'd rather eat here."

So would he, he realized. Being alone with her was more important than flirting in a restaurant and playing footsie under the table. "I guess we've moved past the dating stage."

"Yes, although I don't know what stage we're in."

"We're in transition," he said.

"I suppose we are." She looked at him thoughtfully. "Ready?"

He had the feeling the question had more than one meaning. "Yes."

"Then let's go."

He helped her on with her coat, something he hadn't done since leaving the restaurant Monday night. "I've loved this coat ever since I first saw it, but now I realize it could be sort of a—"

"Witch's cape?" She buttoned it and picked up her purse from a table beside the front door. "My mother gave it to me for that very reason. She has one exactly like it."

"So she's a witch, too?" He held the door for her and waited while she locked it behind them.

"Quite an accomplished one." She tucked her keys back in her purse. "My dad's an excellent wizard."

"When I first met you, you said they were out of the country." He took her hand as they started down the stairs.

"They are, but their work is in the magical realm, not the civilian sector. Oh, and by the way, they don't approve of their daughters dating nonmagical men."

That put a different spin on things. He'd been worried that her magic would be a problem for him. Apparently his nonmagical status could be a problem for her. "Why don't they approve?" He'd never been the object of prejudice before, and he didn't like it.

"They feel it causes too many problems because of the lifestyle differences. I can't tell you how many nice wizard boys they've introduced me to. I couldn't get excited about any of them. I guess it's because I grew up around magic, but being with a wizard is so ho-hum. They don't turn me on."

"Nice to hear."

"Obviously you do." She squeezed his hand as they descended the second set of steps to the ground floor. The space was small and designed chiefly to house the mailboxes lining one wall.

He was happy that she'd admit that openly, but his dick began to react to the conversation. "We might want to change the subject. I'm getting the urge to back you up against the mailboxes."

"Risky business. Anyone could walk through that door."

As if to prove her point, the door opened and Edna Shoumatoff came in wearing her quilted coat and her Cossack hat. She carried a burger bag in one hand.

She stiffened when she saw Anica. "I would ask if you've had that tomcat fixed, but I'm afraid to find out the answer." She glanced sideways at Jasper. "She has a tomcat and refuses to neuter him. Irresponsible, if you ask me."

Jasper gazed at the woman who had nearly had him castrated. He didn't think an operation so final would have been reversed when he changed back. This woman in the Cossack hat had almost ruined his life. His parents' lives, too, for that matter. They hoped he'd eventually give them grandchildren.

"I know about this cat," Jasper said. "He has issues, and now would be a really bad time for him to go under the knife."

"There is no bad time for that to happen. If nothing's been done, I hope the two of you are keeping watch over him day and night."

Anica cleared her throat. "Miss Shoumatoff, I can promise you that someone has an eye on him every minute."

"As long as he still has his balls, anything's possible. But I can see you won't be budged on the matter. You might introduce me to your friend, Anica."

"I'm sorry. This is Jasper Danes. Jasper, this is my neighbor Edna Shoumatoff."

"Jasper?" Shoumatoff narrowed her eyes. "Wasn't that the name of your cat?"

"One of life's little coincidences," Jasper said. "Nice meeting you, Miss Shoumatoff."

"Something fishy's going on. I can smell it. I suppose you've heard the rumor that there's a witch living in the building."

"That's ridiculous." Anica took hold of Jasper's arm. "We'd better get going, Jasper. The cab just pulled up outside."

"You're right. Let's go." Jasper was more than happy to get away from Shoumatoff, but when he stepped out onto the sidewalk he had the strangest thought. *How many stray cats are out here, afraid and alone?*

He'd expected to be worried about himself and his reactions as he moved back into the stream of humanity bustling along the sidewalk outside Anica's apartment. Instead he was worried about cats. He glanced around, as if expecting them to run out from their hiding places.

None did, and he wasn't sure what he would do if that ever happened. He held the cab door for Anica and climbed in after her with a sense of relief. No doubt about it. He might regain his human form, but he would never again be the same person.

Chapter 24

Anica held Jasper's hand through the silent cab ride to Rush Street. She could feel the tension running through him, and he spent most of his time looking out the window as if seeing Chicago for the first time.

When they were almost at the bar, he turned to her. "It's like waking up from a dream."

"I'll bet." At least he hadn't said *waking up from a nightmare*. She hoped that some of his experiences had been good ones. Some of hers certainly had been. "Are you doing okay?"

"Yeah, but it's very weird." He returned his attention to the view out the window. "Before I used to notice the buildings. Now I notice the alleys and the spaces between the buildings, places a cat might hide."

"I know. I found Orion just wandering around one night. If you can believe it, he was skinny then. I'm sure I overfed him because I felt so sorry for him."

Jasper glanced at her and smiled. "Me, too. I'm a bad influence. Listen, I've been thinking he needs another cat around."

"You mean later, after you—"

"Right. Obviously not now. Later. Orion could use the exercise. He loves it when I play chase with him."

"I'm sure he does. I'll definitely think about getting

another cat. You're probably right that it would be a good thing." The cab pulled up to the curb and Anica glanced out her window at the bar with the large neon cauldron over the door. She started to get money out of her wallet.

Jasper put a hand over hers. "Nope. My treat. I'm the one who wanted the cab instead of the bus." He handed money through the window separating the backseat and the front. "Keep the change."

"Appreciate it," the driver said. "You folks have a nice night."

Anica hoped it would be. She could still feel a certain amount of tension in Jasper as they left the relative intimacy of the cab and stood on the sidewalk outside the bar.

She turned to him. "You're sure you're okay?"

"I'm fine."

She didn't think he was completely fine, but who would be if he'd spent most of the past few days as a cat? "I've never mentioned this," she said, "but I like the fact that you're a generous tipper."

"I remember what it's like to depend on those tips. Now it's even more important that I tip big. I'm on a mission to do a bunch of good deeds."

"That's true." Anica had a thought and it might make Jasper less nervous if he had a goal in mind. "I might have a good deed you could do."

"Yeah?"

"Lily's developed a crush on one of her customers, a guy named Griffin Taylor. But he doesn't seem to notice her. I don't know if he'll be there or not, but he might be."

"I'm not sure how I could help that situation along."

"I'm not sure, either. I wanted you to be aware of it, though, in case something occurs to you."

"Like what?"

"I don't know. If the opportunity presents itself, say something nice about Lily, see what sort of reaction you get." She could tell he wasn't keen on this. "Or not. We'll see how it goes."

"If I screw it up, that would make me pretty unpopular with your sister. I don't want to be unpopular with your sister. I already have to worry about being unpopular with your parents."

She was encouraged by the fact he was worried about his standing with her family. That boded well for the future. "You know, we probably shouldn't meddle in this deal with Griffin." She started toward the door. "If it's meant to be it'll happen organically."

"Unless she casts a spell on him."

Anica whipped around to face him, her whole body quivering with anxiety. "She wouldn't do that, not after seeing—"

"Just kidding."

He didn't look as if he'd been kidding. She'd bet he still wasn't totally at ease with the magic issue. And she wasn't totally convinced her sister wouldn't consider trying out her magic on Griffin, either.

"Come on," Jasper said. "Let's go see how your sister handles a martini shaker."

"Okay."

"And thanks."

"For what?"

"Taking my mind off the possibility that I might suddenly turn into a cat again."

The inside of the Bubbling Cauldron was dark and filled with noise and laughter. What light there was had a red tinge to it. Jasper could see how a witch, especially one with Lily's personality, would be happy working here.

He missed his cat vision, which would have made the search for a vacant table a hundred times easier. As he scanned the room, he noted where the bathrooms were. If his calculations were wrong and he felt the change coming, he'd head for the john. He hoped to hell his calculations weren't wrong.

"I see a table." Anica tugged him toward a far corner where a round table with two chairs sat empty.

"Perfect." Jasper had hoped for a spot out of the main flow of traffic. The noise seemed deafening after the relative quiet of Anica's apartment. Had bars always been this loud?

They'd barely had time to sit down before Lily came rushing over. "Hey!"

"Hey, Lily!" Anica hopped up and hugged her sister.

Jasper stood, too, and watched them. The hug seemed real, and not some loose, perfunctory embrace. The Revere sisters seemed to like each other better than Jasper remembered, and he wondered if the transformation problem had brought them closer together.

"So, this is Jasper," Anica said.

Lily thrust out a manicured hand. "It's good to meet you. I mean, *really* meet you. I realize we've met before, but . . ."

"I wasn't myself at the time." He shook her hand.

She laughed. "Well put." Her gaze swept over him. "How does it feel?"

"Temporary," Jasper said. "I *think* I have from six to six, but if I don't, then—" He shrugged.

"You've always had equal amounts of time on either side of midnight," Lily said. "This shouldn't be any different."

"Logically, you're right. I suppose you have a policy about bringing animals in here, though. I'd hate to violate that."

Lily waved a dismissive hand. "It's not gonna happen, but even if it did, we'd bill you as a new street act we invited in. Give people a few drinks, and they'll believe most anything. Speaking of drinks, I need to get back. Why don't you two sit at the bar, so we can talk?"

Anica glanced over at Jasper. He decided to let her make the call.

"I think we're better off over here for now," Anica said. "Jasper's still getting his bearings."

"Oh. Well, that makes sense. What'll you have? I'll send a waitress over with your drinks."

"Sam Adams for me," Jasper said. It hadn't been his brand before, but now that it was associated with Anica and sex, it was his favorite.

"Make that two," Anica said.

"Anything to eat? We have some simple pub grub."

"Onion rings?" Jasper suddenly had a taste for something fried within an inch of its life.

"Sure." Lily glanced at Anica. "Anything for you, toots?"

"I'll share his onion rings." Anica leaned closer to Lily. "Is Griffin here tonight?"

Lily blushed. Jasper hadn't been around Lily much, but he was positive blushing wasn't something she did very often.

"He's at the table closest to the bar," Lily said. "That's the spot he and his friends always take. He's the one in the navy suit."

Jasper glanced over. The guy looked way too conservative for someone like Lily. His hair was cut very short—not quite a buzz cut, but close—and the designer suit was all business. Then the guy laughed, and Jasper could see how maybe Lily was attracted. Griffin had the kind of contagious laugh that said *Let's get this party started*.

Anica nodded. "He's cute, Lil."

Jasper felt a pang of jealousy. He had no real claim on Anica, and yet he sure hated hearing her call some other guy *cute*. Maybe he needed to think about staking that claim if her comment mattered so much to him. Yes, maybe he should.

Lily rolled her eyes. "Duh. You think I'd notice somebody who wasn't? Anyway, trouble over there. Some woman from the law firm has decided to join their little happy hour gathering. I don't like it. I don't like it one bit. Anyway, I have to get back. I'll send someone over with your beer and onion rings." With a wave Lily walked away.

Jasper noticed she chose to walk past the table where Griffin was sitting. He glanced up and glanced quickly down again. Interesting.

"He doesn't want to look at her." Anica sat down but she kept her attention on Griffin.

"Oh, I think he wants to." Jasper settled into his chair. "But he's afraid to."

"Huh?" Anica stared at him. "Since when is a guy afraid to check out a woman? I thought it was the national pastime."

"It is, unless you're worried about the consequences."

Anica's eyes narrowed. "You think he's married? Or engaged?"

"Could be. Or he thinks Lily's too hot to handle. I might have thought from that reaction that he's shy, but nothing else about him comes across that way. What does she know about him?"

"Other than that he floats her boat? Not much."

Jasper pushed back his chair. "Wish me luck. I'm going in."

"You are? I thought you didn't want—"

"I'm curious about the way he deliberately *didn't* look at her. And for purposes of this maneuver, we're going to be engaged, so Lily's my future sister-in-law. That okay with you?"

Anica's jaw dropped. "I . . . um . . . sure."

He left her looking stunned but not horrified. Good. She wasn't grossed out by the idea of an engagement.

He was making this up as he went along, but if he was being honest, the idea of marriage had been hovering in the back of his mind ever since . . . ever since he'd met her. Maybe her remark that Griffin was cute had prompted him to concoct this particular cover story, but he thought the impulse went much deeper than that.

Walking over to the table he cleared his throat. "Griffin? Griffin Taylor, is that you?"

Griffin glanced up in surprise. "Yeah, I'm Griffin." He peered more closely at Jasper. "But I don't think—"

"Jasper Danes. You probably don't remember me. We worked out at the same gym for a while, but then I left and tried somewhere else."

"Mario's?"

Bingo. Jasper had pegged him for a guy who worked out and the gamble had paid off. "That's the place. Anyway, I just wanted to say hello."

Griffin stood and held out his hand. "Good to see you, Jasper. Want to sit down and have a drink with us?"

"Thanks, but I'm over there with my fiancée, Anica Revere." He gestured toward the corner. On cue Anica waved.

"Then go get her," Griffin said with a grin. "Veterans of Mario's torture chamber have to stick together. I left that hellhole, too. I'm over at Fit and Flexible now, just off Michigan Avenue. You should try it. Anyway, go get Anica. We'll make room."

"Okay, thanks." Jasper couldn't keep the smile off his face as he made his way back to where Anica sat. "Come on. We're invited to hang out with Griffin Taylor and friends."

"How did you do that?"

Jasper started to tell her but then thought better of it. "I refuse to answer on the grounds that it might incriminate me."

"What did you tell him besides the fiancée part?"

"I implied that he and I had worked out at the same gym." It wasn't quite like the girlfriend-breakup story, but once again he'd played around with the truth. He waited for the ax to fall.

"You're a smooth operator, Jasper Danes."

He rubbed the back of his neck, not sure if she'd complimented him or condemned him with that remark.

"Then again, I'm not in a position to point fingers." Anica grimaced. "A really honest person would have immediately told her parents she'd turned her date into a cat." She gazed up at him. "I'm hoping it all gets fixed before they come home, so I never have to tell them."

"I can understand that," he said cautiously, not sure if he was out of the woods or not. "So . . . do you want to go over and meet Griffin Taylor?"

She stood and picked up her coat and purse. "I'd love to. I'm sure finding out about Griffin counts as a good deed, even if you had to fib a little to set it up."

Relief flooded through him. "I have to admit the good-deed thing has me worried. I gave away all that money and only got seven hours for it. What will it take to get the other twelve?"

"I don't know. Maybe you have to do acts of service instead of just giving away money."

"Seems like it would have to be something really big."

"Maybe not." She handed him his coat and linked her arm through his. "Let's go get acquainted with Griffin, shall we?"

An hour and two beers later, Anica excused herself from the table and walked over to the bar. Lily had been giving her questioning looks ever since Anica and Jasper had joined Griffin's table. Anica thought Lily deserved to be put out of her misery.

She leaned against the polished wooden bar. "I have info on your boy."

"How did you get chummy so fast? Does Jasper know him from somewhere?"

"No, but he pretended to so he could find out more about the guy."

Lily stopped squirting seltzer into a glass and stared at Anica. "And he would be doing this . . . why?"

"As a good deed. He's paid for two rounds of drinks so far and has given free investment advice to anyone at the table who wants it. He's living in Good Deed City right now. So, do you want to hear what we found out or not?"

"I'm listening. I have to keep working, though. I've been watching you guys too much and I'm a few drinks behind."

"As you already know, Griffin's a divorce lawyer. He also isn't a big believer in happily ever after, which might be about the job, but not every divorce lawyer feels that way so I'm not sure if that's where the attitude comes from."

"I don't care about a happily ever after. I just want a happily right now in bed with that hottie." Lily speared an olive and a pearl onion with a plastic toothpick before floating them in a martini glass.

"Are you sure? Because when we were little, you were the one who always wanted to dress up like a bride."

Lily was silent for a few seconds. "Maybe I wouldn't mind finding a guy like Griffin to marry." She made a second martini and scooted both stemmed glasses across the bar toward a waiter who carted them off on a tray. "I'll bet if I got him horizontal once, I could change his mind about marriage."

"Don't count on it. He's not your type, Lil. Too anal. Too conservative."

"I could fix that."

"Eventually you'd have to tell him you're a witch."

"By then he'll be so blissed out on good sex that he won't care."

Anica sighed. "Don't say I didn't warn you. Listen, Jasper's doing all these minor good deeds, but I think he needs something major, something that will buy him a chunk of hours, maybe even the entire twelve. Any ideas?"

"There's the soup kitchen. It's open twenty-four/seven."

"Which soup kitchen? I'm sure there are several."

"Probably. This is the one I know about and it's only a couple of blocks from here." Lily set up two more glasses and began mixing some drink Anica didn't recognize. "One of my customers is in charge of it and mentioned it so I'd have a place to send anyone who wanders in and needs a meal but doesn't have money."

"Could Jasper just go there?"

"I don't know. I'm sure there's a training program for volunteers, but maybe if I call they'd let both of you come in tonight as a special case."

"That sounds brilliant."

Lily grabbed her cell phone from under the bar and tucked the phone against her shoulder as she continued to mix drinks.

Anica realized she'd never fully appreciated her sister before. Because Lily had a gift for making friends, she also had a million contacts. This one could save the day.

Lily closed up her phone and stuck it back under the bar. "You're all set. Clyde's expecting you."

"That's fantastic, Lil. Which way is it?"

"Go out the door, turn right and go two blocks. It's on this side of the street. Can't miss it."

"Thank you so much. This is huge." Anica hurried back to the table. "Sorry to break up the party, but Jasper and I need to be going."

"We do?" Jasper glanced up at her. He'd ordered a third beer and seemed to be enjoying himself.

"It's either that or abandon that project you told me about. Doesn't it have to be finished first thing in the morning?"

"Yes. Yes, it does." Jasper immediately pushed back his chair and grabbed both their coats.

Some of the guys at the table teased Jasper for his slave driver of a fiancée.

"No, no, she's focused," Griffin said. "I'd hang on to her if I were you, Danes. She'll help you get where you want to go."

"I plan to hang on to her," Jasper said.

Anica knew he had to say that to keep up the facade of them being engaged, but she liked hearing it all the same.

"So what do you have in mind?" he asked as they put on their coats and prepared to leave the bar.

"Lily set this up just now. There's a soup kitchen within walking distance. We can volunteer to help serve for as long as you want."

"All night?"

"I think so."

Jasper rubbed his chin and gazed at her. "This could be it, the thing I need to take me over the top."

"Yes, it could."

"But that means giving up sex for tonight. I think pleasing you in bed might give me points, too, but probably not as much as serving in a soup kitchen."

She smiled. "Probably not."

"More fun, though."

She couldn't disagree with that, and she had been looking forward to a long, slow session with him, one not as constrained by time.

"It's up to you, Jasper," she said. "You're the one in this situation."

"So are you. You're the one with no magic."

True, but she could live without her magic for another couple of days if it meant more time in bed with Jasper.

"I need to do the soup kitchen. But you don't. Let me get you a cab and I'll come home later."

She didn't miss that he'd called it *home*, but she dared not put too much importance on that. "If you're serving in the soup kitchen, I'm serving in the soup kitchen. We're in this together."

He took her by the shoulders and kissed her. At first she thought it would be a quick kiss of gratitude, but then he pulled her closer and delved deep with his tongue. When he finally lifted his mouth from hers, they were both panting.

He gulped in air. "Just a little something to let you know that I almost didn't choose the soup kitchen. Now, let's go, before I change my mind."

As she walked beside him down the street, she couldn't remember a time she'd been happier. She had no magic and she was off to spend the rest of the night serving in a soup kitchen. But she'd be doing it with Jasper, and that seemed to make all the difference.

Chapter 25

"I never want to see another bowl of chicken noodle soup as long as I live." Jasper pulled Anica close as they rode back to the apartment in a cab they'd had the good fortune to locate at five in the morning. "But if it means I don't turn into a cat at six this morning, it'll be worth it. Thank you for sticking with me through all that."

"You're welcome. We need to thank Lily for getting us that gig."

"I will. Your sister's a good person."

"Yep." Anica snuggled close and closed her eyes. "Wake me up when we get there."

"Okay." He kissed the top of her head. He felt guilty as hell for keeping her up all night, but she'd refused to go home and leave him. He hadn't really wanted her to leave, either, just in case something had gone wrong and he'd transformed in the middle of the soup kitchen.

Fortunately that hadn't happened. Until tonight, Jasper hadn't realized there were so many lost souls in the world. They'd been so grateful for a bowl of soup, a slice of bread and a cup of coffee. Yeah, he'd become weary of dishing up the soup, but those folks needed it so desperately.

Maybe once he'd straightened out his life he'd volunteer there again. A different type of soup would be welcome, though. He really was sick to death of smelling chicken noodle. He'd had to eat some, too, because he and Anica had skipped dinner.

As the cab pulled up in front of the apartment building, Jasper got out his wallet and gave the driver what was left in there. He'd made a cash donation to the soup kitchen but saved enough for cab fare. Now it was time to hit an ATM.

He would do that today. All those hours in the soup kitchen had to have an effect. This was going to work out. He had the weekend to get his act together, and then he could go into work Monday morning and let everyone know the flu bug had been hell but he was at 100 percent now.

Coaxing Anica out of the cab, he kept a supportive arm around her as they went up the steps. He ended up being the one who dug the key out of her purse. She was obviously exhausted, which wasn't surprising.

He'd spent some part of yesterday napping, but she hadn't. Thank God she didn't have to go to work today since the coffee shop was open only on weekdays. They could both sleep in, and maybe late in the morning he'd make love to her.

Sometime in the past few hours he'd changed his terminology from *having sex* to *making love*. You didn't simply have sex with a woman who'd stood beside you in a soup kitchen for almost eight hours because she wanted to help you. You made love to that woman and you were grateful for the opportunity.

Jasper got them both inside the apartment. While he locked up, Anica walked sleepily to the bedroom. She hadn't even bothered to take off her coat.

He followed, shedding his coat as he went. Orion prowled around his feet, meowing, and Jasper ignored him. He tossed the coat on a chair before heading down the hall. Anica lay on the bed, fast asleep, coat and all.

Although it took some doing, Jasper managed to get

her out of everything and under the covers. She was deadweight, but he had no problems lifting her so he could undress her. His muscles felt more toned than ever in his life. Maybe that was a carryover from all the running around and leaping he'd done as a cat.

Stripping off his own clothes, he left them in a heap by the bed. He and Anica both needed sleep. Dear God, was it possible that at last he could fall asleep beside her and expect to wake up in the same condition as when he went to sleep? He prayed for that to happen.

But as he climbed into bed he felt a familiar dizzy sensation.

NO! He glanced at the luminous dial of the bedside clock. Five fifty-five.

Ever since Monday night, Anica had dreaded waking up. First the memory of what she'd done would float to the surface. Next she'd think of what had happened since then. Finally she would worry about what had taken place while she'd been asleep.

This morning, though, she went through the familiar progression and ended up with a feeling of hope. She'd slept until ten, and if Jasper had transformed at six, he would have made her aware of that. After all they'd been through, he'd have let her know.

The spot beside her on the bed was empty, but that didn't mean anything. After hours in the soup kitchen, Jasper must have earned his freedom. He was probably sitting in the living room, drinking coffee and reading the paper he'd gone out to buy.

Or maybe he was afraid to use her fancy coffeemaker. Come to think of it, she didn't smell coffee. Time to throw on a bathrobe and go brew some java.

She didn't remember taking off her clothes before going to bed, so he must have done that for her. He was some kind of guy, all right—more caring than she'd realized.

After watching him talk compassionately with the homeless men and women coming through the food line at the soup kitchen, she had a whole new appreciation for his talents. He'd managed to serve up a portion of self-worth along with the soup, bread and coffee. If he hadn't had her heart before, he would have captured it then.

Anica got out of bed and noticed her clothes were in a pile on the floor. No problem. She was grateful he hadn't let her sleep in them.

But then she rounded the bed and discovered Jasper's clothes on the floor, too. Even though they'd become fairly comfortable with each other, she couldn't picture him wandering around her apartment naked.

Dread settled in her stomach as she walked down the hall and stepped into the living room. Jasper, very much a cat, was curled up in his corner of the sofa. He opened his eyes and they reflected pure misery.

Even Orion seemed to have picked up on the mood. Orion, the ultimate chowhound, hadn't been crying for his breakfast even though it was several hours past his mealtime. Orion was keeping Jasper company by curling up on the opposite end of the sofa.

Anica took a deep breath. "I know this is a setback, Jasper, but we didn't know for sure how many minutes you'd get for that soup kitchen gig. You might transform again at three this afternoon! Then you'd have from three until nine tomorrow. It's too early to evaluate your progress. We need to—"

Her cell phone rang. It was still in her purse, which she'd left on the entrance table before stumbling off to bed. The ring wasn't familiar, so it wasn't Lily calling to check on things.

Thinking of Lily reminded her that they'd scheduled another dance lesson this afternoon. Anica wasn't sure that was a good idea now. She had no idea what time Jasper might change back into a man, and she wanted to be available to help in whatever way she could when that happened.

She pulled out her phone and glanced at the readout. Dorcas. Maybe she'd found out whether there was a hierarchy of good deeds, so Jasper could make the best use of his time to earn more minutes. She flipped the phone open. "Hi, Dorcas. Any info for me?"

"Yes. I'm going to guess that Jasper is now on a six in the evening to a six in the morning schedule. Am I right?"

"He was as of yesterday. We spent a lot of hours in a soup kitchen last night, so I'm hoping to see him transform any time now."

"I'm afraid that won't be happening."

"What?" Anica saw Jasper's head come up, and she turned, lowering her voice as she walked into the kitchen. "What do you mean?"

"Ambrose and I need to come up there again. We'll want to talk with each of you privately to explain what's going on, so we should probably time it to get there after six this evening, after Jasper changes into a man again."

Anica lowered her voice. "I don't understand. I thought if he kept doing good deeds, or acts of kindness, that he would keep gaining minutes. He put in eight hours of good deeds at that soup kitchen. Zeus's balls, Dorcas. What's going on?"

"What's going on is that you invoked an ancient, complicated spell. The information we uncovered at first turns out to be only the tip of the iceberg. This is all quite fascinating, actually."

"Not to me!" Anica heard the anger in her voice and worked to control it. This wasn't Dorcas's fault, and she didn't deserve to be yelled at. "I'm sorry, Dorcas. I'm just upset. Are you saying Jasper put in all that time in the soup kitchen for nothing?"

"Of course not. Everyone in the soup kitchen benefited from having both of you there last night. Jasper has a larger understanding of poverty, and I wouldn't be surprised if he volunteers at that soup kitchen again. It's all good, Anica."

"Can I impress upon you how much I *loathe* that happy little phrase right now?" Anica could feel herself losing it again. "This man has worked his butt off trying to break the spell I cast on him, and now you're telling me that what he did isn't good enough."

"That's because it's not." Dorcas's voice remained calm, as if she had no intention of responding to Anica's fury.

Once again Anica felt horrible for giving vent to it. "Forgive me. I have no right to take my frustration out on you, especially when you're kind enough to drive up here to help us."

"We'll be at your apartment as soon after six as we can get there. Ambrose will take Jasper out for a walk, so you and I can talk in your apartment."

Anica leaned her forehead against the smooth door of the refrigerator. "What am I supposed to tell Jasper? I'm sure he's completely demoralized already, and this news isn't going to help at all."

"Tell him what I've told you, that the spell is far more complex than any of us realized, and that we're coming up to offer whatever counsel we can. Tell him there will be a way out."

"What is it?"

"Anica, I can't tell you over the phone. This is powerful stuff, and we have to handle it carefully so that you two don't get stuck in the roles you have now."

"You're scaring me, Dorcas."

"Good. A little healthy fear wouldn't be a bad thing right now. Oh, and don't involve Lily in this. To make sure we have a chance of reversing the spell, the interaction should involve only the four of us."

"I understand. Thank you, again. I . . . well, just thank you."

"You're welcome. See you in a few hours." Dorcas broke the connection.

Anica stared at the phone for what seemed like a really long time. She owed it to Jasper to go in there and give him the latest news, but she dreaded doing that. He'd been so hopeful last night and his attitude had been nothing but positive as they'd struggled through the last hour of soup kitchen duty.

How many times could a person get his hopes up, only to have them dashed by a new set of rules? In his shoes, Anica would be devastated. He'd gone into debt and worked hard for a charitable cause. What more could be asked of him? Was he supposed to donate a kidney?

She thought back to his crime, misleading his girlfriends about the cause of his recent breakup. What a trivial thing that seemed now compared to the threat of spending his days as a cat and his nights as a man . . . forever.

At this point she'd take his punishment upon herself if she could, but she was pretty sure there was no way she could assume his cat shape for twelve hours a day. Dorcas had said there was a way out. She'd cling to that. But for now she had no choice but to go in there and ruin what was left of Jasper's day.

Carrying her cell phone so she wouldn't forget to call Lily, she sat next to Jasper on the sofa and scratched behind his ears. She figured his answering purr was a reflex, something he couldn't control when she was petting him. She doubted he really *wanted* to purr, given his circumstances.

"That was Dorcas," she said. "I have good news and bad news. The good news is that there is a way for you to regain the other twelve hours. The bad news is that it's more complicated than doing good deeds. In spite of the soup kitchen work, you won't change again until six."

Jasper let out a cat sigh.

"I know. I suppose that's what happens when a spell

isn't used for two hundred years. No one's up on how it works, or how it can be broken. When I make a mess, I make a big one."

She rubbed the top of Jasper's head and he moved to take better advantage of the caress. "Dorcas and Ambrose will be here a little after six. That means you have seven hours and . . ." She glanced at the time on her cell phone. "And forty-two minutes left to be a cat. How do you want to spend that time?"

Jasper settled down on the sofa and closed his eyes.

"Got it." Anica stood. "I'll leave you to do that."

Walking back to her bedroom she speed-dialed Lily, who picked up on the second ring.

"I almost called you," Lily said. "So? Is Jasper permanently changed back into a hunk?"

"No. Our eight hours at the soup kitchen were a wasted effort. According to Dorcas, something more is needed to get beyond twelve hours, but she wouldn't tell me what over the phone. They're driving back up tonight so they can interact with Jasper when he's . . . did you call him a *hunk*?"

"Sure did. You latched on to a hottie this time."

Anica narrowed her eyes. "Are you implying my other guys weren't hot?"

"Not like this one. I think he really likes you, too. I was watching him watch you. Major lust going on there, big sis."

A wave of pleasure washed over her. "I really like him, too. I feel so bad for him that he did all that work and got nothing for it."

"I don't get that. Dorcas and Ambrose told you that would work, so why didn't it?"

"I don't know. I guess new info turned up that explains more fully how the spell is broken. Tonight should do the trick, though. Dorcas seemed confident they had the answer now."

"Good." Lily paused. "That's really good. Um, what

would you think if I went back to school and became a paralegal?"

"That you'd lost your mind. That's a very technical field and you've never liked studying, so I don't know why you'd—" Then Anica understood. "You want to impress Griffin?"

"I realize the bartender image probably doesn't work for him, but I could be going to school in my spare time, which would make me look more ambitious. Besides, you're always saying I should latch on to something and stick with it. This would be like ... like a real career."

Anica groaned. "I'd love you to stick with something, but it should be something you like. You'd hate being a paralegal. And to do it just to get Griffin's attention—I think that's a mistake."

"I really like him, Anica. And you're going to think I'm making this up, but I think he's fascinated with me, too. Every once in a while I catch him looking at me as if he wants to do me. Then the minute I look right at him, he looks away."

"Most men want to do you, Lily. You're gorgeous. But wouldn't it be great to find a guy who wants to hang out with you when you're both wearing clothes?"

"Griffin would, once he gets to know me. I just have this gut feeling it would work, but he won't give me a chance."

"Then he's the wrong guy." Anica wished Lily would drop this obsession, but so far she seemed determined to create something with Griffin. And Lily was a grown woman who would have to work this out for herself. Anica couldn't protect her from heartbreak, much as she'd like to.

"We'll see. Listen, I can probably get away from work tonight if you need any help when Dorcas and Ambrose show up."

"Thanks, Lil." Anica was touched that she'd offer. "But Dorcas said it has to be just the four of us. And

I . . . I need to put off that dance lesson. I want to have a clear head when they arrive."

"We don't *have* to drink margaritas, you know."

Anica laughed. "I do. Hey, we'll have another lesson, I promise. You got me hooked. I just need to get through this weekend."

"Okay. So what if I started writing a thriller?"

Anica thought she could get whiplash trying to follow Lily's train of thought. "Why?"

"Lots of lawyers write thrillers and put all this legal stuff in. I could start writing one, which would make me look more interesting and intellectual, and . . . bonus! I'd have to interview Griffin for my research."

"Lily, you hate to write."

"I know." She sighed mightily. "Hera's hickeys, what can I do that will convince him I'm a good prospect?"

"I don't know."

"I'll figure something out. Call me when Dorcas and Ambrose leave, okay? I'll have my cell handy at work tonight."

"Keep your fingers crossed that this works out. If so, we'll come down and have a drink to celebrate."

"Hold that thought. I could fix you each a martini that'll pickle your tonsils."

"I hope that's how it turns out." Did she ever. Walking into the Bubbling Cauldron with Jasper, knowing he wouldn't be changing into a cat again, would be like every birthday present she'd every received rolled into one. Finally she could anticipate the joy of spending time with Jasper, both in and out of bed. At last they'd have a real shot at happiness.

Ambrose slipped a CD into the car's sound system and Frankie Avalon began to croon "Venus."

Dorcas reached over and punched the EJECT button.

"Hey! We need Frankie tonight. This is like a super-duper matchmaking assignment. You know how Frankie inspires me."

"And you know how Frankie makes me break out in hives. You wouldn't want me to go crazy and leap out of this car while you're driving sixty miles an hour, would you?"

He glanced at her. "You wouldn't do that, and you know it."

"It sounded exciting, though, didn't it?"

"I don't see why you get so upset about Frankie." Ambrose looked at her with a sad puppy-dog expression.

"Oh, let me think. Maybe because you've played that blasted CD a thousand times? Could that be it?"

"If I've played it a thousand times, why not once more? I'll keep it low."

Dorcas heaved a martyred sigh. "If you must."

"I must." Ambrose reinserted the CD and as the bouncy little tune began, he tapped out the rhythm on the steering wheel.

Dorcas did her best to shut out the music.

"How much does Anica know about lifting the spell?" Ambrose asked.

"Nothing."

"You didn't tell her about the contracts she and Jasper would have to sign, so she could get used to the idea?"

"That's not something you say over the phone, Ambrose. You don't get used to something like that. She would have freaked out."

"You're probably right. I sure hope this works."

"So do I. I looked through every resource, and even though this is the recommended cure, I couldn't find a single instance where it was employed successfully. But it's all we have."

Chapter 26

At about five thirty, Jasper started watching the clock. He wasn't going to get his hopes up this time the way he had last night, but at least he'd finally meet Dorcas and Ambrose, the witch and wizard who held all the cards. They weren't infallible, though, which meant he might get transformed tonight and he might not. At this point it was a total crapshoot.

A quick stroll into the bedroom reassured him that Anica had laid out his clothes. His shirt no longer reeked of chicken noodle soup, so she must have washed it. Earlier in the afternoon he'd smelled heated fabric, so she must have pressed both his shirt and slacks, since they had no time for dry cleaning. He'd been so tired he hadn't hung anything up, and then he'd turned into a cat who couldn't hang anything up.

Anica bustled around the apartment dusting and fluffing pillows and generally looking nervous as a . . . well, as a cat. That made two of them. He'd given up on his nap and was pacing, since there wasn't much in the way of activity for him.

Anica had lit a few more of her beeswax candles, and the scent reminded him of the great sex he'd had with her in her candlelit bedroom. A bottle of red wine and four glasses sat on the kitchen counter. Jasper assumed that was in preparation for toasting a successful outcome. He hoped they'd use those glasses.

At five fifty-five, Jasper went into the bedroom. Anica could have followed him but she didn't. She'd obviously picked up on his reluctance to be observed during his change. He could only imagine how traumatic that would be. Once implanted, certain scenes could never be erased from a person's mind.

Lying on the bed he waited for the familiar dizziness to come over him. Maybe this would be the last time. He wouldn't want to give up the past five days. He'd learned a lot about himself and the world around him. And he'd come to love Anica with a fierceness that scared him a little.

But he couldn't be what she needed until he became a man twenty-four/seven. As the dizziness began he said a little prayer that the spell would be lifted tonight.

At six, Anica felt a pulse of energy move through the apartment. She must be attuned to Jasper's change because she could almost feel it in her own body. When she heard him rustling around in the bedroom, she knew he was getting dressed.

He appeared wearing the same shirt and slacks he'd worn for a week. It had become something of a uniform.

"Once this is over, you'll probably burn that outfit," she said.

He glanced down at his clothes. "Or keep it forever as a reminder."

"You'll want to be reminded?"

"Of course." He walked toward her and laid his hands gently on her shoulders. "It's been the most memorable week of my life."

She stepped closer and wound her arms around his neck. "I'll bet. *Memorable* doesn't always mean 'good.'"

"In this case it does." He looked into her eyes. "Assuming I don't have to stay half cat, half man forever, I wouldn't trade this week with you for anything."

"I wouldn't trade it, either, although I have to admit I'll be glad to get my magic back. I never realized how much I depend on it. It's more a part of me than I thought."

"I'm sure." He massaged her shoulders. "I can hardly wait for you to get those powers back. It'll be fun to watch."

"Really? You're not freaked about it?"

"How could I be freaked? It's part of you. I cherish everything about you, Anica."

This is the moment. She recognized the emotion in his golden eyes and knew it was mirroring hers. She drew a shaky breath. "Jasper, there's something I want to tell you before Dorcas and Ambrose arrive."

"Hm." His smile was soft. "Might be the same thing I want to tell you."

"Wouldn't that be a coincidence?"

"Indeed."

"Jasper, I—"

The street door buzzer rang. Orion leaped from the sofa and ran off toward the bedroom.

"They're here." Anica gazed at Jasper, wondering if she should put off her declaration, after all. A moment like this shouldn't be rushed.

And yet . . . she'd screwed up the moment before. She decided that he needed to hear it now. "I'm going to say it anyway. I love you, Jasper."

He sighed with pleasure. "And I love you, Anica. I wanted to tell you before, but—"

The buzzer rang again.

"I haven't made it easy. I was afraid this situation was blurring our thinking."

"If anything, it's clarified my thinking."

The buzzer rang a third time.

Anica smiled. "We'd better let them in."

"Yeah."

Anica released the downstairs lock and stepped into the hall to greet the Lowells. As she ushered them into her apartment and made the introductions, she was gratified at the impression Dorcas and Ambrose seemed to be making on Jasper.

And no wonder. As usual, they looked like an ad for successful seniors—Dorcas in her purple cape similar in style to Anica's, and Ambrose in a gray wool coat with a forest green scarf tucked inside the collar. Dorcas had a large black purse over one shoulder and Ambrose carried a small leather briefcase.

Dorcas glanced at Anica and Jasper. "Everything seems to be going well here."

"Extremely well." Anica gave Jasper a quick smile. "Let me take your coats."

"You can have mine." Dorcas set down her purse and began taking off her cape. "But Ambrose will be leaving with Jasper, won't you, sweetheart?"

"Exactly." Ambrose helped Dorcas with her cape. "I noticed a restaurant called La Bohème about three blocks away. I thought I'd buy you a beer, Jasper."

"Hey, it'll be on me, Ambrose. It's the least I can do."

Anica gave him a questioning look. Ambrose had picked out the very restaurant where all of the madness had begun. She wondered if going back there might be painful for Jasper.

"I can give you a key to Wicked Brew," she said. "It's three blocks in the other direction, so it's the same distance, and you'd have complete privacy."

"But then I can't buy Ambrose a beer," Jasper said. "The restaurant's fine with me." He looked strong, resolute, as if he could handle whatever happened.

She understood the feeling. Because he loved her, she could face most anything, too. "All right, then I guess we should let you both be on your way." The minute she said it, she had the urge to grab his hand and beg him not to go.

But that was silly. Jasper would have his talk with Ambrose, and then they'd return.

On his way to the coat closet, Jasper offered to take Dorcas's cape. Then he hung it up and pulled his tweed coat off the hanger.

It was going according to plan, and yet having him leave seemed wrong all of a sudden. "Do you have your BlackBerry in your pocket?"

"Yep." He shrugged into the coat and grinned at her. "Gonna call me? Come to think of it, we could bring food back. Think about what you'd like and we can get it to go."

"That's not a bad idea." But she still didn't want him to leave. Also, she'd never asked why they had to be separated to conduct these discussions. That seemed like an important point.

"How about if we all talk together right here? If we get hungry we could order pizza. I don't see the point in you two leaving. Jasper and I don't have secrets from each other."

"That's wonderful," Dorcas said. "But the reversal of the spell can only take place if you are interviewed without being influenced by the other person."

"So you and I can go in the kitchen and close the door, and Ambrose and Jasper can have the living room. How's that?" The thought of Jasper leaving with Ambrose became more frightening with every passing second.

Dorcas shook her head. "Not far enough away. You'd still sense each other's energy field."

"Then . . . then you and I can go to the end of the hall. It won't take long, right? We can—"

"Anica, it's okay." Jasper finished buttoning his coat and walked over to her.

"I just don't see why we have to be separated." She sounded like a whiny little kid and she couldn't seem to help it.

"If Dorcas says we have to be, then that's how we'll play it. Until now you've shouldered complete responsibility for my welfare, so it's probably hard to let that go."

She searched his eyes, which were so full of love and compassion. "You could be right."

"I am." He dropped a quick kiss on her lips. "Don't worry. This won't take long, and then we can eat some good food and drink that wine you have sitting in the kitchen."

"Okay." She managed to smile, but as he went out the door with Ambrose, she couldn't control the churning in her tummy. No doubt he'd pegged the cause, though. She wasn't used to him going anywhere without her. She'd have to get over that, and now was as good a time as any to begin.

She gestured toward the sofa. "Let's get started."

"All right." Dorcas picked up her purse and carried it over to the sofa.

"Can I get you anything? We could open the wine. I have more. Or I could make coffee or tea, or I also have some—"

"I don't need anything, thanks." She glanced up at Anica and smiled. "Come over and sit down. I have something to explain." She pulled a sheaf of papers out of her purse.

Anica's feeling of dread wouldn't go away. "Something you didn't want to tell me on the phone."

"Right."

Heart pounding, back stiff, Anica perched on the sofa.

"I know you're nervous, and I wish I could tell you not to be, but the fact is that spell has serious consequences. Because I'm a member of the Wizard Council, I have the authority to offer you this contract, which will address those consequences. Ambrose and I have researched this spell using every known resource through magical channels and the Internet. A contract is definitely necessary."

Anica told herself to keep breathing. "But you said Jasper could regain his human form."

"He can, but as the witch who imposed that spell, you must agree to give up something in order for him to return to normal."

Anica's heart felt as if it would hammer its way right out of her chest. "What?"

"Your magic."

She closed her eyes. She'd known it would come to this. Somehow she'd always known. "Forever?"

"Yes, forever."

The sentence was harsh, very harsh, but for Jasper's sake, she'd bear it. She realized that instantly. She would be strong, resilient. "At least I'll have Lily around. I can watch her do magic and get a vicarious thrill."

"That's the addendum, I'm afraid."

"What addendum?" Anica tried not to panic.

Dorcas flipped through the contract. "Here it is. Section four, paragraph six. *Aforementioned witch, having voluntarily given up all use of magic in exchange for the lifting of Transformation Spell Four Hundred Seventy-seven, will hereafter have a negative effect on any magic done in her presence.*"

"A negative effect? What does that mean?"

"You'll give off antimagic vibrations that will interfere with attempted spells. You'll cancel out any and all magic."

"That seems so unfair!"

"It's one of the terms."

Anica swallowed. She wouldn't be able to ask for magical favors, and she thought she could live with that. But could she live with being a pariah, unwanted at any magical gathering?

"I'm sorry, Anica. I wish there could be another way,

but I've researched the spell six ways to Sunday, and this is all we have."

"Right." Anica struggled to accept what must be if Jasper was to be permanently transformed.

"There's one last provision, one that might be even harder on you than the other two."

"I can't imagine what would be harder than being cut off from all magic."

"This is a result of that. Your antimagic vibrations mean that you have to stay completely away from Jasper. Any contact will result in him reverting to his cat form."

"*No!*"

"Those are the conditions."

"I can't accept that! I can't!"

Dorcas shrugged. "Then everything stays the way it is now."

Anica closed her eyes as the bad news hit like a fist to her diaphragm. She was not only losing her magic, she was losing Jasper. Dear Zeus, how this hurt. She hadn't known there was this much psychic pain in the world.

After what seemed like a long, long time, she opened her eyes and took a shaky breath. There was no debate, really. She felt the grief massing an army on the borders of her mind. She'd hold it off for now, so that she could do what needed to be done.

She cleared the emotion clogging her throat and faced Dorcas. "Any contact? Including phone and e-mail?"

Dorcas frowned. "I can't imagine e-mail would matter, but I wouldn't take a chance, if I were you. It says *any contact,* which covers a lot of territory. I might be able to get more clarification, but—"

"Never mind." A phone call or an e-mail would only increase the pain. "I agree to the terms."

Dorcas put her hand over Anica's, which was clenched in her lap. "You're absolutely sure?"

"Of course I'm sure." She met Dorcas's gaze. "I love Jasper. I would do anything to reverse that spell. I would . . ." She swallowed. "I would give my life."

Dorcas regarded her with sympathy. "Giving up your magic and the man you love can't be easy for you."

"This isn't about me. It's about Jasper and what he needs so he can get back to normal."

"And that's your final decision?"

"Yes. I . . . assume Ambrose will make sure Jasper doesn't come back to the apartment?"

"Of course." Dorcas pulled a purple folder out of her purse. "I'll need you to sign this contract, which waives all your rights to practice magic of any kind, and stipulates that you will take every precaution to stay away from the recipient of your spell, Jasper Steven Danes."

"Steven," Anica said softly. "I didn't even know his middle name."

"We had to look it up."

Anica stood, needing to move. "I'll get a pen."

"No, I have a pen." Dorcas dug around in the bottom of her purse. "I know I put it in here."

"Let me get mine."

"No, you need to use this one. Remember, this was a really old spell. Aha. Here it is." She pulled a black feather from her purse.

"A quill? Did you bring ink?"

"The quill produces its own ink, and it's a onetime-use instrument. After you sign and date the contract the quill turns to dust. I have a supplier in Sedona, and fortunately I just got a new shipment."

Anica held out her hand for the pen. Sure enough, after she'd signed and dated the contract, the quill turned to dust that drifted down to the carpet. Then, right after that, the contract shriveled and became dust, as well.

That was fine with Anica. Who would want to have such a horrible document hanging around? "How soon does it take effect?"

"Immediately," Dorcas said. "That pen-to-dust and contract-shriveling magic is the last that will ever work in your presence."

Anica let out a breath. Magic had always been there as a helper, a special friend and a secret ability that made her feel confident and alive. Now it was gone, banished from her life. She wouldn't even have the joy of watching others do it.

Painful as that prospect was, she could think about it, though, and even imagine how she'd deal with the loss. Jasper was another matter. She didn't dare think about him, and she had no idea how she'd face losing him.

No, that was wrong. She knew exactly how she'd deal with losing Jasper forever. She'd concentrate on an image of him happy and healthy, enjoying his human form for the rest of his life. She'd picture the gratitude he'd feel and how precious his days would be for him now that he could live them fully as a man.

She turned to Dorcas. "How about that glass of wine?"

"By all means. I would like to raise a glass and toast you. Not everyone would have done what you have."

"Not everyone's lucky enough to love a man like Jasper Steven Danes."

Walking back into the restaurant felt weird as hell, but Jasper thought it was fitting that the whole thing would end here. He suggested to Ambrose that they sit in the bar at a small two-person booth.

"You seem familiar with this place," Ambrose said as he took off his coat and sat down.

"This is where I brought Anica on our date Monday night, when she ran into my ex-girlfriend, Sheila. After that, the date was completely FUBAR." Thinking of that, Jasper took a quick inventory of the restaurant. He hadn't really expected to see Sheila, but he was relieved to know that she wasn't here tonight.

"FUBAR?" Ambrose frowned.

"Fucked Up Beyond All Recognition."

"Oh. I like that. FUBAR. I've had a few of those situations myself."

"Me, I'm ready for life to get a little less FUBAR." Jasper signaled a waitress, who came, took their order and left quickly.

"I'm hoping you can help me get my life back on track," Jasper continued. "And poor Anica. I know she really misses her magic, and I really miss . . ." He paused to think, and soon he began to chuckle.

"What's so funny?"

"You know what, Ambrose? Other than wanting to be a guy twenty-four/seven, I don't miss much about my former life. I'm wondering if I want to continue chasing market trends for the rest of my days. I'm thinking I might get into fund-raising. There's a lot that needs fixing in the world, and maybe I can pry people away from their money so we can get some of those things fixed."

"It's a worthy goal."

"So, in order to lift this spell, what's my task? Reverse the direction of the Nile? Repair the hole in the ozone layer? Bring about world peace?"

Ambrose smiled. "A sense of humor is good in situations like this." Ambrose reached into his small briefcase and pulled out an official-looking contract. "Why don't you look this over while we wait for our drinks? There's a place for your signature on the sixth page."

Jasper didn't get past the first paragraph. "I can't sign this."

"Why not?"

"You know perfectly well why not. It bans Anica from ever using magic again. It even says she'll have a negative effect on the magic of others."

Ambrose shrugged. "That doesn't seem like such a horrible thing compared to what you'll gain from this document. Sometimes the end justifies the means."

The old cliché ran through Jasper's brain as if he'd grabbed hold of a live electrical wire. That had been his justification for lying to a potential girlfriend. Would the man he'd been a week ago have taken this deal? He hoped to hell not, but he couldn't say that for sure.

"Sorry, Ambrose. I'm not signing this. It would be like sucking the lifeblood out of that woman." He tossed the paper back to Ambrose. "Show me something that allows Anica to get her magic back and I'll sign that."

The waitress brought their beers and a bowl of peanuts. Jasper handed her his credit card because he had no cash. He'd been hoping to remedy that today. Now he was wondering if he needed to stop by an ATM on the way back to the apartment, because at this rate, no telling what tomorrow would bring.

Ambrose waited until the waitress had left. "Here's the situation. Either Anica gets her magic back or you get to be a man again. Your fate became intertwined with hers the minute she placed that spell on you."

A vise tightened around Jasper's chest. "That can't be right. Good deeds were supposed to take care of everything, and once I became a man again, she'd get her magic back."

"Dorcas and I thought so, too. But then we started digging deeper, found a more detailed explanation of the ramifications of this spell, and apparently the good deeds can only get you twelve hours. The other twelve require that she sacrifice her magic."

Jasper stood and grabbed his coat. "Goddammit, is that what Dorcas is telling her? Because I know what she'll do. She'll give it up to save me. I can't have it, Ambrose. I can't let her do that." He started to leave.

"Wait." Ambrose grabbed his arm.

Jasper wondered if there was a penalty for brushing off a wizard. "I don't have time to wait."

"You could sign this instead." Ambrose brought out a different contract.

Slowly, Jasper resumed his seat. "Give me the Cliffs-Notes version. I need to get back to that apartment and make sure she doesn't sign away her magic."

"This says that you agree to live your life as a man for twelve hours and a cat for the other twelve. If you agree to that, it signifies that you've accepted your new role, embraced it, even, and you bear her no ill will. She'll get her magic back."

"Good God." Jasper buried his face in his hands. He didn't really have to think about this. He knew what he was going to do. He just had to give himself a moment to adjust. *Adjust. Was that even possible?* Voices were screaming in his head, reminding him of all he was giving up.

Maybe if he took the first deal Ambrose had offered, he could make it up to her for losing her magic. He'd be fully functioning again. They could have a life together with all the good stuff—kids, house, pets.

And every damn day he'd know that he'd bought all that at her expense, robbed her of her birthright. She would never have pulled out her wand if he hadn't been acting like a shit. He'd goaded her into putting the spell on him, and she shouldn't have to pay for that. He would.

And oh, how he would pay. He'd struggle with the half-cat, half-man thing, but he could do it. That wasn't the toughest part of this deal. What made him ache was knowing that he would give up Anica. If he couldn't be a fully functioning partner, then he wouldn't allow himself to be with her, simple as that. He would spend the rest of his life grieving that loss.

It was settled, then. He would sign the second contract, and Anica would have her magic back. He looked at Ambrose. "Got a pen?"

"Yes." Ambrose pulled a black quill out of the briefcase. "Use this."

Jasper took it. "But it's a feather."

"It'll write."

"Whatever." Jasper scribbled his name with the pointed end of the feather, and ink flowed for some strange reason.

"Date it."

He did, and at that moment the feather disintegrated in his hand, turning to a dusty pile on the table. Then the contract shriveled and went away, too. Jasper didn't get it but didn't really care that he didn't get it. The waitress returned with his credit slip and card. He signed it, pocketed the card and stood. "Get the hell back to that apartment, Ambrose. Make sure Anica doesn't sign anything giving up her magic."

"I'll hurry." Ambrose stood, too.

Jasper hesitated. He longed to give Ambrose a message to take back to Anica, something to let her know how much he loved her. But all that could do was make things worse for both of them. The grief he'd been keeping at bay began clawing at him, threatening to tear him apart.

His throat tightened. "See you around, Ambrose." He left the restaurant while he still had control of his emotions. Outside he scrubbed a hand over his face and it came away wet. Hell. He'd planned to hail a cab, but instead he started walking. His condo was about five miles away, and he was going to need every damn one of them.

Chapter 27

When the doorbell rang, Anica put down her wineglass and leaped up from the sofa.

Dorcas stood and put out a restraining arm. "You'd better let me get it, in case, for some reason . . ."

She didn't have to finish the sentence. Anica was taking no chances that Jasper had insisted on coming back to the apartment. "I'll go in the kitchen. Call me when the coast is clear."

She stood with both hands braced on the counter, breathing hard as she listened to the sound of the door being opened. What *was* she supposed to do if Jasper came looking for her? She would work to stay away from him, but she couldn't control his actions.

"You can come out," Dorcas called. "Ambrose is alone."

Oh, she'd come out all right. She'd come out and get some answers. She barreled back into the living room. "What if he comes to the apartment? Okay, I could refuse to open the door to him, but what if he comes to Wicked Brew? Anyone's allowed to walk in there. I might not notice until it was too late."

Ambrose glanced at Dorcas. "So she signed it."

"Yes."

"So did Jasper."

Anica was ready to scream. "Sign what? I feel as if I'm expected to play a game without seeing the rule book. What sort of contract did Jasper sign?"

Dorcas walked over and laid a hand on her arm. "We can't tell you. But I can tell you that you don't have to worry about coming into contact with Jasper."

"Oh." Anica pressed her fingers against her throbbing temples and paced the room. "Okay, I can figure it out. He signed something promising not to see me, right?" She stopped pacing and looked at them.

Dorcas and Ambrose silently returned her gaze.

"Yeah, I know. You can't say." She returned to her pacing. "But that makes sense. He probably knows that seeing me would turn him back into a cat. If that was in his contract, no way is he coming near me. Which is good. That's exactly what I'd want him to do." She massaged her temples.

Dorcas took a step toward her. "Can we get you anything? If you'd like to go out to dinner, we've found a cute little Italian—"

"That's nice of you, but I'm not really in the mood. You have a car, though, right?"

"Yes," Ambrose said. "We found a parking garage a couple of blocks from here."

"On your way to dinner would you mind dropping me off at the Bubbling Cauldron?"

"We'd be happy to," Dorcas said. "Family can be a big help at times like these."

Anica nodded. "Family and a few wicked martinis."

Six hours later Anica was chock-full of vodka martinis and onion rings. She'd spent her entire time sitting on a stool at the bar, and her fanny would probably be sore in the morning, but at the moment she was feeling no pain anywhere. Even her heart, the most battered part of her body, didn't hurt anymore.

"Come on, sis." Lily helped her into her coat. "We'll share a taxi."

"But you live in the other direction." She peered at Lily, who was slightly out of focus. "Did you move?"

"No, I didn't. But I'm going to make sure you get into your apartment before I go home."

"It'll cost you twice as much."

"Don't care." Lily hustled them out the door and scanned the cabless street. "Wouldn't you know it? Guess I'll have to get us a cab the old-fashioned way." She pulled her wand out of her backpack.

"Won't work, Lil."

"Oh, I don't believe that crap. Just because you've lost your magic doesn't mean you're like some magical Typhoid Mary when it comes to the rest of us. That's crazy."

Ten minutes later, Lily sighed and tucked her wand back in her purse. "I tell you, Anica, that was one bad-ass spell you invoked. Let's walk down to the corner. We'll get a cab easier that way."

Lily managed to get a cab by putting two fingers in her mouth and producing a whistle that nearly split Anica's skull down the middle. She would have a doozy of a hangover in the morning and no magical way of curing it. However, in the morning Jasper would not turn into a cat. That was all that mattered.

Lily behaved like a mother hen as she hustled Anica into the cab. Then she insisted on making the cab wait, meter running, while she escorted Anica to her door. She helped Anica get the door unlocked, too, because Anica's coordination wasn't the greatest.

"Listen, I don't have to work tomorrow night," Lily said. "Call me. We'll do something."

"Thanks, Lil." Anica hugged her. "You mix a mean martini."

"Hey, tomorrow we could do margaritas and salsa!" She produced a shimmy to illustrate her suggestion.

"Sure, why not? I'll call you." With a wave and a lop-sided smile, she closed and locked her door. A cat me-owed, and she glanced down as Orion rubbed against her leg in greeting. "Just you and me, kid." She crouched down and braced one hand on the floor so she wouldn't topple over. Way too many martinis.

She scratched behind Orion's ears. Someday soon she'd look into getting a second cat so Orion could have another playmate. But she'd give it some time. And the cat would not be black.

Jasper spent the night stocking in supplies and making lists. He got cash from the ATM and put gas in his car. Theoretically, if he kept himself busy with details, he wouldn't have to look at the big picture, which tended to make his vision blur. Tonight he was all about trees, not the forest.

At least on Sunday night he'd be able to wear dif-ferent clothes. When he'd thought he had a future with Anica, he'd been fond of the clothes. He wasn't so fond of them now.

At five in the morning he stripped them off and tossed everything but the shoes in the garbage. He couldn't quite bring himself to throw away a pair of Cole Haan loafers that he'd bought last week. If they turned out to be as full of memories as the clothes, then he might, but for now he'd keep them around.

Showering in his own bathroom felt good. He hoped he'd be able to make enough money to keep the condo, but if not he'd adjust. Whenever he got a panicked feeling about his future, he reminded him-self that Anica was okay. She could look forward to the life she'd had before meeting him. He hadn't ru-ined everything for her.

And he would love her for the rest of his life. But he didn't want to think about that right now. He was concen-trating on trees, not the forest. He took inventory of his soap and shampoo. With only twelve hours to work and shop, he'd have to become extremely well-organized.

He wouldn't need to worry about shaving ever again, though. Every night at six he'd transform clean-shaven, and that would take him through until he transformed again at six in the morning. He knew there had to be some sort of bonus to this program, and apparently he'd found it.

At five fifty-five he sprawled naked on his bed and waited. Usually by now he could sense the change coming. Maybe he was just getting used to it, because he didn't feel any different.

At five fifty-eight he turned on his side and stared at the digital clock radio on his nightstand. By now he should be feeling the dizziness that preceded the change. Instead he felt nothing besides a slight drowsiness from being up all night.

He stared at the clock as it switched to five fifty-nine. Something wasn't right. Maybe his clock was off. Leaving the bed, he searched out his BlackBerry, which he'd left on his desk in the den. The BlackBerry read exactly six o'clock.

Putting it down, Jasper went to stand in front of the bathroom mirror. His bearded morning face gazed back at him. He wasn't changing! Could it be? No more reverting to a cat? The rush of pure joy was followed instantly by gut-twisting anxiety. Oh, God. Had Anica's contract gone into effect and somehow canceled his? Had she given up her magic for him?

Or did she give up even more? He had a sudden, awful image of Anica trading places with him. What if her contract wasn't about losing her magic? What if she'd agreed to assume his twelve hours of being a cat?

He had to go over there. Trying to control the shakes that had come on at the idea of Anica turning into a cat, he pulled clothes out of a drawer. In record time he was dressed in a pair of gray sweats and an old T-shirt, along with his running shoes.

Then he grabbed a Bulls jacket out of the closet and crammed a Cubs baseball cap over his uncombed hair. At the last minute he strapped on his watch. If something had gone wacko with the spell and he changed at a different hour, he'd want to know when that was.

He hoped to hell that wouldn't happen. He could be left in a very dicey position if it did. But he'd risk it. He had to get over to Anica's and find out what had happened to her at six this morning.

No doubt looking like a vagrant, he left his condo. A bus that would take him to her street sat at the bus stop a block away. He had to run, but he made it.

The bus was almost empty. Only three other passengers shared the ride with him, but he remained standing and held on to the overhead rail, as if sitting would slow the bus. It seemed to take freaking forever, anyway. He kept leaning down and looking out the window, because it had been days since he'd seen the city at this hour of the morning.

Come to think of it, he'd almost never seen the streets of the city at this hour on a Sunday morning. That was his day to sleep in, read the Sunday *Trib,* meander down to the corner deli for some Danish and coffee, although the coffee there had lost its appeal once he'd tasted Anica's coffee at Wicked Brew.

All those activities seemed too precious and innocent now. He'd been such an arrogant smart-ass, thinking it was just fine for him to manipulate a woman's feelings. When Anica had called him on it, he'd tried to make light of it. He'd even—and this really made him wince—tried to minimize her anger by thinking it could be solved with a kiss.

As the bus neared the stop closest to her building, he pulled the cord to signal the driver and waited impatiently for the bus to slow and the back door to open. Then he leaped down and jogged along the sidewalk. He wanted to run, but that might draw too much attention, especially before dawn. Jogging was normal in the city. Flat-out running usually meant you'd committed a crime.

No lights gleamed in any of the apartment windows. Everyone was probably sound asleep at this hour on a Sunday morning. Too bad. He had to find out for himself what was going on.

Taking the steps at a jog, he leaned on the buzzer. As he waited for her to answer, he ran a hand over his jaw. Man, he needed a shave. What a concept, considering that he hadn't picked up a razor since Monday night.

When she didn't answer his anxiety level hit the roof. He pressed the buzzer again, longer this time, and tried not to imagine a delicate female cat sitting up in her apartment, a cat who couldn't answer the bell.

When she still didn't open the street door or speak into the intercom, he started punching the buzzer in a staccato rhythm. If she didn't come soon, he was calling the police. He'd make up some story that would justify breaking in.

Then he heard her sleepy voice on the intercom and he sagged in delirious relief. She was human.

"Anica, I need to talk to you."

She gasped. "Go away, Jasper! Please, just go away!"

"Anica, I need to see you."

"No! Please leave!"

He couldn't understand the panic in her voice, unless something awful had happened as a result of what she'd signed. He had to get in there somehow. "Listen, did you sign something that said you'd give up your magic?"

No answer. Which was an answer, wasn't it?

"What are you so afraid of, Anica?"

"I . . . just go away. I can't have any contact with you or you might . . . change back!"

That gave him pause, but he was willing to risk anything to see her again and find out what she'd signed. "I'm not leaving until you open this door and let me come up to talk with you."

"You can't!" She seemed terrified. And she also sounded as if she might be crying.

Shitfire. He leaned against the wall next to the row of buzzers and tried to think. The door was sturdy and the lock strong. Not much chance he could break it down. He'd have to use his wits to get inside.

Or Julie. Pushing away from the wall, he studied the list of tenants. Only one Julie. He buzzed her apartment.

Once again, it took three tries before he roused her. "Who is it?" she called through the intercom.

"Julie, it's me, Jasper."

"The cat?"

"I'm a man now, and I'm worried about Anica. I think she gave up her magical powers, or worse, in exchange for me permanently becoming a man. But she won't let me in, so I don't know what's happening. And she sounds scared."

The lock clicked open and Jasper took the stairs two at a time. By the time he got to Julie's door, she'd already opened it. She stood there wearing glasses, kitten-patterned pajamas, and fuzzy pink slippers. "You think she gave up her magic for you?"

"Yes. Would you go down there and see if she'll let you in? I just need to know she's okay. And if you could, please tell her I paid a lot for her to get her magic back. See if you can get her to test her wand."

"Where will you be?"

"Right down the hall."

"Okay. Let me get my key." She disappeared for a minute and returned carrying a cat-shaped key ring. "Let's go."

Jasper made himself walk at her pace, which in her fuzzy slippers was about twice as slow as he'd prefer.

Along the way he decided to fill her in. "See, I signed a contract that I'd stay a cat from six in the morning to six at night, so that she'd get her magic back. If that contract's in effect, I should have changed into a cat at six. I didn't, so I'm worried that the reverse happened and she lost her magic so I could be a man twenty-four/seven. I don't want Anica making that kind of sacrifice."

Julie glanced at him. "Maybe she doesn't want you making one, either."

Jasper blew out an impatient breath. "Right now, I just want to get to the bottom of this. Promises were made, and I want to know if—"

"Gotcha." Julie pointed to a spot by the stairs. "Stay here. I'll signal if you should come in or not."

Jasper wished he didn't have the distinct impression Julie was enjoying this. She probably lived for drama, whereas he wouldn't care if he never had another dramatic thing happen to him. Still, he was grateful that she was willing to help. He propped himself against the wall next to the stairs and prepared to wait.

He couldn't hear what Julie said through the door, but Anica opened it and let her in. He resisted the urge to charge down there and brace the door open before Anica could close it again. That would be another case of the ends justifying the means, and he hoped he'd learned that lesson.

Time stretched out endlessly as he watched the doorway. He clenched and unclenched his hands, resettled his cap on his head about twenty times, and retied the laces on both of his shoes.

After about a hundred years, the door opened and Julie came out. Although the door closed after her, she beckoned him closer.

Julie's eyes were bright with excitement. "Her magic works!"

"It does?" Jasper stared at her. "Then how come I haven't changed into a cat?"

"'Gift of the Magi.'"

"I don't get it."

"You each sacrificed for the other, so you both get what you wanted. It's classic. I'm so glad I got to be part of this!"

Jasper felt a bubble of hope rise in his chest. "So . . . is she going to let me in?"

"No."

"Why not?"

"Dorcas told her that under the terms of her contract, any contact would result in you turning into a cat again."

Stunned, Jasper tried to process that information.

"Personally," Julie said, "I think that part's null and void. If each of you sacrificed for the other, I think you lifted the spell. I mean, neither of the provisions of the contract came true, right? You're still a guy and she has her magic. So I can't believe that she'd turn you into a cat just by looking at you, but she's very scared about that."

Certainty flooded him with warmth. "I'm not scared. I want to see her."

"Then we have to strategize."

"I won't lie to her, Julie. I did that once before and that's how we ended up in this mess."

Julie looked disappointed. "I thought we could cook up a plan that would get her to open the door, and then you'd just step up and there you'd be, looking at each other."

"Nope. I'm going to try the truth and see how that works." He walked to the door and rapped on it softly. "Anica, can you hear me?"

"Yes, but I wish you'd leave."

His heart beat faster. So close and yet so far. "Let's think logically. We each signed a contract giving up what was most precious—your magic and my human form."

"And I couldn't be with you."

"And I told myself I couldn't be with you, either, because I wasn't a worthy partner when I was half cat and half man. But guess what? You have your magic and I didn't change back into a cat at six this morning. So those contract clauses didn't come into play, right?"

"No, but maybe we're not supposed to be together. Maybe that's the price we're supposed to pay."

Jasper leaned his forehead against the door. "I don't believe that. I don't believe that the kind of love that allowed each of us to make that sacrifice is supposed to be tossed aside. If I can't be with you, I might as well be turned into a cat again. But I refuse to believe that will happen."

"I don't know, Jasper."

"How can you doubt the power of our love? Look at what happened because of it. You're magic again and I'm a man again. Don't let fear keep us apart."

"But—"

"Trust that our love is good, and we're meant to be together. I think that's what we're supposed to learn. Open the door. Please." He closed his eyes and concentrated on sending all the love he had through that door.

When the lock clicked open, the sound was more beautiful than a symphony. Slowly the door opened. She stood there with no makeup, her hair mussed from sleep, and her eyes wide with fear. She was so frightened she was quivering, but she stood there.

She was so beautiful and he longed to go to her, but he stayed very quiet, not moving at all. As sure as he was that this would work out, he was no expert in magic. There had to be some risk.

Gradually her eyes grew bright with joy. "You're not changing."

"No."

She launched herself into his arms. "You're not changing!"

"No." He began to laugh. He'd never been so happy in his whole damned life.

"I was so scared. Jasper, I love you, love you, love you!"

"I love you, too, Anica. I couldn't imagine a life without you." He took time to breathe. "It was torture thinking that I would never see you again."

She smiled at him. "For me, too. But now . . ."

"Yes, now." Then he had no need for words, because his kisses said more than his words ever could.

"I'll just be going," Julie said.

He should thank Julie. He knew he should, but he'd have to take care of that later. He backed Anica into the apartment. Much later.

Epilogue

Around ten on a sunny morning in April, Dorcas brewed a cup of tea in her kitchen and headed down the hallway of the renovated Victorian toward her office at the front of the house. At the same moment her black cat, Sabrina, trotted out of the parlor and sat facing the front door, whiskers twitching.

"Ah, the mail must be coming." Dorcas paused, and sure enough, several letters and a gardening catalog whizzed through the mail slot and plopped onto the hardwood floor.

Sabrina waited while Dorcas scooped up the mail and started toward the office. Tail high, the cat followed and leaped to the desk.

Dorcas set her mug on a coaster and located her glasses. "All right, all right. Honestly, Sabrina, I think you have a fetish." Flipping through the mail, Dorcas plucked out an envelope decorated with stars. She slit the flap with a jewel-encrusted letter opener and pulled out the card.

"*Yes!*" She pumped her fist in triumph. "An engagement party for Anica and Jasper. Ambrose will be so pleased. *I'm* so pleased!"

Sabrina bumped her head against Dorcas's hand and meowed.

"Oh, for Hera's sake. You are a strange cat. But I agree, it's the perfect envelope." Dorcas took scissors out of her desk drawer. A few snips here and there and she'd created a paper crown out of the envelope. She placed it carefully on Sabrina's head. "I crown thee Queen Sabrina of Big Knob. Happy now?"

The cat perched on the desk in regal splendor, purring loudly.

Ambrose strolled into the room. "I see the mail came and Sabrina has another crown."

"And we're invited to an engagement party for Anica and Jasper!" Dorcas beamed as she thrust the invitation at him.

"Excellent. I had serious doubts about those contracts, even with the assurances of the Wizard Council, but it all worked out."

"It wouldn't have if they each hadn't chosen to sacrifice for the other," Dorcas said. "We had to go on faith that their love was strong enough to make those unselfish choices. That was one of the scariest weekends of my life."

"Mine, too. So where's the party? The Bubbling Cauldron, I'll bet." Ambrose held the invitation at arm's length and squinted at it.

"Ambrose, for Hera's sake, when are you going to admit you need glasses? One of these days you'll . . ." She paused. "Hold on. There's a note written on the back of the invitation."

Ambrose turned it over and squinted even harder.

"Let me read it." Dorcas snatched it from him.

> *Dear Dorcas and Ambrose,*
> *I appreciate the scrying session you did for me two weeks ago to help Jasper and me find the perfect condo. It's gorgeous, close to Wicked Brew, and has an extra room for an office or a nursery. . . . ☺ But now I need a scrying for Lily.*

*Griffin isn't paying any attention to her, so I talked
her into getting a dog to take her mind off Griffin.
Although Lily loves Daisy, she's still fixated on
Griffin. I'm worried that she'll do something rash,
but I'm not sure what. Can you try to find out?*
  Light and love,
  Anica

Dorcas glanced at Ambrose. "Do you have anything
pressing to do this morning? Because I'd like to get right
on this."

"Sounds urgent to me. Let's do it."

"I don't suppose we could dispense with Frankie
Avalon this one time."

"I don't suppose we could." Ambrose began whis-
tling "Venus" as he left the office and walked toward the
doorway leading to the basement.

Ten minutes later, they had the gas fire lit under the
cauldron, the necessary herbs sprinkled into the water,
and Frankie Avalon crooning on the CD player. Dorcas
made sure everyone—Ambrose, Sabrina and her—were
inside the circle before she closed it.

She was sick to death of Frankie Avalon, but there
was something to be said for the entertainment value
of watching Ambrose's jerky cha-cha as he circled the
cauldron, followed by Sabrina, who had the cha-cha
down pat. Dorcas merely walked around the circle, but
she couldn't help stepping in time with the rhythm of
the song, much as she hated the tune. The steam rose
and Dorcas repeated Anica's wish, to find out what her
sister was up to.

A scene shimmered in the mist. Lily, surrounded
by the vivid red and orange decorating scheme of her
apartment's living room, was on her knees brushing a
golden retriever.

Sabrina went on alert, her tail twitching and her green
eyes focused intently on the dog.

"So that's Daisy," Ambrose murmured. "Seems like the right dog for Lily."

"Uh-huh," Dorcas said. "Shh. Lily's saying something."

"*Daisy, all I want is a guy who's as loving, smart, loyal and good-looking as you,*" Lily said. "*Is that too much to ask?*"

Daisy whined and wagged her tail.

"*Anica has a guy like that, so why can't I find one? I'm at least as pretty, maybe prettier. I think Griffin wants to ask me out but something's holding him back. If only I could break through that wall he's built around himself...*" Lily paused to gaze at her dog. Then she gasped. "*Of course! You're the answer! All I have to do is capture your qualities in an adoration elixir! It's brilliant!*"

Dorcas groaned. "It's sheer stupidity! I'll call Anica. Maybe she can stop Lily before it's too late."

Please read on for an excerpt from

Vicki Lewis Thompson's

Chick with a Charm

Available from Signet Eclipse

In all her twenty-six years, despite being somewhat of a rebel, Lily Revere had never cast a spell on anyone. But dire circumstances called for drastic measures. She needed Griffin Taylor's devoted attention beginning tonight.

That required creating an elixir this afternoon before heading off to work, but her apartment manager would stroke out if she built a fire under a cauldron in the middle of her living room. Technically she could manage the fire without burning down the building, but she might set off the smoke alarm, which would alert the manager, for sure. She was fond of this apartment, located a short bus ride from downtown Chicago.

To avoid possible eviction, she'd abandoned the cauldron and settled for a fondue pot on the floor as she brewed her adoration elixir. She didn't need much of it, anyway. A couple of drops slipped into Griffin's drink during happy hour tonight should start the process.

Her job as bartender would make that easy, and three hours after sipping his drink, Mr. Handsome would be fixated on her. If they had sex within twelve hours, the spell would strengthen, growing more powerful with each sexual encounter. Yummy prospect.

Lily wouldn't have to worry about being too tired

to have sex with Griffin after work tonight. Performing magic jacked her up more than chugging down three triple espressos in a row. It was a side effect not experienced by many witches, but she'd inherited the tendency from a great-aunt and she'd learned to live with it.

While Daisy, her golden retriever, watched expectantly, Lily opened the magic circle that contained the steaming fondue pot and a small basket of herbs.

"Come, Daisy." Lily beckoned the dog into the circle and guided her to sit on one side of the fondue pot. Daisy was critical to the project. She doted on Lily, and that was the quality Lily intended to transfer to the elixir.

It seemed like the only way to get Griffin off the dime. He'd been a happy hour regular for weeks, and only a stupid woman would miss the heat in his hazel eyes when he looked at her.

When he'd failed to go beyond those burning glances, she'd asked around, thinking he was engaged or married. Nope. Finally she'd taken the initiative and suggested meeting for coffee. He'd politely—and with obvious regret—turned her down.

Lily wasn't much given to analyzing a guy's motives, but Griffin flipped all her switches, so she'd made an exception in his case. She'd concluded that his lawyerly self had decided they weren't a good match based on her non-traditional job and cheeky personality. Lily thought that was plain dumb, especially considering the chemistry between them.

Lily hadn't been this interested in a guy in ages. On top of that, her older sister Anica's budding romance with Jasper Danes had become annoying. If conservative, predictable Anica could end up with a hot guy like Jasper, then Lily should be able to snag someone of similar sex appeal.

Griffin Taylor, for example. His close-cropped brown hair and square jaw made him look like a jock, an impression intensified by the way his suit jacket hugged his broad shoulders. Lily knew from barroom conversation that Griffin worked out and would probably look great naked, but he was also smart, and Lily really liked smart men.

Anica and Jasper's engagement party loomed on the horizon, and Lily wanted to go on Griffin's arm. The elixir should guarantee it.

Closing the magic circle, she sat on the opposite side of the fondue pot and gazed at her dog. She'd always wanted a dog, and Anica had convinced her to adopt Daisy, probably hoping that would take Lily's mind off her obsession with Griffin.

Daisy was great—Lily couldn't ask for a better companion, especially because the dog had turned out to possess more than a touch of magic herself. She seemed to understand every word Lily said and apparently could read a bit, too. If Lily asked Daisy to bring her *Vogue* from the magazine rack in the living room, the dog sorted through the rack and brought back *Vogue*.

No doubt about it, Daisy was special and Lily was grateful to have found her. But when all was said and done Lily still wanted what Anica had, a guy who adored her.

"Okay, Daisy, this is it. You must stay very still." Taking a deep breath, Lily picked up a handful of herbs from the basket, sprinkled them in the steaming water and began to chant.

"Pure devotion fills me up. I have found it with this pup."

Daisy regarded her with that wise, brown-eyed stare that was her trademark. Because Daisy was seven years old, she might not appreciate the *pup* reference, but Lily had discovered that very few good words rhymed with *dog*.

She continued with the chant she'd created specifically for this spell. *"Pure devotion, strong and true, makes a lover stick like glue. From the dog into the brew!"*

The mist that had hovered over the fondue pot gradually rose and swirled around Daisy's head.

Lily hadn't tried this particular spell before, so she was pleased that at least something was happening. Daisy snorted, as if the moisture had gone up her nose, but she didn't move from her assigned spot.

Both Lily and Anica, a powerful witch in her own right, had evaluated Daisy after retrieving her from the animal shelter, and they'd concluded Daisy was an unusually sensitive dog in addition to being very smart. Apparently she was used to creating spells, because she'd taken Lily's magical activities in stride.

After the mist had swirled around Daisy's head a while longer, it changed direction and dove into the fondue pot exactly the way a genie would disappear into a magic lamp. Lily was gratified with the results. Anyone watching would have to conclude that something from Daisy had been transferred into the liquid in the fondue pot.

Lily hoped it was the devotion she'd talked about in the chant, and not some other doggie trait like ear scratching or tail wagging. By tonight she would know.

Coming March 2010

Vicki Lewis Thompson

Chick with a Charm
A Babes on Brooms Novel

Ignoring a witch is never wise...

Lily Revere is free-spirited and fun loving—two
dangerous qualities in a witch. Especially while
planning her sister's engagement party, and she
needs a date! She's determined to bring hot Griffin
Taylor, but he's a divorce lawyer who claims his
job has warned him off romance. He may pretend
he's just not into her, but she knows better—
he only needs a nudge in the right direction.

Slipping a love elixir into Griffin's drink may not be
the noble thing to do—but it sure works! Lily's
dreamboat drops all defenses and the two discover
they're perfectly matched in every way. There's just
one problem: Are Griffin's feelings the result of
some truly good witchcraft—or is he really in love?

Also Available

FROM

Vicki Lewis Thompson

Over Hexed

Dorcas and Ambrose, former matchmaking sex therapists for witches and warlocks, are now working for mere mortals—although the handsome Sean Madigan is kind of an Adonis. That is, until Dorcas and Ambrose strip him of his sex appeal and introduce him to his destiny, Maggie Grady. This time winning a girl's heart won't be so easy for Sean. It means rediscovering the charms buried beneath the surface. But what a surface!

"A snappy, funny, romantic novel."
—*New York Times* bestselling author Carly Phillips

Available wherever books are sold
or at penguin.com

Also Available

FROM

Vicki Lewis Thompson

Wild & Hexy

After gaining twenty pounds, former Dairy Festival Queen Annie Winston dreads going back to Big Knob, Indiana, feeling like a dairy cow. But if Annie has changed, so has her quirky home town. A matchaking witch and wizard have moved into the neighborhood—and they've found the perfect man for Annie.

Shy computer whiz Jeremy Dunstan secretly lusted after Annie when they were teenagers, but he never had the courage to pursue her. Now he has a second chance, but only if he can unleash his wild side. It's the sort of transformation that requires confidence, determination—and a little hex.

**Available wherever books are sold
or at penguin.com**